PRAISE FOR ME

"With her wonderful characters and resonating emotions, Melissa Foster is a must-read author!"

—*New York Times* bestseller Julie Kenner

"Melissa Foster is synonymous with sexy, swoony, heartfelt romance!"

—*New York Times* bestseller Lauren Blakely

"You can always rely on Melissa Foster to deliver a story that's fresh, emotional, and entertaining."

—*New York Times* bestseller Brenda Novak

"Melissa Foster writes worlds that draw you in, with strong heroes and brave heroines surrounded by a community that makes you want to crawl right on through the page and live there."

—*New York Times* bestseller Julia Kent

"When it comes to contemporary romances with realistic characters, an emotional love story, and smokin'-hot sex, author Melissa Foster always delivers!"

—*The Romance Reviews*

"Foster writes characters that are complex and loyal, and each new story brings further depth and development to a redefined concept of family."

—*RT Book Reviews*

"Melissa Foster definitely knows how to spin a tale and keep you flipping the pages."

—*Book Loving Fairy*

THIS IS
LOVE

MORE BOOKS BY MELISSA FOSTER

LOVE IN BLOOM ROMANCE SERIES

SNOW SISTERS

Sisters in Love
Sisters in Bloom
Sisters in White

THE BRADENS

Lovers at Heart, Reimagined
Destined for Love
Friendship on Fire
Sea of Love
Bursting with Love
Hearts at Play
Taken by Love
Fated for Love
Romancing My Love
Flirting with Love
Dreaming of Love
Crashing into Love
Healed by Love
Surrender My Love
River of Love
Crushing on Love
Whisper of Love
Thrill of Love

THE BRADENS & MONTGOMERYS

Embracing Her Heart
Anything for Love

Trails of Love
Wild, Crazy Hearts
Making Her Mine
Searching for Love

BRADEN NOVELLAS

Promise My Love
Our New Love
Daring Her Love
Story of Love
Love at Last
A Very Braden Christmas

THE REMINGTONS

Game of Love
Stroke of Love
Flames of Love
Slope of Love
Read, Write, Love
Touched by Love

SEASIDE SUMMERS

Seaside Dreams
Seaside Hearts
Seaside Sunsets
Seaside Secrets
Seaside Nights
Seaside Embrace
Seaside Lovers

STAND-ALONE NOVELS

Chasing Amanda (mystery/suspense)
Come Back to Me (mystery/suspense)
Have No Shame (historical fiction/romance)
Love, Lies & Mystery (three-book bundle)
Megan's Way (literary fiction)
Traces of Kara (psychological thriller)
Where Petals Fall (suspense)

THIS IS
LOVE

Harmony Pointe, Book Two

MELISSA
FOSTER

Montlake
Romance

Published by Montlake Romance, Seattle

www.apub.com

Amazon, the Amazon logo, and Montlake Romance are trademarks of Amazon.com, Inc., or its affiliates.

ISBN-13: 9781542014540
ISBN-10: 1542014549

Cover design by Letitia Hasser

Cover photography by Regina Wamba of MaeIDesign.com

Printed in the United States of America

For my brothers

CHAPTER ONE

THE BRIGHT LIGHTS of New York City shimmered against the backdrop of tall buildings and the midnight blue sky as the driver pulled up in front of the Ultimate Hotel for the Hearts for Heroes fundraiser. In the privacy of the black sedan, actress Remi Divine scanned the entrance. Wealthy couples decked out in floor-length gowns and handsome tuxedos, every bit as breathtaking as the city itself, smiled for the photographers as they made their way up the steps. Remi was surprised her overprotective much-older brother, Aiden, wasn't standing at the entrance waiting for her as usual—as if the two gorilla-like bodyguards he'd hired weren't enough.

Remi had received threatening letters a couple of months ago, and then someone had broken into her house in LA. She hadn't been home at the time, and although her award cabinet had been smashed to pieces, nothing had been stolen other than some lingerie. Though the incidents had died down and she was now staying in Harmony Pointe, New York, while filming the movie *In the Aftermath*, Aiden wasn't taking any chances with the sister he'd raised since she was twelve years old, after their parents were killed in a tragic car accident. Remi owed everything good in her life to Aiden. He was the kindest, most determined man she knew, and she considered herself lucky to have him as her brother and her business manager.

She turned away from the flashbulbs coming from the eager paparazzi and looked past Merrick, the stone-faced bodyguard sitting beside her, to enjoy the beauty of the city for one last moment as she awaited her turn to exit the car. She watched people across the street admiring the hoopla of the event and taking pictures with their cell phones. Sometimes Remi fantasized about being one of those people, rather than the woman in the expensive Jillian Braden gown, draped in diamonds. She loved acting, and she was grateful for her success, but being America's Sweetheart had come at no small price. Over the last couple of years Remi had begun feeling stifled by the scrutiny.

The stalker and the bodyguards had amplified that oppression, which was why she was planning to take a year off after filming wrapped.

The car inched forward, stopping before the entrance.

"Are you ready to exit the car, Ms. Divine?" Porter, the bodyguard sitting in the front of the sedan, asked rather stoically.

Remi's pulse quickened as flashbulbs took aim at her window. "Yes, thank you."

Without another word, the two bodyguards exited the car, swiftly moving into place, flanking her door. She inhaled deeply, silently counting to twenty—the length of time it took the dynamic duo to scan the crowds at these types of events—and her mother's voice sailed through her mind. *Just breathe, Remi. Everything's going to be okay.* Remi sat up straighter, a measured smile sliding into place, and she gazed out the window with ten seconds to spare. Her eyes caught on a broad-shouldered man moving through the crowd with an air of authority. He strode with powerful fluidity, like a puma claiming its territory, parting the crowd with nothing more than a look of sheer confidence and determination.

Porter opened Remi's door, blocking her view of the handsome man she'd spotted. The humid late-August air clung to her skin as she quickly grabbed her clutch and pushed to her feet, forgetting the importance of an elegant entrance. She craned her neck to get a better look at the gorgeous creature who was avoiding the press like a pro. Her breath caught in her throat. He was tall and darkly handsome, as broad and muscular as her burly bodyguards. He stepped into the aisle like he owned it, his eyes moving just as furtively over the crowd as Porter's and Merrick's were.

Just breathe . . .

"Who are you wearing?" A redheaded reporter thrust a microphone in Remi's direction, snapping Remi's brain into gear.

"Jillian Braden, from her Multifarious line." Even as she smiled for the cameras, her mind was weaving a path straight to Mr. Tall, Dark, and Handsome. Her heart had never thudded so hard over the sight of a man. She had to find out who he was.

She scanned the entrance, hoping to catch up to him and strike up a conversation. But he was gone as swiftly as he'd appeared, as if she'd conjured him from wishful thinking. Her shoulders slumped. *Story of my life . . .*

She had the world at her fingertips. She was offered all the best roles, begged by designers to wear their diamonds and dresses. She could buy anything she wanted, but the things she *really* wanted weren't for sale, and they were always just out of reach.

Porter and Merrick ushered her through the hotel entrance and into the ballroom, where the event was already underway. Merrick stood guard at the entrance to the room, while Porter stuck to Remi like glue. Remi's eyes swept over the sea of black ties and fancy dresses, and she spotted Aiden across the room talking with his business partner, Ben Dalton. Ben's sister Willow was the first true friend Remi had ever had. Through Willow she'd become close with Ben's other sisters, Bridgette, Piper, and Talia, and his fiancée, Aurelia Stark. Those women had become like sisters to her. They were her lifelines, there for her in good times and bad.

Remi's heart skipped at the sight of her best friends heading her way. Happiness bubbled up inside her as she lifted the hem of her strapless red dress and rushed toward their open arms, swept into a group hug that had her bodyguard circling like a vulture.

"Remi! You look gorgeous!" Bridgette gushed, her burgeoning baby bump requiring more space than usual as she moved in for another hug. She looked beautiful in a tea-length black dress, her fair hair twisted up in an elegant knot.

"So do all of you! I'm sorry I'm late. Filming has been crazy these last few weeks." Remi hadn't seen her besties since early summer, which was far too long. "I've missed you all so much. I'm bummed Talia couldn't make it." Talia was the oldest of the Dalton siblings. She and her fiancé, Derek, cared for his father, Jonah, who suffered from Alzheimer's.

"Between work, Jonah, and getting ready for the grand opening of their adult-day-care center, they have no time for anything else," Willow explained. She was a vivacious, curvy blonde, and the owner of Remi's favorite bakery, Sweetie Pie.

"I'm sure. They must be so excited to see it finally coming to fruition," Remi said. "Speaking of new businesses, Aurelia, how's your new bookstore?"

"The bookstore is great! You should stop by when you can." Ben and Aurelia lived above Aurelia's bookstore, Chapter One, in Harmony Pointe, though they also owned a large home in Sweetwater, the neighboring town where the rest of Ben's family lived.

"I will. More importantly, how's my favorite little girl? I bet Bea misses me." Bea was Ben's daughter, who he hadn't known existed until she was left on his doorstep a few months ago.

"Of course she misses you," Aurelia exclaimed. "We all do. Wait until you see her again. She's growing so fast, and she's just . . . *perfect*. She and Louie are with Ben's parents tonight, being spoiled rotten, I'm sure." Louie was Bridgette and Bodhi's six-year-old son.

"Can you believe we got Aurelia to ditch her Converse and get all dolled up?" Willow teased.

"Check these out." Aurelia lifted the hem of her sparkly pink dress, showing off a pair of spiked nude heels.

"Wow! Those are hot," Remi said.

"Now that Bea's sleeping through the night and Chapter One is up and running, I actually have the energy to occasionally try to look nice for my man."

"What she really means is now that Bea is sleeping through the night, my brother is no longer blue-balled and grumpy," Piper said with a smirk, leaning in to hug Aurelia again. Piper was only about five two and was thin as a rail, but her brazen personality made her seem much bigger. She and her father owned a contracting business, and she was tough as nails.

"Oh, *please*. Ben gets more action than any guy around here," Aurelia said.

"Not that I want to compete with my brother. *Ew*," Willow chimed in, glancing across the room at her handsome husband, Zane Walker, an actor-turned-screenwriter. "But my man is *very* well taken care of."

Aurelia nudged Remi and said, "Zane's been eyeing the plunging neckline of Willow's dress all night. That man wants to dive into her cleavage and eat his way out."

"If I swung that way, I'd want to dive in, too. Willow's got the best boobs of all of us." Remi winked at Willow.

"I think mine are pretty hot." Bridgette blushed and rubbed her baby bump. "And for what it's worth, Bodhi thinks pregnancy hormones are the *best*." She lowered her voice and said, "I'm like a sex maniac these days!"

"Who needs pregnancy hormones?" Piper looked hot in that sexy tight gold dress. Her pin-straight blond hair gave her a dignified air that conflicted with the lascivious look in her eyes as she ogled Porter. She could have any man she wanted.

"You're *all* getting more action than me, so consider yourselves lucky." Remi had enough pent-up desires to last her a lifetime. She'd been intimate with only two men in her life, but that didn't mean she wasn't aching for more with the right man. A good man. Someone who could see her for who she was, not only for her fame or how much she was worth.

Piper's brow wrinkled. "You have two sexy beasts at your beck and call. What's the problem?"

"*Ugh.* Don't get me started." Remi spoke quietly so as not to hurt her bodyguard's feelings. Although with how stoic he was, she wasn't sure he had any. "They are *so* not my type. I like men who communicate with more than grunts or commands."

"I happen to *love* commands," Piper said. "And grunts, if made in the bedroom. Want me to take the delicious 'Men in Black' off your hands?"

Remi envied Piper's sexual confidence. She'd give anything to know what she *liked* in the bedroom, much less to go after it. She glanced around the room, hoping to catch a glimpse of the mysteriously sexy man she'd seen outside, but it appeared she must have imagined him after all, because he was nowhere in sight.

"Good luck with that," Remi said. "I *swear* I'm going to lose my mind if Aiden doesn't call them off soon. It's a shame, really. If they weren't such robots, I might not mind having them around. It gets lonely in that fortress my brother rented for me."

"Aw, Remi." Bridgette frowned. "I'm sorry you're having such a hard time. Has anything happened with the stalker since you've been here?"

"Not a peep. As I've told Aiden a dozen times, I'm sure he's moved on to his next obsession. If only Aiden would put his laser focus into finding me a boyfriend . . ."

The girls all talked over one another about how Aiden would give Remi a chastity belt if he even thought she was prowling for a man. In his eyes she'd always be the little sister he had to protect.

"But *we* can play matchmaker while you're in town," Willow offered.

"Hey, if Aiden weren't leaving town tomorrow, I'd offer to distract him for you," Piper said, glancing over her shoulder at Aiden. "That brother of yours might be overprotective, but he's scrumptious. He just needs to loosen up and realize he can use that tie for something much more fun than making a good impression."

"Piper!" Bridgette chided. "That's Remi's *brother*."

Piper held her hands up and said, "I'm just trying to do my part to help a friend."

"Let's get back to matchmaking for *Remi*," Aurelia suggested.

"Thanks for the offer, but as much as I would love that, you know how it is when I'm filming. Going out is impossible. I either have fans all over me or the paparazzi trying to make something out of nothing. And with Aiden's army at my back, it's not like I'd have any privacy anyway."

"Maybe you just need less obtrusive security," Aurelia said. "I thought Ben referred Aiden to Mason Swift, the guy he used when he was trying to track down Bea's mother."

"I have no idea who this Mason guy is, but every time I ask Aiden to call off these guys and find me *one* plainclothed bodyguard that won't make me feel like I'm in jail, he says he's *dealing with it*."

"Mason and Bodhi were in the Special Forces together, and then they both worked at Darkbird. According to Bodhi, Mason has a sixth sense for sniffing out trouble." Darkbird was a civilian company that carried out dangerous covert rescue missions for the military. "I don't think Mason does security work anymore, but his employees do. He's here somewhere. You can talk to him if you'd like."

"It doesn't matter. I don't need or want security," Remi said adamantly. "I think even one bodyguard is overkill. I just need space to breathe."

"Like I said, I can keep the hunky hulks busy so you can go have some fun. I'll get them greased up and smiling in no time." Piper winked at Porter, whose expression remained as unaffected as a mannequin.

"Wow," Willow said. "I've never seen a man not react to you at all."

"The night's still young," Piper said snarkily.

"Go for it," Remi urged. "I have a bone to pick with Aiden. But first I need to find a bathroom."

"Out that door and down the hall." Willow pointed to a door in the back of the room. "Want us to come with you?"

"No. I'm good, thanks. One bodyguard is enough. I'll be right back." Remi searched the faces of the crowd as she made her way through the room, hoping to see the mysterious man she couldn't get off her mind.

Disappointed not to have spotted him, she pushed through the doors in the back of the room with Porter on her heels. She strode down the hall toward the ladies' room feeling like a dog on a leash, trying to keep her emotions in check. But between her disappointment and annoyance, it was a futile effort. When she reached the restroom alcove, out of earshot of the other guests, she spun on her heels, leveling Porter with her most threatening stare.

"I'm going to the bathroom!" she hissed. "Do you want to pee for me, too?"

Porter's facial expression remained professional as he said, "No, but I have to check the bathroom before you enter it."

"Of course you do. Go ahead!" She threw up her hands as he walked past.

Remi turned to catch her breath—nearly smacking into the broad chest of the gorgeous man she'd seen outside. She froze, her heart racing. He was even more devastating up close, with perfectly manicured scruff, full, kissable lips, and steel blue eyes that had the knee-weakening triple effect of being intimidating, seductive, *and* regal. She didn't even think that was possible! She'd worked with beautiful men her whole life, and never before had she felt an instant zing of attraction like the one ricocheting inside her now.

She was vaguely aware of Porter knocking on the ladies' room door behind her as Mr. Devastating's narrowing eyes pinned her in place and he said, "Don't worry. I'm not going to pee for you, either."

Shit. Shit, shit, shit. He'd heard everything she'd said.

She opened her mouth to tell him she was frustrated and shouldn't have been so rude, but her mouth had gone bone-dry and she couldn't find her voice. His eyes drilled into her. Disapproving? Amused? She wasn't sure which, until his lips quirked up in a half smile, half smirk. No acting class could have prepared her for the titillating heat this man exuded—*or* the embarrassment overtaking her.

He crossed his arms with a discerning, *arrogant* look in his eyes.

That judgmental look struck a nerve, cooling her desire. She lifted her chin, meeting his steady gaze with an icy look of her own, and said, "Don't you judge me. I'm sure if you were on a leash twenty-four-seven, you'd snap sometimes, too."

Her heart pounded as she pushed through the ballroom doors, storming through the crowd in search of Aiden and mentally preparing her next escape—which would be out of the country if her brother didn't call off his dogs before she completely lost her mind and people started calling her America's Wicked Witch instead of America's Sweetheart.

She whipped through the room, becoming angrier by the second, and finally spotted him through the glass balcony doors, talking on his phone. She stormed outside, glad he was alone.

Aiden pocketed his phone, his brows slanting in confusion. "There you are. Where are Porter and Merrick?"

"They don't matter right now. I'm *done*, Aiden. I can't do this anymore." She paced, arms flailing, frustration flying from her lips. "I feel like a caged rat living with those two guys watching over me. They don't speak to me except when absolutely necessary. I can handle *myself*, and

I swear if you don't get them to back off, you won't be the only one leaving the country tomorrow."

"Remi, calm down." Aiden was twelve years her senior, and he lived in a constant state of calm, which could be infuriating. Even when she was a sad and confused preteen after their parents were killed, he'd never lost his cool. People said he was a dead ringer for David Beckham without all the tattoos, but Remi knew David had nothing on the man who had given up his hopes and dreams, along with most of his life, so she could have hers.

"Calm *down*? That's easy for you to say. You don't have men following you everywhere. I can't even go to the bathroom without one of them standing outside the door." She was pacing again, unable to rein in months of frustration. "I spend my life living under a microscope by the media, and I have *never* given you any reason to believe that I can't handle myself. I can deal with that kind of scrutiny from the press. It's a pain, but I get it. It comes with the territory. But *this*? This constant watchfulness? It's too much!"

"Remington Aldridge, *stop*," he said sharply.

She stilled at his use of her real name, which was the only indication that Aiden was ever at the end of his rope *and* that he'd heard every word she'd said. She crossed her arms and clamped her mouth shut.

"If you'll let me get a word in edgewise, you'll see I have taken care of everything."

"You have not—"

"Have I ever *not* taken care of you?" he interrupted with a sterner tone.

The brotherly love in his eyes tugged at her heartstrings. "No," she said more calmly. "But there's such a thing as doing *too much*."

"Not when your life is on the line," he said firmly, leaving no room for negotiation. "I read every one of your texts. I know you're frustrated, but I had to work out the details to be sure you'd be taken care of."

"I don't need to be taken care of. Whoever sent those letters and broke into my house in LA hasn't done anything in months. Nobody's out to get me, Aiden. The stalker has moved on to his next obsession. You have me locked in a fortress at night, and we have security on set. Just hire a driver to take me to and from set, and I'll be fine." Remi hated to drive, though she knew how.

"Remi, it's my job to keep you safe. If I weren't going out of the country, I'd do it myself. But rest assured, I *hear* you. I know you want one bodyguard, not two."

"Plainclothed."

"Done."

"And not an asshole."

"Porter and Merrick are not assholes. They're professionals."

"That's fair." She huffed out a breath, feeling bad for referring to them that way. "I'm sorry. I just want to be treated normally. Can't you find a guy who can talk to me like a normal person? Someone who doesn't watch me like I'm a *job*?"

"You *are* their job, Remi, and I'm sorry about that. But I did find you the best security there is, at least according to Bodhi." He glanced over her shoulder, and a satisfied smile curved her brother's lips. "Remi, meet your new bodyguard, Mason Swift."

The name rang a bell, and she felt a little relieved, hopeful that Bodhi's friend would treat her like a normal person. She stood up a little straighter, praying Mason had not heard her ranting. She'd had enough mortification for one night.

She turned, and her stomach pitched at the sight of Mr. Devastating's eyes dancing with amusement.

"It's a pleasure to meet you, Ms. Divine. Mason Swift at your service."

Sweet mother of all things hot and annoying, someone really was out to get her.

"Excuse us for just a second," Remi said with what Mason was sure was *practiced* restraint. She grabbed Aiden's arm and spun him around, their backs facing Mason, though it didn't stop Mason from hearing her panicked whispers. "Are you kidding? *Him?*"

"You wanted *one* bodyguard, and he's the best there is. Mason owns the company that Porter and Merrick work for. I fly out tomorrow, Remi, to deal with one of the most important deals Ben and I have ever negotiated. I need to know you're safe so I can be clearheaded and focus on business. It's either Mason, or I tell Porter and Merrick not to move out of your house, which they're set to do before you and Mason leave this event."

Remi looked over her shoulder at Mason, her honey-brown hair covering one keen hazel eye. She was even more stunning in person than on the big screen. Mason had seen her enter the building, moving with the grace of a swan and the cool edge of a movie star, but the minute she'd seen her girlfriends, that practiced facade had fallen away, and quickly thereafter she'd let loose on Porter Lawton. Porter and Merrick were two of Mason's best men. They'd fought with him in the Special Forces, and Porter had followed him to Darkbird. Porter was not only the first person Mason had hired when he'd opened his company, but he was the man Mason called when he was in trouble. He and Merrick were good, responsible, honest men. The only reason they were aloof with Remi was because they were heeding Aiden's directive that they not get mixed up with Remi on a personal level. He didn't want them distracted from their jobs.

Remi narrowed her eyes, lifted her chin defiantly, and turned away to argue with her brother again.

She was a hot little number with a perfect ass, and so fucking pretty, if she weren't such a diva, Mason might have to work at keeping himself in check. But he didn't do clients, and he definitely didn't do divas. Hell, he didn't *do* many women at all.

"Fine," she snapped at Aiden, and then she turned a smile on Mason that had the power to melt a normal man's heart.

Mason was anything but normal.

He didn't usually take on security jobs, but Remi had run through four bodyguards in as many months. He'd stepped in and taken over as a favor to his brother-in-arms Bodhi Booker. Mason had done his homework. He knew Remi Divine—aka Remington Aldridge—had lost her parents when she was twelve, had been raised by her brother, had been acting since she was a teenager, and had won her first Oscar at twenty. Now he also knew that she was far feistier than her low-key good-girl reputation indicated.

"It's nice to properly meet you," Remi said with an air of dignity far more fitting of the A-list actress than her earlier fit about having to *pee*. "I assume Aiden has gone over everything with you? He's told you that I need to be given space?"

"*Remi,*" Aiden warned with a chiding glance.

Aiden was an impressive, well-educated investor. Many billionaires would have hired nannies or shipped their young charge off to boarding school, but as far as Mason could tell, Aiden had dedicated his entire life to raising and caring for his sister. He'd been thorough in hiring security for her, too. He'd not only followed up on every reference Mason had provided, but Mason had heard from colleagues that Aiden had conducted an even more widespread investigation. Mason appreciated Aiden giving Remi's safety the importance it deserved, just as Mason planned to do. He had requested a guest list from tonight's event, and his staff had prepared reports on each and every individual in attendance. Mason had also checked the backgrounds of the women and men Remi had spent time with over the last two years. He had every intention of finding out who was stalking her—and he wasn't knocking anyone off the list until he was certain they posed no threat.

"Don't worry, Aiden. There's nothing I can't handle." Mason met Remi's armored gaze and said, "As far as space goes, I'll give you enough to do my job." He wasn't about to get derailed by the gorgeous spitfire or allow her to compromise his ability to do his job. If his instincts told him something was off, she'd just have to roll with it.

Remi lifted her finely manicured brows, and a glacial smile slid into place. "Well, then, it looks like I can join the others in the ballroom. They're seating guests for dinner. I assume I'll see you after the event?"

"You'll see me before that—" He'd been about to say *Princess* . . . He had no idea why that word had popped into his mouth, but he knew better than to let it slip out. "Would you like me to hold your clutch while you enjoy the event?"

Her brows knitted, but she handed him the clutch. He tucked it into the interior pocket of his jacket.

"Very well, then." She turned to leave.

Mason beat her to the door, holding it open for her. She blinked warily up at him and said, "Thank you."

He leaned in closer, asking for her ears only, "Would you like me to escort you to the ladies' room?"

"Excuse me?"

"It seemed urgent earlier, and you never went."

Her face blanched. "I'm *fine*." She stormed into the ballroom.

"Did I miss something that I should know about?" Aiden asked as they followed Remi in.

"We met briefly when she was chewing out one of my men." Mason scanned the room, keeping a close eye on Remi as she found her girl-friends and began talking animatedly, hands and mouth moving a mile a minute. Her friends looked over, and he lifted his chin, proudly accepting the princess's scorn.

"She's not normally this belligerent. She's been pushing back hard lately in ways she never has before," Aiden explained.

As Remi and her friends settled around a table, Mason said, "Threats and bodyguards have a way of bringing out the worst in people. Nobody likes to lose control of their life. Don't worry, Aiden. I'll take good care of her, and I'll keep you in the loop as I look into tracking the cretin down." He'd already spoken to the detective in LA who was handling Remi's case. Although the LAPD reacted swiftly to the break-in, they had yet to make any headway on catching the culprit.

"I appreciate that. As you know, she's been ditching her bodyguards. You'll need to keep your eyes on her."

Keeping his eyes on Remi wasn't a hardship. Listening to the sass coming from her sexy mouth? That was a different story . . .

CHAPTER TWO

AS THE EVENING wore on, Mason got a much better sense of the pretty princess he'd been hired to protect. She handled herself gracefully at dinner, laughing at all the right times, smiling affectionately, professionally, and in agreement. Although Mason noticed that while she pushed food around on her plate, she ate only a few bites of salad. When she finally headed to the ladies' room, he was right there by her side, making small talk. She'd spoken to him without exuding too much of an attitude. Remi was an actress, all right, but even her superb acting skills couldn't cover up her biggest reveal of the night, which had come later. Aiden would be overseas for several weeks. He and Remi had talked privately for a long time, and Remi's facial expressions had been camera ready during their entire conversation. It wasn't until Aiden had embraced her that Mason had seen the love and adoration of a younger sister toward the older brother who had raised her. The break in her facade had lasted only a few short seconds before Aiden stepped back, kissed her cheek, and headed for the door. Remi had stood pin straight, shoulders squared, looking elegant and gorgeous, but the fear in her eyes as her brother walked out the door was inescapable—and it had disappeared as quickly as it had come.

Remi had returned to her friends, spouting happiness about finally being *free* from Aiden's watchful eyes, as if that fear hadn't existed. But now, more than an hour later, Mason was still thinking about what he'd seen in her eyes when Aiden had left.

One by one Remi's friends left the table to dance with their significant others. She watched them with longing in her eyes, a look that made Mason's chest tighten and brought a desire to take away that longing. As a private investigator and bounty hunter, Mason dealt with all sorts of people, from the rich and famous to the dregs of society. He'd been hit on by the best of them, but he lived by a strict moral code and never crossed professional boundaries, which was why he shoved the oddly intimate sensation down deep.

Mason had been watching a powerful and arrogant investor who had been eyeing Remi while also chatting up a blonde. The man left the blonde and approached Remi. Mason stepped out of the shadows, a few feet from where Remi was sitting. She and the arrogant prick talked for a moment before the guy offered his hand. Remi took it, allowing him to lead her to the dance floor.

The hair on the back of Mason's neck stood on end. He'd assumed a sass-mouthed bodyguard ditcher would have a nose for bullshit. He should know better than to assume and made a mental note to school her on the issue. He moved closer to the dance floor, positioning himself so he had a clear view of Remi. She was smiling, but it was the practiced smile Mason had already cataloged, not the genuine one her friends and their significant others had elicited. The man said something, and she laughed, but it wasn't the carefree laugh he'd heard her use with her friends.

Dude, she's not into you.

The guy leaned closer, speaking into her ear. Remi's smile faded, and Mason's muscles flexed, his senses on high alert. Remi shook her head, and the guy's grip on her tightened, his hand slipping closer to her ass. Remi's eyes darted around the room, but Mason was already on the move, parting the dancing crowd like it was the Red Sea. He didn't want to embarrass Remi, but in his experience there was only one way to deal with arrogant pricks who thought that because they had money, women were their due.

He leveled the prick with an iron-cold stare and said, "Unless you want to lose that hand, I suggest you remove it from Ms. Divine's body."

Remi's eyes widened.

The prick scoffed, a nervous sound slipping through his thin lips.

Mason stepped closer, speaking through gritted teeth as he said, "*Now.*"

The guy took a step back, and Mason inserted himself between the man and Remi, leaving no room for mistaking how far he was willing to go to protect her.

The guy mumbled, "Asshole," and walked away.

Mason drew Remi into his arms, and as he'd known she would, she draped her arms around his neck and fell into step, camera ready.

"What are you doing?" she hissed, somehow managing to keep a smile on her face while visually throwing daggers. She was like a sexy little snake, just wicked and fierce enough to get herself into trouble.

"I didn't like the way he was getting handsy with you."

"I can take care of myself, thank you very much."

He ground his back teeth to keep from replying that maybe she could, but he wasn't taking the chance that the prick got a handful of her first. Instead, he said, "Then I guess I misread the way your eyes were skating around the room, searching for a way out."

She clamped her mouth closed, as she'd done earlier, and they finished the dance in a silent battle of wills. He tried not to think about how good she felt in his arms, or her breasts brushing against his chest. But mostly, he tried to figure out why having her safe in his arms felt a hell of a lot more perfect than any other woman ever had.

"You shouldn't have cut in," she said, a little less angry.

"Duly noted. We need a signal."

She rolled her eyes, and he noticed the daggers had dissipated. "Like a safe word, Christian Grey?"

"You are a pistol, aren't you, Princess?" *Aw, hell.* He hadn't meant for *Princess* to slip out.

She pressed her lips together, eyes narrowing. "I'm *not* a princess."

He didn't bother to argue, focusing on the more important issue. "From now on, if someone makes you uncomfortable, scratch your neck, just below your ear, like this."

He reached up and ran his nails lightly down her neck. Her eyes darkened, and at the same time they widened innocently. *Damn.* That was the sexiest thing he'd ever seen.

"Like this?" she said sweetly as she reached up, tilting her head ever so slightly, and dragged her nails down her neck.

His eyes were riveted to hers, but in the next second they dropped to her tongue sweeping over her lower lip. Scratch his earlier thought. *That* was the sexiest thing he'd ever seen.

She rolled her lower lip between her teeth and said, "Was that right?"

"Perfect."

"And then you'll rescue me?" she asked softly, blinking guilelessly. "No matter what?"

The longing in her eyes hit him with the magnitude of an earthquake. She had him skating a dangerous line, and she'd done it as easily as taking candy from a baby.

He steeled himself against her seamless transition from *charge* to *seductress*, loosening his hold on her and putting space between them as he said, "No matter what. That's my *job*."

Her eyes narrowed lethally, washing away the veil of innocence. "I don't need *rescuing*, Mr. Swift." She stepped from his arms, nervously smoothing nonexistent wrinkles from her dress. "I have to be on set early tomorrow for a meeting. I'd like to say goodbye to my friends and call it a night." She strode off the dance floor with an air of loftiness.

It seemed the princess had momentarily fallen off her throne. It was good to know she could climb right back on.

Remi wove through the crowd toward Willow and the rest of her friends, wondering what the hell had just happened. She could walk the red carpet without missing a step, mingle and charm high-powered media executives, and flawlessly carry out the role of any character. So why did one touch from her new bodyguard make her heart race? He was even bigger, broader, and harder up close, easily six three or six four. And those eyes . . . Holy moly, they made her stomach go all sorts of squirrelly. But that wasn't the worst part. When he touched her, his hard gaze had *softened*, making the *rest* of her—the parts that hadn't reacted to a man in ages—take notice.

She hoped her girlfriends hadn't seen her fall from grace.

"Hey, cheeky girl," Piper said. "What the heck was *that?*"

"It was . . ." She wasn't about to admit that they'd witnessed her losing her mind over a man for the first time *ever*.

Before she could form a response, Piper said, "It was impressive as hell, that's what it was. Mason sent that jerk packing. I like a man who knows how to take charge."

Apparently so do I.

Remi had been pissed when Mason had stepped in as if she couldn't take care of herself. But she'd been even angrier at the way her mind had turned to dust from his touch. She was used to bodyguards treating her like she was a fine diamond and keeping her locked away. But Mason hadn't hesitated to pull her into his arms and dance with her, keeping the scene to a minimum. And what she was trying to convince herself *hadn't* taken place had actually happened—he'd noticed the look in her eyes and he'd reacted to it. The same way he'd noticed when she hadn't gone to the ladies' room. She'd had to pee so bad before dinner, it had killed her not to have him escort her right away, but she had her pride. She'd waited a solid ten minutes before finally heading in that direction. And he'd been right there by her side, asking her if she was having a good time with her friends instead of trudging beside her like a wall of oppression.

"Aiden finally listened to you," Bridgette said. "Mason will take good care of you."

"I'd like to take good care of *him*," Piper said under her breath, earning a glare from Bridgette.

Remi felt a stab of jealousy, which was utterly ridiculous. She must be exhausted, because she hadn't been jealous a day in her life.

Well, that wasn't exactly true.

When she'd first met Willow and her sisters, she'd been a little jealous of their charmed, small-town lifestyles. They had each other and parents who adored them and were still alive. But that jealousy was short-lived. As she'd come to know them and, in time, the rest of their friends and family, she loved them like family, and they returned that love in spades. She'd quickly learned that nobody's life was what it seemed and that *charmed* was only the way their lives appeared at first glance. Bridgette had lost her first husband shortly after Louie was born, and Bodhi's father had been killed in the line of duty when he was young. Zane's family wasn't always kind to him, and Aurelia's mother had died during childbirth. Aurelia had been raised by her grandmother, Flossie McBride, a woman who had such a kind, generous heart, she'd embraced Remi as a surrogate granddaughter. Remi knew she was lucky to have had Aiden and to be welcomed so freely into the lives of so many warm and wonderful friends.

But even so, she'd never been jealous over a man—until just now when that unfamiliar clutch of the green monster gripped her.

"Do you like Mason more than you liked the last two bodyguards?" Willow asked.

"He talks to me. That's a plus," Remi said in a tone that was lighter than she felt. He hadn't *just* spoken to her—he'd heard the things she *hadn't* said. But the way he made her feel was confusing, so she tried to shrug it off and said, "Besides, it's easier to ditch one bodyguard than two."

Her girlfriends exchanged a concerned look.

"What . . . ?" Remi asked.

"I can think of many things I'd like to do with Mason, but ditching him definitely isn't one of them," Piper said, eyeing him.

Remi stole a glance at Mason, who stood by the doors watching her like a hawk. Irritation—at herself and at him—pecked at her nerves. "That's because he's not holding *your* leash. I thought he was devastatingly hot when I first saw him, too, but that was before I realized Aiden had left him in charge of me like I'm a child."

"Or like your life might be in danger," Willow said thoughtfully, reminding Remi of the real reason Aiden had hired him.

Aurelia's brow knitted. "It hasn't been that long since someone broke into your house, and we're worried about you."

"I know you are." Remi tried not to sound exasperated. "I understand everyone is worried. I'm not blowing off the possibility that some freak is still stalking me. But that was thousands of miles away from here. All I'm saying is that I don't think I have to worry so much here. I haven't seen anyone weird hanging around the set, and the 'Men in Black' didn't seem concerned about anyone in particular." They'd stuck to her like glue, but they had never ushered her away from a person as if they posed a threat, or stepped in the way Mason had. But she didn't want to think about Mason's bodyguarding abilities right now, because that led to her thinking about the way he'd made her hot all over when they'd danced. "I have to be on set early tomorrow, and Mason still needs to get settled in, so I'm going to take off."

"Are we still on for a girls' night Friday evening?" Willow asked, pulling Remi into a tight hug.

"Yes. Six o'clock at the fortress?" Remi joked. The three-story, six-bedroom stone-and-brick gated estate where she was staying was gorgeous, even if it felt like a prison and was too elaborate for her taste. She knew Aiden had her best interests at heart, ensuring there was a gym, a pool, and a hot tub, which she enjoyed almost every evening after a long day's work.

After sharing enough hugs to fill up a little of her well, Remi headed for the burly bundle of hotness watching her cross the floor.

Mason squared his shoulders, looking more like a movie star than a bodyguard in his tuxedo. He stepped toward her and placed his hand on her lower back. "Excuse my hand, but your handsy dance partner has you in his scope again."

She realized he hadn't been just watching her. He'd been taking in everything around her. She glanced over her shoulder, and she got chills at the hungry look on the face of the man with whom she'd danced.

Mason's hand pressed firmer against her back. "It's okay. I've got you. I'll help you learn how to spot those types of guys. We have a long drive. Do you want to use the facilities before we go?"

You'll help me spot them? That was definitely *not* in his job description, but hey, she'd be happy to listen to his advice. "No, thanks. I'm fine. You?"

"I'm good, but thanks for your concern."

"What are you, a camel?" she teased as he led her through the lobby, his all-seeing eyes scanning their surroundings.

"Catheters come in handy."

"No way." She saw the tease in his eyes and said, "Oh, you were kidding."

"Was I?" He cocked a brow and reached for the door. He followed her into the brisk night air.

While he gave the valet his ticket, Remi walked to the far end of the steps, gazing out at the lights of the city. The thought she'd done such a good job of ignoring trickled in.

Aiden was leaving tomorrow.

As overprotective as he was, Remi was always a little anxious when he traveled. Not that she needed to keep tabs on him, but she'd breathe a little easier once he'd landed and checked in, safe and sound.

She focused on the beautiful lights of the city, working hard to force her worries away. She loved the city, and the sights and sounds at night usually calmed her, though she worked so often, she got to enjoy them only in snippets. New York was much more appealing to her than LA had ever been. When her parents were alive, they'd taken her to the city every year. They didn't stay there, though. They stayed in their family's rural cabin outside the city, because her parents liked the privacy. She had nothing but good memories from those trips—memories of the days before Aiden had given up much of his own life and stepped in to parent her. Even though he was much older, she had fond memories of a less serious brother, a brother who spent more time teasing and joking around than worrying.

The truth was, she'd not only lost her parents in the car accident, but she'd lost her brother, too, and had gained a man who walked a fine line between father figure and sibling. She often wondered if Aiden missed his old role as much as she did. She knew he didn't see her as a burden on his life the way she saw herself, but she couldn't help worrying that one day he would realize he did see her that way. She wanted him to be happy, and as she got older and understood more of what he'd given up, she realized his taking care of her had hindered his ability to find his own happiness. That weighed heavily on her, and it might even be part of why she fought so hard for her freedom.

She felt Mason's presence before he said a word, and she steeled herself for a sharp command to get in the car, or a reprimand for walking too far away.

"Did you want to take a walk or something before we leave the city?" he asked.

She was sure she'd misheard him. "I'm sorry, what?"

"You were looking out at the street like you wanted to go somewhere."

Surprised he'd noticed, she said, "I just love the lights, and I don't get to see them very often."

"Do we have to rush home? I know of a few places with great views."

She couldn't suppress her smile. "You wouldn't mind? My previous bodyguards ushered me from cars to buildings like I would melt from outside elements."

"That's no way to live. I'm starting to understand why you've gone through four bodyguards in as many months. If you want to see the lights, let's go see them."

Finally, somebody understood her plea for normalcy, or at least claimed to. "You're not worried about the stalker?"

"I would only be worried if I didn't think I could protect you, and trust me, that's *not* a problem."

A bud of excitement bloomed inside her. Her life had become so closed off. Outside of work and occasionally seeing her girlfriends, she didn't have much to look forward to. "I'd like that, thank you."

"You're not afraid of heights, are you?" Mason asked.

"No. Why?"

"Just making sure. Parking is a bear, but we'll manage."

"I'd rather walk, actually."

He looked at her heels. "You're okay walking in those for several blocks after being on your feet all night?"

She appreciated his unexpected thoughtfulness, but she didn't want to appear anything less than capable, even if her feet were a little achy, so she said, "I can walk in my heels for days. Please don't underestimate me. I'm just as tough as you are."

He held his hands up in surrender, an amused smile softening his features, making him look younger than Remi's guess of midthirties.

"My apologies," he said. "I know of two great spots with incredible views."

"I'd like to see the *best* view possible."

"We can do that, but while I'm perfectly confident and comfortable taking you there, you might get spooked at the neighborhood."

She crossed her arms and said, "Nothing spooks me except ornery bodyguards who don't give me credit for being able to handle myself."

"You sure about that?"

"Do I *look* sure about that?" she said confidently. "If you're genuinely confident in your skills, you should be able to accompany me anywhere, and I should feel one hundred percent safe. Treat me like you would any other *regular* person."

The muscles in his jaw bunched. "All right, then, *Fearless*. The *best* view it is. Let me take care of the car." He went to speak to the valet, and a minute later he was by her side, his hand pressing reassuringly and protectively on her lower back, guiding her down the sidewalk.

The sounds of cars and the din of people hustling along the sidewalk broke the silence as Mason navigated the city like he knew each street by heart. He directed Remi with a nudge on her lower back, or a nod of his head in the direction they were going. When she put her arms around herself to ward off the chilly air, he shrugged off his tuxedo jacket and helped her put it on, taking a moment to roll up the sleeves to her wrists.

Mason hadn't said a word since they'd left the hotel. After a while, the streets became darker, less populated. She had a disconcerting thought that Mason could be the stalker and she'd fallen right into his hands. Her heart rate kicked up, and horrific visions of torture slammed into her. She glanced at Mason, noting that his watchful eyes continuously scanned their surroundings, and she realized he was completely focused on keeping her safe. Aiden's penchant for worrying must be rubbing off on her.

"Here we are." Mason stopped by an old apartment building. He must have noticed how hard she was breathing, because he studied her face and concern rose in his eyes. "Are you okay? Do you need a second to catch your breath?"

Before she could respond, a craggy voice called out from the shadows. "Mason? That you?"

"Yeah," Mason said without turning his attention away from Remi. He stepped closer to her, and her heart tripped for a whole different reason. His masculine scent penetrated her fear. He placed his large hands comfortingly on her upper arms, looking deeply into her eyes. "You're safe with me, Remi, but if you're uncomfortable, we can go back."

"I . . . um . . ." She caught movement over Mason's shoulder, and a man with bushy white hair and a scraggly beard ambled into the light coming from the apartment building. He was disheveled, wearing two shirts, both too large for his slight frame, and a pair of baggy pants. His face was mapped with wrinkles, his heavy-lidded eyes underscored with puffy dark crescents that told of a difficult life. Remi stepped backward, hating the judgments taking place in her head, but unable to avoid them.

Mason must have supersonic senses, because he didn't turn around, didn't give any indication that he realized the man was approaching other than saying, "Chuck, give us a second, will you please?"

The man retreated silently into the shadows.

"Chuck's harmless," Mason said. "He lives here and sits outside because he was in the war and doesn't like confined spaces. I didn't mean to scare you by bringing you here, Remi."

She wanted to say she wasn't scared, but it would be a lie. She was totally out of her element, and she *was* scared, despite believing Mason would never let anything happen to her. The truth in that thought surprised her. She'd never really felt safe with anyone other than Aiden before. But now, as Mason looked at her like he'd swoop her into his arms and carry her back to the car if she needed him to, she truly believed she was safe.

"The view I wanted to show you is right upstairs," he said. "But you're spooked. I'll call a car to take us back to the hotel. This probably wasn't the best—"

She was being ridiculous, and she certainly wasn't showing him that she was brave. She mustered all of her courage and said, "I'm *fine*. Please show me what we came here to see."

He studied her again, searching her eyes for something—signs that she was lying? That he needed to get her home before she lost her shit and went off on him like she'd gone off on Porter?

She inhaled a deep breath and blew it out slowly, her eyes drawn to a scar on his left cheek, just below his eye, and another barely visible just above the scruff on his right cheek. *Why am I noticing those minute details at a time like this?* She didn't have to look far for answers. Maybe because Mason was the first man who had ever really seen her—the *real* her, not the actress—and what she had achieved, and that was remarkable regardless of their circumstances.

"I'd like to see the view," she said. "I'm fine, Mason. I just got a little rattled."

"Okay," he said gently. "There's nothing wrong with being rattled, but you need to know, and wholeheartedly believe, that I would never take you anywhere if I didn't fully believe I could keep you safe. If this relationship is going to work, it's got to be a two-way street. You have to trust me as much as I have to trust you."

Trust was hard for Remi. With the exception of her few closest friends, most everyone wanted something from her. She wasn't naive. She knew that most people who worked for her weren't doing it because they wanted to help her succeed or because they liked who she was as a person. Even her assistant, Naomi, was an aspiring actress. Those people might like her, but that didn't supersede their need for money, or a leg up on their résumé. But for some strange reason, she sensed she could trust Mason with *more* than just her safety. That was a little unsettling, so instead of blindly handing that trust over, she said, "I trust you'll keep me safe."

"Then you can probably take your nails out of my forearms." He glanced at her fingernails drawing blood through his shirt.

"Oh my gosh." She released his arms, leaving little red stains on his crisp white dress shirt. "I'm so sorry. I didn't realize . . ."

"I didn't even feel it." He gave her a reassuring look, unleashing butterflies in her stomach. "Let's go see that view."

As they headed up the walkway, Mason stopped in the light and said, "Chuck, please say hello to Ms. Divine."

Chuck rose from a chair Remi hadn't noticed earlier and stepped out from the shadows, his beard twitching with what she assumed was a smile. He nodded and said, "Pleased to meet you, ma'am. I'm sorry if I frightened you."

"Hi. It's okay. It's nice to meet you, too." She lifted her hand in a half wave, wondering how Mason knew him.

"How're you holding up?" Mason asked him. "Taking your medications?"

"As often as I remember."

Concern brimmed in Mason's eyes. "Do I need to sic Estelle on you again?"

Chuck waved a hand dismissively, making a disgruntled sound. "That woman's all over me all the time."

"Then you're a lucky man, my friend. She's a good wife." Mason hiked a thumb toward the sky. "We're heading upstairs. Do you need anything?"

"No, thank you. It's good to see you with a woman, though. Don't blow it." Chuck stepped back into the shadows.

"She's my *boss*," Mason said as they turned to go inside.

"All women are," Chuck called out.

Remi's fear of Chuck now waylaid, they headed inside. The building smelled like fresh paint. There was no lobby, just a hallway straight ahead of them feeding apartments on the first floor and a staircase to their left. Remi lifted the hem of her dress as they took the staircase up several stories. She followed Mason down a hallway to another set of stairs, and they climbed two more flights. When they reached the final landing, Mason pushed open a steel door, and she followed him onto the roof of the building.

A sea of lights sparkled in the darkness, snaking along the streets with the cars below and dotting the windows of tall buildings like thousands of secrets against the night sky.

"Mason . . ." Words failed her as she wrapped her arms around herself, taking in the gorgeous skyline, the mazes of streets, and the plethora of smells rising around them. The city was like a world all its own, so different from Harmony Pointe. Goose bumps rose on her arms despite wearing Mason's jacket.

Mason stepped closer with a look of restraint, as if he wanted to reach for her, to put his arms around her, but he remained six or eight inches away, his body heat sizzling in the air between them. Remi had been all over the world, seen gorgeous cities and iconic locations in the company of some of the most sought-after celebrities. And yet the rooftop of this old building she hadn't even known existed, with a man who had been inserted into her life against her will, felt like the most romantic place on earth.

"This is beautiful," she said softly. "Can we stay for a while?"

"We can stay as long as you want, Remi. You're the boss."

There it was again, a reminder that she was nothing more than a job to him. She'd gotten carried away by the breathtaking views and by the man who was not only off-limits, but who made her emotions take flight. She *really* needed to get a life.

"How did you find this place?"

"You live in the city long enough, you get to know its little secrets."

She wondered how many secrets *he* had. "Why did you bring me here?" she asked.

"You wanted to see the city lights, and in my opinion, this is about as good as it gets."

They admired the view for a long time, the sounds of the city floating up around them. After a while, Remi was so relaxed, she sank down to the rooftop and slipped off her heels, tucking her feet beneath her dress for warmth. Being up there, above the rest of the world, without fears of stalkers, paparazzi, or exuberant fans, Remi felt like she could breathe for the first time in forever.

"You should probably sit on my jacket, so you don't ruin your dress," Mason suggested.

"Then I'd ruin your jacket." She looked up at him standing sentinel over her, jaw set tight, biceps straining against the material of his crisp white shirt, bloodstains marking his forearms. His thick thighs were outlined by the thin material of his slacks. Lord help her, because she couldn't resist allowing her eyes to graze over the bulge at the juncture of his thighs. Lust pooled low in her belly, and she once again reminded herself that he was off-limits. Aiden would fire Mason faster than she could blink if he knew she was even the slightest bit attracted to him.

She forced her eyes away, but she was too drawn to Mason, and like a moth to a flame, she found herself looking again . . . and *again*—at his face, at the strong ridges of his jaw and nose. The closer she looked, the more curious she became. Not just about how his arms would feel wrapped around her, or about why she had the urge to take his gorgeous face in her hands and taste his kissable lips. Those curiosities had been simmering since she'd first seen him outside the hotel. But now they were joined with other curiosities, like why he had taken this job when Bridgette said he didn't do security work. And what was behind the eyes that looked like they had seen more than any one person ever should? And the most curious of all, why did she get the sense that he might be just as lonely as she was?

CHAPTER THREE

IT WAS AFTER two o'clock in the morning when Mason drove through the gates of the massive estate where Remi was staying and crawled up the long, winding driveway. The estate was located down a dead-end street, and the road and the gate were monitored by security cameras. Aiden had provided Mason with a map of the property, floor plans, and a detailed security-system rundown when his company had first taken on the job. Mason had access to the security cameras from the vehicle and from his phone. He turned them on now, and images of the interior rooms of the house flashed on the LED screen on the dashboard. He navigated to each of the rooms and then to the exterior cameras. The property boasted six bedrooms, six full and two half bathrooms, two formal living rooms, a formal dining room, a gourmet kitchen, an office, a lower-level recreation room with a wet bar, a home theater, a gym, and a three-car garage. There was also a courtyard with a swimming pool and a hot tub. Mason wondered if the elaborate setup was chosen by the demands of the princess he was hired to watch or by her brother.

He glanced at Remi, fast asleep in the passenger seat. His tuxedo jacket swallowed her petite yet curvy body. Her feet were tucked up on the seat beneath her pretty gown. She was an anomaly to him. He could usually get an instant read on people, but there seemed to be so many sides to Remi, he wasn't sure *she* even knew which one was real. But he sure as hell wanted to find out. She'd further intrigued him when he'd opened the back door of his armored Escalade for her and she'd shot him a disapproving look and climbed into the front seat. She'd made a few comments about his vehicle being *overkill*, and then she'd promptly fallen asleep. He felt guilty waking her when she looked so peaceful after going through so many emotions over the course of the evening—from angry charge to polished actress to worried sister, happy friend, and finally, on the rooftop, to a softer, more relaxed woman he had a feeling the rest of the world wouldn't recognize. Even in her beautiful gown, with probably half a million dollars' worth of diamonds resting against her flawless skin, she looked younger and more vulnerable than her twenty-five years.

She was truly, captivatingly beautiful, a fact he should not be noticing.

He climbed from the SUV, doing a quick visual sweep of the property as he walked around to the passenger side. He opened the door slowly, so as not to startle Remi, but he needn't have worried. She was fast asleep. He wanted to lift her into his arms and carry her to the safety of her bed, but he still had to secure the inside of the house, and knowing Remi, she might sock him in the jaw if he startled her.

That thought made him smile. He liked her fierceness.

He touched her arm, catching sight of the thin red crescents she'd left on his skin. She must have apologized fifty times when he'd rolled up his sleeves and she'd seen the cuts she'd caused. He had plenty of scars on his body. He'd proudly wear the marks of the first woman to stir something inside him that he'd never known existed.

Remi didn't rouse, so he shook her arm. "Remi," he said softly. When she didn't wake, he ran his fingers down her cheek and leaned in closer, saying, "Remi," a little louder.

She murmured in her sleep, snuggling against the seat.

She was so damn adorable, it took everything he had not to lift her into his arms. He leaned close again, inhaling her feminine fragrance, which he'd been trying to ignore all night. It was a unique combination of sweetness, flowers, and *Remi*.

"Remi," he said louder.

She wrinkled her nose, tucking her chin low.

This was useless. Thank God her stalker hadn't broken in when she was sleeping. That thought sent a pang of unease through his gut.

He scooped her up, and she wound her arms around his neck, nestling against his chest. That simple move made his protective urges surge. He pondered that sensation, using it as a distraction from how incredible she felt in his arms as he carried her into the house.

"My bedroom's upstairs," she said sleepily as he closed the door behind them.

"You're *awake*?"

She blinked up at him, a small, insanely sexy smile curving her luscious lips. "You jostled me when you unlocked the door."

Damn. That innocent-but-sexy look nearly did him in.

"Sorry, Remi, but I can't carry you up to your bedroom."

Her lower lip pouted out, and his chest constricted.

"I have to check the house." He set her on her feet, instantly missing the weight of her in his arms. Pushing that unfamiliar longing aside, he said, "I need you to wait here."

"*Here?*" she said, coming fully awake and sounding annoyed. "I'm going up to my room while you do your thing."

She took a step past him and he grabbed her arm, stopping her in her tracks. Their eyes collided with such intensity he had to fight the urge to haul her into his arms and kiss the challenging look off her beautiful face.

"I'm here to *protect* you," he said sternly as a reminder to himself as much as to her. "If you fight me every step of the way, it's going to be a long few weeks."

Her eyes dropped to his mouth and then to his hand on her arm, lingering there. She lifted her other hand and ran her fingers over the cuts on his forearm. Then those bottomless hazel eyes found his again, soft and alluring, sending desire and empathy coursing through his veins. He wanted to give her what she wanted, to take her in his arms again and carry her upstairs just to see that little smile one more time.

"Sorry about your arms," she said softly. "I'll wait here."

He was going to get whiplash trying to keep up with her sass, challenges, and suddenly sweet disposition. He released her arm, struggling to pull his mind out of the *Remi haze* consuming it, and focused on securing the house. "What's your phone number, Remi?"

Confusion wrinkled her brow. "I'm right here. Just talk to me."

He pulled out his phone and waved it in front of her. "I need to check out more than eight thousand square feet. I want you to have my number in case you get spoo—" He worried saying the word *spooked* might set her off, so he said, "In case you need me, you can just push a button."

"Do you think someone is in here?" Fear rose in her eyes.

"No, but I need to be sure."

She rattled off her phone number, and he called it from his phone.

"My phone is off, in my clutch," she said nervously.

He lifted the lapel of his jacket, which she was still wearing, and withdrew the clutch from the inside pocket, handing it to her. "Please turn your phone on and check it."

She did as he asked, and added him as a contact. "There's no one in the house. Aiden has me gated in like a criminal."

"Or maybe like a sister he adores," he said. "If you call, I'll be here in three seconds flat."

"Not if you're in the basement," she said challengingly.

His eyes narrowed. "Try me."

He left her by the front door as he checked the house, starting on the lower level and searching every nook and cranny. He was in security mode, every sense on alert, his body buzzing with readiness as he moved from room to room. He wasn't surprised that none of the rooms looked lived in, except for the last one he checked, a third-floor bedroom and bathroom where Remi was staying. He didn't allow himself to slow down or get tripped up as he thoroughly inspected her rooms, looking under the bed and in the closets, which were filled with boxes. It wasn't until he was sure both rooms were clear that he breathed easier.

His eyes swept over her bedroom one last time, seeing it for the first time through the eyes of a *man* and not just a bodyguard. He felt like he'd walked into the very heart of her. Where he'd expected to see expensive perfumes, jewelry, and makeup, the dresser was covered with framed pictures of Remi and Aiden and the girls she'd spent time with tonight and their significant others. A worn and frayed stuffed golden retriever lay on the nightstand, and a flowered blanket that had seen better days was draped across the arm of an equally well-loved leather recliner by the window. An old book with a pink bookmark rested against the arm of the chair. But it was a collage of pictures in a larger frame propped up against the wall on the second dresser that held his attention. It was full of pictures of Remi as a little girl with Aiden and their parents, whom Mason had seen pictures of during his due diligence.

In one picture Remi looked to be no more than three or four years old, dressed up in a frilly rose-colored dress with shiny white shoes and socks with lace trim. She clutched the stuffed golden retriever, which looked new. In another picture she stood in front of her tall, distinguished father, who Aiden closely resembled. Her father was holding both of Remi's hands. She had her head tipped back and was smiling up at him as he gazed down at her with love in his eyes. Another picture showed Remi and her mother, a honey-haired, hazel-eyed beauty. Remi, a little girl of maybe five or six, sat on her lap in front of a Christmas tree, holding a present with a big red bow. Another picture showed Remi and Aiden standing with their father. Remi was dressed in a leotard and tutu, holding a certificate that was too small for Mason to read, but her ear-to-ear smile and the pride in her brother's and father's eyes told him it was an important one.

Mason tried to swallow past the lump forming in his throat.

It was one thing to never know your parents and a completely different thing to *see* the love she'd lost. His heart broke for the sweet, sassy, confident woman waiting downstairs.

He'd expected Remi to call thirty seconds after he'd started searching the house, just to test him. But she hadn't, which made him wonder if that meant she trusted him. As he descended the grand staircase, he saw her sitting on the floor, sleeping by the front door. She was leaning against the wall, her feet tucked beneath her dress again, clutching her phone between her hands.

"Hey," she said, sleepily pushing to her feet as he approached.

She stumbled, and he caught her around the waist, steadying her. She was barely up to his chest in her bare feet. She sighed, making the kind of soft, enticing noise women made when they were about to be kissed. Electricity sizzled in the space between them. She licked her lips, sending heat searing down the center of his body and snapping him back to reality.

He had no idea if she meant that lip lick seductively, or if that was just Remi being *Remi*, which was an even more worrisome thought. Resisting seduction had never been difficult, but how did a man resist what he never saw coming?

He took a step back. "The house is clear. I assume you want me to stay in the room at the other end of the hall?"

She shook her head, holding his gaze with that innocent-vixen mix that wreaked havoc with his senses, and said, "Too far away. Just in case, would you mind staying in the room across the hall from mine? Oh, and I have a meeting at seven fifteen tomorrow morning. We should leave by six forty."

"Sounds good."

She stepped toward the stairs and stopped to slip out of his jacket and hand it to him. "Thank you for tonight. And you were right earlier. I *was* looking for an escape."

It took him a moment to realize she was talking about when she was dancing with the handsy prick. "That's what I'm here for."

On her way up the steps, without looking back at him, she said, "I'm glad you're here, Mason."

Given her need for control, he imagined those were tough confessions for her to make. He waited until he heard her bedroom door close before retrieving his bags from the car. As he carried them to his bedroom, he was grateful that he'd never needed much sleep. He had a feeling that when he closed his eyes, he'd see her alluring hazel eyes staring back at him.

CHAPTER FOUR

MASON LOOKED UP from the reports he was reading on his laptop at six thirty the next morning when Remi breezed into the kitchen looking sexier than should be legal in a slinky yellow sundress and flat strappy sandals. Her hair was still wet from her shower, and she was fresh faced, without a speck of makeup, at least as far as Mason could tell. Any other woman would look exhausted after only a few hours of sleep, but Remi had an aura about her that radiated like the sun, sprinkling just-wait-until-I-open-my-mouth energy as she flitted over to the table and plunked an oversized leather bag down beside his laptop.

"What are you doing?" She went to the refrigerator and grabbed a bottle of water.

"Working," he said as she took a drink. He'd been up for an hour and had already walked the perimeter of the property, looking for signs of prolonged visitors: litter on the ground, broken branches, or flattened grass. He had security notifications set on his phone and would be alerted day or night if there was movement on the property or inside the house, but he wasn't taking any chances.

"We have to go. *Chop, chop,*" she said as she screwed the cap onto her water bottle and shoved the bottle into her bag.

He closed his laptop. "You have to eat. You barely ate last night."

"What are you, the food police? There's a food tent on set."

She reached for her bag and he snagged it. "I've got this. There are six boxed meals in the fridge from Saturday and Sunday. Please tell me you ate your meals at the tent the last few days, with the exception of last night's dinner."

"Clock's tickin', nosy guy." Ignoring his question, she breezed out of the kitchen.

He grabbed his laptop and followed her out. "I can't have you fainting on me."

"Don't worry. I'll be on set. You'll be on the sidelines."

"Is that how we're playing it? If you faint on set, it's okay?" He'd wondered how she would act toward him today. She was obviously reclaiming control, and he was okay with that, as long as it didn't impede his work.

They went out the front door, and as he locked it, she said, "How we're *playing it* is that I'm a big girl and I'm in a very unforgiving industry. I know what my body needs to survive, and in case you're wondering, I've *never* fainted. Why are you worried, Mr. Three Seconds Flat? If I faint, I'm sure you'll be right there to catch me."

He didn't bother replying. They both knew she was right.

She sat in the front seat on the way to the set, texting with a mischievous expression on her face. He was curious about who she was texting and told himself his curiosity was purely security related.

He was a fucking liar.

He'd been up half the night thinking about her across the hall in that room with all the pictures, wondering if she was okay, or if when her head hit the pillow, without the distractions of events or filming, she sank into a darker state of mind, missing her family. Or . . . was she lying awake thinking of him, too? He'd told himself things would be different this morning, that they were drawn to each other last night only because of the situation they were in. But he'd been in close proximity with other beautiful women, and never once had he felt anything beyond a professional duty. The truth was, he'd never taken anyone to that rooftop before, and he wasn't sure why he'd taken her, except that she'd looked lonely and he'd wanted to ease those feelings.

He glanced at her thumbs tapping out a text and said, "According to your schedule, you have your meeting, and then you start filming at eight, which runs until six. Is there anything else on your docket I should know about?"

"Filming won't end at six," she said without looking up from her phone. "Probably more like eight. We're doing a grueling scene this afternoon, and I have serious doubts about me and Raz being able to nail it on our first—or *fifth*—try."

He'd already checked out Duncan "Raz" Raznick, another A-lister and an ex-boyfriend of Remi's. Like many celebrities, Raz had a spotty dating history, dating various women for short periods of time, but when he wasn't filming he spent time in Pleasant Hill, Maryland, with his family. Mason's investigation hadn't sent up any glaring red flags, but Raz's prior relationship with Remi left that door open.

"No problem," he said as he came to a stop sign. "According to the information I have, you don't have an assistant with you?"

"Nope. I hardly ever bring Naomi, my assistant, or Shea, my publicist, when I travel. I touch base with them throughout the day, and they make sure I'm kept abreast of my schedule. There are always people on set I can turn to if need be, but I told you, I'm perfectly capable of taking care of myself and making sure I'm where I'm supposed to be."

She lifted her chin, underscoring her determination, but when their gazes collided, the temperature in the SUV spiked, and a blush spread over her cheeks. She shifted her eyes away.

He hit the gas. *Holy hell.* Whatever was brewing between them hadn't dissipated one bit. It had gotten stronger, *hotter*, even more intense.

He'd spent a lifetime so adept at distancing himself from others, he'd become used to those walls. So much so, he'd forgotten they existed or that there were other ways to live, until Little Miss Challenge began chipping away at them. Remi was smart, sexy, and feisty, which wasn't so unusual, but she had an underlying vulnerability, belying the chip on her shoulder, which she wore like a medal. And apparently that was a deadly combination for Mason.

He had to nix this attraction fast. If it could multiply threefold in a few hours, what would happen in a few days?

As he drove toward Beckwith University, the small private college where most of the filming was taking place, he fought to push aside the unfamiliar feelings.

Mason had studied the layout of the various filming locations at the university and in town. Even though Porter and Merrick had already met with the head of security for both and apprised them of the situation Remi had faced in LA, Mason had done the same prior to taking over the position. The university had beefed up campus security, and the studio also had their own security on staff.

He turned onto the main road leading into campus, mature trees casting shadows over the car as they drove past manicured lawns and areas that were to be used for filming, which were corded off with tape and low concrete barriers. Throngs of college students lined the sidewalks, holding up their phones to take pictures and videos of the film's *base camp*. Trucks and trailers were lined up for cast and crew, creating boundaries along the far side of the property. Mason drove through campus, passing academic buildings on the left, residence halls to the right, and circled around to the sports complex. He had long ago learned not to overlook the obvious, and he took mental notes of vehicles and pedestrians, which he would do daily in case he spotted someone or something out of the ordinary.

"You passed the tent where they're holding the meeting," Remi said with a hint of annoyance.

"I'll have you there on time. I just want to get a read on the crowd."

She sighed. "The stalker isn't *here*. I've been filming for weeks. If he was going to do something, wouldn't he have already done so?"

"You'd be surprised. Some crazies can lay dormant for months, then come out of the woodwork in a blaze of fury." He glanced at her, noting the disbelief—and the underlying fear she was trying hard to mask. "Don't worry. You're in good hands."

"Mm-hm. I'm fine. Let's just get to the meeting."

As promised, they parked by the tent with nine minutes to spare. A crowd of eager fans waved papers, shouting Remi's name from the other side of the barricades.

Remi headed for them, smiling and waving. Mason moved closer, speaking low and clear so she was sure to hear every word as he memorized the faces of the cheering crowd. "Keep enough distance so they can't touch you. Don't put yourself in a compromising position. Say my name, and I'll get you out of there."

"You've seen too much television. They're my *fans*. This is called promoting the movie."

In her world that was true. In his it was called *dangerous*. He stuck to her like glue, stopping grabby hands as fans shouted, "I love you, Remi!" and "Are you single?" Mason shut that dude down with a glare, putting the guy who had asked on the top of his *watch* list. Remi handled herself like a pro, signing and smiling, though she didn't listen to Mason's suggestion and leaned in for selfies with fans. When a shaggy-haired guy grabbed her arm, Mason clutched his wrist, twisting his arm up and causing the guy to stumble backward, cursing.

"Hands off," Mason commanded.

Remi glowered at Mason and then quickly schooled her expression for her fans. Another guy reached for Remi, and Mason stepped between them. A group of twentysomethings, most of whom were guys, rushed toward them, and a girl was climbing over the other end of the barricade. Mason put his arms out in front of Remi, aiming his command at the crowd. "Stand back." He glared at the climber and said, "Other side *now*."

As the girl scrambled back to the appropriate side of the barricade, Mason said, "Ms. Divine has to get ready to film now." He took Remi by the arm, dragging her toward the tent as fans tried to lure her back with pleas of affection.

"I love you, Remi!" "We'll wait for you!" "You're hot!"

"What the hell?" Remi snapped.

"Things were getting out of hand, and you don't have time for that." He nodded toward the tent. "You've got two minutes to get to your meeting."

She wrenched her arm free and stormed into the crowded tent. Mason registered the faces of Raz and several supporting actors, the assistant director, producers, and a few miscellaneous people whose identities he would nail down promptly.

"I'll be by the door," he said.

"I'm fine. You should go get coffee."

He arched a brow at the ridiculous idea that he'd actually leave her unprotected.

"God forbid you leave my side," she said sarcastically.

Mason stood a few feet away as actors and crew settled into chairs, and Remi sat beside Raz. Mason didn't like the pitch in his gut at how cozy she seemed with the square-jawed, chisel-faced actor, whispering and smiling flirtatiously. He wondered if there were renewed sparks between them, and he didn't like the fact that he cared. He kept an eagle eye on them as the meeting began, and then he walked the perimeter of the tent, taking in the faces of the people milling about. He spoke to a security guy who was hanging around, and then he returned to the interior of the tent for the remainder of the meeting.

When the meeting ended, Remi shouldered her bag as she and Raz headed out. Mason fell into step behind her. A larger group of fans had formed by the barricades, and they were calling out "Remi!" "Raz!" "There they are!" and "Over here, Remi! I love you!"

Raz glanced at Mason over his shoulder, and Remi waved at fans as she said, "Raz, this is Mason, my bodyguard." *Thank you, Aiden.* "Mason, this is Raz."

Mason nodded in greeting, expecting Raz to snub him.

Raz's blue eyes lit up, and he thrust a hand in Mason's direction, flashing the smile that Mason was sure melted every pair of panties in its path. He shook Raz's hand, gritting his teeth at the thought of Remi being in that path.

"Nice to meet you," Raz said. "What happened to the other guys?"

"I told Aiden I was *done*," Remi said. "One guy, plainclothed." She motioned toward the overzealous fans and said, "I'm signing. You?"

"No. I've got to catch up with Patch." Mason knew from his research that Patch was Raz's assistant. Raz looked at Mason and said, "Take care of our girl. She's a sneaky one."

Our girl, my ass.

When Raz took off, Remi made a beeline for the fans.

"You need to eat before you get to the set," he reminded her.

"I'm fine," she said.

He could see this was going to be a trying job.

The afternoon passed in a cycle of standing guard, fending off fans, and watching Remi perform. She was playing the role of a woman who'd lost her young son to a stray bullet in a gang-infested area and falls in love with the intended target, a recovering drug addict, played by Raz. Remi was a consummate professional, hitting the mark with every emotional high and devastating low. After two of the scenes, the crew had applauded. She blew Mason away, even if she had been keeping her distance and avoiding eye contact with him since they'd left the house.

It was better this way, easier for him to concentrate on keeping her safe.

By the time she wrapped for the day, it was after seven, she was irritated with the producer for something that had happened on set, and she had to be exhausted. But on the way to the parking lot, she stopped to sign more autographs, her typical radiant self, as if she'd just come from a rejuvenating afternoon at the spa. She was impressive as hell, dedicated enough to put on a great face even if she was stressed and tired—and had a stalker hunting her down that she was pretending didn't exist.

How she managed to pull it all off was beyond Mason. Especially since she had eaten only an apple and had rebuffed his reminders for lunch and dinner.

I'm fine had quickly become his two least favorite words.

CHAPTER FIVE

ON WEDNESDAY AFTERNOON Remi flopped back in the SUV and closed her eyes as they drove home after a long day on set. The last three days had been mirror images, with long, exhausting days on set, made even more so because she could barely concentrate with Mason standing a few feet away at all times. She was used to distractions while she was working, but nothing could have prepared her for the way he infiltrated her every thought. She'd spent the last few nights thinking about the combustible heat between them, which multiplied with every passing day. He was always *right there*, making sure she was not only safe, but had whatever she needed. If that wasn't bad enough, when she finally fell asleep each night, Mason was front and center in her dreams.

Fantasies.

They were definitely fantasies.

Dark and *dirty* fantasies, in which she'd *tasted*, *touched*, and *discovered* every naughty thing she wanted. She'd woken up hot and bothered every morning since he'd moved in. This morning a cold shower hadn't helped, and she'd had to take her pleasure into her own hands just to make it through the day. She'd thought that would allow her to pull off acting calm, cool, and collected around Mason, but the last three mornings, the second she'd seen him sitting at the kitchen table in his tight T-shirt, those steel blue eyes had connected with hers and all bets were off. She could have melted an iceberg from the inferno he'd caused. She'd spent her days avoiding those omniscient eyes.

But there was no avoiding his thoughtfulness or the ruggedness he exuded.

"Why don't we stop and pick up a pizza or a salad or something? You haven't eaten all day."

There it was again. He'd asked after her all day, offering her food, water, to take a walk between sets—all of which she'd wanted but had refused. She wasn't used to having someone notice so many things about her, and this wasn't exactly a man she should be interested in. Mason was under Aiden's thumb, on his payroll.

He was another thing she wanted that was just out of reach.

"I'm fine," she answered, her mind turning to Aiden.

She still hadn't heard from him, and that added a little extra anxiety to her day. They relied heavily on email when they were traveling, but he always called when he first settled in. She'd breathe easier once he touched base.

She didn't need to look to know Mason's jaw was clenching and those sexy muscles in his jaw were flexing from her response to his suggestion they stop for food. She could feel tension buzzing in the air. She'd seen that look on him so many times today, she'd actually become fond of it. It was almost as appealing as the jealousy she'd sensed when Raz had tracked her down between scenes and they'd spent an hour running lines. Raz had a great personality, and they had fun, but that was as far as it went. Their relationship had had no spark.

Unlike the sizzling chemistry heating up the interior of the SUV.

"You have to eat, Remi. You can't exist on an apple when you work as hard as you do."

She looked at his large hands gripping the steering wheel, deep-set eyes focused on the road, biceps twitching, and her insides got hot. Now, *those* were sparks.

He glanced over, and his lips quirked into an *almost* smile. She really liked his *almost* smile. It was mysterious, like him, and it was real, unlike most of the smiles she saw on people's faces.

"What'll it be?" he asked. "Burger? Eggs? We can hit the grocery store."

"Didn't anyone ever teach you that when a woman says no, it *means* no?"

That earned a rough laugh that skated beneath her skin. "Princess, the word *no* hasn't come out of your mouth, and you have to eat something. You expended thousands of calories today, and you can't weigh more than a buck ten soaking wet. You'll wear yourself out at this rate."

She stared out the window and said, "Spoken like a man who has probably *never* been told what to do."

"I spent years in the military. If you think I haven't been told what to do, you're sorely mistaken. How about a protein shake? You don't even have to chew."

"*No*, thank you."

He stopped at a red light on the corner and pointed to Chapter One, Aurelia's bookstore. "Doesn't your friend own that place? She sells baked goods from your other friend's bakery. How about a cupcake?"

Shocked, she said, "How do you know about Aurelia and Willow?"

He glanced at her out of the corner of his eye and said, "It's my job to know who you're in contact with. I'd rather have you put some meat in that smart mouth of yours instead of sugar, but at this point I'd be thrilled to get anything inside you."

Her mind went straight to the gutter, and the way his eyes locked on the road and he white-knuckled the steering wheel, she had a feeling he was thinking the same thing.

"I'm fine," she said quickly. "Let's just get home, please." *Before the images your comment conjured get me even hotter.*

When they got home, Mason checked the house while Remi waited by the door, which seemed ridiculous to her, but whatever . . .

She needed to get him out of her head, and the farther away he was, the better. The man sucked the oxygen right out of her lungs when they were alone.

"All clear," he said as he came down the stairs. "Why don't I whip up one of those boxed meals you've got in the fridge?"

The image of Mason wearing nothing but a pair of leather briefs and carrying a whip slammed into her. *Holy crap.* She was definitely losing her mind.

She pushed past him, heading up the stairs, and said, "I don't need you to whip anything, thank you. I'm going to change and relax in the hot tub. You can eat my box if you want." It wasn't until she reached the landing that she realized what she'd said. Mortified, she spun around and said, "The *meal!* I meant the *boxed meal!*"

He chuckled.

Damn him for having that effect on her!

A little while later, Aiden called while Remi was standing in her bedroom wearing her bikini and looking out the window at Mason traipsing along the perimeter of the yard. Relief swept through her at the sound of her brother's voice.

"How are things going with Mason? Are you two getting along?"

She swallowed hard and said, "He's fine, very *intuitive.*" She watched Mason stop by the tall iron fence. He pulled out his phone, clicked a picture of something through the fence, then continued walking.

"Good. His references were excellent. Anything troublesome happening?"

You mean like the way he makes my heart race? "No. I told you. I really think all that stalker nonsense is over." As the words left her lips, she realized that once Aiden finally believed her, he would let Mason go. A heavy feeling settled in her chest.

"Let's hope so, Rem. And how are you? How's filming going?"

"Good. We're on schedule so far."

She and Aiden talked a little longer about filming and how good it had been to see their friends at the fundraiser. She wished him luck with his business deal, trying to concentrate on their conversation, but she couldn't shake the uneasy feeling that accompanied the idea of no longer seeing Mason. How could that have happened so fast? One day Aiden would realize the stalker was no longer a threat and Mason would move on to his next assignment. Then she'd be left pining over a man she never could have had. She was an idiot.

An idiot with a crush, but an idiot all the same.

When they finally ended the call, her mind was whirling. She had to find a way to stop thinking about Mason like the delicious hulk of hotness he was, and since that seemed impossible when he was around, she needed to get away from him. *Fast.*

She sent an SOS text to Willow. *Busy? I could use some fun.*

She waited until Mason headed for the front yard before grabbing a towel and going down to the hot tub. Willow's response came through as she stepped out the patio doors. *Sorry! Can't. We're having a couples night with Bridge, Bodhi, Talia, and Derek. Want to join?*

That was just what she needed—to be the third wheel with a bodyguard in tow. She thumbed out, *That's okay. Have fun! I need to be without male company tonight.* She added a smiley-face emoji and sent the text.

She set her phone on the side of the hot tub and climbed in, determined to figure out a way to put space between them, even if she had to hole up in her room.

Ahh. This was just what she needed. She closed her eyes, reveling in the solitude. She could just hide out here and relax while he did his *traipsing.*

"Share a sandwich?"

Her eyes flew open. Mason stood by the hot tub holding up a sandwich.

"Where did you get that?"

"A gentleman never eats and tells," he said with a smirk.

"*Ohmygod.*" Laughter burst from her lungs.

He waved the sandwich and said, "I'm sorry. I shouldn't have said that, but I sure do like your laugh better than the 'I'm fine' you've been doling out all day."

"Sorry about that, but I really was fine. I don't eat a lot when I'm on set," she explained. "I can't afford to get reflux or feel or look uncomfortable or bloated."

"I understand where you're coming from. In my line of work, I can't afford to be weighed down, either. There are things you can eat that won't make you feel or look that way but will fuel your body and keep you healthy."

"I can't afford to gain weight, either. Cameras are very unforgiving."

"In my opinion, you could gain thirty pounds and still be stunning, but I hear where you're coming from. Like I said, there are things you can eat that'll help maintain your figure and still fuel that smart brain of yours."

You think I'm smart? Most guys wrote actresses off as brainless beauties.

"Trust me," he said. "I know what I'm talking about."

He lifted his shirt, flashing toned abs and a treasure trail she wanted to follow all the way down to paradise. Her mouth watered, and she looked away, hoping he wouldn't notice. *Just breathe . . .*

"Come on, Remi. Aiden would never forgive me if I let you starve." His tone softened. "Please tell me you're not one of those women who tries to survive on air."

"I'm not. I like to eat, and when I'm not filming, I eat a *lot.*" But she'd never been around a guy who noticed or cared what food she put in her mouth. Although she'd been around plenty of men who wished she'd put certain body parts of theirs in her mouth.

Great, now she was thinking about having *Mason's* certain body part in her mouth, which was weird, because she'd given exactly one blow job in her life, and it hadn't been the best experience.

"Glad to hear it. Come on, Princess, make me feel better. Take one bite."

She'd been momentarily struck dumb when he'd first called her the endearment her mother had used so often. This time *Princess* came out soft and seductive, so different from the way he'd said it at the fundraiser. She met his compassionate gaze, and her stomach fluttered.

God . . . She was crushing on him like a naive girl of eighteen instead of a grown woman who had resisted more advances than she cared to remember.

He wiggled the sandwich, his eyes narrowing. "Sure you don't want a bite of my big, meaty sandwich?"

Holy cow, did she ever. She grabbed his hand, pulling the sandwich forward to take a bite in an effort to stop thinking about his other big meaty thing she wanted.

"Oh my goodness," she said as sweet and spicy flavors exploded on her tongue.

He winked and said, "Attagirl." Then he took a bite, too.

"That's the best thing I've ever had. Where did you get it?" She reached for his hand, taking another bite.

"La Love Café. One of the guys on set turned me onto it, and I had the sandwich delivered while you were filming. I figured if I ordered something different every day, I might find *one* thing you like."

Her thoughts stumbled. "You would do that? Just to get me to eat?"

He shrugged and leaned on the edge of the hot tub. He didn't look at her breasts or steal a glance at the rest of her nearly naked body, like most men did. He looked only at her face, like he wanted her to know he saw her. Didn't he know she'd gotten that impression the second he'd offered to walk her to the restroom at the fundraiser when he'd noticed she'd never gone?

He reached for her face, his rough hand cupping her cheek, his eyes locked on her mouth, stealing her ability to think past what it would be like when his lips touched hers. She felt like she'd been wanting him for months, rather than days. He leaned in, and she closed her eyes. His thumb brushed over the corner of her mouth. *Yes, kiss me . . .*

"Crumbs," he said as his hand slipped from her cheek.

The air rushed from her lungs at the same moment her phone vibrated. She jumped, knocking her phone from the ledge. Mason caught it in midair.

"Just breathe, Princess." He handed her the phone and walked a few feet away, giving her privacy to read her text.

She was flustered and more turned on than ever. Mason had not only gotten under her skin, but he definitely had superpowers and was figuring out all her secret vices. Lord help her if he ever actually kissed her. With her luck she'd probably melt into a puddle of liquid heat and slip away, rendering him just out of reach *forever*.

She opened Piper's text with trembling hands. *Willow said you're down to party. I'm getting ready to ditch a sucky date and head to Decadence. You in? Bring your hottieguard!*

Remi choked out a cough at the thought of Piper and Mason. The last thing she needed was to watch Piper hit on him all night.

Mason spun around with concern in his eyes. "You okay?"

No! I'm hot and bothered and seriously need to get away from you because you look like last night's delicious fantasy and I know just how incredible that was!

"I'm fine," she said as she sent a response to Piper. *I'm suffocating from his hotness! Pick me up?*

Piper's response was immediate. *What about your stalker?*

Nonexistent! Please!? Remi added a kissing emoji and sent it off.

Piper agreed with a firm *I've got your back!* Remi had thirty minutes to get ready and sneak out. She felt a little guilty ditching Mason when he'd been so nice, but if she stuck around, she'd end up eating a lot more than his sandwich.

She climbed out of the hot tub, secretly planning her escape.

Mason handed her the towel. "You okay? You weren't in there very long."

"Yeah. I'm exhausted." She feigned a yawn. "It's been a really long day. I'm going to take a quick shower and go to bed. Thanks for sharing your sandwich. I'll see you in the morning. I have tomorrow off, so sleep as late as you want."

"Great. I think I'll hit the shower, too. If you need me, just bang on the door or text."

In her head she twisted his response to *If you need to bang me, just text*.

Yep, he'd turned her brain to dust.

It was a damn good thing she was leaving.

She told herself she wasn't really ditching Mason. She was preserving her sanity.

Remi stood in front of the mirror, second-guessing her frayed skinny jeans and black T-shirt. She wanted to fit in at Decadence, an upscale nightclub that featured male and female dancers. It was classier than a strip club, but *classy* meant something much more casual in the small town than it did in LA. Remi had gone with Piper and the girls a few months ago to see Talia's fiancé, Derek, dance. Remi tried to channel her inner *Piper* and figure out what her tough-as-nails friend might wear on a date. She stripped off her jeans and put on a short, hip-hugging black skirt with a zipper running from the middle of her thigh to the waist, which lay just below her belly button. Remi usually wore that particular skirt with a nice sweater, but in an effort to look nothing like herself, she pulled on a black crop top and shoved her feet into chunky black boots. She twisted her hair up and pulled on a black baseball cap.

She shoved her phone and keys in her pocket and opened her bedroom door. The house was silent, and Mason's door was ajar. She tiptoed across the hall and heard the shower running. *Perfect.*

She ran downstairs and out the front door. The cool night air stung her skin as she sprinted down the driveway, feeling the familiar rush of freedom that overcame her every time she'd ditched her previous bodyguards. Only this time it was followed by a heavy dose of guilt for ditching this particular bodyguard.

Her lungs burned as she rounded the first curve. She'd never noticed how long the driveway was! As she hurried around the second bend, she realized she'd forgotten to open the gate. She'd climb the damn thing if she had to. With one hand on her hat, she navigated to Piper's phone number and called her.

As the gate came into view, "Hello, Princess," sounded in her ear, rich, smooth, and masculine as hell. *Mason. No, no, no!* She must have called the wrong number! She poked at her phone, trying to end the call. Panting, she shoved the phone in her skirt pocket and grabbed the cold iron gate to catch her breath—and her stomach sank at the sight of Mason leaning against the hood of his SUV on the other side, arms folded over his broad chest, legs crossed casually at the ankle, and an angry look in his eyes.

Piper stood beside him in a pair of black skinny jeans and sky-high heels. "Looks like someone's gonna get spanked," she said with a smirk. "Hope it's me."

Mason handed Piper her phone and pushed from the hood of the car. "Feeling restless, Princess?"

"How did you get down here?" Remi panted out, her heart racing. She was angry, annoyed, and oddly intrigued that Mason had figured her out so easily. "You were *just* in the shower."

"That was a test." He stepped up to the gate, glowering down at her. "Guess who failed?"

"I'll happily fail a test if you'll wait for me in the dark," Piper chimed in.

"Piper!" Remi snapped. "That's *not* helping."

"Piper tells me we're going to Decadence. All you had to do was tell me you wanted to go and I'd have driven you." His gaze raked down her body, leaving a heat wave in its wake. "You're going to a nightclub wearing that?"

"It's a disguise," she snapped. "I'm trying to fit in."

"You look like the nineties threw up on the eighties." He turned to Piper and said, "I'm going to take Remi back up to the house, turn off my shower, and get her into some clothes that are fitting of who she is. We'll meet you at the club. Cool?"

"I'd be cooler if you said you were going to get my friend *out* of her clothes and leave it at that, but whatever floats your boat." Piper stepped up to the gate, pressing her face close to the bars, and whispered, "Take your time with hottieguard." She put a hand on her hip and narrowed her eyes at Mason. "I'd never let anything happen to her. I know the owner and bartenders at the club. I'd make sure she was safe."

Eyes on Remi, Mason said, "Not as effectively as I will."

After Piper took off, Mason brooded in silence on the drive up to the house. His jaw was clenched as he parked, and they stepped from the car. His face was a mask of anger and something else that felt a lot like disappointment. Remi could handle anger, but the disappointment sent regret slicing through her.

"I'm sorry," she said at the same time he said, "What the hell was that?"

He rubbed the back of his neck like she'd caused a pain there, and then he crossed his arms. "What's this about, Remi? I'm here to protect you, and I can't do that if you don't trust me."

"I *do* trust you!"

"Bullshit. Trust means coming to me, telling me that you need to get out of the house. You want to go to a club? I'm there. You want to dance with a dude? I'm there to make sure you're treated right. You want to hook up with a guy?" His hands fisted as he said, "Just give me a few minutes to check him out first. I'm not here to judge you. Your personal life is your own. But I *am* going to protect you with everything I have, and I'm *not* going to play games. You're either going to trust me, or we're going to find you a new bodyguard, because I will not chase you down like a child."

"I'm not a fucking child."

"I know you're not, which is why I don't understand this. I thought we were getting along pretty well."

"We were." *Too well.* Regret settled on her shoulders like a lead shawl.

"Then what is this? Some form of rebellion? Didn't you ever sneak out as a kid?"

She swallowed hard, unexpected emotions welling up inside her. "No."

His expression softened, and she felt a lightening in the tension around them. "Well, lucky for you, I'm awesome at it." His eyes shimmered with an unexpected playfulness. "You want to have fun? I'll help you have fun while keeping you safe. I'll school you in the ways of the wicked, but I won't allow you to put yourself in danger."

"What does that mean? You'll teach me to sneak out?"

"If that's the itch you need to scratch, yes."

He stepped closer, looking deeply into her eyes as he said, "Let me keep you safe, Remi. Trust me." It came out as a plea as much as it did a demand.

Now she was breathing hard for a whole new reason.

He eyed her outfit. "If tonight is about going incognito and you're comfortable in what you have on, then go for it. But know that you don't have to. I'm here so you no longer have to live your life in a box. I'm not going to shuffle you from car to building and lock you away. That's no way to live when there's a whole world out there waiting for you to light it up."

She didn't know exactly how to respond beyond "Thank you." *I'm sorry* felt too pat, and there was no way she was going to admit *why* she'd wanted space from him, especially now, when space was the last thing she wanted.

"Just tell me one thing," he said in a gentler tone. "Were you testing me? To see if I'd quit?"

"No," came out fast and loud. She tried to soften her vehemence to a more casual tone and said, "I like you. I don't want you to quit."

He exhaled loudly. "That's a start. I'm on your side, Remi."

"Thank you. I'm not used to being around someone like you. You *see* things about me, *in* me, that other people don't."

"It's part of the job. No big deal."

It was a very big deal because he saw what she *needed*, what she *wanted*. "I'm sorry. I didn't mean to worry you or make you angry."

"I'm only angry because you could get hurt. I'm sure it's frustrating for you to have someone breathing down your neck all the time. But if that scumbag followed you from LA to New York, then your life could be in danger every moment of the day. Like it or not, Remi, you need me. And guess what, Princess? I need you, too."

"Somehow I doubt that," she said softly, wondering why *Princess* sounded sweeter now, like an endearment.

"I've never failed at a job, and you hold all the cards. You fire me and I fail. See? It goes both ways." He motioned toward the door. "We'd better shut off the shower and get going so Piper doesn't get the wrong idea." As he unlocked the front door, he eyed her skirt and boots and said, "So, are we partying Madonna-style tonight?"

"I think so. I need a night when nobody knows my name."

"I'm cool with that, as long as *you* know who you are." He placed his hand on her lower back as they walked inside and said, "Because once you lose sight of that, you're screwed."

Remi had always believed she knew exactly who she was: Aiden's younger sister and an actress. It wasn't until she'd met Willow and formed a circle of real, true friends that she'd realized how much richer life was with them in it. She'd added *friend* to her short list after *sister* and *actress*. As her friends fell in love and started forming their own families, Remi had begun taking a closer look at her own life and realized—or finally acknowledged—how lonely she was and that she wanted to be more than a friend, sister, and actress.

Achieving Oscar-winning, America's-Sweetheart status took a perfect storm of elements. She'd gotten lucky with her career. If only she could get as lucky in her personal life.

Mason had never been a fan of nightclubs, though he understood the draw of a place to let down one's guard and connect with another lonely soul with whom to hole up for an evening of meaningless sex. It had been a long time since Mason had stepped foot into a place like Decadence, where bad decisions lingered in every drink. Testosterone-laden men and scantily clad women bumped and ground to the pounding beat, the scents of lust and foreplay drawing them closer, the haze of alcohol taunting them into submission. Mason stood by the crowded dance floor where Remi and Piper had been dancing and chatting since they'd arrived more than an hour ago. At six four, he had a clear view of the room. He sized up men and scrutinized women, cataloging the faces of every person in the place, just in case he needed to draw upon them later.

The combination of dim lighting, lust-filled hazes, and Remi's hair tucked beneath her baseball cap seemed to do the trick of hiding her identity. She was sexy as sin in that skimpy leather skirt, her toned stomach peeking out, begging to be licked with every sway of her hips. She'd seemed nervous when they'd first arrived, but she'd downed a shot of tequila, and the liquid courage had done its job. The girl had *serious* dance moves.

Moves he'd like to see in the privacy of a dark bedroom.

Moves he should *not* be thinking about.

The door to the club opened, and a group of guys blew in, loud and boisterous. They headed directly to the bar. The door opened again, and Remi's friend Willow walked in with her husband, Zane. Zane Walker was an actor-turned-screenwriter and had starred with Remi in a romantic movie last summer.

Willow scanned the dance floor and pulled Zane through the crowd toward Remi and Piper. Remi squealed when the curvy blonde appeared before her. The girls fell into a giggling group hug, and then Remi hugged Zane. Jealousy clawed up Mason's spine. He had no business caring who Remi hugged, and Zane was married, for God's sake. She obviously wasn't interested in him. What the hell was wrong with him?

"I didn't know you were coming!" Remi exclaimed.

"Bridgette and Talia called it an early night, and I wanted to dance. Piper texted me earlier," Willow said loudly. "I hear you got caught sneaking out!"

"I was hoping she'd at least get spanked for it, but apparently hottieguard is a gentleman," Piper said.

"That's my cue to leave you girls alone." Zane said something in Willow's ear, kissed her, and then he joined Mason off to the side. "You're Remi's new bodyguard, Mason, right? Bodhi's friend?"

Mason shook his proffered hand. "Yes, but we're keeping the bodyguard thing on the down low tonight. Remi's here incognito."

"That explains the baseball cap. I'm Zane Walker."

"I know." When Zane's brows slanted, Mason said, "Part of the job. Background checks on people close to Remi."

"Oh, right. I guess that makes sense."

A guy danced over to the girls, and Mason readied himself to intervene, but as the guy leaned closer to Remi, Piper inserted herself between them, shaking her head, and the guy backed off.

Zane chuckled. "Has she been doing that all night?"

"Pretty much." He liked Piper, despite her role in Remi's attempt to sneak out. She'd been watching over Remi since they'd arrived, and when their friend Everly had shown up briefly, she'd watched out for her, too. Piper seemed to have a nose for sniffing out douchebags, and she had no problem shutting them down.

Remi glanced over, as she'd done several times. Mason tried to convince himself she was just making sure she was safe, but there was no mistaking the sensuality in each and every furtive glance, or the spike in temperature they caused.

"Don't let Piper's size fool you," Zane said. "She's the fiercest of all the Dalton girls. She's everyone's protector, including Remi's and Aurelia's."

Mason had studied people long enough to know there was more to the brazen siren than she cared to let people see. The same way he knew Remi was a hell of a lot more than just a gorgeous actress.

"But don't let Remi fool you, either," Zane said. "She gets prickly, but who wouldn't? I hated all the bullshit that came along with being a celebrity, and I never had a stalker. She's been dealing with a lot these past few months. She's an incredible person—you should know that. She's got a big heart, and she would do anything for her friends."

"Yeah, I get that impression." Mason spotted a guy watching Remi from across the room, and the hair on the back of his neck stood on end. He didn't like the way he was looking at her.

Zane lowered his voice and said, "I hear Remi gave you the slip earlier."

"She *tried* and *failed*," Mason said distractedly as the guy he was watching wove through the crowd, his eyes trained on Remi. Remi was too busy dancing with Willow to notice, and Piper was now dirty dancing with a dark-haired dude.

"Excuse me," Mason said to Zane and strode onto the dance floor behind Remi, locking a threatening gaze on the guy. Mason put his hand on Remi's waist, and her head whipped around, eyes wide. Mason didn't miss a beat, dancing as if they were together as he spoke directly into her ear. "There's a guy at ten o'clock heading your way. I don't like the look of him."

The actress in her must have taken over because she fell effortlessly into a seductive dance. Her hips swayed and her ass brushed against his groin, making him hard as steel despite his focus on the guy, who was now standing still, watching them. Remi's arm snaked into the air, blindly finding the side of Mason's face, and slithered down his neck to his shoulder. She turned in a hip-swaying, shoulder-rocking dance. Neon lights rained down over her beautiful face, reflecting in her eyes as they danced thigh to thigh, chest to chin. She moved sensually, *hungrily*, against him, meeting every thrust of his hips with a seductive move of her own. Mason knew he should put space between them, but the guy was still watching—and Remi felt fucking incredible.

Mason noticed several other men watching as her hands slid up his chest and down his arms. He was quick to shoot them warning glares, though he was sure there was also pride in his eyes, because holy hell, Remi was *hot*. She moved like she was born with rhythm and sensuality coursing through her veins. Every sway of her hips amped up his arousal as she turned around again, brushing her ass against his cock. His hand belted around her waist, pulling her closer, *staking claim* as he lowered his chin, shooting a darker, even more menacing look at the original ogler, sending him retreating with a sheepish look in his eyes. Remi's ass pressed against him, her hands sliding down his outer thighs. Their bodies moved in perfect harmony, brushing and taunting. If she were anyone else, he'd be taking her to his bed tonight.

On that thought, he stepped back, putting space between them. Remi glanced lustfully over her shoulder. Her gaze quickly morphed to confusion, and then something akin to hurt brimmed in her beautiful eyes. *Fuuck.*

With the threat alleviated and a knot of guilt burning in his chest, Mason strode off the dance floor.

"Whoa, hottieguard has moves," Piper said loudly.

Fucking hottieguard. He didn't want to be anyone's hottieguard, but he couldn't deny the possessiveness pulsing inside him, the desire to make Remi *his*, to protect her from all the ogling assholes and help her find the life she so desperately wanted and didn't quite know how to live. He gritted his teeth, watching the guy across the room to be sure he wasn't dumb enough to approach her again.

"Damn, dude," Zane said. "The way you two looked out there, I'd have sworn you were a couple."

"All part of the job." The lie came easily, but he wasn't fooling himself. Remi Aldridge had the power to slay him, and if he was going to protect her, he couldn't let that happen.

As the night wore on, Remi's glances came more often, hotter and more intense than ever. Suddenly the music died down and the din of the people rose. Women cheered and guys shouted.

Mason moved closer to Remi just as the room went nearly pitch-black. He swept her into his arms, his senses buzzing like live wires, ready to fend off any threat. In the next second a fast, staccato beat rang out and neon lights flashed over the stage. Women screamed, and the crowd surged forward amid whistles and catcalls. Smoke rose at the back of the stage, and a muscular dark-haired guy burst through a curtain wearing a bow tie and skintight pants.

Women waved dollar bills, chanting "Geno! Geno!"

Mason's eyes dropped to Remi, who was clutching his shirt and looking up at him with those entrancing hazel eyes like *he* was the main event.

Holy. Fuck.

There was a half-naked man tearing off his clothes onstage, and the most beautiful woman in the room wanted only him. But damn it, that momentary blackout was a perfect reminder of why he needed to keep his hands off her.

He released his grip, but she fisted her hands tighter in his shirt, snagging a few chest hairs. The beat of the music accelerated, competing with the pounding of his heart.

"Dance with me," she said heatedly.

She rolled her plump lower lip between her teeth, her hazel eyes darkening and widening at once, pleading with him as they had when they were dancing at the fundraiser, chipping away at his resolve.

He gritted his teeth and said, "I'm here to watch your back, Remi."

"How about you watch my *front*, instead?" she practically purred.

She began swaying seductively, still clinging to his shirt. The beat slowed, but Mason's engine revved faster. Blood pounded through his veins as he tore his eyes from Remi and scanned the crowd of dancing, cheering women and men. Zane's arms were around Willow, and Piper was waving dollar bills. The song came to a crescendo, causing another surge toward the stage. A group of women knocked into Piper, sending her stumbling into Remi and knocking Remi's hat off. Mason steadied them both.

"Is that . . . ?" A woman pointed at Remi and yelled, "It's Remi Divine!"

Several people whipped around, converging on them like walls closing in. Fear rose in Remi's eyes. Thinking fast, Mason said, "My girlfriend gets that all that time!" He hauled her against him as he pushed toward the door, knocking people out of the way with his broad shoulders, clearing stragglers with a powerful sweep of his arm. Piper, Willow, and Zane were on their heels as they burst from the bar into the cool, dark night. Mason kept Remi close as he blazed a path toward the SUV.

"Holy shit!" Zane exclaimed as a few people stumbled out the door behind them.

"That was insane!" Willow said.

Piper said, "Hottieguard, you're pretty kick-ass."

Mason had Remi tucked safely against his side, but there was nothing funny about the way his insides were thrumming or about what could have gone down if he'd given in to his desires and been caught off guard.

Another excellent reminder of why he needed to keep his python in his pants.

CHAPTER SIX

THURSDAY MORNING REMI awoke feeling rejuvenated and refreshed. She'd heard her girlfriends talk about inescapable lust and combustible heat, but Remi had never actually experienced any of those things until she'd met Mason. Now that she'd experienced the heart-pumping, toe-curling *thrum* of white-hot desire, she wanted *more* of it. She'd left the door wide open last night when she'd asked Mason to dance, and though he'd sent a clear message about being there to watch her back, not to cross professional boundaries, she knew in her heart that he felt their connection just as strongly as she did. She just wasn't sure what to do about it.

She dressed in a sports bra and yoga pants, hoping to work off some of her sexual frustration, and then she combed through emails, taking care to respond to all of Naomi's messages. When she finally headed downstairs to the gym, every step made her vibrate with excitement about seeing Mason. It was more than physical attraction that had her flying high. It was *everything* about him—even the fact that after only a couple of days, he knew her well enough to be waiting at the bottom of the driveway when she'd tried to sneak out.

The man paid attention to details.

And, *sweet heavens*, he knew how to dance. Her heart raced just thinking about the feel of his body against hers, his hand splayed over her belly, his hard heat pressing against her ass.

Her pulse quickened as she peeked into the kitchen, expecting to see him there, but the room was empty. She looked out the patio door, but he wasn't walking the property line, either. He was usually right *there*, wherever she was. He definitely had Spidey senses. She headed down to the gym on the lower level, wondering where he was. She knew he wouldn't have gone far.

His voice floated out of the open doors to the gym. "I know, sweetheart. I'm sorry," Mason said. "I hate that I have to cancel, too."

Remi stopped cold, listening despite knowing she shouldn't.

"I'll make it up to you after I finish this job." He paused, and then he said, "A few weeks. Three, maybe four. Then things will go back to normal."

He had a *girlfriend*? Why on earth had he danced with her the way he had?

"I miss you, too. Okay. See you soon, sweetheart."

Back to normal? Sweetheart? Tears burned her eyes. *I'm such an idiot.* He was just doing his job, and she was throwing herself at him. His voice whispered through her mind. *I'm here to watch your back, Remi.* She leaned against the wall, feeling sick. How could her radar be that far off?

Just breathe, Remi. Just breathe, and everything will be okay.

She had to fix this, to find a way to make things okay without totally embarrassing herself. If she needed a bodyguard, she wanted it to be Mason, even if they could only be friends on a professional level. She trusted him, and she liked him. The clink of weights jostled her brain into gear. Maybe she was worrying too much. So what if she'd misread him? He was hot, and he'd danced like he'd *wanted* her, even if he'd been doing it just as part of his job. *Any* other woman would have thought the same thing. She told herself she had nothing to be embarrassed about, and even if she didn't quite believe it, she was a professional actress. She could save face like a pro.

She pushed from the wall, rolled her shoulders back, and forced a smile. *Piece of cake.* She flexed her hands a few times, and with a bounce in her step, she entered the gym.

And nearly swallowed her tongue.

Holy mother of hotness.

Mason Swift was delicious wearing jeans and a T-shirt. He was devastating in a tuxedo. But he was *intoxicating* curling barbells in a room full of mirrors while wearing nothing but a pair of black shorts. His jaw flexed with each curl. A sheen of sweat glistened off his tanned, sculpted muscles. She'd never seen a man whose body looked like a work of art.

Mason was that man.

Her mouth went dry as her eyes trailed over his sculpted pecs. The word *Goodbye* was tattooed over his heart. She wondered about that, but she couldn't hold on to the thought as her eyes drifted down to his abs. Forget bouncing quarters off them. She wanted to *lick* them. And his thighs? *Thick* didn't begin to describe the power straining against those shorts.

"Never seen a guy work out before?" he asked with a smirk, snapping her from her Mason-induced trance.

She tore her gaze away. "I just didn't expect to see you in here."

He didn't look like he believed her, but *whatever.* She had bigger things to deal with. Like figuring out how to make her heart stop racing. She stretched her arms over her head, then out to the sides, trying to distract herself from her tingling nerves and the lust pooling inside her. God, she was a terrible person. He had a girlfriend and she was still getting turned on by him.

"Did you sleep okay?" he asked.

Back to business as usual.

Okay, she'd take it.

"Yes. Sorry I got a little tipsy last night. I'm a lightweight. I almost never drink. I shouldn't have asked you to dance."

"No sweat, Princess. I know you couldn't help yourself." He grinned and pumped out a few more curls. When he set the weights on the rack, he said, "Seriously, though, I hope you had a good time with your friends."

"I did. Thank you for getting me out of there before there was a scene. Pictures of me at a club like Decadence would definitely make for some ugly headlines."

"That's what I'm here for." As he loaded weights on the bench-press bar, he said, "There is something else we need to talk about."

She began stretching her legs, praying he wasn't going to bring up the way she'd practically thrown herself at him.

"*Food*," he said flatly.

Oh thank God!

She stepped onto the treadmill and increased the speed to a fast walk to warm up.

"I'm not going to harass you about what you're eating, or rather, what you're *not* eating. But you've got no eggs, milk, bread, or meat. I'm a big guy. I need to eat, and you said you're having your girlfriends over for a party tomorrow night. What are you going to feed them?"

"You can have my boxed meals today and we can order you meals from the service from now on. I'll just order something in tomorrow."

"I prefer to cook my own meals." He finished loading up the bar and lay on the weight bench. His shorts pulled tight across his groin.

Everywhere she looked she saw that bulge reflected in the mirrors, making it impossible not to think about it. It was like the universe was paying her back for trying to sneak out on him. *Geez!*

He lifted the bar from the rack, his muscles straining as he said, "I thought you told Aiden you wanted to be like a regular person."

"Jesus, do you remember every word I ever said?" She told herself to calm down. At least he wasn't embarrassing her about last night. But really, gym shorts should be banned for that man.

"Usually." He gritted his teeth through several more reps.

Remi increased her speed to a run, trying to distract herself from all the hotness wafting off him as he stood and stretched. But when he guzzled water from a bottle, she caught sight of his Adam's apple sliding up the center of his neck, and for some reason it made him even sexier.

He's taken.

Taken, taken, taken!

"You know, most normal people cook for their friends," he said as he lowered himself onto the bench again. He gritted and flexed, his arms shaking as he pushed out a few more reps—the last one with the sexiest groan she'd ever heard.

She amped up her speed to a sprint, trying not to think about how that groan would sound in her dark bedroom as he lay naked on top of her, his muscular thighs pressing down on hers.

Mason pushed to his feet and sauntered over to the treadmill. She swallowed hard, sure he could sense her desire like he sensed everything else about her.

He eyed the digital display. "Nice pace. So, was that all just talk about wanting to be treated like a regular person?"

"No." She scrambled through her memory bank, trying to remember what they were talking about. *Food. Tomorrow night. Got it.* "I never learned how to cook."

"Slow down to a walk," he said. "If you do interval sprints, you'll get more out of your workout. Do you usually work out with weights, too?"

She turned down the speed, and he reached over, reducing the speed even more.

"I don't do much with weights." She panted, trying to catch her breath. "I think it's more feminine for women to be toned but soft."

A wicked smile curved his lips. "I couldn't agree more."

He needed to stop looking at her like that, and *she* needed to stop noticing.

After another minute he said, "Kick it back up to a run. How long do you usually do aerobics?"

She quickened her pace. "An hour." He looked concerned, and she wondered if he expected her to say *two*.

"Don't you have a personal trainer?"

"I did, but it seemed silly to pay someone to watch me work out. Why?"

"Because an hour on the treadmill for someone your size, who eats like a bird, is ridiculous. You really do need me, Princess. I can help you tune up your workout so you aren't wasting your time. A few weights, the *right* aerobics, and you'll feel better and have more energy. You need resistance training as you get older anyway, for bone health. It's easier to get into the habit at twenty-five than it is at forty."

After three minutes, he motioned for her to turn down her speed again, which she did. She completed two more intervals of running and walking, already more winded than if she had been running the whole time. She was also less stressed about last night. He obviously wasn't going to bring it up, and for that she was beyond thankful.

"I have a few years before I hit forty," she panted out. "How old are you?"

"Thirty-four. Why do you get meals brought in if you don't eat them?"

"Aiden feels better knowing I've got three square meals at my disposal, but it's too much food, and I don't always feel like eating what they send."

"I'm glad to hear he's thinking about your nutrition, but it's no good if you aren't eating. What do you say we hit the grocery store, stock up on fresh food? I'll show you how to cook for your friends and how to make a few things that won't add to your waistline but that you might actually eat."

"It's such a pain going to the grocery store."

"Regular people grocery shop."

"I don't mean because it's an errand. Regular people don't have fans taking pictures of their cart and then selling them to rag magazines so they can print headlines about how they only eat carrots or they must be bingeing and purging. Normal people don't get stopped every ten minutes for their autograph. I love my fans, I really do, but sometimes it's just easier to order in."

He motioned for her to increase her speed again. "Last run. You don't like living in a glass house, and I get that. But you can't go through life pleasing everyone else and making yourself miserable."

"I'm not miserable."

"I didn't mean it literally. I mean, you have to be able to live your life, not avoid it. Eating premade meals from boxes isn't living your life. But I've got an idea. You have access to great makeup artists. They're on set today, even though you're not filming. Let's head over and get you a disguise that's better than a baseball cap. We'll hit the grocery store, and then I'll show you how to cook a few things. See how you like the life of a regular person. If you like it, great, then we'll start working on boundaries next."

"Next? So you think I need to be fixed?"

"No, Princess. I think you want to live your life, but you've created a life that makes that difficult. People approach you so often because you make yourself approachable."

"It's called catering to fans. And please don't think I'm not grateful for my position, because I *am*."

"I realize that. But did you see Raz or the other actors signing autographs between *every* scene? Once a day is great, admirable even. It gives your fans something to look forward to, and it gives you a chance to breathe between doing other activities that require your focus and energy. But you signed autographs *four* or *five* times nearly every day this week. I think it's fantastic that you want to be available to your fans, but not at the risk of losing yourself. If you can't even go to the grocery store without being mobbed, then you're on the fast track to becoming a hermit."

He paused, as if he were letting the words sink in. They did more than that. The truth in them rocked her a little off-kilter.

"You're always going to be Remi Divine. Maybe it's time to take control of what being Remi Divine means for the rest of the world." He motioned for her to decrease her speed.

Mason seemed intent on protecting more than just her physical being, and even though he was taken, she couldn't stop her budding emotions from blooming. She slowed to a walk, wondering if she could keep her emotions in check enough to remain in the friend zone without getting hurt. She gripped the side rails, trying to halt the discomfort of that thought, when for the first time in her life she wanted so much more.

He covered her hand with his and said, "What do you say, Princess? Grocery store, cooking, and maybe work on some of those fan-related boundaries?"

She tried to ignore the way his caring made her insides warm. "Even if I wanted to, I don't know how to start creating those types of boundaries without looking like a bitch."

"That's where I come in." There was that grin again, the one that said he was a man who knew exactly what he was doing. "Trust me?"

He had no idea how loaded that question was.

Later that morning, Mason paced outside the makeup trailer, waiting for Remi. He'd touched base with Aiden last night and checked in with his contacts to ensure there was no funny business going on at Remi's LA residence. He had two of his top men monitoring her other residences—a cottage on Cape Cod and a rural cabin about an hour from Harmony Pointe. There had been no movement at any of them, but while that should give him some peace of mind, he knew better and kept his guard firmly in place.

The trailer doors opened, and a young guy stepped out. Frayed jeans dragged past the heels of his black sneakers as he descended the steps. His scruff was unkempt and shaggy, a few colorful tattoos decorated his left forearm, and he had a trendy haircut, longer on top, shorter on the sides. He wore a maroon T-shirt with a picture of a mustache and MY MUSTACHE MY RULES written beneath it. A black backpack hung over one shoulder. He shoved his hands in his pockets, his narrow shoulders rounding with the insecurities of a younger man as he nodded at Mason and said, "What's up?"

"How's it going?" Mason crossed his arms, sizing him up.

The guy shrugged, kicking at the ground with the toe of his sneaker. He lifted his gaze, meeting Mason's eyes. It took only a second for Mason to recognize Remi's sweet hazel eyes, and it took less than three seconds for the undercurrent of white-hot lust to stain Remi's cheeks.

"Damn, woman. You make one hell of a guy." Mason chuckled.

Remi lowered her eyes, shyly touching the scruff glued to her cheeks. "You could tell it was me? I thought they did a better job than that."

"They did a hell of a job. If you'd been anyone else, I wouldn't have been able to tell."

"What does *that* mean?" she asked, kicking at the ground again.

He stepped closer and her breathing hitched. He shouldn't enjoy that as much as he did, and he definitely shouldn't be leaning in even closer and saying, "I think you know what I mean." But *man*, the desire in her eyes was so blatant, so captivating, he wanted to memorize it. Hell, he wanted to see it long after he was done being her bodyguard.

She made a soft sound, a cross between a whimper and something else, and that small sound jerked him back to reality. Realizing he'd crossed a line he shouldn't have, he stepped back, cleared his throat, and said, "What's in the backpack?"

"Makeup remover." Her eyes shifted from him to the trailer. "They used glue for the facial hair."

He focused on *facial hair* to get himself under control. "Sounds like you're all set. Ready to hit the grocery store?"

She nodded, kicking her toe at the ground again.

Fuck. She was so freaking adorable, even in that getup, he wanted to pull her into his arms and kiss the embarrassment off her face.

What the hell? He was attracted to her even in male form? He ground out a curse at how far gone he was as they headed for the parking lot and said, "Don't kick your toe."

"Okay. Why? Too girlie?"

"Too *Remi.*"

She giggled. "Don't clench your jaw."

He arched a brow.

"Too *Mason.*" Another giggle slipped out, and in a rougher, lower-pitched voice, she said, "Let's go pick up some chicks."

Christ, this was going to be interesting. It was like a secretive game, where he was the only person who would know that beneath that masculine exterior was a gorgeous, smart-mouthed, vulnerable woman.

Remi took selfies on the drive to the grocery store, making stern faces, which she probably thought made her look tough. Now that Mason knew it was her beneath the makeup, he saw even more clearly her plump lips, her adorably pointy chin, and the wariness in her eyes she tried so hard to cover up.

When they got to the grocery store, she shoved her hands in the front pockets of her jeans, pulling them tighter across her ass.

Great. Now he looked like he was checking out a dude's ass.

"I'm nervous," she whispered on the way in.

He started to put his hand on her lower back but quickly realized his mistake and pulled back. "You look great. Just act like a guy."

"Like this?" she said in a low, husky voice. She clenched her jaw, her brows slanting.

"Yeah," he said. "Something like that."

"Why do you scowl and clench your jaw so much?"

Because it's hard to shift my focus from you as a woman to you as a client. He grabbed a shopping cart outside the entrance, and as they went inside, he said, "Habit. Let's hit the veggies first."

There were several other shoppers making their way through their lists and checking over vegetables and fruits. Nervous energy buzzed around Remi.

"Here, you push." He relinquished the cart.

"Why?" she asked softly, in her normal voice.

"Because you need something to focus on. What's on tap for tomorrow evening?"

"I don't know. You're the cook," she whispered.

"Do your friends like guacamole and pita bread?"

"I *love* guacamole," she said excitedly in a high-pitched voice, causing two women to glance over. Her hand flew over her mouth as she said, "Shoot!"

"It's fine," he said for her ears only. "Just breathe. You've got this."

In a deeper voice, she said, "Yeah, guac is cool."

"There you go. Roll with that." He grabbed a few tomatoes, then moved to the next area and selected several avocados. "Channel your inner dude."

"My inner dude, got it."

"We'll make skinny guac to keep the calories low. How do you feel about grilled chicken and shrimp kabobs?"

"They're cool," she said huskily.

"Awesome. Making progress. Cobb salad? Gazpacho?"

"Yum!" Her eyes widened, and she lowered her voice again. "Um, I mean, *great.*"

After gathering fruits and vegetables, they worked their way down each aisle. Mason made suggestions of meals they could make during the week, and Remi seemed open to everything. As they walked through the aisles, Remi became more confident in her getup and her male voice.

"Hey, man, how'd you learn to cook?" she asked as Mason looked over cuts of meat.

"Chuck taught me." He tossed a few packages into the cart.

"Really? Are you related to him?"

"No."

"Oh," she said softly. Then, in a rougher voice, she said, "How do you know the guy?"

He headed for the fish and said, "I lived downstairs."

"He was your neighbor?"

"Yup. What kind of fish do you like?"

She looked over the choices in the display case and said, "Anything except eel. You?"

"Same," he said, though he'd never tried eel. It didn't sound appealing. He gave the guy behind the counter his order and said, "How do you feel about egg-white omelets?"

"I try not to eat a lot of cheese. Does your family live in New York? Is that where you grew up?"

Did she really think she could sneak in questions without him realizing it? Disregarding the question, he grabbed the fish from the counter and said, "I make omelets without cheese. Just spinach and other veggies. Cool?"

"Cool. Did you grow up in New York?" she asked again.

So much for ignoring the question. "Yeah."

"That must have been amazing. There's so much to do there," she said in her normal voice, then quickly realized her error and lowered her pitch. "Do your parents still live there?"

He ground his teeth together, fighting the urge to shut her out like he did most people when they asked personal questions. He didn't usually let anyone get close enough to feel comfortable asking about his family, but Remi had been different from the start.

"You don't have to tell me," she said softly. "I'm sorry if that's too personal. You're so easy to be with, I forgot this was just a job."

Her disappointed tone tugged at his heartstrings, and the truth came out. "I never knew my father, and my mother's gone."

"Oh, Mason." She turned a compassionate gaze on him, and his insides went soft. "I'm sorry."

"Don't be. She was a drug addict. I was taken away from her when I was six. I grew up in the foster-care system, went into the military at eighteen, then worked at Darkbird. Started my business five years ago, and now here I am, all grown up and doing great. So, how about we finish our grocery shopping?"

He'd tried to keep his tone light, but the look in her eyes told him he'd failed miserably. He could tell she had more questions, but he needed to get this shopping trip back on course. "Sorry, but I don't usually talk about that stuff."

"It's okay. We don't have to."

They shopped in silence for a while, and as they walked past two pretty women, Remi leaned closer and said, "Did you see the ass on that redhead?"

He chuckled, glad for her levity. "Actually, I wasn't looking."

"Dude," she said huskily. "You missed out." She grinned, laughing softly.

She had the greatest laugh, and Mason wanted to hear more of it.

They grabbed eggs, hit the spice aisle, and headed for the registers. When they passed a display of cantaloupes, Remi picked up one in each hand, holding them in front of her chest, and said, "Check out these melons."

"Speaking of *melons*." He glanced at her chest and said, "How'd you pull that off?"

She set a melon in the cart and said, "They're all strapped down. Look." She thrust her hips forward and pulled her jeans tighter, revealing a masculine bulge between her legs.

A surprised "Holy shit" burst out before he could stop it. He cleared his throat and said, "Seriously?"

"Aiden taught me never to do anything halfway. Might as well nail the part, right?" She cupped her crotch, jiggling it. "I don't know how men manage with all this hardware. It's so uncomfortable."

You have no idea . . .

CHAPTER SEVEN

AFTER THEIR GROCERY excursion, Remi scrubbed off her makeup and tattoos. She'd always wanted to get a tattoo, a small JUST BREATHE on the inside of her wrist. She was afraid of how much it would hurt, but maybe one day . . .

She changed into her favorite cutoffs, the dark ones, frayed at the edges and torn across the right hip, and her softest army green tank top, and headed downstairs, excited for her foray into cooking.

The scent of something delicious met her on the way into the kitchen. Colorful peppers, chicken, shrimp, and a host of other foods they'd bought were spread across the center island. Mason stood by the stove, his head bopping to the beat of music streaming from his phone, reminding Remi of the way he'd danced behind her last night. The memory of his hard body brushing against her and his hot breath washing over her cheek sent a scintillating shiver skating through her.

"How long are you going to stand there staring at me?" He glanced over his shoulder, grinning. His gaze slipped appreciatively down the length of her, and his jaw clenched.

She put her hand on her hip and said, "Now who's staring?"

"You were." He turned his attention back to the stove. "Good thing you don't still have your *male hardware* on, or the rise caused by all that ogling you're doing would be all the proof I'd need."

"I was *not* staring at you."

"Whatever you say, Princess." He carried two plates of omelets to the table and said, "Have a seat. Before we get started we both need to eat."

She sat down and said, "That looks amazing. You just whipped that up?"

"No, the food fairies came in while you were upstairs." He grabbed silverware from the drawer and handed her a fork with a wink. "Sweet peppers, egg whites, sliced mushrooms, zucchini, and seasonings. Quick and easy."

She took a bite, and an explosion of delicious herbs kissed her tongue. "Mm. What *is* that zing I taste?"

"Dijon mustard. I whisked it into the eggs with chives and parsley."

"You might just make me fall in love with eating."

He lifted his gaze to hers. "Good. You could use a little love in your life."

"Is that a dig or an observation?" She ate another bite.

"Neither," he said, eyes on his eggs. "Just an off-the-cuff comment."

She didn't believe Mason made off-the-cuff comments, but she didn't want to get into her nonexistent love life, either, so she let it go. "You and Raz seemed pretty cozy at that meeting. Is it hard to work with your ex?"

"We're friends. It's not weird."

He lifted serious eyes to hers and said, "Do you have any reason to believe he might be the person who is stalking you?"

"Raz? No way. He could have any woman he wanted."

He shoveled eggs into his mouth. When he finished the omelet, he carried his plate to the sink and said, "Maybe you're the one he wants."

"Hardly. We went on two dates and the press made it seem like we were planning our wedding."

"So what went wrong?" he asked as he washed his plate.

"Nothing really. My publicist, Shea, set us up on a whim, but we had no chemistry. We're good friends now, as I said, so something good came of it."

He reached for her plate and said, "I need to ask you something personal, for the investigation. I did a background check on Raz, and he seems like he's on the up-and-up, but you never know about scorned lovers."

"We weren't lovers. I just told you we had no chemistry."

"People sleep together for lots of different reasons, and chemistry doesn't always play a part."

She snagged a piece of pepper from the cutting board and popped it into her mouth. "True, but for the record, chemistry is everything in my book. I have to feel it to kiss a guy, much less have sex with him, which is why I have such a hard time with intimate scenes. Anyway, what was your question?"

"You've already answered it."

"Wow, that was easy. Now can we take Raz off your stalker list?"

"Possibly. I didn't come up with any other guys you went out with in the last two years. Is there anyone else I should check out?"

"As lame as it makes me sound, *no*. I've been pretty busy filming and keeping up with my appearances and other commitments. The little downtime I've had I've spent catching up with my friends, or just catching my breath. But I'm really looking forward to learning to cook things like the omelet you made me."

"It will probably be the easiest thing you've ever done." He picked up his phone and said, "Any preference for music? I need it on while I cook."

"Something danceable."

As he navigated on his phone, he said, "You are just trouble waiting to happen, aren't you?"

"I never get in trouble."

"Four bodyguards in as many months and a baseball cap tell me otherwise." As Rihanna's voice rang out, Mason put his phone on the counter and said, "Time to light up your taste buds."

Mason cooked the way he did everything else, with complete focus and unflappable confidence. He sliced, diced, peeled, mixed, and steamed, while patiently explaining every step to Remi. And his choice of music was just as good. Remi grooved to the beat as she followed his instructions, cubing chicken, chopping vegetables, and mixing herbs. She swayed to "Sexy Love" by Ne-Yo, watching Mason's butt move to the beat as he rinsed the shrimp for the kabobs, reminding herself that despite how well they got along or how much fun they were having, he was still just doing his job. Friends were all they would ever be.

Did it make her pathetic that she'd gladly take just that? Because when she was with him, she was happy. He made her think, and feel, and want to discover more about herself.

"How's that rub coming?" He looked over his shoulder, catching her checking him out. *Again.*

"It's ready." She turned back to the counter to avoid his all-seeing eyes.

She told herself that just because she enjoyed *looking* at him didn't mean she was like the evil, slutty girl in movies trying to scam on someone else's boyfriend.

"Great. Now let's get those pretty hands dirty," he said. "How are you at handling meat?"

Her mind tramped down a dirty path as he moved beside her. *Okay, maybe I need to stop looking at you that way.*

"Have you ever applied a rub to it?"

"That's a little personal, don't you think?" she joked.

His amusement climbed his features, dancing in his typically serious eyes. "You've got a dirty mind, Princess. I was talking about *chicken.*"

"Mm-hm. That's what all the guys say." Oh yeah, she could *totally* do this friendship thing. She just had to stop looking at his butt. And his arms. *And those eyes . . .*

"I'm nothing like *all the guys*, and trust me, you're nothing like other women, either. How many women could pull off being a dude at the grocery store?"

"I did make a pretty good guy, didn't I?"

"The *hottest*. Now, how about we get your mind back on cooking and spread some of that rub on the chicken." He sprinkled a spoonful of the rub she'd made over a chicken breast, and then he began rubbing the herbs and spices into the meat. "You can't be afraid to get dirty. Apply it generously, covering the top and bottom. Go ahead—you try."

She washed her hands, and then she sprinkled rub over a few more chicken breasts and began rubbing it in the way he'd shown her. "It doesn't stick very well."

"Here, let me show you." He moved behind her, covering her hands with his. "The oil will make it stick, but you have to press down as you spread it." His hands swallowed hers as they spread the rub over the breasts, oil and spices coating their fingers.

"You're getting it," he coaxed, adding more rub to the chicken. "Don't be afraid to put a little pressure into it."

"I'm being taught by a master in the kitchen. You make it look easy," she said.

He wrapped his fingers around hers, curling them around the chicken breast. She imagined her fingers curled around his hard length and closed her eyes, letting him guide her. His chest pressed against her back, his hot breath coasting over her cheek, their fingers intertwined. She couldn't help but wonder if he was a master in the bedroom, too.

"You're a natural." His gravelly voice seeped beneath her skin like a caress. "Have you enjoyed your trip down Normalcy Lane today?"

"Yes," she said softly.

"Maybe we can try it again someday soon without the disguise, and work on those boundaries we talked about."

He stepped to the sink to wash his hands, and her eyes flew open.

Boundaries.

Holy shit, my heart is racing over someone else's man.

I am the evil friend after all!

CHAPTER EIGHT

FRIDAY-AFTERNOON SUNSHINE TURNED to evening clouds, but Remi would take a cloudy night with her closest girlfriends over a sunny day alone any day of the week. The fun hadn't stopped since the moment Aurelia, Willow, Piper, Talia, and Bridgette arrived two hours ago carrying six-packs of her favorite cocktail, Kinky Pink, a box of Willow's famous Loverboys, a delicious cross between éclairs and cupcakes, and the warmth of good friends. Now, with empty plates littering the table, their bellies full of food Remi had actually helped make, music filling the air, and smiles on their faces, Remi and her besties sat by the stone firepit. At times like this, Remi wished she could walk away from her overburdened schedule for good, give up the glamour and glitz for nights spent sharing secrets and planning their future families. But on the heels of those wishes came others, like her desire to do *more*, although she really had no idea what *more* might entail. Take on more meaningful, complex roles? Earn a Golden Globe? Or something completely different?

It didn't matter, because reality always crept in.

While her girlfriends were planning futures including significant others and babies, Remi was in a holding pattern, trying not to think about whether her stalker would suddenly reappear and wondering if she'd ever have a real relationship. Would she ever find someone she could trust enough to laugh *and* cry with? To share these types of thoughts with? Someone she'd look forward to seeing as much as she did her girlfriends?

She looked across the lawn at Mason, who was walking along the fence line again and glancing back at her every few minutes, and her pulse spiked.

Someone who isn't off-limits?

Mason was acutely aware of everything about her, whether he was working on his computer, standing guard outside a door, or traipsing through the yard. She knew he was always watching out for her. Last night after they'd prepared the food for the party, she was looking over scripts her agent had sent her and Mason had enticed her into binge-watching *Daredevil* on Netflix. She would never watch that show by herself, but with him she enjoyed it. Of course, she spent much of the night watching him instead of the show, but still, she enjoyed what she had seen—of *both*.

"Remi, can you email me your recipe for skinny guacamole?" Bridgette asked, bringing Remi's mind back to their conversation. Bridgette rubbed her belly, looking cute in maternity jeans and a peasant-style blouse. "The way I've been eating, they'll need to roll me into the delivery room."

Aurelia pulled out the hem of her shirt, which had FEED ME AND TELL ME I'M PRETTY emblazoned across the chest, and said, "I'm getting you one of these shirts. You know, if Bodhi had been more of a horndog like Ben, you could have skipped the whole pregnancy thing, like me." She sat with her black Converse propped up on the edge of the firepit, her dark hair pulled up in a high ponytail.

"You say that so casually, but I know it wasn't easy when you found out about Bea." Talia pushed her glasses to the bridge of her nose and leaned back in her chair. She was the most careful of the Dalton sisters and had always been the voice of reason. "Ben is truly lucky to have you. I don't even want to *think* about Derek with other women."

"People have sex, Tal, and pregnancies happen. It's not like Derek was your first," Piper said. "Get over it already. It's just sex."

"I know, but . . ." Talia shrugged.

"I'm with Talia on that front," Bridgette said. "I hate thinking about Bodhi and any other woman, but I also love him so much, if a baby he'd fathered appeared on our doorstep tomorrow, I'd gladly raise it as my own, just as he's raising Louie."

"Oh, that's not what I meant. I'd absolutely love any child of Derek's no matter who the mother was," Talia clarified. "I just meant that at first it would hurt thinking about him having a baby with someone else."

"It did," Aurelia confessed. "But all it took was a few hours with Bea and Ben to know genetics didn't matter. I love them so much it hurts sometimes."

As the girls talked about loving their families, Remi tried not to think about Mason and his *sweetheart*, but this conversation wasn't helping.

"I can't imagine my life without either of them," Aurelia said, "and hopefully I'll never have to."

Remi took the opportunity to redirect the conversation. "Aurelia, did you find a dress for Bea for your wedding?" Aurelia and Ben were getting married in a small family ceremony at the end of November.

"Yes! I can't believe I forgot to show it to you at the fundraiser. We also got a new outfit for her to wear to Flossie's birthday party next Sunday." Aurelia pulled out her phone as they chatted about being excited to celebrate Flossie's birthday. After finding the pictures she was looking for, she passed the phone around. "We did a photo shoot with Bea in her new dress and made it into a keepsake book for Flossie. We're going to give it to her on her birthday."

"Flossie will love that. Bea's so stinking cute, I just want to kiss her little face!" Remi's heart melted at chubby-cheeked Bea in Ben's arms, wearing a frilly pink dress with white stockings. She handed the phone to Willow, and her gaze caught on Mason heading toward the house.

She wondered how serious his relationship was with his girlfriend. Were they thinking of marriage? Having a family?

Willow handed the phone to Talia and said, "One day we'll have babies. Right now we're keeping our eye on the prize—getting Zane's movie made."

"Looks like Remi's got her eyes on *another* prize," Piper said, jarring Remi enough to realize she was staring at Mason *again*.

"What? Sorry." Remi tipped her bottle back, taking a long drink.

"First he *protects* you by dirty dancing with you, then he teaches you to cook, and now he's got you spacing out," Willow said with a curious look in her eyes. "I'm thinking you're keeping secrets we need to know about."

"Then you're thinking wrong." Remi sucked down the rest of her drink. "He's been very clear about *boundaries*. The man is intent on keeping me safe, which I'm thankful for, but . . . I told him he didn't need to hang around tonight, and he scoffed at me. He said he'd give me space, but that I wasn't getting rid of him that easy." She got up and grabbed another bottle of Kinky Pink, then flopped down in the chair with a sigh. "The problem is, getting rid of him is the *last* thing I want to do." If she couldn't be honest with her friends, who could she talk to?

Piper kicked her booted foot up on the edge of the firepit and said, "I do not see a problem with that scenario. That hottieguard is *living* in your mansion. You're Remi Divine—you know how to seduce a man."

"First of all, no I don't, not really. I know how to fake it pretty well in movies, but I've never actually *tried* to seduce anyone off set. And more importantly, Mason is *taken*."

"No way!" Willow snapped. "The man danced like he was ready to lay you down on the dance floor. If he's taken, I feel sorry for his girlfriend. Are you sure?"

"Yes, I'm sure. I heard him talking to her on the phone, and you know what? It shouldn't surprise me. I mean, come on, you guys. Look at him. I saw him walking into the fundraiser when I first arrived, and I swear . . . You know how they say the earth stands still when you find *the one?* Well, apparently when you find someone else's *one,* the world quakes beneath your feet. He's just another thing that's out of my reach. The suckiest part is that we're literally together *all* the time, and I *like* being around him way too much, which makes me an awful person because he's got a girlfriend. I know I have to stop being attracted to him, but how can I when I like *everything* about him? We binge-watched television for hours last night, like old friends. I keep telling myself, 'friend zone, friend zone, friend zone,' but turning off the attraction is like trying not to breathe. I know a *gazillion* people, and I've never met a man who sees me the way he does, or sees things in me that *I* didn't even know existed."

"Like the *hot dude* in you," Willow teased.

Remi smiled, thinking of how Mason had known it was her beneath the disguise after one quick glimpse of her eyes. "Now I understand what you guys mean when you talk about how strongly you're attracted to your men. There's this hum, a *vibration* inside me that I feel every time I think about him. I can't explain it. But if Aiden catches wind of my attraction to Mason, he'd probably blame Mason *and* slaughter him."

"You're not doing anything but being female," Piper said. "Besides, Aiden needs to get a life of his own, separate from watching over you— which, by the way, I've offered before and I'm offering again: I'd gladly distract that delicious brother of yours."

"Piper!" Bridgette rolled her eyes. "Remi, why do you have to *explain* anything? Emotions aren't meant to be explained. They're meant to be felt. *Period.*"

Remi sighed. "Yes, but I've never felt anything like this before *and* he's off-limits. I keep hoping it's just a crush and it'll go away, but I swear it gets stronger by the minute, like right before a tsunami when the water gets sucked back into the ocean. That's me getting sucked in every time I think about him. I feel like a jerk, too, because he's got a girlfriend, and I am *not* the kind of person who hits on another woman's man." She threw her hand up and said, "See how confused I am? He makes me laugh and he makes me think about things I haven't wanted in a very long time."

"Like really hot sex with a muscled hottieguard?" Piper said. "The kind of sex that leaves you too spent to move. Oh yes, I can definitely see that."

Remi swatted her, because now *she* could see it, too, and that was the last thing she needed. She was having a hard enough time trying to forget what he'd looked like half-naked in the gym. "He's making me a hot mess, but at the same time, he's helping me understand myself and my life better, which is weird, right? I mean, he hasn't even known me very long. But the things he says, the things he notices about me, about what I need . . ." She shook her head, overwhelmed by the intensity of her emotions.

"Maybe he's your *one*," Talia said thoughtfully.

"But we've known each other only *five* days, and he's someone *else's* one," Remi said in a sharp whisper.

"Maybe he's not that into her, because for you to feel this way, he has to be sending you the same vibes, right? And stop fretting about how long you've known him. I knew the second I saw Bodhi I wanted him," Bridgette reminded her.

Piper smirked. "We *all* knew you wanted him."

Talia tucked her dark hair behind her ear and said, "I never believed it before Derek, but love happens fast, when you least expect it, so don't discount all those things you're feeling."

Remi's eyes bloomed wide. "Whoa. I'm not in *love* with him."

"*Yet*," Talia said. "I didn't think I would ever be attracted to a long-haired dancer who took his clothes off for a living, but when you meet the right person, something inside you changes. Actually, your view of yourself and your world changes."

"It's true," Aurelia said. "Look at me and Ben. Did you ever think Ben would want to live in a two-bedroom apartment above a bookstore? The man has more money than God himself, and he wants nothing more than a simple life with me and Bea."

"Remi, look at how much you're already changing. You *cooked*, and you don't want to ditch him anymore," Bridgette added.

"I'm happy for you lovebirds, but I say forget *love*," Piper said. "Why does Remi need forever? Just because you chicks drank the Kool-Aid doesn't mean she has to. Stick with me in the Single Ladies Lust Club. It's a fine place to hang your panties."

"*Ohmygod!* Nobody is hanging my panties anywhere! Did you not register the *he's taken* part of this conversation? Forget I said anything. Can we please change the subject?" Remi gulped down more of her drink as Mason stepped onto the other end of the patio and began poking away at his computer. He was like a swooping eagle, hovering and making her heart race but never getting quite close enough to her nest for her to attack. That was probably a good thing. She pushed to her feet, pulling Willow up beside her, and said, "Dance with me. I need a distraction from all this love talk."

The rest of the girls joined them, dancing in a circle, and Remi's lustful thoughts fell away as she lost herself in the fun of her girlfriends. Piper stepped into the middle of the group, shimmying up to each of them. Talia shocked them all when she joined Piper, wiggling her hips and whipping her long hair around.

"Go, Tallie!" Willow cheered.

"Derek showed me a few moves," Talia said, blushing furiously.

Piper danced over to Remi and said, "Hey, five-foot-two, don't look now, but hottieguard's eyes are on you."

Remi didn't have to look. Now that she was thinking about him again, she could feel his electric gaze on her. She'd probably go straight to hell for it, but she couldn't resist turning up the heat of her hip-swaying, shoulder-rocking dance. Piper whistled, and the girls cheered

Remi on as her arms snaked over her head in a dance of pure seduction. She tried to lose herself in the music again, to fill the empty places inside her she'd always kept secret and Mason had unearthed—the loneliness no amount of Kinky Pink, sexy dancing, or cheering girlfriends could ever fill.

Mason had prepared for an all-nighter with Remi and her girlfriends, since Remi didn't need to be at the set until midafternoon tomorrow, but they surprised him and called it a night around ten fifteen. The girls shared so many hugs as they said goodbye, he wondered if Remi's friends were leaving on a six-month excursion without her. Afterward, he stood by the open gates as her friends drove away, to ensure no unwanted visitors slipped in. He kept an eye on Remi via the live feed from the patio camera on his phone. She was pushing in the chairs around the table. Her shoulders were rounded forward, and the bounce in her step was gone as she sauntered over to the firepit and stared forlornly into the ashes.

As he got into the SUV, he watched Remi walk to the edge of the patio and tip her face up toward the cloudy sky, looking young and vulnerable in her frayed cutoffs and the T-shirt she'd knotted at her hip.

What was she thinking? Even though he knew he shouldn't, he wondered if she was thinking about him.

He drove up to the house and parked in the driveway. As he climbed from the SUV, the faint beat of music pulsed in the air like rain threatening to fall. He made his way inside, keeping an eye on the video. Remi began swaying to the music. She was a sensual, energetic dancer, but this was different. *She* was different. Her face was still tipped up toward the clouds, and there was nothing energetic about her movements. It was as if she'd turned on for a role when her friends were there, and now she'd switched off. But he knew better. The sensual dancing, the laughter, the carefree smiles that had lit up the darkness—that was *all* Remington Aldridge. She hadn't been acting then any more than she was acting right now as she wrapped her arms around her slim body, swaying to a lonelier beat.

She sank down to the patio steps and kicked off her sandals.

Mason pocketed his phone, grabbed the long cardigan she'd left hanging over the back of the couch, and went to her.

"How's it going, Princess?" He handed her the sweater. "I thought you might get chilly now that the fire's died down."

"Thank you."

She spread the sweater over her legs and turned her beautiful face toward him. There was no mistaking the loneliness welling in her eyes despite the small curve of her lips. Her sadness seeped between the cracks of his armor, straight down to the emotional dungeon he'd thought he'd sealed off long ago. He wanted to hold her, to fill whatever void she was feeling. Remi had made those emotions rise to the surface so often, he was starting to expect them.

"Did any creepers sneak in?" she asked softly.

He sat beside her on the stone steps. "Not this time. Did you have fun?"

"Mm-hm."

"Post-party letdown?" he asked carefully.

She shrugged, looking out over the yard. "Have you ever not wanted to clean up from a good time because you didn't want it to end?"

"I've never hosted a party, but I understand what it's like not to want something good to end."

Confusion rose in her eyes. "But you knew exactly what to do to prepare for tonight."

"Sure, I know how to cook. I've had to do it forever. My life has never been conducive to entertaining, but I'd imagine not wanting to clean up after a good time with your friends is similar to meeting really great foster parents and not wanting to unpack your bag because once you do, you hear a timer ticking and know the short time they'll keep you isn't going to be long enough. And you think, 'If I leave everything just as it is, maybe it can stay this way forever.'"

"Yes," she said just above a whisper. "That's exactly how I feel. I hate that you know that feeling. I'm sorry."

He sat up a little straighter, unable to believe he'd just revealed so much of himself. "It's a sucky feeling, but unless your friends are going off to war, I'm pretty sure you'll see them again soon."

She lowered her eyes, fidgeting with her sweater. "Did you go through many foster homes?"

"Enough to know the difference between good ones and bad ones." He gritted his teeth against the memory of years of discomfort, anger, and loneliness pushing at those dungeon doors.

"Mason?"

"Yeah?"

"Can I ask you something personal?"

He turned, meeting her sorrowful, curious gaze, and steeled himself against the walls stacking up inside him like Legos. He didn't want to shut himself off from her, and that reality scared the hell out of him. "You can ask, but I can't guarantee I'll answer."

"I understand. How long were you in foster care?"

"Twelve years. Ten homes."

Sadness washed over her face. "That must have been awful."

"Awful is relative, I guess. I see awful as being homeless, or watching your buddies die and not being able to save them. I was one of the lucky ones. I made it off the battlefield alive."

"I'm not sure watching someone die is lucky," she said in a thin, shaky voice. "The images never go away."

His senses reeled. "Remi, that sounds like you're speaking from experience."

She nodded, and tears slipped down her cheeks. "I was there when my parents died," she whispered. "In the car."

CHAPTER NINE

MASON'S GUT SEIZED, and he swore he felt his heart tearing right down the center. The thought of Remi having been in the car with her parents when they were killed slayed him.

"I don't understand," he said, trying to put the pieces of Remi's past together. "The articles about your family indicate that you were home with Aiden when your parents were killed."

She shook her head. "It's not true. That was Aiden's doing, to protect me from the media. I don't know what it was like for you in the military, but I'll never forget that day. It was February, freezing rain, and I was supposed to have a big ballet recital that night. Aiden was living in California, running a West Coast office for my father's company. I didn't know it at the time, but he'd come home to surprise me and attend the recital with us. He was always doing things like that when I was growing up. Anyway, I was out with my parents when Aiden called to tell my dad he was home. He later told me that when he called, my father said we were only ten minutes away. I remember my dad looking at me in the rearview mirror after he took the call. His eyes were always so serious, like Aiden's. But sometimes they would fill up with happiness so bright, when he looked at me I felt like the sun had risen inside me."

Christ, that was exactly how Mason felt when Remi looked at him.

Her eyes teared up, and she touched the center of her chest.

"I'm so sorry, Remi."

"It's okay." She inhaled a shaky breath. "I realized after the accident that my father looked so happy because he'd kept Aiden's arrival a secret, and he was excited for me not only to see the big brother I idolized, but to hear about the gift Aiden had gotten me. Aiden knew how much I wanted to be an actress, and he'd gotten tickets to a Broadway show. He'd pulled some strings with a friend's family and arranged for me to go backstage and meet the actors. I know that doesn't sound like such a big deal these days, but when I was growing up, even though we had money, we lived a really simple life. When my parents were first married, my father lived paycheck to paycheck, but my mom had some savings. My father started investing the little money they had, and when my grandfather, who had raised him, passed away, my father invested the life insurance money. It turned out he had a knack for investing. Aiden has that same innate ability. Anyway, my father started investing for other people—on the side, not like a business at first—and he got lucky. By the time I was born he was worth millions, but I don't think our neighbors or anyone else knew it. My parents were very private people. We lived in a modest farmhouse on a few acres in the hills of West Virginia. My parents took me to New York City once a year, and our lives were very *normal*. I went to public school, and we vacationed on Cape Cod each summer. Going to the city was a really big deal, but we never stayed there overnight. We always stayed in our little cabin about an hour outside of the city. Anyway, Aiden later told me that our parents felt that if they indulged me too often, it would demystify the magnificence of the city."

He remembered the way she'd gazed longingly out at the lights the night of the fundraiser. She must have been thinking about her parents. "It sounds like they wanted to give you the world without stealing the stars from your eyes."

She nodded, and he reached for her hand, squeezing it reassuringly. As he pulled back, she curled her fingers around his, holding on tight.

"The roads leading to our house wound up the mountain with sharp curves and harsh drop-offs," she said softly. "I remember my mom putting her arm over the seat back and smiling at me. She was beautiful and as vivacious as my father was serious. I can still hear her saying, 'I'm so proud of you. You're going to shine tonight, Princess.' That's what she called me. *Princess.*"

He winced for the pain he'd probably caused every time he'd called her Princess. "I didn't realize . . . I won't call you that anymore."

"No, I like it when you call me that. It makes me think of my mom, like she had a hand in you being here. Anyway, everything happened in an instant after that. Some deer ran across the road, and my father swerved to avoid them, but it was icy and the car spun. I remember screaming, and the sound of my mom yelling for me to hold on." Tears spilled down her cheeks. "Then the car was rolling down the hill. Every roll brought thunderous sounds like the earth was exploding, metal tearing and crunching, glass shattering, our cries of terror. When the car slammed into a tree, it was on its side, and the sound, the impact . . . I can't even describe it. I have no idea how I survived. I was sort of hanging there in the seat belt. The rest of the car was crushed except this bubble of space around me. My memories come and go after that. I see flashes of my father's mangled arm crushed beneath metal. There was so much blood. I remember knowing he was gone and telling myself it was a nightmare and when I woke up he'd be fine. It felt like the car was still rolling, even after it stopped, and I had horrendous pressure in my chest." She rubbed her chest. "I don't know if that was from the impact, or . . ."

"*Remi* . . ." Mason's voice cracked as he put his arm around her, holding her against him. She was trembling, tears wetting her cheeks. Wishing he could erase her pain, he pressed a kiss to the top of her head and said, "You don't have to say anything more."

"I want to," she choked out. "I couldn't see my mom. The car was too mangled. But I heard her voice. It was so quiet, and you know how you can hear pain in someone's voice?"

Like I do now? "It's deafening."

She nodded. "My mom kept saying, 'Just breathe, Remi. Just breathe and everything will be all right.' You say that to me a lot," she said a little absently. "I remember holding on to her voice like it was tangible and could wrap around me and keep me breathing, save me. I don't remember much else except that I was freezing and drenched from the rain. It felt like forever before I heard Aiden calling my name, and then he was pulling me from the wreckage, checking to see if I had broken bones, holding me, telling me I was okay. I was so traumatized, everything else is foggy. I don't know if Aiden bribed the EMTs and doctors or what, but he managed to keep the fact that I was in the car out of the media. He was only twenty-four, but he'd always come across authoritative. People listen when he talks, plus he had money even then. He told me later that he didn't want me to become known as *the girl who survived* and have that define who I became."

Mason was floored by Aiden's foresight.

Remi gasped a breath. "Aiden said he'd waited forty-five minutes for us to come home, and then he went looking for us. He drove by the scene of the accident twice before he noticed the trampled shrubs and torn-up grass along the side of the road and realized we'd gone over the side. We'd rolled too far down the mountain to see from the road. I . . ." She paused, breathing hard. "I remember begging him to save our parents, even though I'm sure I knew he couldn't."

She was breathing too fast. Mason cradled her face between his hands and brushed her tears away. "Focus on me, Princess. Take a deep breath." When she did he said, "Attagirl. You're okay, Princess. I've got you." He wrapped his arms around her and whispered, "I've got you. You're safe."

Remi blinked several times, coming out of the fog of memories that had consumed her. She pulled back a little, though not completely out of Mason's arms, savoring his comfort. She had never shared those details with anyone. She didn't know what had compelled her to tell Mason, but she didn't want to stop. She wanted to tell him everything that had followed that awful night and explain that was why she didn't like driving. But she was pouring her heart out to someone else's man, and that wasn't fair to him or to his girlfriend. He was her *bodyguard*, and he was stuck listening to her sob story, which was definitely *not* in his job description.

She forced herself to break from his embrace and stuffed her painful memories down deep, as she'd learned to do long ago. Swiping at her tears, she tried to calm her racing heart. "I'm sorry. I didn't mean to fall apart. It's been a long time since I . . ." *God, I'm pouring out my heart again.* She steeled herself against that urge and said, "I'm sorry. That was way too much information to dump on you."

He placed his hand over hers, stirring the feelings for him she was trying to ignore, and said, "Remi, don't apologize. I appreciate you sharing that with me. I had no idea how much you'd been through, and I'm so sorry for your loss. For all of it. Anytime you want to talk, I'm here."

The sincerity in his eyes and voice made her want to say more, and it hurt knowing she shouldn't. She felt awkward, having revealed so much of herself to a man who shouldn't be burdened with it. She could only imagine what he'd say to his girlfriend about the *fucked-up celebrity* he was *babysitting*. That thought stung, too, but mostly because she didn't believe he was the kind of guy to think that way, much less say it.

She pushed nervously to her feet, pulling on her sweater as she headed for the table to clear away the dishes, and said, "I've taken enough of your time, but thank you."

She began stacking dishes, and he did the same, watching her intently. Her emotions were all over the place. "You don't have to help," she said as they carried dishes inside.

"I don't mind. Rain's moving in. It's best to get this stuff indoors before it starts."

Once the table was cleared, they put away the leftovers, the silence broken only by the music streaming through the speakers on the wall. She was glad for the noise, even though it couldn't completely drown out her thoughts. She hoped it might distract Mason from all that she'd told him.

When she began washing the dishes, he said, "I'm going to secure the house. I'll be back in a few minutes. Are you okay?"

"I'm fine, and I appreciate you asking, but please don't think I need pitying because of my family. It was a long time ago. I'm fine, really. I don't even know where all that came from." Her stomach knotted. It *was* a long time ago, but talking about it had brought all of those painful memories to the surface.

"Remi, what I'm feeling is nothing like pity. I just wanted to be sure you were okay before I left you alone."

"I'm good. Thank you."

He went to secure the house, and she scrubbed the hell out of the dishes. Her mind played games with her, sifting through their afternoon at the grocery store, the way they'd danced and joked as they cooked, and the heated looks and closeness they'd shared.

She was putting detergent in the dishwasher, thinking about the stricken look on Mason's face when she told him she was in the car with her parents, when he strode back into the kitchen looking hot and delectable. Was it possible for one man to be her best *and* her worst distraction?

"What's that grin for?" he asked.

"Nothing." She wiped her hands on a dish towel, scolding herself for thinking of him that way again when he had a girlfriend. Maybe she needed to get that off her chest and acknowledge that he was taken in order to stop thinking about him as if he were a single man. Yes, that's exactly what she needed to do.

She mustered the courage and said, "I heard you talking to your girlfriend on the phone this morning. You shouldn't have to turn your life upside down because of me. I can stay with Ben and Aurelia or Willow and Zane for a night so you don't have to miss your date."

His brow knitted. "My *date*? I have no idea what you're talking about."

She moved around the kitchen, scrubbing the already-clean counters to work off her nervous energy. "Mason, you're allowed to have a life. God knows someone around here should."

"That's good to know, but again, I have no idea—"

"Come on, Mason. Unless you call your secretary or the guys who work for you *sweetheart*, I'm pretty sure I know what I heard."

He touched her hand, stopping her from scrubbing the finish off the counters. She dropped the sponge and folded her arms, then quickly unfolded them.

An amused smile lifted his lips.

"What's that smile for? I'm sorry if I seem nosy. I just feel bad for your girlfriend."

"You feel bad for her? Well, that's nice of you, and I'd let her know that if I *had* a girlfriend. What you overheard was me talking to Brooklyn, the ten-year-old daughter of a buddy of mine who was killed in the line of duty. She lives about twenty minutes from here, and I try to see her once a month and take her out for a movie or dinner. It gives her mom, Krista, a break, and it gives me a chance to tell Brooklyn stories about her dad to help keep his memory alive. It's the least I can do, since I survived and he didn't."

"Oh . . ." She understood all too well the burden of survivor's guilt. How many other brothers-in-arms had he lost? How many other families did he visit?

"Now I feel stupid *and* guilty for overhearing your phone call and for you missing out on seeing her. I'm sorry. I just assumed . . ." *You had a girlfriend.*

But you don't.

That reality had her revisiting everything that had gone on this evening—every touch, the kiss on her head, the way he'd held her hand and comforted her.

"It's fine," he said tightly.

"No, it's not." Her mind spun, twisting everything around until she was too conflicted to think straight about the two of them. But she saw one thing very clearly: She didn't want a fatherless little girl to miss out on seeing Mason. "I'm sure Brooklyn looks forward to seeing you, and her mom has probably been looking forward to a night off. Aiden never had time off from taking care of me when I was younger, and I know how much of a burden I was to him." *I still am in many ways.* "Like I said, I'll go stay with Ben and Aurelia for a night so you don't have to worry about me."

"Let it go, Remi. I'm not leaving you to take Brooklyn to the movies."

"Then why don't you bring her here for dinner and to watch a movie? She can roast marshmallows over the fire and go swimming if she wants."

"That sounds nice, but I would never put her in danger."

"Danger?" She looked around the kitchen. "Of what? The stalker obviously isn't around. Besides, you didn't have an issue with my friends coming over."

"They're adults. They make those decisions for themselves. Their boyfriends and husbands know the score."

"Well, there has to be a way for you to see her. I don't like knowing you're letting Brooklyn down because of me. How about if we both take her out? I'll sit at another table or something."

He shook his head. "I know you don't think you're in danger, but I'm not taking any chances by dividing my attention between you and Brooklyn. That's not safe for either of you."

She realized he was right, even if she didn't believe the stalker had followed her from LA. But that didn't take away the sting of knowing he was letting Brooklyn down because of her. She pulled her sweater tighter around her and said, "I'm just trying to help. I'm going to figure out a way for you to see her."

"Brooklyn will be fine. You, on the other hand, worry me. You've just bared your soul, and I know how that can unearth unwanted emotions."

If he didn't care about her as a woman, as opposed to just a job, would he bother saying that? If she didn't get out of there fast, she was liable to make a fool out of herself and *ask*. "I'm okay, thanks. I think I'll go to bed."

She headed for the steps, hope fluttering inside her like birds dancing toward the sky.

"Remi?" he called after her.

She turned with her heart in her throat. "Yeah?"

"I'm just trying to do my job the best way I know how. You know that, right?"

Talk about killing two birds with one stone.

Her hope deflated like a balloon. *No girlfriend doesn't mean no boundaries.* "Of course. Good night."

She stalked into her bedroom feeling stupid for even playing with the idea of there being something more between them, for thinking too much about his comforting touch and all those glances she was obviously misreading. She washed her face and changed into her silk sleeping shorts and tank top as the skies opened up and lightning and thunder crackled and boomed outside. She looked at the rain pummeling her window, and the memories she'd unearthed came rushing back. The flash of headlights on the deer as they darted in front of the car. The skid that sent the car careening down the hill. Her heart pitched as more thunder clapped, shaking her from the horrid memories.

With tears in her eyes, she retrieved her crafting supply boxes from the closet and set them on the floor by the bed. As she laid out one of her father's favorite books, along with her supplies—a razor, a stapler, glue, construction paper, a wooden cutting board, and hemp—her mother's voice trickled in. *Just breathe, Remi. Everything will be okay.*

"I'm trying," she mumbled to herself.

Her mother had loved crafting, and she'd taught Remi to make paper ornaments, bouquets, and cards from the pages of books and construction paper. She made them whenever she was sad or anxious.

Or, apparently, sexually and emotionally frustrated.

There were several boxes of ornaments and other things she'd made in the closet. She took them with her when she traveled. It comforted her to have them nearby. Though she owned several homes, she'd never felt grounded in any one place. She stole off to Cape Cod for a few weeks here and there, usually by herself to decompress. Sometimes she spent time with her friend Parker Collins-Lacroux, who ran a children's charity and owned a house in Wellfleet. She holed up in her rural cabin not far from Harmony Pointe when she wanted to be alone or needed to center her mind. They'd long ago sold their childhood home in West Virginia. The sadness outweighed the good memories there. But here, near her friends in Sweetwater and Harmony Pointe, was where she finally felt her roots trying to take hold.

She wiped her tears away, listening to rain drumming against the windows as she used the razor to carefully cut pages out of the book. The measured drag of the razor gave her something to focus on. She set several pages on the cutting board and began marking off one-inch strips with the ruler and pen.

Just breathe, Remi. Just breathe and everything will be okay.

She'd been old enough to have her first crush the December before she lost her mother. Johnny Templeton had broken her heart by asking someone else to the school's holiday dance. When Remi's mother had found her crying in her bedroom, her face buried in her pillow, her mother had said, *There will be lots of boys like Johnny Templeton in your life. They're for practice. Nobody is born knowing how to handle everything in life, and the Johnny Templetons of the world help us learn about all types of things, including protecting our hearts. But I promise you, Princess, one day there will be a special guy who will take one look at you and know without a shadow of a doubt how incredibly special you are. He might drive you crazy, because boys are not quite as smart in the love department as we girls are. But mark my words: When he comes along, you'll know it and so will he, because when true love hits, it's inescapable. Your heart will soar, and the pit of your stomach will get all knotted up. You might even want to outrun those feelings, but no matter what direction you turn, he's always going to be there.*

Thunder boomed at the same moment a knock sounded on Remi's bedroom door, startling her, and the pen she was holding tore through the paper. *Perfect. What else can go wrong?* Maybe Mason wanted to hammer the boundary thing home? Put her hopeful thoughts in a coffin and nail it shut?

She pushed to her feet and threw the door open. Mason stood before her, jaw tight, shoulders slightly rounded, looking sullen and angry at once.

"Hey," he said gruffly.

She swallowed hard and croaked out, "Hey."

"I, um . . ." His gaze shifted to the mess on her floor.

"I craft when I'm anxious."

"You're anxious . . ." He uttered a curse, and his serious eyes found hers again.

Without a word, he pulled her into an embrace, holding her tighter than she could ever remember being held—except maybe by Aiden the night of the accident. But this was different. This wasn't the embrace of an older brother. It was the embrace of a lover. The kind of embrace she'd acted out dozens of times in movies, only this wasn't an act. It was endless and beautiful. She didn't know why he was holding her like that, and she didn't question why she was letting him. She was too thankful for the comfort she'd always known existed but had never found in the arms of another.

His heart beat sure and steady against her cheek. Their closeness should have made her more anxious, but as she stood in the confines of his protective arms, her breathing calmed and her tension melted away. She closed her eyes, soaking him in like a sponge.

"I'm sorry for all you've lost and for all you've gone through," he said without releasing her, his voice tight, *visceral*, potent enough to make her legs weak. "And I'm so fucking glad you survived." His muscles tensed, and he stepped back, his stormy eyes catching hers for only a second before he strode into his bedroom, closing the door firmly behind him.

With whispers of hope in her head and feeling more than a little confused, Remi retreated into her bedroom. She closed the door and leaned back against it, her heart racing, wondering if she wouldn't be putting a nail in that coffin after all.

CHAPTER TEN

REMI? COME ON, Princess. Remi was having the best dream *ever.* Mason was in her bed, whispering her name, his breath coasting over her cheek as he pulled her closer. She reached for him, her fingers trailing over his prickly scruff, into his hair. She could practically taste his mouth on hers.

"Remi!"

Her eyes flew open at the very *real* whisper, and she bolted upright, smacking into Mason's chest.

"We have to go," he whispered urgently, helping her out of bed.

Panic flared inside her. She grabbed her sweater from the chair and shoved her hands into the sleeves. "*Why?* Is it the stalker? Is he *here?*"

"No," Mason whispered loudly as he darted into her closet, returning with her Ugg boots. "Put these on. We're sneaking out."

"Sneaking out?" she snapped, shoving her feet into the boots.

"*Shh!* We have to go." He took her hand and hurried out the bedroom door, speaking in urgent whispers. "You have a late call tomorrow, which means you can sleep in."

"Why are we *whispering?*" She tried to keep up as they rushed down the stairs.

"Because that's what you do when you sneak out."

She laughed and whispered, "You aren't like any bodyguard I've ever known."

"I'll take that as a compliment."

They snuck out to the SUV, and she stole glances at him as he drove through town. He was wearing his normal attire of jeans and a T-shirt, but his cocky grin made him look even hotter than he had in her midnight fantasy. She looked down at her silk pajama shorts and tank top, unable to believe they were sneaking out! In the middle of the night! Together! This was *so* different—better, more mysterious—than ditching her bodyguards.

"Do you always rouse your charges in the middle of the night?" she teased. "Is it your way to get a peek at their *goods*?"

"Their *goods*?" He chuckled. "Do I look desperate to you?"

"*Desperate* is not the word I was thinking of." *But I'm pretty sure telling you that sneaking out with me makes you sexier than ever would only get me in trouble.*

He drove to the edge of town and turned off the main road, navigating through side streets.

"Where are we going?"

"You'll see."

She couldn't stop smiling. It was after midnight, which officially made it Monday morning. They'd gotten so close in the days since she found out he didn't have a girlfriend and she told him about the night of the accident, it was getting even more difficult to hide her feelings for him. She'd taken him up on his offer to help her with her exercise routine, and they'd been working out together in the mornings. She'd never been so excited to face a new day as she was knowing she'd spend it with Mason. She even looked forward to making breakfasts and cooking dinners together, which was not only fun, but it gave them time to get to know each other better. He was helping her understand and take care of herself, but not in a controlling or demeaning way. He didn't push too hard, and it was clear that he wanted her to understand *why* she might want to consider doing things differently, like developing boundaries. He'd even carefully suggested she sit down and have a talk with Aiden about the way he handled her without taking away from her gratitude toward him. Most people thought she should break away from Aiden totally, or just be thankful for the way he cared for her. Remi appreciated that Mason saw both sides of the equation. She never knew everyday things like cooking could be so fun—or that a man could be so enlightening *and* enticing.

She gazed out the window as Mason drove down a narrow road and parked at the edge of an open field. A water tower loomed in the distance. He grabbed a backpack from the back seat and came around to the passenger side to help her out. The cool air brushed over her legs, but she was warm with her sweater and Mason's hand pressing against her back.

"I assume you've never had the pleasure of climbing a water tower?" he said as he guided her into the field.

"I haven't, but I've always wanted to. Isn't it illegal?"

He flashed that grin again, and her pulse quickened. "A federal crime."

She froze. "I can't do that, and neither can you!"

"Do you really think I'd let you get in trouble? I've got your back, Princess." He took her hand, tugging her toward the tower. "I told you I'd help you do wicked things *and* keep you safe. I have connections. We're both cleared to climb. As long as you don't fall off the tower, we're cool."

"Wow! Where were you when I was a teenager?"

She wasn't surprised he didn't respond. He was too busy scanning the grounds as they neared the tower. Ladders snaked up the side in long segments with landings in between, which made her much more comfortable than if it had been one continuous ladder that went straight from the ground to the top.

She gazed up at the massive tower, her heart racing. The rusted metal legs stirred memories of the children's movie *The Iron Giant*. She imagined the tower morphing into a giant spider and scaling the chain-link fence surrounding it with its big metal legs. "It's so much taller than it looks from the road."

"Too high for you?" he asked. "We can go hang out on the high school football field, sneak into neighborhood pools to skinny-dip, or toilet paper one of your friend's houses."

"Have you *done* those things?"

"I'll never tell." He looked up at the tower and said, "You game, Rebellious Remi? I hear there's a hell of a view of the lights of Harmony Pointe from the top."

Her heart leapt that he'd remembered her love of lights. "I'm in. But how will we get past the fence?"

"We could climb over it."

Visions of cutting herself on the barbed wire at the top danced in her head.

"Or we can walk through it." He unhooked the lock and chain, dangling it before her.

"Smart-ass," she said as she walked through.

"Told you I had your back. It's called trusting me, Princess."

Mason stayed close behind her as they scaled the ladder. She was nervous enough climbing so high, but it didn't help knowing Mason had a view of her butt. She wasn't wearing panties under her pajama shorts. He was probably too focused on being there to catch her if she fell to even notice.

They stopped at each landing, taking in the views. Each time they stopped, Mason asked if she was okay, making sure she was comfortable enough to continue their climb.

When they reached the top, the breeze was stronger and the view of the town was breathtaking. It was different from New York City, where the streets were constantly busy and big-city noises and smells filled the air. Remi could see all the way from the sleepy town of Harmony Pointe to the lights of Sweetwater and the mountains beyond. It was exhilarating knowing they were wide-awake when practically every house was dark. She felt safe up there, like she'd left all her troubles below, and being with Mason made it that much sweeter.

Mason stood beside her at the railing, watching *her* as she took in the view. He did that a lot, openly watching her. She wondered what he saw and what he was looking for, but she didn't dare ask. She had a feeling he sensed all of her inner thoughts.

"This is seriously beautiful," she said. "How did you even know this was here or that we could do this?"

"When your life and the lives of your teammates depend on knowing every possible place an enemy can hide from the second you land on the ground until you're out of enemy airspace, you learn a thing or two."

She reached out and traced the scar just below his left eye. His jaw clenched, his eyes holding hers captive as she touched his other scar, just above the scruff on his right cheek. "Is that how you got these?"

"Yeah," he said roughly.

"What was that like for you, all those dangerous missions?"

He stood rigid and silent for a long moment, and then he shifted his eyes away, looking over the field as he said, "I needed the structure of the military, a direction that wasn't going to land me in jail." When he met her gaze again, she saw some of the tension in his face dissipate. "I'm not going to lie and say it wasn't terrifying. It was. But I didn't think about that out in the field. Out there, the only thing that mattered was the mission and the safety of my team, doing everything I could to make sure they made it back alive." A shadow of sadness washed over his face and he said, "Many didn't, but we all knew the risks."

"Do you know a lot of kids like Brooklyn? Other families?" She had an idea of a way for Mason to see Brooklyn, but she didn't want to bring it up and derail their conversation, and she hadn't figured out all the pieces of that puzzle yet.

Mason pulled a blanket from his backpack and laid it on the metal floor as he said, "Unfortunately, there are lots of kids like Brooklyn and women like Krista, who have lost a parent or a spouse in the service.

There are guys who have lost wives, parents who have lost their grown children. The fallout from war is ruthless, but with charities like Hearts for Heroes, those who are left behind don't have to go it alone."

"I didn't realize you got to know them through Hearts for Heroes." Hearts for Heroes helped grieving families who had lost family members in the service. They held quarterly get-togethers for the families. Remi gave generously to the cause.

"I didn't. I was with my buddy Shelton, Brooklyn's father, when he took his last breath. He asked me to make sure his little girl didn't forget him, and I promised to be there for his family."

He tucked the blanket over the edge, and then he took her hand and helped her sit with her legs dangling.

"If we were kids," he said as he sat beside her, "we'd probably drink beer and smoke a joint. But since we're too smart for that . . ." He pulled a bottle of sparkling water from the backpack and set it beside him. Then he withdrew a pack of Skittles and tore it open.

"I didn't peg you as a *joint* kind of guy."

"I got in a fair amount of trouble as a kid." He held up the bag of Skittles and said, "I hope you like these. I figured chocolate had too many calories and chips were too salty since you're filming tomorrow."

Not many men would put that much thought into a snack. But as Mason had said, he wasn't like other men. "I love them. Thank you."

He poured Skittles into her hand and then doled out some for himself and set the package down, tossing a few candies into his mouth.

"I can't imagine you getting into trouble." She ate a Skittle.

"Nothing good comes from uprooting a kid every few months. Being the new kid in school sucks enough. Add trying to figure out new family dynamics at the same time, and that's a lot of stress for kids. It was easier not to make friends in school or at home than to find a buddy and know at any time you could be moved away."

"I can't imagine how difficult that was."

"It made me tougher. It's all good." He tossed a few more Skittles into his mouth.

"No, it's not *all good*," she said earnestly.

He half laughed, half scoffed, his eyes flicking up to hers as he said, "You're right. It wasn't."

He ate the rest of his candy, and she had a feeling he was deciding if he should say more, so she waited patiently.

When he finished eating, he said, "It was hard, and as a kid I didn't really understand why I was being moved around so much, so I acted out. As you can imagine, the more I acted out, the more often I was moved. I wasn't smart enough to realize *I* was the problem."

Her heart ached for him. "I don't think it had anything to do with lack of intelligence. You had to be angry and scared. You *weren't* the issue. You were just a young boy. The adults who were supposed to be caring for you should have been focusing on helping you get through being taken away from your mother. Any kid would be hurt and angry and act out. The one person who should have put you above all else didn't. How can a kid process that without help?"

"Yup." He got a faraway look in his eyes and gazed into the distance.

She put her hand over his and said, "I guess we both know what it's like to be separated from the people we love."

He looked soulfully at her as he turned his hand over, lacing his fingers with hers, and said, "We're stronger for it."

She wondered if he meant their pasts or their connection.

They sat in silence for a while, sharing the rest of the candy, his past settling in around them.

"You know, Remi, when you said you wanted control of your life, I *got* that. As a foster kid you don't have control of your life. Where you live, who you live with, the schools you attend, when everything will change, that's all governed by others. It wasn't until I was seventeen and one step away from juvie, when I met Chuck and his wife, Estelle, that

I began to understand that I *could* control my life. Maybe not as a kid, but I could control what happened moving forward."

He gazed up at the sky and said, "You were lucky to have Aiden step in after you lost your parents, and I got lucky when I met Chuck. I owe him a hell of a lot. When I lived in that building I took you to, my foster parents had three other foster kids and they fought a lot. I used to go up to the roof to escape the chaos. One day Chuck followed me up. It had been a particularly rotten week. The one thing I'd had from my mother, my grandfather's silver pocket watch, went missing. I knew without a doubt that one of the other kids had taken it. It wasn't particularly valuable, but it was the only link I had to my family. It had my grandfather's initials on it, *MS*. I was named after him. I used to hold the damn thing when I went to sleep, and after it went missing, I looked it up online and found that it was a Junghans watch. After that I hit the pawnshops every week looking for it, but I never did find it. Anyway, when it went missing, I got in a fight with the kid who I thought took it and the other kids raced in, and we brawled. It was a mess. I went up to the roof to try to clear my head. When Chuck came up, he hung back at first, giving me space, not pushing me to talk. The very first thing he ever said to me was 'Some people suck.'" Mason chuckled. "It was the perfect way to break the ice. It took him hours, but eventually he broke through my barriers and I told him what I'd been through and about the trouble I was getting in. He'd gone into the service at eighteen and was medically discharged at forty-eight. I'll never forget the way he looked me dead in the eyes and said, 'You've got two choices, Mason. Be a loser and blame your mother, or make something of yourself, save lives instead of being part of the problem, and blame your mother.'"

He cocked his head, looking at Remi with a serious expression, and said, "He probably saved my life that night, and he followed me up there nearly every night thereafter until I left for the service."

"The family you lived with sounds awful. Thank goodness for Chuck. This is embarrassing to admit, but I was afraid of him when I first saw him. I thought he was homeless, and I didn't know what to expect. That was horribly judgmental, and I'm ashamed to have thought it."

"It's not every day you're dragged into a questionable area by a guy you've just met. Add in a disheveled man coming out of the shadows and I'd say you had a right to jump to assumptions. But he's a good guy, and he saved my ass."

"I'm glad you had him. Did you ever try to find your mother?"

He nodded. "When I was twenty-six I tracked her down, but she'd overdosed a few years earlier."

"Oh, I'm so sorry. You never got to make peace with her or say goodbye? Is that why you have *Goodbye* tattooed on your chest?"

"The most painful goodbyes are the ones we never get to say. My mom, my military buddies who lost their lives. It's for all of them."

Remi tried to swallow past the emotions clogging her throat, but thoughts of her own parents made it even more difficult. She finally managed to say, "I'm so sorry."

"It's life—and death."

"I wish I had told my mom how much I loved her in the car that night." Her eyes teared up. "That's my biggest regret, not saying the important things before she died."

He put his arm around her, pulling her closer. "I'm sure your mom knew. I'm sorry for making you sad."

"It's okay. My world can be so superficial, I appreciate you sharing some of your life with me. Can I ask you a stupid question?"

"Is there such a thing?"

She nudged him. "How bad does a tattoo hurt? I really want to get *Just Breathe* right here, but I'm afraid." She ran her finger over the underside of her wrist.

"That spot will probably hurt, but not the way losing your parents did."

She lay on her back, staring up at the stars, thinking about everything he'd said and gone through. "How do you feel about your mom now? Are you angry with her?"

"If I am, I don't feel it anymore." He lay down next to her and said, "Addiction is a beast. You know from the movie you're filming that it's a daily battle even for those who think they've beat it."

Remi had researched for her role as the supportive and harried girlfriend of a recovering addict and had learned all about the complexities and struggles of addiction and the strains the disease put on those around them. To think that as a small child Mason had been around an addict was horrifying, but knowing how far he'd come spoke volumes about his strength and determination.

"The addiction was stronger than she was," Mason explained. "She was a seventeen-year-old kid when I was born, and I really believe she tried to be a good mother." He looked at Remi and said, "I remember her reading to me, holding me when I was sick. But I also remember strange men coming in and out of the places we stayed and finding her passed out cold more than once. I have no way of knowing how many of my memories are real, or if I fabricated the happier memories to make myself feel better. But that doesn't matter. There are no do-overs or take-backs in life. All we can do is learn from our mistakes and move forward."

"It sounds like you've learned from yours."

"And it doesn't sound like you had many chances to make mistakes. When you were growing up, Aiden held the reins pretty tight, didn't he?"

"He never had to. I was always well behaved, afraid to do anything that might lead to either of us getting hurt. I don't even like to drive, though I know how."

Pain rose in his eyes and he said, "That's understandable."

"It's only been the last couple of years that I started feeling too hemmed in. But also, I know what you meant about being unsure of how real your memories are. I wonder about that sometimes. Aiden did such a great job of keeping our parents alive for me—telling me stories about them, making birthdays and holidays as special as my parents always did. Sometimes I wonder if my memories are real or not, too. And that makes me wonder how those memories, real or fake, impacted how I turned out. I think about that a lot. Do you? Are you happy with your life now? Is your job and your life fulfilling?"

"Sure, my job is fulfilling in terms of accomplishments."

"And are you pretty busy, or do you have a lot of downtime? I feel like I'm always busy, and even my downtime is broken up by events and appearances."

"Downtime? I'm not sure what that is," he said sarcastically. "When I stepped in to take over for your security, I was working with two PI clients and preparing to take on a bounty-hunting job, all of which I delegated to my staff. So, yeah, I'm pretty busy."

"Do you ever meet your buddies for drinks? Hang out and watch football games or do other guy stuff?"

"I'm not a sit-around-and-watch-football type of guy."

She turned to face him. "Then it sounds like you live in a box, too, only you don't have a bodyguard making sure you stay in it. It's a self-imposed box."

His brows slanted. "How do you figure?"

"You're a workaholic. That's your box. What do you do for fun?"

"Catch bad guys," he said snarkily. "How about you, Ms. Divine? And while we're sharing, how'd you come up with your screen name?"

"My parents loved old movies with Marilyn Monroe and Rita Hayworth, and my mom used to say, 'These ladies are so divine!' When I started acting, Aiden suggested I not use my real name, but I love Remi and I didn't want to give it up. I'd already lost enough of my family. But then my agent said Aldridge wasn't a strong screen name, so I went with Divine, to honor my parents."

"That's a nice way to do so. And what makes you happy, Remington Aldridge?"

Loving that he used her real name, she said, "I'm still figuring that out. My friends and Aiden make me happy, even though he drives me bonkers sometimes. The stalker made Aiden even more protective, and the combination of the two are a big part of my decision to take time off after filming this movie. I'll still have to do promotional engagements, but I'm not going to make another movie for a while. Acting makes me happy, but something's still missing, and being stuck under a microscope isn't helping me figure out what it is. That's why I'm trying to get out of my virtual *box* more often. Thank you for tonight. I like being here *with you*." She said *with you* softer, a little worried about admitting it but not wanting to hold it back.

They gazed into each other's eyes, and Remi felt a light come on inside her, like she was finally exactly where she was meant to be—lying beside Mason on their secret-sharing perch over the town, their hands touching on the blanket between them. Maybe she was wrong for all these years thinking she had the world at her fingertips. She had the overwhelming sensation that she was only just discovering the world in which she belonged.

"Mason?" she said softly.

"Yeah?"

"Maybe *I* should be *your* bodyguard and drag you out of your workaholic box every once in a while."

He was quiet for a long moment, and then his fingers moved silently over hers and he said, "You already have."

CHAPTER ELEVEN

MASON WAS LIVING in hell, and it was all his fault. He'd opened the gates when he'd told Remi he'd help her with her exercise routines, and all sorts of trouble had flooded in ever since. Remi had spent the last three mornings prancing around in skimpy tops and shorts as they worked out together, and the evenings swimming in the tiniest fucking bikini he'd ever seen because he'd mentioned that swimming would tone her entire body.

Big mistake.

Nothing compared to the sight of Remington Aldridge climbing out of a pool dripping wet, her gorgeous body begging to be touched, tasted, and *worshipped*. Even now, as he waited for Remi outside her trailer, he saw the whole damn scene in his mind in slow motion—Remi tossing her wet mane over her shoulder as she bent to pick up a towel, blotting the water from her neck and chest, and then lying down on a lounge chair, her wet bikini leaving nothing to his imagination. He gritted his teeth against the white-hot lightning burning through him.

He'd like to see her come all right . . . on his *tongue*.

If all of that wasn't bad enough, sneaking her out of the house had totally backfired on him. He'd wanted to help her experience something a little rebellious to make up for all that she'd missed as a kid, and then he'd gotten lost in the moment, telling her all his long-held secrets. *What the hell?* When they'd finally made it home, he'd felt like he'd known her forever and he'd been *this close* to kissing her good night. It was one thing to be sexually attracted to her, but this was a whole other level of attraction. He never expected to have so much in common with her or to feel so drawn to her.

"Hey, Mason," Carl Welch, the second assistant director, called out as he strode determinedly toward Mason carrying an iPad, his ever-present headset efficiently in place. "They need Remi in makeup."

Mason had done a background check on Carl and had found nothing concerning about the married father of a young son. "No problem."

Carl poked at his iPad and headed for another trailer.

Mason knocked on Remi's trailer door. When she didn't answer, he knocked again. She'd been in there a long time, and he wondered if she'd finally conked out and fallen asleep. She'd been running herself ragged, working twelve- to fifteen-hour days, signing autographs for overzealous fans, and practicing her lines long after she took her nightly drive-Mason-crazy swim. At least he'd convinced her to eat. They'd gotten in the habit of making breakfast together after their workouts, and although she was never very hungry at night, he could usually get her to eat a salad with some form of protein on it. He took that as a win in the keeping-Remi-healthy department.

"Remi?"

Answered with silence and knowing time was of the essence, he opened the door and found her sitting in the middle of the floor, concentrating on cutting a piece of paper. He could hear music coming from her earbuds. No wonder she hadn't heard him knocking. Dozens of paper hearts littered the floor, some covered in gold glitter, others cut from construction paper, the remnants of which were also scattered about. A book lay on the floor with an X-ACTO knife sticking out from between the pages, which explained why some of the hearts had text printed on them. A few feet from where she sat were several stacks of hearts, the largest on the bottom, smallest on top, with colorful strings attached at the top.

Mason realized she was making ornaments, *and* more importantly, that Remi was anxious.

He tapped her on the shoulder, startling her. Her gorgeous eyes shot up to him, and then a heart-pounding smile appeared and she took out her earbuds.

"Hey," she said lightly.

"Sorry to interrupt, but Carl was just here. They need you in the makeup trailer."

"Okay." She put her earbuds back in and continued cutting.

Remi was meticulous about being on time, and now that he knew she was anxious, he wasn't going to stand back and wait to find out why. He'd been watching her like a hawk. If someone had spooked her or treated her badly, he'd have seen it, which meant there was something going on in that pretty head of hers.

He crouched beside her and took out one of her earbuds, ignoring her scowl. "What's going on, Princess?"

She pressed her lips together, turning those beautiful eyes back to her project, working the scissors with a vengeance. "Nothing. I just want to finish this before I go."

He covered her busy hands with one of his and said, "Why are these ornaments more important than your next scene?"

"Because my mother taught me how to make them."

Although he noted the importance of the project, he wasn't buying that as a reason for her to delay getting to the set. "Not a good enough reason to hinder your reputation. Try again. Does today have a special significance? Are you giving those ornaments to someone? Using them on the set?"

"I don't ever give them away, and no, they're not coming with me to the set. Making them helps me calm down." She put down the scissors and pushed to her feet, pacing.

Her brooding mood fit the outfit she was wearing for her upcoming scene—skintight black jeans and a too-small black tank top, revealing far too much cleavage and the lace bra that barely contained her breasts.

"I didn't see you bring these from home. Do you keep craft supplies in your trailer?"

"Yes. I never know when I'll need them, so I bring them every time I'm filming."

"How long have you been using this as your stress reliever?" He could think of a hell of a lot of better ways to relieve stress, but they mostly involved Remi naked.

She shrugged. "Since I was little."

The importance of what she said dragged him from his dirty thoughts. "You must have boxes full of things you've made."

Her cheeks pinked up, and she crossed her arms defensively. "So?"

He went to her, carefully walking around the pretty ornaments. "I'm not judging you, Remi. I'm just trying to figure out what's going on. Maybe I can help."

"It's stupid. I have to do a kissing scene with Raz, and I hate kissing scenes with a passion. Like truly, madly *hate* them."

Mason chuckled. He remembered her saying something about having trouble with intimate scenes, but he hadn't imagined she meant *kissing*. "Seriously? *That's* what's causing your anxiety? A beautiful woman like you must have kissed dozens of men." He hated how it felt to say that, but as much as he wanted Remi all to himself, he knew that wasn't an option. What mattered was helping her get over her anxiety and to the set.

She threw her hands up and said, "I've kissed dozens of men *on-screen*, not off. But that doesn't make it any easier."

"Come on, Remi. Raz is a good-looking guy. How hard can it be to kiss him? Is it because he's your ex? Is that freaking you out?" As he said the words, he remembered something else she'd said when they were talking about Raz. *For the record, chemistry is everything in my book. I have to feel it to kiss a guy, much less have sex with him.* Damn, why couldn't he have remembered that before he'd opened his mouth?

"No! It doesn't matter that he's my ex. I should *want* to kiss him, right? I mean, he's America's hottest heartthrob. Women would give anything to kiss him. But kissing is intimate, and it's never been easy for me to fake."

"I know you told me that. I'm sorry I didn't remember earlier." He stepped closer, lowering his voice, trying to reassure her. "Remi, you're an incredible actress. I saw you go from serious to bawling your eyes out on set yesterday, then today, laughing so hard you were doubled over after having a seething argument with the producer. I'm sure you can nail this scene."

"You think it's easy?" She was pacing, with a feral look in her eyes.

"I didn't say that. I just believe in your acting abilities."

"I swear just thinking about it makes me feel like I have spiders crawling on my skin." She stopped in front of him and put her hands on her hips. "Let me show you what I have to do. You'll see how it comes out stilted and uncomfortable. Here's the setup. Raz has just come in from an NA meeting and he's feeling down, like he's a total failure despite being clean. It's a really emotional time for him, and for *us*."

"I saw the script when you were running lines the other night. I know the gist of the scene." He figured this would be a challenging scene for Raz, but the idea that Remi had trouble with kissing scenes still sort of shocked him, despite all she'd said.

"Good, because I need you to act frustrated and pace around a little, like Raz will."

He was so sexually frustrated his balls were close to exploding. He didn't have to reach far to let that frustration roll out.

Remi closed her eyes, breathing deeply. When she opened them, they were softer, concerned, matching her expression. Mason had learned how to differentiate Remi's real emotions from those he witnessed when she was acting. When she acted, she tended to keep her chin a tad higher than normal, and her movements were graceful, lacking the nonchalance of not being filmed. Her smiles were effervescent on set, but when she was off set, they lit up the sky. And her eyes? He could go on for hours noting the differences between the deep, inescapable emotions he'd witnessed the other night after her girlfriends had left and on the water tower, and the surface-level emotions she drew upon when she was acting. He was sure to anyone else, what they saw on the big screen was raw and magnificent, but Mason had seen the woman behind the veil; he'd gotten lost in the unrelenting pain and sorrow he'd seen in her eyes and felt billowing off her like the wind.

He raked a hand through his hair, allowing the silent war that had been raging in his head, and his heart, for days to take control. He strode across the floor, hands fisting, his insides twisting as he mentally toyed with the fine ethical line he'd nearly crossed too many times with Remi. He'd been burying his emotions so deep, it felt good to let them brew.

"Why do you keep doing this to yourself?" Remi pleaded, closing the distance between them. "You're a good man, a *great* man. You're doing all the right things."

And thinking all the wrong ones.

"Look at me," she said seductively. "Do you *see* how much I want this? How much I want you? Us? Let me *in*, Lenny." With pleading eyes, she pressed her hand to his chest. "You think you need walls to protect yourself from your past, but don't you see? Your past is what brought you here, to *me*."

She grabbed his shirt with both hands, a sea of emotions swimming in her eyes. Mason's hands circled her waist, and he felt her entire being sway closer.

"All those years of hurt and anguish, when you lost yourself in drugs, when you turned away from everyone who reached out to you, didn't make you any less of a man." She tightened her grip on his shirt with one hand, reaching up to caress his cheek with her other, her voice turning soft as velvet. "You're stronger and *braver* than any man I've ever known, and I want to know *all* of you."

I want to know all of you, too.

He gritted his teeth, telling himself she was only acting, despite knowing—*feeling*—the difference. His nerves were strung tighter than guitar strings. He was too hyped up to trust his judgment.

"I want you, Lenny." She pressed her body against him, and he was an asshole, because he couldn't stop himself from holding her tighter. "I want the good, the bad, and the parts of you that *you* don't even want to acknowledge." She went up on her toes, breathing heavily, her eyes so dark and hungry, the gold and green flecks shone like stars in the night sky. "*Stop* holding back. *Take me* with everything you have."

Mason was stuck between heaven and hell, with Remi's luscious mouth *right there*, begging to be devoured. Her chest rose against him with every heated breath, tauntingly enticing. She pressed impossibly closer, so not even air could fit between them. The only thing *stilted* or *uncomfortable* was behind his zipper. He lowered his mouth toward hers, fighting with everything he had to keep himself from taking what he wanted. He forced himself to stop short and practically growled, "I'm not seeing a problem here, Remi."

A knock sounded on the door, but neither of them moved.

Remi rolled her lip between her teeth, doing that cock-hardening innocent/hungry thing with her eyes that clawed at his self-control.

"Because I'm not acting," she said soft as a whisper—and loud as a hurricane.

Several hard *thuds* sounded at the door, and it swung open. Carl peered in, and Mason released Remi, stepping back across the line he'd nearly crossed. *Fuck. Fuck, fuck, fuck.* The mixture of shock and relief in Remi's eyes tore at his gut. He had no idea if that look meant she was relieved he'd stepped back, or relieved she'd said she wasn't acting.

"Sorry, um . . ." Carl stammered. "They need you—"

"I'm coming," Remi said quickly, and hurried out the door with Carl.

Mason followed her down the steps, leaning close enough to say, "Remi . . . ?" for her ears only.

She looked over her shoulder and hissed, "Don't look at me like that! It's not my fault."

Before he could respond, Carl started going over a schedule with Remi, closing the door on any hope Mason had of conversation. He kept his eyes peeled, mentally ticking off the names of the crew as they passed, memorizing the face of every bystander. All the while *Because I'm not acting* fought for his attention.

He struggled with that thought as Remi went through makeup. She came out of the trailer and looked sheepishly at him as handlers ushered her toward the set. *Damn it.* He had to nix that embarrassment so she didn't mess up her lines. He bided his time as she went through the camera rehearsal, where they told the actors where to stand and move so the camera crew could ascertain their positions and lighting. Then the actors met with the assistant director, and they were asked to hang around, which meant filming wasn't far off.

Mason kept an eye on their surroundings while Remi talked with two supporting actors. The need to talk with her about what had happened magnified with every passing minute. When Remi finally broke away, Raz sauntered over and put a hand on her shoulder. Mason had the urge to shove Raz's hand off her, but he could tell by Remi's expression that she wasn't bothered by it, which made Mason an asshole for even thinking it.

After Raz walked away, Mason went to her, unwilling to wait another minute. He guided her away from prying eyes, feeling her nervous energy. "Everything okay?"

"Raz knows I hate kissing scenes. He was just trying to ease my nerves."

She looked at the set, the other actors, the director, *everywhere* except at Mason, and that killed him. He knew what he had to do and stifled the gnawing urge to talk about what had happened in the trailer. Instead he said, "You've got this, Remi. You'll nail the scene."

They called Remi to the set.

"You think so?" She looked a little disappointed. "How? Pretend he's you?"

No fucking way. Biting that back, he said, "If that's what it takes, *yes*. You're a pro. Don't let whatever happened in the trailer get under your skin."

"Too late," she said softly.

Everything she did got under *his* skin. He stepped closer and took her by the shoulders. She looked longingly up at him, the air between them pulsing with lust and something much deeper. He fucking hated doing the right thing.

But he had to build her up, to help her get the scene done well despite wanting to lower his mouth to hers and kiss away the disappointment in her voice, so he said, "Then *use* it, Remi. Do whatever it takes to get out there and blow that fucking scene away, you hear me? Don't ever let anyone or anything stand in your way of getting everything you want and deserve in this world."

CHAPTER TWELVE

MASON HAD CARRIED out dangerous covert operations without a single hesitation. He'd tracked seemingly untraceable people and brought justice crashing down upon some of the world's most hardened criminals without a second thought. So how was it that sweet little Remington Aldridge could practically bring him to his knees with nothing more than a few simple words? Even on the battlefield he'd never felt as vulnerable as he did when they were alone together. She'd effortlessly stripped him of his defenses, and now he was so tightly wound, he was ready to tear someone's head off.

As he watched Remi and Raz work up to their kissing scene, it was mainly Raz's head he wanted, but anyone's would do.

Remi nailed her lines, proving why she was an A-lister. Every sentence was perfectly intoned, every action poignantly carried out. Mason noted the looks of awe and appreciation from the crew. Even Raz was phenomenal. Mason couldn't hate the guy for being good at what he did or for having once been with Remi, because any man in his right mind would want to be in his shoes.

The hair on the back of Mason's neck stood on end as he scanned the grounds, catching sight of a group of fans forming across the field at the edge of the parking lot. Remi was still dead set on signing autographs at every opportunity, though this morning she'd made a comment about *maybe cutting back*. About fucking time. The woman gave her all to everyone else, and from what he'd seen, she did very little for herself.

He turned his attention back to Remi as the critical kissing scene began. Mason's chest constricted when her hand landed on Raz's chest, but at the same time he was rooting for her, hoping she'd not only pull it off, but blow everyone away.

And as he watched, she did just that.

She went up on her toes, and Raz's mouth came down over hers, so real and impassioned, jealousy streaked through Mason. His hands fisted by his sides, but the second they yelled "Cut" and applause rang out, Mason was right there with them, pumping his fist and cheering. He was so damn proud of her he could barely see straight.

Remi's eyes darted to his, and she *ran* toward him. Before he could get his bearings, she launched herself into his arms, crushing her lips to his. A surge of heat consumed him as her tongue thrust into his mouth, and then all bets were off. He *took* and *tasted*, their tongues tangling, his mind spinning. In those few scorching seconds, nothing else existed. But the sound of whistles and cheers quickly broke through his reverie, and his brain began firing again. He tore his mouth away, lowering Remi to her feet, taking in the prying eyes all around them, the fans aiming their phones in their direction. *Fuck.*

"You're done here?" Mason said roughly.

Remi's cheeks were flushed, her eyes wide and *wanting* as she trapped her lower lip between her teeth and shook her head.

Christ, she was going to be the death of him. "*Filming*, Remi. That was your last scene for today, right?"

"*Oh.* Yes," she said absently, and then a big-ass smile appeared and she bounced on her toes. "I *nailed* it."

"You sure did." *And you nailed me, too.* "Let's go." He took her by the arm, leading her toward her trailer, shielding her from fans with his body. His mind reeled with too many thoughts to hold on to any one of them beyond the most important. He needed to get a fucking grip, because what just happened could not happen again.

Inside the trailer, he walked around her ornaments and paced, trying to wrap his head around the situation. Remi stood by the door with a sexy-as-sin grin, desire practically seeping out of her pores. It took every ounce of his control not to pull her into his arms and take everything he wanted.

"What was that?" he snapped.

She tilted her head innocently and said, "A really hot kiss?"

"No shit, Princess. But this *can't* happen. Your brother is paying me to keep you safe, and what happened out there"—he pointed at the door—"that fucked with my head. I wasn't thinking about *protecting* you, Remi. I was thinking about . . ."

"Touching me?" she asked huskily, closing the distance between them.

She reached for him, and he grabbed her wrist. "Remi," he warned. "You're playing with fire."

Desire brimmed in her eyes. "I've waited twenty-five years to feel this, and you can't tell me you don't feel it, too," she said sharply. "I know you do, Mason. I see it in your eyes. I feel it eating up the space between us."

He stepped around her and sank down on the couch. "It doesn't matter what I feel. What matters is your safety." He gritted his teeth against the emotions stacking up inside him, telling himself her safety *had* to come first.

"So don't kiss me in public," she challenged.

"You don't want that, Remi, and you sure as hell don't deserve to be someone's dirty little secret."

She looked at him and sighed. "Then what will you do, Mason? Because *you're* the one I want."

Her words sent bullets of desire firing through him.

"No one can keep me safer than you can." She moved closer, her leg brushing against his. "You told me you were the best person to protect me, and I've seen the way you are. You don't miss a thing. You *care* about me, Mason. Maybe it started as a job, but you don't fool me."

"Remi, you have no idea how dangerous this is."

"Don't I?" she said seductively.

She held his gaze as she straddled his lap. He knew he should push her away, stand up and put space between them, but as she sank down on his lap and took his face between her hands, her pleading eyes rendered him powerless to resist her.

"Just kiss me," she whispered.

He ground out, "Remi," and he crushed his mouth to hers, taking her in a penetrating kiss, turning all his confusion, all his resistance, into white-hot desire. She dug her fingernails into his flesh as he tangled his hands in her hair, angling her face and taking the kiss deeper. She arched into him, and then their hands were everywhere at once, groping and caressing as they ate at each other's mouths. She pushed her hands into his hair, moaning longingly. The sexy sound tore through him, unleashing all the pent-up desires he'd been holding back. He lowered her to the cushion, coming down over her, his thoughts a tangle of dark desires.

Her hips rocked against his hard length as he intensified their kisses. She tasted sweet and hot, like sunshine and whiskey, and *holy fuck*, he wanted to get drunk and live in the sun. The feel of her hands pressing against the back of his hips and those sweet lips devouring his drew him deeper into her. Somewhere in the back of his mind, warning bells were going off. He tried to ignore them, but they only became louder. He forced himself to pull away, but she was looking at him like he was everything she ever wanted, and *man*, she was that for him.

"Mason" fell from her lips like a secret.

He wanted to know *all* her secrets, all her lies, all her truths, and all her dreams.

She reached for him as he reclaimed her mouth, more demanding this time, greedily needing her to feel—to *know*—how much he wanted her. He was vaguely aware of something ringing, but between the blood rushing through his ears, the pounding of their hearts, and the throbbing of his cock, he was too caught up to think straight. He trapped her lower lip between his teeth, and she rubbed against him like a cat in heat, moaning and mewling. He'd been dying to do that since the first time she'd rolled that plump lip between her teeth, and *fuuck*, it'd been worth the wait.

"*Again*," she pleaded.

He captured her mouth in another scorching kiss, and when he tugged her lip, she made a sinful sound that wound lustfully through him. The ringing sounded again. He'd heard about fireworks going off when people kissed, but he'd never actually experienced it until now. Ringing, fireworks . . . His body was ready to explode.

When the ringing continued, he realized it was coming from her phone, and forced himself to break away. She tried to pull his mouth back to hers, but his neurons were firing again, and reality hit him like a bullet.

He sat up, both of them breathless, and scrubbed a hand down his face. "That's your phone. Sounds like it could be important. It might be Aiden."

Remi's head was spinning. She didn't want to think about Aiden, not when she'd just experienced the hottest kisses of her entire life. Her lips tingled, and her body was on fire. She felt *primal*, fiercely *feminine*. How could she have gone her whole life without ever once feeling this type of connection, this unrelenting passion for another human being? This was what the stories her girlfriends told her were made of, and she wanted more of it, more of *Mason*.

She reached for him, pulling his mouth back to hers. But even as they kissed, she felt him pulling away.

He put an arm around her without breaking their connection, bringing her up beside him and into his arms. "Princess, that was—"

"*Don't.*" She pressed her lips to his to avoid hearing the words she'd never believe.

He kissed her deeply, eagerly, and when their lips finally parted, her nerves were buzzing like live wires. "I know where you stand, Mason, and I care about your strong moral bearings, but I also care about the unstoppable connection between us. If you say this was a *mistake*," she said sharply, "I will never forgive you."

He kissed her again, slow, sensual, and so sweet she lost her train of thought. He trailed a series of lighter kisses along her lips. His face was so close, she could feel his breath on her lips.

"How do you feel about the word *incredible?*"

Happiness soared inside her, and she pressed her lips to his again, grinning like a lovesick fool.

"You could never be a mistake, Remi. But *this?* It's dangerous and tricky. We need to think it through."

Her phone chimed again, and as she came out of her lust-filled delirium, she realized her phone had chimed several times. She had to check it, but she didn't want to move.

"What does that mean?" she asked.

"I don't know, but we'll figure it out. Until then, we can't let what happened out there happen again. I have to protect you with everything I have, or I have to quit and bring someone else in to take over."

The thought of losing him after she'd only *just* found him brought a rush of panic. She clung to him and said, "*No.* I don't want someone else *and* you. I want only you."

"You can't make all the rules, Remi. How about we figure it out together?" He pressed his lips to hers. "*After* you see why your phone is blowing up."

Together. She loved the sound of that, and she loved that Mason didn't treat her like she couldn't make decisions for herself or like she was just a *job.* Feeling like she'd won a Golden Globe, she snagged her phone from the table. There were four text message bubbles on the lock screen. The sender's phone number appeared as all zeroes.

She quickly scanned each text bubble.

I saw you.

This will stop.

He won't have you for long.

The last bubble was blank.

Panic flared in Remi's chest as she sank down beside Mason and opened the first message, which caused all four to open. Four images of Remi and Mason kissing popped up, with a single line of text above each one, except the last image, in which Mason's face was crossed out with an angry red slash.

"Mason! What does this mean?"

"Motherfu—" Mason took the phone and pulled her trembling body into his arms. "We've pissed him off."

"But what does it *mean?* He wants to *hurt you*, not just me?"

"I don't know, Remi. But we're sure as hell going to find out."

"I thought this was over," she snapped, clinging to him. Anger and terror twisted inside her. "How did he get my number? Can you trace the messages? This is all my fault."

Mason pulled back, holding tightly to her upper arms, his serious eyes boring into her. "This is *not* your fault."

"I kissed you in front of everyone! Of course it's my fault. I was just so overwhelmed with what happened between us, and then I nailed that scene. I did what you said and pretended Raz was you. It's like the stupid stalker *knew* I was finally truly happy and he needed to rip it to shreds!"

"Remi, listen to me. Whoever this is, he's sick, obsessive, and we're going to stop him—or her. If he didn't focus on the kiss, he would have found something else, so don't you *ever* think anything he does is your fault."

"I get that his psychotic behavior isn't my fault, but that doesn't ease the guilt of knowing I've put you in danger. I've been such an idiot, thinking the stalker had moved on and I was in the clear. Aiden has been trying to protect me for months, and you, Porter, Merrick, the bodyguards before them . . . *Everyone* was doing their best to protect me, and I was sneaking out, acting like a spoiled brat. I could have been killed, and I could have put every one of them in danger."

"You were acting like a woman who didn't want to live in a box. And I don't want you to live like that, either. But, Remi, listen to me. We can't undo what's done. We can only learn from our mistakes and be smarter as we move forward. Remember those boundaries we talked about? It's time to start figuring them out."

The fact that he'd used *we* didn't go unnoticed. "Okay. What should we do?"

"Most stalkers use more than one means of approach. There were letters in LA, he broke into your house, and now these texts. He's getting bolder, showing us just how close he is. We need reinforcements. I'm calling in a team."

"A team of what?"

"My guys—security, IT professionals, *muscle*. I want every angle covered. I'm not taking any chances that someone slips through the cracks." He pulled out his phone and said, "We need to contact the police, talk to the director. The film crew needs to be apprised of the situation."

"But it's probably one of them! I kissed you right by the set."

"One of them, *maybe*. But that's *one* person out of everyone out there—directors, producers, makeup and costume staff, film crew, runners, craft services. The list goes on. Better to have all those people looking out for you than to keep it under wraps. It could be someone on set, yes, but the picture could have been taken by someone on the sidelines. Hell, there were plenty of fans watching. Any one of them could have taken it, posted it to social media, and the asshole could have downloaded it."

"That fast?"

"That fast. We'll check out every angle. Lots of people had their phones out. If the picture has already surfaced online, we'll do what we can to shut it down. But my gut tells me the guy we're looking for took this particular picture, and if I'm right, he'll probably keep it to himself. He wants *you*, Remi, and typically obsessives don't share. They hole up in a basement somewhere."

"That creeps me out." She tried to swallow the bile rising in her throat as images of a Remi Divine shrine slammed into her.

"It should. We need to get moving. Somebody might remember seeing someone strange or unfamiliar take a picture of us kissing. I also need to meet with campus and set security and get online to start tracking down where the text originated. That's easy to mask, so I don't hold much hope for it leading us to the culprit. If it's the same guy who broke into your house in LA and disabled your home security system, then he knows his way around technology and security."

"Mason, what if he gets into the house?"

"I've got that locked down tight, with several layers of security."

"But you just said—"

He pulled her against him, one hand on the back of her head, the other around her waist. "I've got backup security on all the windows and doors, Remi. I will never, *ever* let anything happen to you. Do you hear me?"

"Yes," she croaked out. "But if he's *here*, on set, he could be anyone."

He pressed a kiss to her temple and said, "We'll find him. But I need you to promise me you will not go *anywhere* without me. Got it? No walking into trailers without me checking them out first. If you have to go the bathroom, I'm right there with you to make sure it's clear."

"Okay," she said against his chest.

"You're not going to like this, but no more signing autographs for a while. Remember the guy who tried to grab you?"

Ice-cold terror flared in her chest. "You think it was *him?*"

"I don't know, but I intend to find out."

He brushed her hair away from her face, his expression softening the slightest bit, the first crack in the granite armor that had overtaken him the moment the threat arose.

"Listen to me, Princess. I'm going to arrange for you to have a new phone by tonight. I need this one. But I don't want you giving the new number out to anyone other than Aiden and your closest girlfriends, and they need strict instructions not to share it. Anyone else can call my number to reach you. Got it?"

She nodded. "Yes, of course."

"Good. Now, I assume you want to help catch this guy?"

"Oh my gosh, yes!" As scared as she was, she was still thrilled not to be treated like a damsel in distress.

"We're a team, so I'm glad to hear that. I need you to get on the phone with Shea and tell her to quash this story. We don't want it hitting the tabloids. Pay them off . . . Do whatever you need to do—just get it *shut down.*"

"Okay. I'll call Naomi, too."

"Good. I need to get online and put these plans into motion. Can you pick up your crafts? If you need to use them to ease your nerves, then please do it in the bedroom. We'll need this space. Your trailer is about to become our headquarters."

CHAPTER THIRTEEN

"COME ON, YOU fucker, give me something," Mason seethed through gritted teeth as he scanned reports on his laptop. Beside his bed was another laptop with live feeds from the home security system, streaming videos from each of the cameras.

It had been the longest day of his life. After meeting with local police and security, he'd assembled a team of eight of his best men, who would be on set when Remi was filming and available at his beck and call to accompany them anywhere Remi wanted to go. He'd brought Porter and Merrick back and explained to Remi that they'd previously been under strict orders from Aiden to keep their distance. She seemed okay with bringing them back and irritated with Aiden for making her seem off-limits for even normal conversations. He didn't blame her, and he'd already corrected that situation with his men. He'd connected with his top IT guys, who were not only running the gamut on the text messages but were also retracing the steps of the initial detectives who had handled Remi's case in LA. His recon team had pulled social media posts with recent pictures of Remi and were tracking the origination of the photos, though they had yet to find the exact picture that had been sent to Remi. He also brought in a photography expert to review the picture in the text to try to discern the possible location of the photographer.

Mason had already spent hours going over campus security footage that covered the parking lots near the set, looking for *anything* out of the ordinary, and he'd been racking his memory for the faces he'd cataloged since the night of the fundraiser. There were too many possibilities. He needed a fucking bread crumb. *One* clue as to where the asshole was holing up.

When he found him, he was going to tear him apart.

He rested his head against the headboard, eyeing his open door and thinking about Remi. His chest physically ached over how brave she'd been as her world was turned upside down. She'd vacillated between fear and anger throughout the afternoon and evening, with a hundred other emotions surfacing in between. By the time she'd turned in for the night, she was emotionally and physically exhausted. He'd wanted to take her into his bed, to hold her in his arms and make sure she was safe. But he didn't want to increase her fear or inadvertently put pressure on her about their budding relationship. She needed to know she was safe in the house and that she had control over whatever happened— or didn't happen—between them. Lord knew she needed control of something.

He couldn't help thinking he should have kept his distance from the get-go and made extra efforts to shut down the attraction between them, but that would have been like trying to stop a speeding train. Their connection was too powerful, too *real* to turn off. But he *should* have stopped the kiss, even though he knew that wouldn't have stopped the stalker from rearing his ugly head. The asshole would have found another impetus for his threat.

Fuck.

That kiss.

And all the incredible kisses that followed.

He'd thought working with Remi and not being able to touch her was hell. Man, was he wrong. He was frustrated, angry, and yeah, he was fucking scared. The thought of something happening to her? Of some dirtbag getting his hands on her and doing Lord knew what? That was *hell*. And the fear he'd seen in her eyes? That was an image he'd take to the grave—and willingly give his life to erase.

He heard Remi's bedroom door open and sprang to his feet, meeting her in the hallway. Anger and hurt twisted inside him at the fear welling in her eyes. She hadn't torn down his barriers. She'd effortlessly peeled them back until she'd exposed his raw underbelly and burrowed her way into his heart. How could he ever go back to the life he'd had before her lips had touched his? Before he'd held her?

"I keep hearing things," she said softly, fidgeting with the hem of her pink sleeping shorts. Her matching pink top stopped just above her belly button, revealing a path of toned, tanned stomach.

Defenseless against her bottomless hazel eyes, which told him everything she felt without words, he reached for her. "Come here, Princess."

A flicker of apprehension shone in her eyes, and then those gorgeous eyes trailed down his bare chest, to the gray sweats he'd thrown on after his shower. She took his hand, stepping willingly into his arms. He felt mildly guilty for taking pleasure in her soft curves melding to his hard frame. If she couldn't tell he was commando before, there was no hiding it now. He tried to shut off the part of his brain that wanted to dance with the sexual devil and focused on helping her feel safe.

"I've got you," he reassured her. "You're hearing the wind, the house settling. Nobody can get anywhere near you."

She lifted troubled eyes to his and said, "Can I lie with you just for a little while?"

"Of course." He led her into his bedroom, moved his laptop to the nightstand, and pulled the covers back.

As he turned off the lights, she climbed into bed. He lay beside her and gathered her in his arms. Her cheek rested on his chest, her hand on his stomach, and she sighed, a long, relieved sigh, like she'd been holding it in for hours. He felt the same way. Every minute they'd been apart was torture.

"You have cameras all over?" She pointed to the security videos on the laptop.

"Inside and out."

She was quiet for a few seconds before asking, "In my room?"

"No. Just the hallway. Your window's too high for someone to break in." He kissed the top of her head, inhaling her feminine scent, like sweet apricots. "There's a control room on the lower level with live feeds from each camera, but I didn't want to be that far from you."

"Aiden told me about it." Her fingers moved over his stomach and ribs. "I couldn't have gotten through today without you," she said softly. "Thank you for making sure I knew everything that was happening. Is it always that intense with your job? When you're doing investigations?"

"Sometimes, but this one is a bit more complicated."

"How so?"

Honesty came easily for Mason, but there was nothing easy about the truth he was about to expose. "Because this time I stand to lose something important to me. The stakes are higher."

She angled her face, the fear in her eyes replaced with warmth. "You do care."

"I do, Remi. You've gotten so deep under my skin, I can't fight it anymore. But what we both want and what you need are two very different things. There's no margin for error."

"I know." She pressed a kiss to the tattoo on his chest. "You've made that clear."

He smoothed his hand down her back, hoping to hell she wouldn't hate him for what he had to say next. "I don't like having to suggest this, but for now, even with my team in place, we should keep this— *us*—private. I hate to be that guy, and I sure as hell don't want to be him with you, so if you want me to keep my distance until after all this is over and you're out of danger, I'm okay with that."

Hurt shone in her eyes. "Are you? Okay with that?"

"If I have to be in order to keep you safe, yes."

"That says a lot about you."

She traced the hair down the center of his stomach, sending a rush of heat to his cock, and her fingers slipped beneath the waistband of his sweats. He touched her wrist, their eyes meeting with a blaze of fire.

"This is dangerous territory, Remi."

"I want to be dangerous with you," she whispered.

"We riled up that guy today. I will not *knowingly* put you in danger, so are you sure you're okay with keeping us private—a *secret*—for now? Because the last thing we need is for that asshole to strike out because he sees something between us."

"Yes," she said, her eyes darkening. "I'm okay with it."

He shifted onto his side, bringing their mouths a whisper apart as he said, "Once we cross this line, we can't undo it. There are no takebacks, Princess."

"I want you to *take*," she said seductively. "And I want to *give* you *everything*."

His mouth came hungrily down over hers.

Mason was a force to be reckoned with. He kissed like he did everything else—passionately, *thoroughly*, as if pleasuring Remi was his sole focus. He seduced her with a penetrating rhythm, lulling her with sinful sounds of appreciation as he intensified the kiss. His tongue probed soft and rough at once. He tasted rugged and manly, like nothing she'd ever experienced before, and it was utterly addicting. She was dizzy with desire, her body pulsing and clenching as he rocked his hard length against her center. His hand moved over her heated flesh, pushing beneath her shirt, and he cupped her breast, rolling the taut peak between her finger and thumb. She moaned into their kisses, arching beneath him, craving so much more. He drew back and traced her lower lip with his tongue, drawing a needy whimper from her lungs.

"You do me in, Princess." He brushed his lips along her cheek and whispered into her ear, "You make me cross every line, and I don't know what that says about me, but I sure as hell know how special that makes you."

He crushed his mouth to hers as he swept her beneath him, like he couldn't wait another second to devour her. His mouth left hers abruptly, kissing a path down her neck and between her breasts. Then those devastatingly blue eyes caught hers, and he stripped off her shirt, tossing it to the floor. His gaze swept over her face and slowly down her chest, as if he were committing every inch of her to memory.

"Oh, my sweet Remi, you are *divine*," he said in a gravelly voice that sent shivers of heat skating along her skin.

He lowered his mouth to her breast, kissing, licking, and teasing her into a needy, writhing mess. When he sucked the peak into his mouth, he moaned, as if he were savoring the taste of her.

"I want all of you," he said hungrily.

"Take me, Mason . . ."

His heady groan moved over her skin as he lowered his mouth to her other breast, giving it the same toe-curling attention. He sucked and teased, sending her entire being into a torrent of desire. Just when she thought she'd lose her mind, he rose and captured her mouth in a plundering kiss. Their bodies ground together, his glorious muscles flexing deliciously against her chest and stomach. He was so big, so broad and athletic, and yet somehow his weight was perfect bearing down on her. When he eased his efforts, kissing her intoxicatingly lighter, heat streaked down her limbs, tingling from the very tips of her fingers to the ends of her toes. She felt like she was floating and grounded at once, overwhelmed by the emotions taking root inside her.

"*Princess*," he breathed against her neck, pressing a kiss there. He brushed his nose along her cheek and whispered, "Oh, *my Princess*, I will protect you with my life."

He sealed that promise with another passionate kiss, and she believed him with every iota of her being. He whispered sweetness against her skin as his magnificent mouth moved down the center of her body—"*So beautiful . . . Only you . . . Kiss you forever . . .*" The honesty and longing in his voice made everything more intense. She fisted her hands in the sheets as he stripped off her shorts. He nudged her legs open with his broad shoulders, kissing from the crook of her knee all the way up to the joint at her hip, and goose bumps raced up her flesh. His hands curled around her waist. She'd never experienced anything as sensual as the warm press of his lips, the whisper of his breath over her skin, and his rough and then demanding caresses. She was trembling all over, high on anticipation. Her body tingled and burned as he pressed the feathery kisses to the juncture of her thighs.

Her hips bucked involuntarily, and a whimper escaped before she could stop it. Her eyes were closed, but she could feel his gaze on her face. He kissed her softly all around the place she needed it most, until she was unabashedly begging for more.

The first slick of his tongue was so slow, so exquisitely erotic, she cried out. He must have liked that, because he did it again and again, making her swell and ache as he teased her right up to the edge of madness.

"*Mason*," she pleaded, and he brought his hand into the mix, playing over her most sensitive nerves with deadly precision. "Oh *God . . .*"

He sealed his mouth over her sex, thrusting his tongue, teasing her with his thick fingers, until she was gasping for air, drowning in pleasure. He did something wicked with his mouth, and she spiraled over the edge, bucking wildly, a stream of indiscernible sounds flying from her lungs. Just as she started to catch her breath, he did it again—and repeated the pattern until she was delirious, unable to concentrate on any one sensation. The anticipation of finally having him inside her was unbearable. Like an addict needing a hit, she begged for more, clawing desperately at his shoulders, ready to sell her soul to the devil if it meant she'd get more of him.

"Mason, I need *you*—"

He crawled up her body, taking her in a fierce kiss. He tasted of *her*, and she didn't care. She pushed at his sweats, and he tried to take them off while they kissed, but it was awkward and impossible.

"How do we make it look easy in movies?" she said playfully as he moved to the edge of the bed. "*Hurry!*"

She went up on her knees, kissing the back of his neck, her arms circling his waist as he tugged off his pants. She took his thick length in her hand, stroking him as she kissed his neck and shoulder. She'd never been this aggressive with a man before, but with Mason she didn't want to hold back. He swelled in her hand, and a low growl escaped his lungs. He tackled her to the bed, both of them laughing.

"Greedy girl," he said. Then he kissed her.

"I never was before *you*. You must have had lots of practice at all that stuff to be so good at it."

His brows knitted, wiping the smile off his handsome face. "No, Princess. I'm not like that. I've only been with a handful of women, and it's been an embarrassingly long time since I've been with anyone."

"I didn't mean . . ." He was being so honest, she didn't want to lie. "I *did* mean that, but I wasn't judging you. It's been a long time for me, too, and I haven't been with a *handful* of men, unless you have a very tiny hand."

He kissed her again, slow and sweet. "Tell me you're on the pill, Princess. I'm clean, and I want to feel all of you."

"I am," she whispered. "And I want to feel you, too."

Their mouths connected, and their bodies came together slowly, his girth stretching, pushing, *claiming* until he was buried to the hilt.

Mason buried his face in her neck and said, "*God*, you feel so good."

How could five little words make her feel so special? She couldn't speak, could only *feel* as they found their rhythm. They kissed, whispered, *pleaded*, hips grinding, hands searching, nails piercing, as he stroked over the magical spot that sent her soaring so high she felt like she was flying. Mason was right there with her, protecting her even as she lost her breath, breathing air into her lungs. He cradled her face between his hands, kissing her deeply as he loved her. And *oh*, how he *loved* her. He was tender and dominating in equal measure, lighting her up like she'd been living in the dark. But she felt his restraint in his corded muscles, and when he gazed into her eyes, she saw it in the punishing intensity of them.

"Let go with me, Mason," she pleaded, needing to feel all of his emotional power.

He touched his forehead to hers. "I don't want to hurt you. I'm a big guy, and you're so small. If I let go and lose my mind, hold you too tight . . ."

"You won't. I trust you. Do you trust *me*?"

"Yes, of course," he said.

"Then take away all of my fear, anger, and hurt by showing me with everything you have. Believe in *my* trust in you. Two-way street, remember? Lose yourself in us, Mason. Let me feel what you feel."

"*God, Princess.* What stars had to align for me to deserve you?"

He slanted his mouth over hers and proceeded to love her like she'd never been loved before. Slow and deep, then fast and hard, like storms colliding in the night. Their kisses were urgent and messy, teeth clanking, tongues dancing. They moaned and groaned, laughed and gasped, tickled and clawed, in a frenzy of discovery, every single touch bringing them closer together. When she lost control, he captured her cries in toe-curling kisses, and then he followed her over the edge, reveling in their ecstasy.

After the last aftershock jerked through their bodies, Mason gathered her in his arms, both of them panting between kisses. Their bodies were covered in a sheen of sweat. Mason's skin had red scratch marks from her nails, and she was sure she'd wake up tender in places she'd never imagined being sore. But as he moved one of his legs over her hip, grinning against her lips, and said, "I've got you, Remington Aldridge, and I might never let you go," she had a feeling that the place deep in her chest that had always been lonely and scarred would never feel that way again.

CHAPTER FOURTEEN

MASON AWOKE TO Remi's beautiful ass nestled against his hips, her back cocooned by his chest and arms, and the delicate fingers that had stroked and taunted him before they'd made love for the third time interlaced with his.

Oh-dark-thirty had never looked so good.

He listened to the even cadence of her breathing, wondering how he could feel so much so fast. Sex had always been a release, a way to satisfy a physical urge. But with Remi everything had been different from the moment he'd seen her searching for an escape on the dance floor. And what they'd done last night? That wasn't *fucking*. He'd wanted to pleasure her until she didn't remember a single man who had come before him. He didn't want her to just forget the nightmare bearing down on her, but to *be* her escape, her safe haven. Last night had changed more than their relationship. He wanted to get her out from under the shadow of her life belonging to others and help her spread her wings in all the ways she not only deserved, but wanted.

Guilt threaded into his thoughts. He was hired to protect her, and he'd broken his cardinal rule. An even more uncomfortable thought occurred to him. What if she woke up and regretted what they'd done? He'd be forced to walk away and let other men take care of the only woman he'd ever cared about.

His gut told him there was no way she would regret last night, but what the hell did he know about women and relationships? His own mother had loved drugs more than she'd loved him. And that wasn't the worst of it. He was a protector. He'd seen things no man should ever see, and he couldn't turn that part of himself off. Not even for Remi.

She made a sweet, sleepy sound. A smile lifted her lips as she blinked awake. He told himself to hold back, to try to read her feelings beyond that welcoming smile, but he was no match for the emotions trampling through him.

He kissed her cheek and said, "Good morning, beautiful."

"What time is it?" she asked groggily.

"Too early for you to be awake."

She made a warm, pleasure-filled sound, turning in his arms to face him, and said, "But in a few hours I won't be able to do this." She pressed her lips to his.

"Oh *yeah*, I like doing that." Relief swept through him as he kissed her, but there was a nagging thought in the back of his mind. Remi could have any man on the planet. She needed to know what type of man she was getting involved with, and he forced himself to break the kiss. "Princess, I need you to be sure that you want this, that it's not just your emotions running high because you're scared, or—"

She touched her lips to his again in another sweet kiss. "I told you, I'm *in*, Mason. I like you. After everything we did last night, why are you questioning us?"

"I'm not questioning us. You put your heart in my hands, and I just want you to be happy. I want this, and I want *you*, but you need to know something about me."

"That you tried to fight what's between us? Because so have I, and luckily we both sucked at it."

He chuckled. God, he loved her sense of humor.

"I have a confession to make," she said softly. "Before we were introduced, I saw you outside the fundraiser, and I swear my heart skipped a beat. I'd never felt anything like that before. I wanted to be on your arm that night."

"I love knowing that. And I'm sure you could probably tell when I carried you in that night that I wanted to carry you to my bed."

Her cheeks flushed. "I thought maybe, but . . ." She buried her face in his chest.

He lifted her chin, pressing his lips to hers. He could kiss her from morning until night and it would never be enough. "All of that underscores why I have to tell you this. I know how to protect and to give my all to my team, but I'm not sure I'll be a very good *boyfriend*. I can't just turn off my protective nature, and you hate being suffocated."

"There's a difference between being shuffled around like an object and being cared for, looked after like a person with feelings who has a life to live. You've already proven that you know the difference. Whether you realize it or not, you care too much to suffocate me."

"You have a lot of faith in me, Remi. *This*, waking up in a bed with you, it's new for me, and I don't want to mess it up. I know how to strategize a mission with weaponry and men. But this is a whole new world for me, having feelings for you, wanting to protect *and* touch you. Holding back when we're in public is not going to be easy."

She caressed his cheek and whispered, "For me, either. I wouldn't feel like this if you were overbearing, so stop worrying. You're an amazing man, and I've seen that behind that hard exterior is a heart of gold. But also, in case you haven't noticed, I have a big mouth. I'm not afraid to tell you if you cross a line and start to suffocate me."

"Good, because the last thing I want to do is walk away from us, but I would if you needed me to."

"There are no take-backs, remember?" she said sweetly.

"I remember, and speaking of no take-backs, I need to touch base with Aiden. I can't lie to him."

She groaned. "I believe in honesty, but he's not going to like this. Can't we just tell him when he comes home? He's working on a *huge* deal. He doesn't need to be distracted by something he has no control over, and trust me, he'll want control."

"He might get wind of a picture."

"He never looks at social media. He's been dealing with it my whole career. He's above all the hype."

"Remi, it's never a good tactic to do damage control *after* the damage has been done."

She sighed, looking adorably determined. "*Fine.* I'll tell him the truth. I was excited about nailing the scene and I kissed you. He knows I'm impulsive, so he'll buy that if he sees a picture of us kissing on set. But this is my life, Mason, my body. That's all he needs to know until he's here and we can tell him about us in person. Okay?"

He couldn't deny that truth. She was an adult, and Aiden had no say over her sexual decisions, but he imagined as a man who had taken on the role of father to Remi, Aiden would be pissed that she'd waited to tell him. But it was her decision to make, as long as Mason's ability to protect her wasn't compromised. With all his worries about crossing lines, he'd thought his ability to protect her might be clouded by his emotions. But now he knew he'd been wrong. If anything, he was *even more* determined to keep her safe.

He shifted over her and laced their hands together, loving the hitching of her breath and the darkening of her eyes. "I respect your decision, but my gut tells me Aiden's still going to be pissed. You are playing another dangerous game, Remi."

"A *greedy* game," she said seductively, her hips rising to meet his arousal. "And from now on, Aiden stays *out* of our bedroom."

"*Our* bedroom . . . ?" Damn, he liked the sound of that. "As I recall, *your* bedroom is across the hall, Princess."

"My castle, my rules." Challenge glimmered in her gorgeous eyes. "But if you're having second thoughts . . ."

He shifted, nestling his cock against her wetness. She angled her hips, her fingers clinging to his, as he entered her.

"I'm having thoughts about *seconds*." He kissed the corner of her mouth. "And *thirds*." He slicked his tongue along her neck, earning a sharp inhalation. He ran his hands down her sides. "I want everything you're willing to give, Princess. I might not be Prince Charming, but I'll always have your back"—he clutched her ass, squeezing tight—"your front"—he thrust hard and deep—"and everything in between."

Later that morning, Remi sat in her trailer talking on the phone with Willow, waiting to be called to the set. They were in the center of town, where they were shooting today's scenes. She'd filmed there two weeks ago, and at that time, although they'd closed off the streets, pedestrians had been allowed to watch the filming. Today Remi felt like she'd arrived in an alternate universe. Enormous screens had been erected to block fans from watching. Mason had met with all the key players and security, and clearly word had spread about the offending texts because everyone Remi passed, cast and crew, asked if she was okay.

"I hate being in this position," she said to Willow. "I feel like a trapped rat, but I don't know if the snake who wants to eat me is *inside* or *outside* the box. I've known most of these people for years, and now I can't look at any of them without wondering if they want to lock me in their basement."

She knew she had to keep her relationship with Mason under wraps, but she trusted Willow implicitly to keep it between them, and she was dying to tell her about last night. But she was too discombobulated by all the changes to give their relationship the happy announcement it deserved, even if that announcement could only go to her best friend. She knew Willow would be happy for her, because earlier in the week when she'd told Willow that Mason didn't have a girlfriend after all, Willow had made comments about Remi following her heart.

"I can't even imagine how that feels. Does Mason have any idea who sent the texts?"

"No. He said they used an online program, and he—or she—knows their way around technology because they've used VPNs and proxy servers. I don't understand all the technical stuff, but apparently technology is *so* good it's easy for tech-savvy people to evade detection. You've got to love the internet," she said sarcastically. "Mason's got his best guys following every lead, tracking down fans the crew has seen hanging around, delivery people who have come by the set, basically anyone who had a chance to take the picture. He even has guys reviewing the pictures of the set that have surfaced that I'm *not in* to check out any of the people they caught in the background."

"At least he's being thorough, Remi. I know you hate it, but it sounds like he's doing the right things to protect you."

"I know, and I'm glad," she said with a sigh. "I thought having a bodyguard was weird, but Mason has brought in an *army*, including Porter and Merrick, my last two bodyguards. Did you know they work for him?"

"No. Honestly I don't know much about Mason other than what you and Ben have told me, and that he and Bodhi go way back."

"Well, they work for him, and Aiden basically told them not to talk to me on any personal level, which I'm going to give him grief about." Remi pushed to her feet and paced. "Anyway, Mason is meeting with a group of local police right now, and Porter is *armed* and standing guard outside my trailer door."

"That's a little terrifying. Do you still want me to confirm the date for that surprise we talked about? And are you still going to Flossie's birthday party this weekend?"

She'd been working on a way for Mason to see Brooklyn. "Everything is still up in the air, but yes, please confirm the date. As far as Flossie's birthday goes, Mason and I talked to Ben and Aurelia about it this morning," Remi said, remembering their conversation about boundaries and the need for extra protection when they were out in public. "I don't want to put anyone else in danger, but the party is going to be at Ben's house in Sweetwater, and he has a security system. Mason's guys will check it out before we go, and his guys will stand guard during the party. They all seem to think it'll be okay. I swear, Willow, I've gone from being afraid to being pissed. Can you believe I need people to *stand guard*? It's so unfair that *one* crazy person can upend not just my life, but everyone else's, too."

"One psycho nobody can find," Willow reminded her. "You don't know how crazy this person is. Maybe he's just making empty threats, but based on that picture, it kind of seems like *Mason* needs a bodyguard."

"I know. I hate that kissing *me* put *him* in danger. I know I should wish I never kissed him because of that, but . . . I can't, and I know he can take care of himself. I haven't seen him physically take anyone down, but he warned that guy off at the fundraiser, and I have no doubt that if that jerk had made a move toward me, Mason would have torn him apart. Someone would have to be seriously stupid to mess with him."

"Yeah, but there's more to him, isn't there? From what you told me about the night at the water tower and everything he's done to help you, I think he sees you clearer than any of us ever has."

"He does," Remi said with a sigh.

"I'd apologize for that, because it makes me sound like a crappy friend not to see you as clearly as he does, but I think men we're close to see us differently than anyone else in our lives. But I have to ask . . . I've never seen you kiss a man off-screen—*ever*—much less a guy who's supposed to be protecting you. What's going on there?"

"Something extraordinary, but you can't tell anyone. Mason's worried about making the stalker even more irate." It felt incredible to say that out loud.

"I knew it!" Willow said excitedly. "I want all the details, and don't worry—your secrets are all safe with me. I haven't even told the girls that Mason doesn't have a girlfriend. I figured they'd get that out of you themselves."

"Thank you for that. He's amazing, Willow, and not just in bed, which he totally is. He treats me like I'm a regular person, but a really special-to-him person. I know how weird that sounds, but he listens and cares differently than anyone else seems to. I mean, I know you guys all care, but it's not the same." Thinking about the night she'd told him about the car accident, she said, "I've told him things I haven't even told you, and he's done the same with me. I think we were meant to meet. I know you believe in soul mates, but I think Mason is even more than that."

"I don't know what 'more than a soul mate' means, but that's how you know this is real, Remi. I'm so happy for you."

"Yeah, me too. I'm not sure what I meant by it, either, but that's how deep things feel with him. Hey, do the girls still get together at your bakery before work?"

Willow arrived at work around dawn every morning to bake for the morning rush, and her sisters and Aurelia stopped by when they could.

"Aurelia and Talia don't come as often since they live in Harmony Pointe now, but Piper and Bridgette are there almost every morning. Come by the next time you have a day off."

"I have Monday off. Me and my entourage of burly men will try to make it."

"I'll be sure I have lots of goodies on hand."

Another call rang through, and Aiden's name flashed on the screen. "Aiden's calling. Can we catch up later?"

"Of course. Love you. Be safe."

Remi switched over to Aiden's call, wondering if he'd gotten wind of everything that was going on. "Hi, Aiden."

"Hey. Are you all right? I called to check in with Mason a few minutes ago and he was in a meeting with the *police*. He said there was another threat?"

There was a knock at her door. "Hold on one sec."

Aiden grumbled on the other end of the phone as she answered the door. Carl stood beside Porter, looking about as uncomfortable as Remi felt having an armed guard looming over her friends. The first thing she'd done that morning was apologize to Porter and Merrick for the way she'd treated them. They were very kind about it, and though they could be gruff, focused, and definitely intimidating, they seemed friendly.

"We need you on set, and I need to go over a few things with you on the way," Carl said.

She held up one finger as she descended the steps from her trailer. Porter flanked her on the way to the set as she updated Aiden. "I got a text with a picture yesterday. Don't freak out or anything, but Mason helped me study for a scene and when I nailed it, I was so happy I ran off the set and kissed him. The stalker saw it, took a picture, and sent it with a red slash through Mason's face."

"Shit. I'll leave tonight. I can be there by morning."

"No! Mason has an army of guys following us everywhere. Remember Porter? He's *armed* and walking beside me right now." She held the phone up to Porter and said, "Please say hello to Aiden."

Porter cracked a smile, softening his chiseled features as he said, "Hello, Mr. Aldridge. I've got Remi covered."

She put the phone to her ear and said, "Did you know Porter *smiles?* That's right, Aiden. Bodyguards can actually be friendly to the people they're keeping safe without losing focus." She tried to stop the angry knots forming inside her at the way Aiden had made her seem like she needed to be kept in a glass box, but it was impossible. Instead, she tried to calm her tone. "Please stay there and finish your work. I know how important this deal is for you, and there's nothing you can do here to keep me safe that these trained professionals can't do better."

Aiden cursed under his breath. "Damn it, Remi, you're more important than this deal. If anything happens to you—"

Carl stopped walking and tapped his watch.

"It won't! You hired the *best*. You said it yourself. Now let him do his job. I have to go. I love you, and don't worry. I'm well taken care of." She ended the call and said, "Sorry, Carl. What did you want to go over?"

"Are you okay? Do you want to delay filming?"

"No. That's the *last* thing I want. I cannot wait to be done. I swear I'm going to hole up in my cabin where things like stalkers and horrendous texts aren't part of my life."

Carl nodded. "You and me both. I can't wait to get back to Samantha and Timmy. Samantha has a big audition coming up for the lead in an indie film, and she's really nervous."

"Auditions are definitely nerve-racking. Tell her I'm pulling for her." Remi had known Carl and his wife, Samantha, who was also an actress, long before their five-year-old son, Timmy, was born.

As Carl filled her in on the changes to next week's schedule, Mason came around the corner, unraveling the knots her conversation with Aiden had caused. Their eyes met for only a second, but it was long enough for her insides to sizzle. She hoped no one else noticed.

"Everything okay here?" Mason asked, eyeing Carl and Porter.

Porter nodded.

"Carl was just going over the changes to the schedule," she explained. "We're still on schedule to wrap a week from Wednesday, and I have Monday off, but some of the filming times have been adjusted."

"Got it," Mason said.

"The updates have been posted to the online schedule. Your team can download them." Carl looked at Remi and said, "I've got to get Raz to the set. Are you good to go?"

"Yes. Thanks, Carl. Tell Sam I hope we can catch up soon."

"Will do. She'll be excited to see you again."

After Carl walked away, Mason said, "Porter, why don't you get the new schedules out to the team."

"Sure thing, boss."

Mason waited until they were alone before stepping closer. "How are you holding up?"

"I'm fine. I talked to Aiden and told him about the picture. It's a good thing we're waiting until he's back in town to tell him about us. I didn't realize how angry I was at him about the things he said to your guys. I got a little riled up. Hopefully I'll be less angry by the time he returns."

"I'm glad you told him about the picture, but don't be too angry with him. He was just doing his best to keep you safe. Do you want to talk about it? To get it off your chest?"

"God, no. I have a feeling there are more riled-up feelings waiting to come out, and we don't need that kind of stress on top of everything else."

"Okay. Well, we might have some good news. We have a lead on the fan who grabbed you. One of my guys found a picture and I think it's him. It's blurry, and unfortunately facial recognition software failed, but we're circulating it, trying to track down his whereabouts."

"That's great, *if* he's the one who has been doing this."

"I know. We're checking pictures from your last three productions to see if he was hanging around." His eyes warmed, though he remained a respectable distance from her.

She wished he could hold her, kiss her. When she was in his arms she felt like nothing could hurt her.

"Are you sure you're all right, Princess? I know how much you hate having so many eyes on you." He was always thinking of her safety and her well-being.

"I'm okay. A little wound up over everything. I think I just need some downtime. I'm looking forward to Flossie's birthday and having Monday off. I know what's between us is new, but assuming we're still together when filming wraps, I would love to go on a quiet getaway together. I'd really like to go to my cabin. It's only about an hour from here, and I could use some *Mason* time."

He made a purely *male*, greedily sexy sound and spoke in a low voice as he said, "I want nothing more than to take you in my arms right now. You know that, don't you?"

"Mm-hm. I can feel it," she said softly.

He squared his shoulders, putting a little more space between them as he said, "But I don't think we'll have the luxury of a *quiet* getaway until the stalker is behind bars."

She wrinkled her nose. "I hate that."

A devilish grin lifted his lips and he said, "But that doesn't mean we can't go away and enjoy ourselves. My guys know how to stand watch and keep their distance."

"I'll take it!"

CHAPTER FIFTEEN

MASON COULD COUNT the number of birthday parties he'd been thrown as a kid on one hand. He'd attended even fewer parties as an adult, much less *for* an adult, which was why he was blown away by the birthday celebration for Aurelia's grandmother, Flossie McBride, Sunday evening. In addition to Ben's sisters and their significant others, Ben's parents and Bodhi's mother were there, along with Derek's father, Jonah, who had Alzheimer's.

Mason stood in Ben and Aurelia's massive kitchen talking with Bodhi and the guys after dinner, while Ben washed the dishes and Zane heckled him. Bodhi nudged Mason's arm, motioning toward the dining room, where his six-year-old son, Louie, an adorable and inquisitive brown-haired boy, sat on Jonah's lap, showing Jonah his baseball card collection. At the other end of the table, Flossie sat with Ben's mother, Roxie, a vivacious curly-haired blonde, and Bodhi's mother, Alisha, a reserved silver-haired woman, poring over a photo album of Bea that Ben and Aurelia had given Flossie for her birthday. During dinner, Talia and her fiancé, Derek, had announced that they'd decided to have a small wedding around the holidays, so Jonah could attend without the risk of being overwhelmed. Now Remi and the girls were chatting in the living room, looking at wedding dresses on Talia's phone.

It was a scene out of a big-family movie, and Remi looked like she was in heaven. Everyone had greeted her with tight hugs and concerned questions about the stalker situation. Mason was glad she had so many people who cared about her, but he hadn't expected the warm embraces *he'd* received. Apparently the Daltons' close-knit family extended to those around them, and his association with Remi meant he was now part of their inner circle.

"You don't have to wash them first," Zane said to Ben, pulling Mason from his thoughts. "That's why it's called a dish*washer*."

"I'm embarrassed to say we practically raised you, Zane," Dan Dalton, Ben's father, teased. In his slacks and dress shirt, he looked more like the retired college professor he was than Piper's partner in their custom-home-building business. "Didn't we ever teach you how to do dishes?"

"He was too busy scoping out Willow to pay attention," Ben said, earning a smirk from Zane.

"That's something I don't want to think about." Dan headed into the dining room, joining Roxie at the table.

"What was that about?" Mason asked Bodhi. "Did Zane live with them?"

"Practically. Zane's parents were less than present when he was a kid," Bodhi explained. "He spent a lot of time with the Daltons when he was growing up, and he and Willow had a secret tryst."

"Seems like it worked out well for them." Mason had noticed that Zane and Willow couldn't keep their hands off each other. They were always kissing, holding hands, or whispering, like the rest of the couples there tonight.

Except for me and Remi.

Longing washed over him, and he tried to school his expression. Mason had never been a fan of public displays of affection, but he'd give anything to stop pretending there was nothing between them and hold her, *kiss* her, in front of the people who loved her like family. He wanted them to know that she had someone who adored her just as much as their significant others adored them. Hell, he'd give anything to be able to wink, or blow her a kiss without worry, like they had last night, when they'd cuddled on the couch in the rec room and watched a movie. They'd been making love for days. It was heaven when they were home alone and he was able to openly hold and kiss her. She needed that type of normalcy in her life, and with Remi, he craved it. But since Ben and Aiden were business partners and Remi didn't want Aiden to get wind of their relationship while he was away, Mason was stuck pretending he was nothing more than her bodyguard.

Derek sauntered into the kitchen. Mason had gotten to know Derek throughout the evening, and although Derek was a handsome guy with longish brown hair and an athletic build, Mason had a hard time reconciling his serious disposition with a guy who danced at Decadence. Mason had nothing but respect for the man who was not only caring for his ailing father but also opening an adult-day-care center to help others in the same type of situation.

Derek placed a cup next to the sink and said, "Found that in the living room. Want me to finish up the dishes?"

"Nah, I've got them." Ben motioned toward Zane and said, "But I'll pay you to drag his ass out of here before I knock him upside the head."

Derek took Zane by the arm. "Let's go. No head knocking on Flossie's birthday."

"I prefer *headboard* knocking anyway, right, Wills?" Zane said loudly as Derek dragged him out of the kitchen. He headed directly to his wife.

"Don't we all?" Piper chimed in from her perch on the couch beside Remi.

Before dinner, Remi and the girls had been huddled together talking, and they'd glanced over so many times he'd wondered if he was the topic of conversation. Now, as they gushed over wedding dresses, Remi held Ben and Aurelia's adorable baby, Bea. Every few minutes Remi pressed a kiss to the baby's cheek, holding her lips there and closing her eyes like she was soaking in the feel of her baby-soft skin. He wondered if Remi had dreams of a white wedding and babies. She sure as hell deserved everything she'd ever dreamed of.

As the girls huddled closer to get a better look at Talia's phone, Remi pushed to her feet. She looked beautiful in a white tank top and peach capris, with a pair of sexy leather sandals. She smiled at Mason as she snuggled with Bea. Her smile reached all the way up to her eyes, but it didn't wash away the longing in them. She rolled her lower lip between her teeth, the nervous habit he'd learned she had when she was contemplating dirty thoughts. That made his ache to be closer to her even stronger.

Roxie breezed into the kitchen, her long colorful skirt flowing around her ankles. "Ben, are you just about done? Piper's getting antsy. I think we should get to the cake."

Ben wiped his hands on a dish towel. "Just finished."

"Great. Thanks, honey." Roxie lovingly patted his shoulder.

An unexpected yearning moved through Mason. He didn't spend much time around families, and witnessing the love between the Daltons brought feelings he'd thought he'd buried too deep to ever resurface. But in the past two weeks, Remi had unearthed so many other emotions, he shouldn't be surprised that more were creeping out from the dungeon.

"So, Mason." Ben leaned against the counter and crossed his arms. "This shit storm started with a kiss?"

Mason had liked Ben from the moment they'd met, when Ben had come to him searching for Bea's mother. He was a brilliant businessman, and it was apparent that his love for his daughter was impenetrable. It was also apparent that Ben could read between the lines, which was why Mason wondered if he'd noticed a look passing between him and Remi. He thought he'd been careful not to give anything away, and now he made a mental note to be even *more* self-aware.

"No, actually," Mason said. "The stalking started when Remi first received letters months ago in LA. This seems to be a continuation of the same."

"Ben, I don't think you should ever connect a kiss to a *shit storm*." Roxie winked at Mason and said, "Remi should be able to kiss whomever she pleases without worrying about what anyone else thinks."

Mason had to work to keep his agreement under wraps.

Bodhi said, "I think Aiden might have a different opinion."

"Poor Aiden," Roxie said thoughtfully. "This stalker business is killing him. He tries so hard to do the right thing by Remi, and he has done an excellent job as a surrogate parent *and* a big brother. But all the running away Remi has done recently is a cry to be heard."

Ben pushed away from the counter and said, "I understood why Remi ditched her bodyguards earlier in the summer, although I wasn't happy that she didn't tell Aiden where she was. But now that I have Bea, I also understand where Aiden is coming from. If anyone threatened Bea, I'd keep her under lock and key until I tracked the bastard down and either killed him or put him behind bars for good."

"Oh, honey, I'm not talking about the stalker." Roxie reached into the cabinet for plates and said, "Obviously Aiden has to do the right thing when it comes to protecting her. But those tight reins were being held long before the stalker came out of the woodwork. If you pen in a tigress too long, eventually she'll have no choice but to break free."

She raised her brows in Mason's direction as she set the plates on the counter and said, "Remi is a smart, capable woman, and Aiden has hired the perfect person to watch over her. Now Aiden needs to open that cage and trust the two of them."

"Remind me not to let you hang out with Bea when she discovers boys. I plan on locking her cage until she's *thirty*." Ben chuckled and headed into the living room.

Roxie sighed. "Why do men act like they were never the boys girls were interested in?"

Mason chuckled.

"Bodhi, your little man is having a ball with Jonah." Roxie pushed a wayward curl from her cheek.

"They have a special relationship." Pride shone in Bodhi's eyes as he glanced at his son.

"I'll say. The universe brought my grandson a wonderful gift the day Talia met Derek."

Bodhi nodded. "I think that gift goes both ways, Roxie."

"I still can't get over how much your life has changed, Bodhi," Mason said. "You were the lone wolf for so long. Now you have a little boy, a beautiful wife, and a baby on the way."

"I'm a lucky guy," Bodhi said. "I never expected to fall in love, and with Bridgette, there was no turning away."

Mason wanted to tell him he knew the feeling, but instead he said, "Very lucky, indeed."

"Mason? Are *you* on the market?" Roxie waggled her brows. "I can help you find your one and only true love. I've helped *lots* of people find their forever loves, including Bodhi and Bridgette."

Mason arched a brow.

"Roxie makes soaps, fragrances, body wash, and other things, and she sells them around town. But she's famous for her love potions," Bodhi explained. "I wasn't a believer until it happened to me."

Roxie sidled up to Mason and lowered her voice as she said, "Don't let this get out, but I've been sneaking my potions into Piper's lotion bottles for months. I don't usually take a sneaky route, but she's a stubborn one, unlike our Remi. The last time Remi visited we had a long talk about love, and I gave her my special apricot body wash and bubble bath. Did you know that apricots do a lot more than just *protect* your heart?"

Mason froze. He and Remi had been showering together for days. He loved lathering her up almost as much as he loved the effects his slippery hands had on her. They'd been drenched in apricot at least once or twice every day since they'd first come together.

Roxie put a hand on Mason's shoulder and said, "A handsome guy like you who helps other people for a living shouldn't still be single. You must have pretty thick walls around your heart to have fended off women for this long." She leaned closer and whispered, "Just say the word, and I'll get you fixed up." She *sniffed*, and her eyebrows shot up with a curious—and *pleased*—look in her eyes. She started humming, picked up the plates, and headed into the dining room.

"You're in for it now," Bodhi said with a shake of his head. "Once Roxie gets you in her sights, you haven't got a chance in hell at dodging her bullet."

Mason glanced at Remi and said, "Who says I want to dodge anything?"

"Yeah? You got a girlfriend I haven't heard about?" Bodhi asked.

Before he could respond, Piper burst into the kitchen and said, "Let's get this show on the road. I'm meeting a friend at Dutch's and I don't want to be late." She picked up the birthday cake from the counter.

As they followed her out of the kitchen, Bodhi said, "That's code for Piper having a date. She always meets her dates at Dutch's Pub, which drives the owner, Harley Dutch, crazy."

Piper glanced over her shoulder and said, "Safety first, right, Mr. Bodyguard? Never meet a first date someplace private and all that?" She set the cake on the table as everyone filed into the dining room.

"More like drive Harley batty so he never knows if he's coming or going," Willow said as she sat down at the table.

"He'd like to be *coming*," Piper said under her breath, taking a seat beside Willow.

"Piper Dalton," Roxie snapped. "Watch yourself!"

Piper chuckled.

"I'm sure the girls will hear *all* the details about your hot date tomorrow morning at their morning gossip session at the bakery," Talia said as she and Derek sat down by Jonah. "Someone will have to fill me in."

"Me too. I can't make it tomorrow," Aurelia said.

"I wish I could go to the bakery tomorrow!" Louie exclaimed as he jumped down from Jonah's lap and scrambled into a chair beside Bodhi.

"Another morning, buddy." Bodhi kissed Louie's head. "Tomorrow you, me, and Dahlia have a date with Fletch and Molly, remember?"

Dahlia was their Great Dane, and Mason knew Fletch was Ryan "Fletch" Fletcher, who taught at Beckwith University with Talia. His name had come up as someone Remi had spent time with while she was visiting her friends.

"Oh yeah, I forgot! Dahlia loves Molly! Molly's Fletch's dog. Do you have a dog, Mason? Maybe you can come with us!" Louie asked excitedly.

"No, I'm sorry to say I don't, and I need to be with Remi tomorrow morning. But thank you for thinking of me."

"Okay. Maybe you can get a dog one day. We're meeting them at Chiffon Park *really* early," Louie explained. "Fletch said that's the best time to let the dogs run wild."

"I'd like to meet Fletch at Chiffon Park," Piper said sassily.

"Paws off my friend," Talia said with a scolding look.

Piper rolled her eyes.

"Now, Talia, you know there's nothing wrong with your sister pursuing a man," Flossie said with a wink. "Piper shouldn't need to wait for an invitation."

Flossie was a whirlwind of energy, unlike any other senior citizen Mason had ever met. She stood just shy of five feet tall and had long silver hair and a flair for fashion, as evidenced by her ankle-length black skirt, leopard-print blouse, and bright red lipstick. She wore large pearl earrings and a matching pearl ring. She was warm and outgoing. Mason had overheard her talking throughout the evening, and she had something insightful and wise to say to everyone. When they'd first been introduced, Flossie had taken one look at him, poked him in the chest, and said, "Life is too short for all that tension you're carrying around. Find the person who helps you breathe, then hold on to her and *never* let her go."

He glanced at Remi, still cuddling Bea. She helped him breathe all right . . .

"I agree," Alisha, Bodhi's mother, said. "If we women waited for men to make all the right moves, the whole human race could die out."

Ben, Zane, and Derek spoke over one another, arguing that point, until Roxie clapped her hands and said, "Okay, boys. We get it. You're macho."

The girls giggled. Mason chuckled.

"How did we get on this conversation anyway?" Roxie asked. "Oh yes, the bakery. Remi, have you seen the renovations Willow's made yet?"

"That would be *me* who made them," Piper reminded her. "The day Willow wears a tool belt is the day I'll wear an apron."

Willow pushed to her feet and said, "Dad? Where's your tool belt?"

That earned another round of laughs.

"I haven't seen the renovations yet," Remi said. "But I hear they look fantastic." She tickled Bea's chin, her gaze drifting to Mason. "I forgot to mention that I'd like to go to the bakery with the girls tomorrow. We need to be there by six in the morning, though. Is that okay?"

"You're the boss—" Mason noticed Roxie watching them and stifled *Princess* before it came out.

Ben glanced at him and said, "Poor guy. You'll have to sit through gossip central."

"I'll be *outside* the bakery," Mason clarified. He was glad Remi was making time for her friends, and he had no intention of suffocating her.

"Be sure to try the Loverboys," Zane said. "They're the most delicious éclair/cupcake combo you've ever had, and they're named after me, so you know they're awesome." He lifted Willow's hand and kissed the back of it. "Although anything made by these talented hands is delicious."

Zane and Willow kissed, and Ben said, "Get a room."

As the others settled in around the table, Remi handed Bea to Aurelia.

Mason pulled out a chair for Remi and whispered, "You looked like a natural with that baby in your arms." He didn't know where the comment had come from, considering he'd never given a thought to having a family of his own.

When Remi met his gaze, he swore everyone could feel the intensity of their connection.

"I'm pretty sure she could make anyone look like a natural," she said as they sat down.

The lack of contact was killing him. He brushed his arm against hers. The intimate smile curving her lips should have taken the edge off his need to be closer, but it only drove the need deeper.

"Aurelia? Ben?" Flossie motioned for them to join her at the head of the table.

Ben towered over Flossie. She put her arm around him and Aurelia, and then she kissed Bea's forehead. "As most of you know, this is my first birthday without my husband, and while not a day passes that I don't miss him, tonight there's not much room for loneliness. I'm blessed to be with all of you, and this year we have a lot to celebrate. In addition to all of the newfound love around the table, we have Bridgette and Bodhi's little one on the way."

"Uncle Ben and Auntie Aurelia are getting married!" Louie chimed in. "Mommy said 'It's about damn time!'"

Everyone laughed.

"Louie, watch your language," Bridgette said.

"Your mom's right, Louie, but you're right, too," Ben said. "It's about damn time."

"Yes, we're all very happy that our two lovebirds are *finally* standing on the same branch," Flossie agreed. "What a joy it is to share this special day with all of you and with the bright new faces around the table—Jonah, who reminds us how precious life is, and our newest little bubbelah." She tickled Bea's foot, earning sweet baby giggles. She looked at Remi and said, "Fate was certainly on our side, bringing my faraway girl to us tonight. As you all know—but Mason may not—when Remi escaped her bodyguards earlier this summer, she came straight *home*." She put her hand over her chest and said, "Home is where your heart feels safest, and it pleases me to no end, Remi, that you've embraced our family as we've all embraced you."

Remi blushed, and Mason had to once again squelch the urge to put his arm around her or show his affection in any other intimate way.

Flossie turned to Mason and said warmly, "And my faraway girl brought us a lovely gift: Mason, her brawny protector and probably the only man on the planet she doesn't want to run from."

All eyes turned to Mason, including Remi's, and holy hell, she was looking at him like he'd hung the moon. He curled his fingers into fists to keep from reaching for her and showing everyone just how glad he was that she was no longer running.

The curious looks around the table compelled him to say, "I think Remi understands the seriousness of her situation."

Flossie held his gaze as if she weren't buying a word of it as she said, "I for one am very glad that you're taking care of our girl. Every strong woman deserves to have a good man watching over her. Remember what I said, Mason. Everyone deserves time to *breathe*."

When she winked, Mason was sure she was onto his and Remi's secret relationship, but he didn't have more than a second to think about that before the celebration continued.

"Here, here." Alisha held up her wineglass and said, "To the wisest woman I know. Happy birthday, Flossie."

Everyone lifted their glasses, clinking them to those around them, and then Louie began singing "Happy Birthday."

Remi touched Mason's pinkie beneath the table, and though he knew he shouldn't take the risk, he covered her hand with his. He never knew one look could be so powerful, but the way Remi was looking at him bored so deep, he felt it coursing through his veins.

Surrounded by joyous voices and the warmth of family, Mason was once again swamped with emotions. When they sang the last words and Flossie blew out her candles, Mason made a wish right along with her, one for not only Remi's safety, but *their* future.

What was it about witnessing the love between others that stirred a strange mix of happiness and melancholy? Remi pondered that question on the drive home. Mason had been quieter than usual tonight, which said a lot since he wasn't a very talkative guy in general. He'd taken a few calls while they were out, and she wondered if he had received news about the stalker. She also worried that when she'd touched him under the table, she'd made him uncomfortable, but she'd spent all evening watching her friends love up their significant others, and she wanted that, too. She wanted the world to know how she felt about him, and it infuriated her that one crazy person had the power to stop her from doing that.

Mason's thumb brushed absently over her hand as he parked in front of the house. When he cut the engine, ending the video feed from the security cameras on the dashboard, he climbed from the SUV. Remi watched him scanning the yard as he helped her out. He was in full protective mode, muscles flexed, ready to spring into action at any second. It had to be hard to live like that, but she was sure glad he could, because she felt perfectly safe with him.

As Mason did his nightly check of the house, Remi's thoughts turned to Aiden. He'd ensured her fortress was equipped to keep people out, and he'd unknowingly brought in the one man who made her feel so much more than *safe*.

"All clear," Mason said as he came up from the lower level.

She reached for his hand. "Why don't we relax in the hot tub tonight?"

"I'd love to, Princess, but when we're outdoors I like to keep an eye on things. If we're in a hot tub, I won't be able to keep my eyes off *you*, much less my hands or *mouth*." He drew her into his arms and said, "It was hard enough pretending I didn't want to do this tonight."

He lowered his lips to hers, and she went up on her toes, wanting more. He crushed her to him, deepening the kiss. "But I promise you," he said between long, steamy kisses, "when the stalker is behind bars, we'll make up for all the hot-tub time we missed."

"I'm holding you to that." She was elated that she didn't seem to be the reason he'd been quiet earlier. "Forget the hot tub. I have a better idea. Now that we're locked up safe and secure, give me ten minutes, then meet me in my bathroom."

Remi rushed upstairs. She'd never taken a bath with a man before, and while their showers always ended up with them slipping and sliding in each other's arms, she was excited to surprise him with a little romance. She gathered candles and set them around the luxurious master bathroom as she filled the tub with bubbles. Her mind drifted to their joint showers. She'd always imagined shower sex would take serious thought to work out the logistics, but the minute they were naked, they were drawn to each other like metal to magnet and they never *thought* at all.

She began stripping off her clothes, remembering how Mason's slippery hands had felt that morning as he'd slid down to his knees in the shower, pleasuring her so thoroughly, she'd had to cling to the wall and door just to remain standing. She'd wanted to repay the favor, but he'd been too desperate for her, and he'd lifted her into his arms and lowered her onto his shaft.

A streak of heat shuddered through her as she stepped out of her capris. She was vaguely aware of the scent of warm apricots, but it was overpowered by the memory-induced smell, and taste, of *Mason*. She squeezed her thighs together to try to quell the needy ache the memories brought. Before she could slip into the tub, Mason appeared in the doorway, further rousing her passion with the lecherous look in his eyes. She turned off the faucet, getting more turned on by the second as he openly watched her, his gaze lingering on her breasts, then skating lower, to the juncture of her thighs. He took off his shirt, and chills danced along her skin as she reached for the button on his jeans.

"Help me get these off," she said, emboldened by her naughty thoughts.

"In a hurry?" He grabbed the wall as she yanked his jeans down and he kicked them *off*.

She wanted to say so many things, to tell him how badly she wanted him, how she hoped that he wasn't kidding about spending time together after the stalker was arrested. But she was too hungry for him to form a single word. She didn't even try to hide what she wanted as she went down on her knees, her heart beating wildly. She wanted this with him more than she wanted her next breath, and even though she wasn't quite sure of exactly what she should do or what he liked, she *wasn't* going to chicken out.

She looked up at him, and he must have seen uncertainty in her eyes, because he stroked her jaw and said, "You don't have to do this."

"I want to, I just . . . I want to make you feel good."

"Anything you do will feel good because it's you, Princess."

He was such a burly guy, when his tender side came out like that, her heart stumbled. She pressed her hands to his muscular thighs and dragged her tongue along his hard length. His cock jerked, and she stole a glance at Mason's face. He was watching her intently, his eyes an erotic mix of protective and animalistic. His whole body seemed to rise up and inflate as she wrapped her hand around his shaft, guiding it into her mouth. She sucked slowly at first, taking him deeper with each pass, stroking tightly with her hand.

"*Fuck*, Remi." He grabbed the sides of her head, threading his fingers into her hair and guiding her a little faster. "That's it. Squeeze tighter. Damn, that's it. You okay?"

He stopped guiding her head and she nodded. Wanting him to continue showing her, she put her hand over his and took him in deeper. He got the hint.

He closed his eyes, and a rumbling moan fell from his lips as she followed his lead, squeezing tighter, sucking harder, driven by the tensing of his muscles. She slowed to catch her breath, teasing the head, and he hissed out a breath. She took him deep again, and a sexy, guttural noise accompanied nearly every thrust of his hips. She loved the power that came from the control, and she sucked harder, moved faster. The appreciative sounds streaming from his lips emboldened her, but the tensing of his muscles and his short thrusts told her he was holding back. She clung to his thighs, giving full control over to him, but he continued with measured movements.

He was being careful, and she didn't want *careful*. She wanted wild and passionate. She wanted Mason to lose control. She dug her fingernails into his thighs.

He withdrew from her mouth with one fast jerk backward. "Did I hurt you?"

The panic in his voice touched her deeply. She pushed to her feet. She hadn't realized she was shaking until she stood on wobbling legs. "No, and I know you never will. *Let go*, Mason. I want to cross every line with you, including this one. Make me yours."

He crushed his mouth to hers in a possessive, rough kiss. God, she loved his kisses. He didn't just kiss her. He explored her mouth like he wanted to live inside it, consumed it like it was *his*.

She tore her mouth away, knowing exactly what she wanted, and said, "I want you to take my mouth like you do when you kiss me. Don't hold back."

She kissed her way down his body, and this time when she took him in her hand, she was confident. She let him lead, and he was careful at first, despite her plea. But she'd expected that. This was Mason after all. He didn't take chances with her. But soon his body took over, and he loved her mouth the way he ravaged her body. His thick shaft pushed fast and hard through her lips. She felt tension mounting in his legs. He tightened his grip on her hair, creating a scintillating sting of pain and pleasure. His breathing became choppy.

"*Remi*—" The harsh warning flew from his lungs.

She gripped his thighs harder, letting him know she wasn't backing off. When the first warm jet hit the back of her tongue, her throat constricted, and she thought she was going to gag, but she quickly regained control, opening to him as "Princess, Princess, *Princess* . . ." fell from his lips.

Her body was on fire. He was breathing hard when he pulled her to her feet and gathered her against his heaving chest. He kissed her forehead, her cheeks, and finally, his hot mouth covered hers, his tongue sweeping deeply and sensuously without hesitation. That was a total turn-on. She'd never realized she could become so aroused from pleasuring a man, and she knew it had everything to do with this particular man, who was brushing his lips over hers and gazing into her eyes.

"You obliterate everything else around us, Remi. That's as incredible as it is dangerous."

"Should I fire you as my bodyguard?"

He kissed her softly. "No, Princess. I'll never let anything happen to you. But I've never experienced anything like this. I just need to be aware, that's all. I'm not used to letting my guard down, but when we're alone like this, it's easy for me to get lost in you."

"But we're safe inside, so that's a good thing, right?" She loved when he couldn't hold back what he was thinking and spoke directly from his heart. She knew he'd keep her safe, but she really loved knowing how lost he got in them. She felt it, but hearing him say it made it even more real.

"A very good thing." He took her hand, leading her to the tub and helping her in. As he climbed in behind her, he said, "Now it's my turn to make all your troubles disappear."

His arms circled her body as he kissed her neck. She closed her eyes, relaxing against his chest as he caressed her breasts. Her nipples tingled from his touch, and she bent her neck to the side, giving him better access.

"You're so beautiful, Remi," he whispered between spine-tingling kisses. "So soft and feminine, you're all I can think about."

One hand teased her breast as the other moved down her belly and between her legs, expertly homing in on the spots that made her legs go numb. The air left her lungs in one long sigh, and she closed her eyes, her hips pulsing in a slow rhythm.

He slicked his tongue along the shell of her ear and whispered, "Kiss me, Princess."

She angled her face to the side, and his mouth came down hungrily over hers. His tongue and fingers moved in tandem. Tingling sensations skated up her limbs, and lust coiled tight and low in her belly like a snake readying to strike. Her entire being flooded with desire, and she felt like she was speeding toward a cliff, chasing her release. He stroked over that magical spot, and the world tilted on its axis. She cried out in long surrendering moans, her body bucking and clenching until she collapsed, boneless and sated, in his arms.

He lavished her with tender kisses as her erratic heartbeat calmed. She wanted to lie right there forever, nestled in his arms, surrounded by warm water, romantic candles, and the scent of sweet apricot.

When he began lovingly bathing her with a washcloth, she said, "We *are* dangerous together. A woman could die from this much pleasure."

As he bathed along her thigh, he said, "Death is nothing to joke about, but it would be an incredible way to go." He pressed a kiss to her temple. "I wish we could be this close all the time, not just in private. It was hell not being able to reach for you tonight at the party."

"Is that why you were so quiet?" She rolled onto her side so she could see his face. He pressed his lips to hers, but he didn't answer, so she said, "Did you get news about the stalker?" The muscles in his jaw tensed, giving her the answer. "I can take it, Mason."

"That's not why I was quiet, but I did get an update. We thought we'd tracked down the fan who tried to grab you the first day I was on set with you. Remember, I mentioned that we found a picture that looked like him? It wasn't the same guy. That kid's been out of state all summer. It was another dead end, but don't worry. We'll find him. I just found you. I'm not going to let anything happen to you."

"I know you won't, but aren't you worried he'll go after *you*?"

"Let him try. I welcome it. I'll tear the fucker to pieces." He grimaced. "I don't want to scare you. I'm not a killer, Remi. I just—"

"Stop. I understand. But if that's not why you were quiet tonight, did something else happen? Was it something I did?"

He ran the washcloth along her shoulder and down her arm and said, "No."

"You're not a fan of birthday parties?"

"I don't have much experience with them. I'm sure I must have celebrated my birthday a time or two, but I honestly can't remember ever having a birthday party when I was a kid."

"When is your birthday?"

"January fifteenth."

She made a mental note of the date. "So tonight's party made you sad?"

"No, it made me *think*. When you grow up the way I did, you forget things, like what normal families do for each other. There was so much love in that house tonight, it was a little overwhelming."

"In a bad way?"

"Not really, just eye-opening. Seeing Bodhi with Bridgette and Louie hit me hard. You get to know guys when you're in the field, because you never know if you'll be one of the lucky ones to make it out alive."

"I hate thinking about you in those situations. I mean, I know what you did was important for the country, and for yourself, but I wish I had known you then."

"Trust me, you don't. Leaving someone behind is hell for both parties."

"But it must have been hard having no one waiting for you back home." She put her arms around him and hugged him. "I'm glad you made it out alive."

"Thanks, Princess," he said in a strangled voice. He kissed the top of her head as she embraced him. "Bodhi was always a lone wolf, like me and lots of other guys we knew. His father's death had a huge impact on him. I never imagined him falling in love, much less having a family. But he's living a normal life, and he's happy. He's proof that people can overcome just about anything." He moved the washcloth absently over her skin. "But at the party, seeing all that love and support, all those families and generations coming together to celebrate, made me think of my childhood and how sucky it was to grow up feeling unimportant, *disposable*."

"It breaks my heart that you felt that way."

"I'm not looking for empathy, Princess. I'm thinking about other kids going through the foster-care system. I mean, how hard is it to bake a cake for a kid on their birthday?"

"If Aiden can do it, anyone can. For as long as I can remember, Aiden has made or ordered my birthday cakes. Even when my parents were alive, he would make or order the funkiest cakes. When I was seven, he ordered this gorgeous cake with a Barbie that had a billowing pink dress made from beautiful rippling pink-icing roses. I got up in the middle of the night and ate half of it. I remember sitting at the table with the box and a huge serving fork. It was *so* good, and he got so mad. I don't even remember why I did it. I think all that frosting was calling out to me in my sleep."

"So, even back then you were a little rebellious thing. I thought you said you never got in trouble?"

"I *was* a pretty good kid in every other way, especially after we lost our parents. It was too hard being in the house where my parents had lived, surrounded by all those memories, so we moved to California, where Aiden lived. He hired a great therapist for me and brought in tutors, so I wouldn't have to relive our parents' deaths by explaining it to kids at school. He also hired an acting coach for me. Everything he did was to help me *forget* what I'd gone through. But probably the best thing he ever did was make me feel like any other kid on my birthdays. We'd invite a few friends over and have cake and ice cream. Even as a teenager when I'd get in a mood and say I didn't want a party, he'd still bake a cake and invite friends over. It was the one day each year that I could just be normal and not the girl who was trying to forget what she'd lost. There's something wonderful about being celebrated, wearing silly hats, blowing out candles."

"Exactly," Mason said. "I was thinking about that tonight, wondering what kind of impact that had on me, if any, and if things might have been different if I'd had that one day a year to feel special. That sounds stupid and needy, but moving around as a foster kid was tough. There should be some things every kid can count on, like hearing 'happy birthday.'"

"That doesn't sound stupid at *all*. You have the biggest heart beneath all that brawn, and I think we should make it happen."

His brow furrowed. "Make what happen?"

"I don't know. *Something* birthdayish for foster kids. We could put together birthday boxes and fill them with gifts." She sat up on her knees, splashing water out of the tub as she turned to face him, excitement bubbling up inside her. "I know so many people who would donate gifts. My PR rep, Shea, is always setting me up for events. She'd probably love to help us put something like this together. My friend Parker Collins-Lacroux runs the Collins Children's Foundation. They work with foster kids and run a program that's sort of like a summer camp, giving foster kids a chance to come back together every summer with other foster kids they've bonded with in different foster families to keep those friendships alive. I bet she could help us, too, and maybe Bodhi and Shira will have some advice." Shira was the president of the Hearts for Heroes foundation. She was not only a brilliant accountant and businesswoman, but a badass martial artist and one of Bodhi's closest friends.

"You're really something, Princess, thinking of all that. I've heard of CCF, and I know Shira and Bodhi would probably jump right on board. I love this idea. But you're busy with filming—"

"Oh, please! There's always time to help other people. We can do it in the evenings, right here at home. We can arrange for everything to be delivered to the set so you don't have to worry about delivery guys showing up here at the house. I bet Willow and the girls will want to help. I'll talk to them when we go to the bakery. Speaking of tomorrow, can I tell my friends about us? Would you mind? Just the girls? Aurelia won't be there, so Ben won't find out."

"Whoa, slow down."

"I can't!" She straddled his lap and wound her arms around his neck. "I want to do this for foster kids with you. I can see how happy the idea makes you."

"It does, Princess. And so do you. You make me happy."

He pulled her closer, sealing the words that made her feel good all over with a kiss. When their lips parted, she continued holding him close, their lips touching as she whispered, "You make me happy, too."

She kissed him again, feeling him grow hard beneath her as he drew out the kiss. She lifted up without breaking their connection and sank down on his hard length. He held her so tight, cheek to cheek, unmoving, their bodies as close as two people could get.

"God, Remi," he said in a long breath. "Every time we're close, it's better than the last."

"I know," she whispered. "That's why you can't expect me to keep how I feel about you bottled up all the time." She gazed into his eyes and said, "I want to brag to my girlfriends about the incredible man in my life, and I'll have to tell Parker. I can't pretend we're not together. She's a good friend, and as an actress, she knows the score."

"Incredible might be stretching it. I told you I might suck at this relationship stuff."

"Oh, you do *suck . . . perfectly.*"

He made a guttural noise in his throat, his hips rocking beneath her. "The word *suck* coming from your sexy mouth is an evil combination."

"Suck, suck, *suck*," she teased, earning a warning glare. She gave him a chaste kiss, giggling as she said, "I've never been someone's *woman* before, so we'll figure it out together, and while we're at it, we'll give lots of foster kids very special birthdays. *After* I give you the best belated birthday gift you've ever had."

He touched her chin, lifting her face, and said, "I'm already looking at her."

CHAPTER SIXTEEN

"YOU LOOK LIKE you're going to burst," Mason said as he parked behind Sweetie Pie Bakery early the next morning.

"I'm just excited to tell my friends about us and about our ideas for the birthday boxes." They'd stayed up late talking about their ideas. Every time they closed their eyes, more ideas would pop into their heads. It felt beyond wonderful to be planning something together, and she'd noticed that Mason had a new brightness in his eyes since deciding to move forward with their idea.

"I'll call Bodhi later this morning to see if he has some advice on how to get started." He climbed out of the SUV and came around to open her door.

"I'm going to call Parker, too," she said as he helped her out, wishing she could reach for his hand. "I hate not being able to touch you. Why can't we just lure the stalker out of his creepy basement?"

"Because there's no way in hell I'm using you as bait."

"Think about it, Mason. We could quietly let it get out that I'm sunbathing down by the lake, but really you and your guys would be nearby waiting to catch him."

He scowled. "No."

"What's he going to do?"

Mason crossed his arms, glowering at her. "It takes seconds for a knife to slice through skin or a bullet to cross a field."

"Are you *trying* to scare me?"

"Yes, out of thinking about doing something stupid. Remi, this guy's going to slip up, and when that happens, we'll be there to get him. Okay?" He stepped closer and said, "And if you think I'd stay far enough away from you for anyone to think you're alone while you're baring your beautiful body in a skimpy bikini, you're sorely mistaken."

She giggled, loving the serious look in his eyes. "I just want to catch the guy so we can be a normal couple." She put her hand on his stomach, and he immediately scanned their surroundings, silently reminding her that she had to be careful even if it was the crack of dawn. Remi reluctantly dropped her hand.

"I want that, too," he said as Piper's truck pulled into the parking lot. "More than you can imagine."

Piper parked and came around the front of her truck in work boots, faded jeans with a hole in the knee, and a T-shirt that had LET'S GET BANGIN' written over a picture of a hammer. "You two going in, or waiting for an invitation?"

Mason lifted his chin in greeting. "Good morning to you, too, Piper."

"*Hottieguard,*" Piper said.

My hottieguard, thank you very much. "Calm your jets, girlie," Remi said. "How was your date last night?"

"Harley scared the guy off." Piper looked at Mason and said, "He loves doing that shit."

"So why meet them there?" Mason asked as he opened the door.

Piper scoffed. "Because it's a great way to weed the weak from the strong. The one guy who sticks around will be my keeper."

They followed her inside.

"Remi, you made it!" Willow was on the other side of the kitchen, pulling a tray of croissants from the oven. Her cutoffs and gray T-shirt were speckled with flour, and her hair was braided in a thick plait down her back.

"Where's Bridgette?" Remi asked as Piper snagged a pastry off a tray on another counter.

Willow set the croissants on the metal table in the center of the kitchen and closed the oven. "She'll be here."

"You don't mind if I look around, do you?" Mason asked, heading for the door between the kitchen and the bakery.

"Feel free," Willow said. "Everything is locked up tight until I open the bakery." She moved to another counter and began frosting yellow cupcakes with blue icing.

Piper hoisted herself up on a counter, and as soon as Mason was out the door, she said, "That is one fine specimen of a man. You two looked like you were ready to rip each other's clothes off out there. Is his girlfriend out of the picture?"

Bridgette came through the door with one hand on her burgeoning belly. "*Please* tell me you made Loverboys. I have been craving them all night, thanks to your husband, Willow."

Willow pointed to a plate of Loverboys on the far side of the counter, and Bridgette practically dove for them.

"Getting back to hottieguard and the girlfriend . . ." Piper made a hurry-up motion with her hand.

"There is no girlfriend. It was a misunderstanding," Remi explained as Mason came back into the kitchen.

"All clear, Prin—*Remi*." He clenched his jaw.

He was so cute, dead set on being the perfect bodyguard. "You guys, I have something to tell you." She walked over to Mason, went up on her toes, and kissed him smack on the lips. She felt his surprise in his rigidity. Last night he'd agreed to let her tell the girls and Parker about their relationship. She hadn't planned on doing it this way. He had Piper to thank for that—and she wasn't nearly done. She wound her arms around his neck, kissing him longer. He finally must have figured out what she was doing, and his arms circled her waist.

Sometimes a girl needed to stake her claim.

When their lips parted, she felt exhilarated, and Mason looked just as invigorated. Willow was grinning from ear to ear, while Bridgette stood frozen with her mouth agape.

"Damn, woman," Piper said. "How long have you been holding *that* in?"

"Too long," Remi said.

"Far too long," Mason agreed, reaching for Remi's hand. He tucked her beneath his arm, leaning down for another kiss.

"And hottieguard goes in for seconds." Piper took a big bite of her pastry.

Remi smirked at Piper and said, "He's *my* hottieguard, thank you very much."

"Aiden's going to have a cow," Bridgette said. "Have you told him yet?"

Mason's expression turned serious again.

"We're waiting until he's back from overseas," Remi explained. "And you can't tell Aurelia because she'd have to tell Ben, and I can't ask either of them to lie."

"But she can ask us to," Piper pointed out.

"I'm not asking you to lie. I'm asking you not to spill the beans," Remi said.

"Relax, *Prin*—Remi," Piper teased. "I assume that was for *Princess*, which is seriously cute coming from a beast like Mason, and I'm only giving you shit. Nobody needs to run off and ruin your fun." She pointed at Mason with a threatening stare and said, "I'm glad the two of you are together, but if you break her heart, you'll have me to deal with. And be warned, I carry a big hammer and I know how to use it."

"I'd yell at her, but she's not kidding," Bridgette said with a shake of her head.

"Got it, Piper," Mason said evenly.

Remi could see he was holding back a smart-ass remark, and she appreciated it. She'd seen Piper give men hell, and she knew Piper would put their friendship above any man any day of the week.

Mason's gaze moved from one friend to the next as he said, "Don't worry. We have every intention of telling Aiden about us. We're just trying to do what's right for everyone."

"That's good, because I hate keeping secrets," Willow said.

"Wait. Did you *know*?" Bridgette asked.

Willow made a zip motion across her lips and tossed away the imaginary key.

Bridgette said, "That's it. I need *details*. How did this happen? When did you two get together?"

Mason kissed the top of Remi's head and said, "I'm going to let you girls chat. I'll be right outside."

They all watched him leave, and the second the door closed, the girls peppered Remi with questions.

"How? When?" Bridgette said.

"Is he as hot in bed as he looks?" Piper asked.

Willow glared at her. "That's private, Piper."

"Says the girl who told us about the incredible view of the ceiling she had on her honeymoon," Piper reminded her.

"Remi, come on," Bridgette pleaded. "I want to know everything."

"Okay, let's see. Remember the kiss that sparked the stalker texts? Well, we've pretty much been together since then, and yes, Piper, he's incredible in bed—though I hate telling you that, because you've been drooling over him since the first time you saw him. But after listening to all of you rave about your men, I am proud to *finally* have my own." She wrapped her arms around herself, unable to stop gushing. "You guys, I've never been so happy!"

"Good sex releases endorphins," Piper chimed in.

"It's *so* much bigger than that. I don't even hate my fortress any-more. I think I hated it because I felt so alone and locked away, but having Mason there and the two of us doing everything together has given it a whole new feel. It's warmer, homier."

Piper licked the cream from the center of her pastry and said, "There are so many dirty jokes I could make right now. But I won't, because you're already way too giddy."

"I *am* giddy," Remi agreed. "You guys remember how frustrated I was the night you came over, wanting Mason and not being able to show it. Now I get to wake up next to him, kiss him, touch him, and be hugged by him. Oh my gosh, *nothing* compares to his hugs."

"That's not saying much about his . . ." Piper arched a brow.

"Okay, let's set that record straight. The man has magic hands, a talented mouth, and a wondrous *pleasure wand*. Got it?"

"Pleasure wand?" Piper snort-laughed. "It's just us, babe, and we're not eighty years old. You can say 'cock.'"

"Whatever! I was being funny. Anyway, we have common interests, which I want to tell you about, but the absolute best thing about him is how he treats me. He communicates about *everything*, and he's patient. He respects me and doesn't treat me like I don't need to know all the facts. I can't explain it, but I'm just so happy."

"That's the best news ever," Willow said. "You deserve to be treated like gold, Remi."

Bridgette lowered herself into a chair and said, "I couldn't be happier for you. Bodhi made a comment after the birthday party that Mason had hinted at having someone special in his life. I guess that was you."

Remi hadn't expected that, but she was glad to hear it.

"What happens after you're done filming? Or after he catches the stalker?" Piper asked.

"I don't know. We haven't gotten that far. Everything is happening so fast."

"Well, yeah," Willow said. "You guys live together. How can it not?"

"You should thank Aiden," Piper pointed out. "That'll get his goat." She chuckled.

"I don't want to think about Aiden right now. I have a lot of guilt for not telling him when Mason and I first got together. But you know how Aiden is. He'd storm home, thinking Mason took advantage of me. I can't deal with that right now. And I have *more* news to share. Mason and I are starting a project together, a really important one." She didn't want to share too much of Mason's private life, so she said, "He grew up in foster homes, and he didn't have great experiences. One of the things that he missed out on was celebrating birthdays."

"Aw, poor Mason," Bridgette said.

"I know. He was moved around a lot. I don't know if that's typical or not. He blamed himself because he acted out, but even if he did, it sounded like he was a product of the system. It makes me sick to think of him—or any child—being uprooted all the time." Her heart hurt anew talking about what Mason had gone through.

"No shit," Piper said angrily. "I'd like to go find those foster parents who passed him on to other houses or didn't celebrate his birthday and give them hell."

"Me too, and I love that about you," Remi said. "But there's no sense in going backward, right? Mason and I came up with an idea of how we can help other foster kids. It's small in the grand scheme of things, but I think it's a start. We want to make birthday boxes and fill them with gifts. At least that way, any of the foster children who might not get a gift will have something special to look forward to."

"I love that idea!" Bridgette said. "Maybe Shira can help you figure out how to go about it."

"Mason's calling Bodhi later this morning. I'm sure between him and Shira, he'll get some ideas." She told them about her friend Parker and CCF. "We're thinking about starting small, like doing it for local foster kids first, until we figure out all the logistics. I'm glad I planned on taking a break after this movie wraps. I'll have plenty of time to devote to this, and I'm excited that Mason and I are doing it together."

"Can we help?" Willow asked. "I'd love to be involved."

"Me too," Piper and Bridgette said in unison.

"Really? We'd love that. I have today off, so I'm going to contact Parker and then make some calls and see if Shea Steele, my publicist, has any ideas. I'm sure I can use my connections to get donations."

"You should include Stackables," Piper suggested. Stackables were like Legos, only they came in a bigger variety of sizes and shapes. "They were my favorite toys as a kid."

"Good idea," Bridgette said. "Coloring books, dolls. Can you find a toy company to donate those things?"

"Wait. I need to get Mason in here." Remi rushed out the door, so excited she could hardly stand it.

Mason was leaning against the hood of the truck. He pushed off as soon as she came out the door. "Everything okay?"

"Yes! I told them about the birthday boxes and they want to help. They have some great ideas. Would you mind coming in?"

"They want to help?" he asked excitedly. "That's fantastic."

It took all her willpower not to leap into his arms and celebrate.

As soon as Mason stepped inside, Willow said, "We love your idea! I can talk to the woman I buy my bakery boxes from. I bet she can give you a good deal on something cute to use for the birthday boxes. And we can put together cake mugs for the elementary school–aged kids, so they can make their own cakes."

"Cake mugs?" Mason had no idea what that was.

"They're mugs with all the ingredients for a single serving of cake inside," Willow explained. "You just add water and microwave them."

He shook his head. "They definitely didn't have those when I was a kid."

"That's a great idea, because if they don't get a cake, they'll have that one," Bridgette said. "Louie has always loved little cars and action figures. And for babies you can put in rattles or maybe one bigger toy like a music box. Will you make boxes for babies?"

"I think we should make them for all kids. Being excluded sucks," Mason said.

"What about backpacks for school-aged kids?" Piper asked. "But cool ones, with some fun toys packed inside. Or is that too much like a necessity and not a toy they'd enjoy?"

"I'm not sure what the system is like nowadays, but I'd have given anything for a cool backpack. I carried my belongings from house to house in a trash bag," Mason said.

The kitchen went silent, four sets of sad eyes locked on him. Damn, he hadn't meant to evoke pity.

"Oh, Mason." Remi wrapped her arms around him. She kissed the center of his chest, and then she looked up at him and said, "You know what we have to do?"

"Make everyone stop looking at me like I'm a six-year-old boy carrying a trash bag?"

"Sorry," Piper mumbled, and the others looked away.

Remi shook her head. "We have to make duffel bags for the kids, too, with all the necessities—toothbrushes, hairbrushes, shampoo, all the stuff they need."

"I love that idea," he said, unable to believe their little idea was growing such strong legs. "We buy bags for our security guys from a company in Colorado. I'll call our rep and see if they have any interest in donating."

"We need to include comfort toys," Bridgette added. "A teddy bear or something to hold at night. I wonder if the distributor I use for my bouquet stuffed animals can cut us a deal. I'll ask."

"Good idea. I wish we could do pajamas," Willow said.

"Maybe we can," Remi said excitedly. "I'll call Mia Stone at JRB Designs, Josh and Riley Braden's assistant."

"The famous fashion designers?" Willow asked, wide-eyed.

"Yes. I wear their stuff all the time for events. They just launched a children's clothing line, and they're really into giving back and paying it forward. I bet they'd love to donate pajamas. I might have to do a commercial or something in exchange for it, but I can't imagine a worthier cause to use my celebrity status."

"I'm as excited as you guys are, and I hate to put a damper on things, but have you looked into the legal aspects of this? I'm sure the foster-care system has rules and regulations about this type of thing," Piper pointed out.

"Not yet. But I'll get the scoop from Parker this afternoon. I need to make some notes." Remi pulled out her phone and began typing.

"I bet Mom would love to donate something to the boxes," Bridgette said. "She'll probably whip up a happiness potion, but the more the better."

"Yes!" Remi exclaimed. "That would be great! I think we need *big* boxes and duffel bags. We have a busy day ahead of us." She glanced at Mason. "But don't worry, we'll make time to go to the grocery store." To her friends she said, "We're going to the store without a disguise—not even a baseball hat—to work on forming boundaries. Mason's been schooling me on ways to give myself space from fans without coming across bitchy."

"Good. She needs that," Piper said. "She is *such* a pleaser."

Remi's cheeks pinked up, and she quickly busied herself focusing on thumbing out notes on her phone. Mason knew her mind was chasing his down a dirty path, thinking about how eagerly she pleasured him.

"Why don't you come with me to the farmers' market instead?" Bridgette asked. "I'm meeting Bodhi and Louie when we're done here, before I open the flower shop." She owned the Secret Garden, a flower shop right next door to the bakery. "I think the butcher will be there, so you can probably get everything you need and skip the grocery store, and the market is only open from seven to eleven, so you'll have plenty of time to make calls."

"I heard one of the Loves' rescue dogs had *puppies*," Piper said with a taunt in her eyes. "Deirdre is going to be there trying to find homes for them."

Remi turned pleading eyes to Mason. "Can we go? Please? Do we need to call Porter or Merrick to come? I'm totally okay with it if we do. Or do you need to be at your computer earlier to do your PI stuff? It's okay if you do. We can hit the grocery store later instead. Maybe we can see the puppies another day. The Loves own an orchard. We can go by anytime."

There wasn't a chance in hell he'd keep her from those puppies.

"It's a great market, and not too busy," Willow said. "They set it up across the street by the lake. If you peek out there now, I bet you'll see the vendors' canopies."

"I have some time this morning. I'll go as extra muscle and keep an eye out for creepers," Piper offered.

Mason was touched by how they rallied around Remi. "I think we can fit that in," he said, and the girls cheered.

"Thank you!" Remi launched herself into his arms and kissed him.

As strange as it was for him to make a public display of affection, Remi—and her supportive friends, who were currently whistling and making silly comments—helped him over the hurdle.

They brainstormed while Willow finished baking, and by the time they were done, Remi had a list of ideas a mile long.

Mason pulled Remi into his arms and said, "We've only just come together and you're willing to put your name on the line for children you don't even know."

"It's going to be incredible!" Remi said.

He glanced at the women, who were quickly becoming like the not-afraid-to-give-him-shit sisters he'd never had, and said, "All of you are willing to give your time and use your business names to help. I think this effort will make a world of difference in so many lives. I don't know how to thank you."

"No thanks necessary," Willow said. "We love doing this stuff. And if you decide to go bigger and offer birthday parties, I'll donate the cakes!"

Remi gasped. "Yes! We *have* to do that! We could hold quarterly birthday parties for all the kids in the area who have birthdays during that time period."

"We have to find a big place to rent," Bridgette said.

"Slow down, idea churners," Piper interrupted. "First we have to figure out what we're legally allowed to do and what kind of red tape we have to untangle to get approvals."

As the girls talked about quarterly birthday bashes and what they would like to do at them, Remi looked at Mason and said, "I bet you never realized *sisterhood* could be as strong as *brotherhood*. Welcome to life with the Daltons."

Bridgette and Piper flanked Remi as they crossed the cobblestone street to the farmers' market. About a dozen white canopies were set up on the grass, with colorful signs announcing fresh fruits and vegetables, meats, breads, and other goods. Mason followed close behind, taking in the glistening lake and the charming small town. Sweetwater was nestled in the foothills of the Silver Mountains and boasted old-fashioned store-fronts, a marina, and from what Mason could see, lots of friendly looking residents milling about the farmers' market. He'd messaged Bodhi, who had assured him that the market was small, and he was bringing Dahlia, his Great Dane. Dogs were great deterrents, and a person would have to be a fool to try to get near Remi with Mason around, much less Mason *and* Bodhi.

"Bridge!" Bodhi called from the parking lot by the market.

Dahlia pulled at her leash, barking, and Louie clung to Bodhi's other hand, waving as he looked up and said something to Bodhi. Bodhi nodded and let go of his hand.

"Brace yourselves," Bridgette said as her little boy sprinted across the grass toward them. "I have no idea who he's going for."

Remi crouched and opened her arms. "I hope it's me!"

Just like that, Mason fell a little harder for her.

Louie ran into her arms and hugged her. "Guess what, Auntie Remi? Dahlia and Molly had a race and Dahlia won!"

Auntie Remi? Had Louie called her that last night? He couldn't remember, but it was about the cutest thing he'd ever heard.

"She did? Well, that's not surprising. She has those long legs, and she's *your* dog after all. Look how fast *you* are!" Remi ruffled Louie's hair.

As she rose to her feet, Louie took her hand like it was the most natural thing in the world for both of them. For all Mason knew, it was. Bodhi and Dahlia joined them, and Remi loved up the dog, hugging her big head and letting her lick her face.

Bodhi kissed Bridgette. Then he rubbed her belly and said, "Everything okay with our little man?"

"Or little lady," she reminded him. "Yes. I feel great."

"When's the baby due?" Mason asked.

"The middle of October," Bodhi said. "Five or six more weeks."

"Can you believe these two haven't found out the sex of their baby?" Piper said. "If it were me, I'd want to know."

"Not me. I like surprises almost as much as I like dogs," Remi said as she bent to kiss the top of Dahlia's head.

"Good. Let's surprise you with food. I have half an hour before I need to get to work, so let's get your pretty little butt moving." Piper looped her arm with Remi's and said, "I'm your new hottieguard. Don't get too handsy."

As they headed for the canopies, Bodhi turned a more serious gaze to Mason and said, "Everything cool here?"

"Yeah. The market seems tame. Thanks for letting us crash your time with your wife."

"I never thought I'd say this, but I like the company. We rarely go anywhere without one of Bridgette's sisters or Ben and Aurelia. *Family*, man, that's what it's all about."

"I can see that." He glanced at Remi, who was talking with the girls as they picked vegetables from a stand. Louie dropped a yellow pepper into Remi's bag. "Listen, man, I have to tell you something in confidence. Remi told the girls this morning, and I don't want Bridgette to have to keep it a secret from you. Remi and I are together."

Bodhi treated Mason to a rare smile. "Really? That explains you not wanting to avoid Roxie's love potion. I'm happy for you, man. Remi's a great person, and she's lucky to have you."

His accolades meant the world to Mason, because they'd teamed with some awesome guys over the years. "Thanks. But honestly, I'm the lucky one. Everything's still new, and we have to keep it under wraps from the public because of all the shit she's going through, but I wanted you to know." He scanned the grounds as the girls paid for their vegetables.

As they followed them toward the butcher's booth, Bodhi said, "Have you told Aiden?"

"Not yet, and Aurelia wasn't at the bakery, so she and Ben don't know." He explained that Remi wanted to wait until Aiden finished his business dealings to break the news to him.

"That makes sense," Bodhi said. "Remi and Aiden have been through a lot, but you know that already. The girls are excited that she's sticking around for the next few months."

He glanced at Remi, who was leaning on Piper. Mason felt himself smiling and said, "I think she needs these women in her life. Speaking of which, I wanted to talk with you about something Remi and I are putting together."

As they walked through the market, Mason told him about their ideas for the birthday boxes, duffel bags, and the possibility of hosting quarterly birthday parties. "What do you think?"

"I think it's a great idea, but you'll get further with a nonprofit than you will as well-meaning individuals. I can talk to Shira and see about coordinating those efforts through Hearts for Heroes. Our focus is military families, so it would mean branching out and dealing with divisions that handle foster care. But that's doable if you want to go that route. Or you could always set up your own nonprofit, if you think this could lead to a large enough effort. Are you looking at something local, while Remi's here, or in the city? Or are you thinking of going bigger, taking it national?"

"I'm not sure. We just came up with the idea. We talked about starting small, seeing what's involved, but the girls are pretty stoked about it. I'll talk to Remi and see what she thinks. She also has a friend who runs a nonprofit that works with foster kids, and I know she wants to see what she has to say, too."

"If you decide to open a nonprofit, talk to Shira," Bodhi said. "She can go over the complexities with you. Let me know when you figure it out. I'd like to get involved any way I can."

"Thanks, I will," he said as the girls stopped by a booth with five energetic puppies in a penned-in area. "I appreciate the offer to work through Hearts for Heroes."

"Can I get in there, Deirdre?" Remi asked the blonde sitting by the pen.

"Absolutely! These babies need some love." Deirdre opened the gate, and Remi and Louie went in.

They plopped down on their butts and let the puppies climb all over them and lick their faces. Remi giggled as much as Louie did. She was a sight for sore eyes.

"Looks like you might be taking home a puppy," Mason said to Bodhi.

"Nah. Louie knows the rules. Dahlia's a big dog and takes a lot of love." Bodhi loved up Dahlia. "Besides, you can't actually take home a puppy. They go through a whole process of evaluating families, just like when you adopt a child."

"That's good, because if Remi asked for every one of them, I'd have a hard time saying no." He took out his phone and snapped a few pictures of Remi. He didn't want to forget a second of those smiles.

"Want to hold one, Mason?" Remi asked, cuddling a puppy.

"No, thanks. But it looks like you want one."

She kissed the pup on its snout and said, "Nope. I just wanted to love them up. A dog I could handle, once it's past the chewing-everything stage."

After a long goodbye that included dozens of sloppy puppy kisses, they left the pups. A blond woman walking by said, "You look just like Remi Divine." She gasped and said louder, "Oh my gosh! You *are* Remi Divine, aren't you?"

Three women who were walking by hurried toward them.

Piper and Mason stepped beside Remi at the same time. Bodhi stood close by, clearly aware that those women didn't seem threatening.

"I can't believe you're Remi Divine, here at our little farmers' market!" one of the women exclaimed.

"Can we have your autograph?" another woman asked.

Remi flashed a gorgeous smile and Mason fully expected her to agree, which he knew would cause the other people who were now closing in on them to ask for the same.

"Actually, I'm shopping with my friends, so it's really not a good time," Remi said a little tentatively. She quickly added, "But if you go to my website and email my publicist, she'll be glad to send you an autographed picture."

"Thanks!" one of the women said. "We love your movies!"

Remi waved and hurried toward another booth, whispering, "Are they still looking? Are they mad?"

Holy shit! She did it! Mason wanted to take her in his arms and spin her around, celebrating her strength. "No, but even if they were, we've got your back, Princess. How do you feel?"

"Nervous." She put her hand over her stomach and began petting Dahlia like she was a worry stone. She lifted her beautiful eyes to Mason and said, "But good. Really, really good."

"Aw hell," Piper said. "Look at them. They want to *hug.* You two are . . ." She moved between them and hugged Remi. "Pretend I'm six four and sexy as hell." Then she turned to Mason and hugged him as she said, "If the stalker is watching, he'll be thoroughly confused."

"I want in on that," Bridgette said, and she hugged Mason, causing everyone to laugh. "Thanks for helping Remi learn about boundaries." She put her arms around Bodhi and said, "Can't leave out my own man."

After a few minutes of banter, they went to finish their shopping. Two more people recognized Remi, and she handled each one with a little more confidence than the last.

As they crossed the street, two young girls came out of the bakery and pointed to Remi. Through the front window, Mason noted how crowded the bakery was.

Bridgette said, "You didn't get to see the renovations Piper made to the front of the bakery. Do you want to go in?"

Bodhi shot a look at Mason, clearly conveying *This might not be a good idea,* which confirmed Mason's gut feeling. He wasn't worried that the stalker was inside, but he was worried about Remi being in a closed environment with what could turn out to be too many overzealous fans.

But he'd also promised her she wouldn't live in a box while under his watch. This was her decision to make.

Remi touched his fingers, like she needed grounding. Then she quickly pulled back, as if she'd realized what she'd done, and said, "I think I've had enough boundary practice for today. I'll come see the renovations another time."

"Good, because I've got to haul ass to my job site." Piper pulled her into an embrace and then said to Mason, "You done good, hottieguard. Keep it up."

"I'm never going to live down the hottieguard thing, am I?"

"Not a chance." Piper sauntered off with a bounce in her step, as if she'd just dropped the mic and left the stage.

CHAPTER SEVENTEEN

REMI WAS ON a mission to bring her and Mason's ideas to fruition. After they arrived home and put away their groceries, they sat at the dining room table armed with phones, laptops, and notebooks, making lists of the people they wanted to contact and ideas they'd come up with at the bakery. Though they loved how enthusiastic everyone was about their idea, they were both passionate about the project and wanted to remain hands-on every step of the way.

"We need to decide where we're starting," Remi said. "In the city, since that's where you grew up?"

"I think we should help kids here, locally, since this is where you'll be for the foreseeable future."

Remi's nerves prickled at the question vying for release. Mason must have seen something in her eyes because he took her hand between both of his and said, "What's going on in that beautiful mind of yours?"

"I'm just thinking about the foreseeable future," she said softly. "We're making plans like we're a given. What will happen to us after the stalker is caught? I assume you'll have to go back to business as usual in the city?"

He slid a hand to the nape of her neck, drawing her closer as he gazed into her eyes, and said, "*You* are my foreseeable future, Remi. I can work from anywhere, and drive into the city when need be. The last thing I want to do is to walk away from what we have."

Happy tears burned her eyes as he pressed his lips to hers in a sweet kiss.

"You mentioned going away after filming ends. Do you still want to do that?"

"Yes, definitely."

"Good. I'm on board with the idea, and I'm talking with my men about ways to make it happen where you won't feel so oppressed but will ensure your safety." He looked at the lists in the notebooks and said, "The other day you asked me if I was fulfilled. I thought I was, but at the time I didn't realize some things were missing. You and this project are two of them. I am one hundred percent behind us and this project. The idea of giving kids something I never had makes me as happy as knowing we're doing it together." He brushed his thumb over her neck and said, "You know how you're working on boundaries?"

"Yes."

"I am, too. You were right when you said I was a workaholic. I'm thinking about ways to strike a balance there, too, once the stalker is behind bars. And that new direction, my sweet Remington Aldridge, is because of *you*."

Grinning, she grabbed the front of his T-shirt and tugged him in for another kiss, which was interrupted by a phone call.

Mason groaned as he pulled out his phone. "It's Porter. He has to drop something off. I asked him to call on his way here. I'll take it outside." He headed for the front door as he answered. "Hey, Porter. How far away are you?"

Remi got started making calls, the first of which was to Naomi. She caught her up to speed on their ideas, handled a few other lingering business issues, and then she called Shea.

"This is the best news I've heard all month," Shea said. She was one of the most successful PR reps in the industry, and she'd been repping Remi for years. "How long have I been asking you to find something you were passionate about *besides* acting?"

"A long time, but nothing fit. This feels right. Can you help?"

Remi pictured her blond friend leaning back in her chair, kicking her high heels up onto her desk, her keen eyes narrowed in a *let's do this* expression.

"Absolutely! I'll put together a list of companies you've worked with and see who I think we can talk to about donations for birthday boxes and duffel bags, and support in general, because these things take *funds*. Did you talk to Aida yet?" Aida Strong was Remi's attorney.

"No, but I will after I call Parker."

"Which reminds me, I need to take a trip out to the Cape to see her! Her little girl is so freaking cute, she almost makes me want one." Parker's daughter, Miriam, had her daddy's dark hair and her mommy's blue eyes.

"Your baby will be born with a to-do list," Remi teased.

"Nothing wrong with starting them young. Listen, babe, I've got to go, but before I do, is there something I should know about you and Mason Swift?"

"Yes, but nobody can know," Remi confessed.

"Hey, who do you think stopped the tabloids from rolling out a story about the photographs and threatening texts? I pulled a Ray Donovan and paid them off, *thank you very much*. I've got your back."

They talked for a few more minutes, and then Remi called Parker.

"Remi! It's been too long. How are you?"

Remi could hear the happiness in her voice. They hadn't seen each other since early spring, when Remi had gone to Cape Cod for a week to destress. "Hi. I'm well, but my schedule has been crazy. Sorry I haven't called in a while. How's Miriam?"

"Only the most amazing child on the planet, of course. She's *walking!*" Parker gushed. "She has Grayson wrapped around her little finger, though. You should see them together. It's mama porn for sure! But more importantly, did they ever catch the guy who broke into your house?"

"No. I'm in Harmony Pointe, New York, filming, and we think he might be *here*, but we don't know for sure. He sent me threatening texts with pictures from the set. They're following all leads, of course, but they said he could have gotten the picture off social media, and maybe he's *not* here. I've got an army of guys watching me." *And I'm falling for one of them.*

"Oh, Remi. I'm so sorry. I don't miss that attention *at all*," Parker said. She hadn't taken on an acting job since getting pregnant with Miriam. "The third-best thing I ever did was take a step back from Hollywood."

"I'm guessing the first was marrying Grayson and the second was having Miriam?" She knew the answer. Parker was so in love with her handsome artist husband and her adorable daughter, just being around them had always made Remi want to fall in love.

"Of course. What about you? Has Aiden given you the key to your chastity belt yet?" Parker teased.

Remi trusted Parker not to expose her secret, and she wanted to be honest with her. "There is someone special in my life, and his name is Mason, but we have to keep it quiet until the stalker is caught, so please don't mention his name anywhere that could carry it in the wind. You'll like him, Parker. He's smart and loving, and he's got the biggest heart."

"I'm so happy for you. Does he get along with Aiden?"

"Yes, but Aiden is out of the country, and he doesn't know we're together. I'll tell him when he returns."

"Good plan. Otherwise he'll hijack a plane to come make your official relationship rules. He's never really had to do that before. That should be interesting. When are you coming to the Cape? I missed seeing you this summer."

The idea of going to the Cape with Mason brought a smile. "I'm not sure, because Mason and I are embarking on an exciting new project, which is why I'm calling, actually."

Parker had also been brought up in the foster-care system, which had been the impetus for the Collins Children's Foundation. As Remi filled her in on their project, Parker told her about a company that did something similar to what Remi was suggesting, but they didn't have birthday bashes. That alone made Remi more determined to host the parties. Parker gave her the lowdown on how CCF worked and the hoops Remi could expect to jump through if she and Mason opened a nonprofit.

"Why don't you run it through CCF?" Parker suggested. "We have relationships with the offices that oversee foster care in every state. Why reinvent the wheel?"

"That's so nice of you, but Mason and I really want to be hands-on. He grew up in the system, and this is really a passion project for both of us."

"I didn't mean that I would take your idea and run with it. I meant that you and Mason could remain in control of developing and running the program to whatever extent you'd like. But doing it through CCF will allow you to avoid jumping through all those time-consuming hoops. You'd have full control, and we'd just help guide you when you need it."

Remi was beside herself. "You wouldn't mind? That's so generous. I'll have to talk to Mason, but that sounds smart to me."

"Of course I don't mind. I'll support this endeavor any way that I can, and I'm happy to speak with Mason and answer any questions he has. I'm so glad you're doing this. The foundation changed my life, and the lives of so many children. Anything you can do to help foster kids is a good thing."

They talked for a long time, and after they ended the call, Remi was so excited, she wanted to tell Mason. She went to the front window and saw him talking with Porter in the driveway. Her stomach growled and she realized it was already almost one o'clock. She couldn't believe

Mason's internal clock hadn't sent him searching for food. The man fueled his body like the well-honed machine it was.

She went into the kitchen and made a salad for herself with sliced hard-boiled eggs, peppers, and mushrooms. Then she made a sandwich for Mason and one for Porter in case he hadn't eaten. She took a picture of the food and sent it in a group text to the girls with the caption *Feeding my man.*

As she carried the plates of sandwiches outside, it struck her that what she was doing felt very domestic and natural, which was weird, because she'd never been domestic before.

The men were no longer out front, though Porter's truck was still there. She walked back inside and called Mason's name in case she'd missed them. Answered with silence, she went back outside and around to the courtyard. They weren't there, either. Her pulse quickened as horrible thoughts whipped through her mind. What if the stalker got them? *Ohgodohgodohgod.* Mason would never leave her alone like this.

"Mason?" came out as a choked whisper as she hurried around to the back, scanning the yard, which was also empty. She dropped the plates on the patio table, her heart racing as she cried out, "Mason!"

Mason bolted out of the trees at the edge of the yard with Porter at his heels. "Remi!"

The air rushed from her lungs as Mason gathered her in his arms.

"What happened?" His gaze darted to the yard as Porter yelled "Clear" and ran toward the front of the house.

"I got scared," she panted out. "I didn't see you and I thought . . ." Tears filled her eyes as her panic flooded out. "I thought I lost you."

He held her tight, her cheek pressed against his hammering heart. He lifted her face, wiping her tears with the pads of his thumbs. "You'll never lose me, especially not to some dirtbag."

"I didn't realize I was still so scared about the stalker. I'm sorry, but as silly as I feel for worrying over nothing, it *wasn't* nothing. This is *real*, Mason. He could hurt either of us."

"Listen to me. I'm here, you're safe, and nobody's going to take me down. This is a stressful time, and I know you have things to keep you sidetracked, but it's perfectly normal for the fear to swallow you up sometimes. Don't ever apologize for that. That's why I'm here. And I don't mean as your bodyguard—I mean as your man."

Relief and renewed panic gripped her at the ferocity of her emotions. She stepped back and pressed her hand over her heart. "I don't want anything to happen to you."

"It never will."

"You can't *know* that." She inhaled deeply and blew it out slowly, trying to regain control of her rampant heart. "You came running so fast."

"Three seconds flat, that was my promise to you." He shot a look toward the front of the house and pressed a kiss to the top of her head. "We need to get you a better text notification sound on your phone."

"Why?"

"Because I texted you to let you know Porter and I had to take care of something out here."

She pulled out her phone and saw Mason's text, along with texts from Piper and Bridgette. "Now I feel really stupid. I had notifications off while I was making calls."

Porter came around the house and yelled, "All clear, boss. Want me to check the house?"

"No, we're cool," Mason said. "Remi just got scared when she couldn't find us. Even a brave front has to crack sometime."

"Don't I know it." Porter put his hands on his hips, smiling as he said, "I'm glad everything's okay. I needed to get my heart rate up anyway. Thanks for that."

A nervous giggle tumbled out. "I'm sorry, Porter. I made you guys sandwiches. Does that help make up for it?"

"Sandwiches and a heart attack, the perfect lunch. Thanks, Princess." Mason put a hand on her back and said, "I told Porter about us, but I'm pretty sure we can trust him."

Porter winked.

The guys sat down to eat, and as Remi went inside, she turned on her notifications and read Mason's text first. *Porter and I have to take care of something in the woods out back. Text if you need me.* She warmed all over, and just as quickly that uneasy feeling took over. Mason was right: She had been putting up a brave front. She couldn't believe she'd ever suggested that they use her for bait. This was no joking matter, and it turned out that when it came to Mason's safety, her brave face wasn't nearly brave enough.

She opened and read Piper's text, closing the door firmly behind her and leaning against it. *When I feed a man, I'm usually naked.* She chuckled at Piper's text, wondering if Piper was all talk, like guys who pretend to play the field. Then she read Bridgette's message. *Now I'm hungry. For FOOD, not what Piper's insinuating!*

She was glad for their levity.

A text from Mason rolled in. *Sure you're okay? The sandwiches are almost as delicious as you are.*

She thumbed out, *I'm okay. Sorry for overreacting.* His response came fast. *You didn't overreact, you reacted, and that's good.* She typed *Thank you,* added a kissing emoji, and sent it off. She pushed from the door, feeling calmer.

When she'd first moved into the fortress, she'd barely noticed the rooms and floors, much less the beautiful home in which she was living. Now, as she stood in the entryway, instead of seeing sterile white marble floors and big, lonely rooms, she saw Mason chasing her up the stairs from the gym, catching her, and tickling her ribs as he had the other evening after they worked out, and she saw him picking her up and laying her on the couch as he came down over her, kissing her breathless.

She went into the dining room to eat her salad, recalling his laughter from when they'd come downstairs for a midnight snack last night. After weeks of living there, the fortress finally felt less like a prison and more like a home.

CHAPTER EIGHTEEN

MASON WAS IN and out of the house throughout the afternoon, dealing with the investigation as Remi worked on gathering information and reaching out to influential people. He popped into the dining room for kisses, which she loved, or to work on his computer, which also included kisses. Remi had called Parker back several times during the course of the afternoon to ask more questions and to ensure she was going about things properly when dealing with her contacts. Things were moving right along, and although this was just the beginning, the project already felt real. She updated Aiden via email on the latest events in her life, leaving out her relationship with Mason. When Aiden said he was proud of her for putting herself out there in such a meaningful way, it made the project even more special.

Late in the afternoon, Mason came into the room, and she tilted her face up for a kiss. She could get used to this. Work a little, kiss a little . . .

"Hey, beautiful. I've got news."

"Is the news that they caught the guy, so we can be a couple in public?"

"I wish. This is a long shot, but my guy who's watching your LA house saw a drone flying around and tracked it down to a techy college kid who lives about a mile from your property. He's not the stalker, but he's got footage from all his flights and they're obtaining the footage from the night of the break-in."

"Seriously? We might catch the guy?"

"Like I said, it's a long shot, but we're checking into it. And if he's not on that footage, they'll check out the footage for the few weeks prior. If we get lucky, he'll have caught something—the guy, a car parked too long nearby, or something else."

"That's great news."

"We hope so. I also put a few calls in to my military buddies who are now out of the service. It looks like we'll have all sorts of volunteers to help with the project when we're ready. And I contacted my supplier for the bags, and they suggested different bags for younger children and teenagers, which makes sense. They're sending a few samples."

"That's great! I've made headway, too. I found out there are eighty-one foster kids in Harmony Pointe and another sixty-three in Sweetwater. I think we should do birthday boxes for all of them. I also talked to Mia Stone, from JRB Designs. I was shocked she got back to me right away, but that woman has more energy than the Energizer Bunny. She's going to present the idea to Josh and Riley Braden. She said it's right up their alley, and she can't imagine that they'd turn down a chance to help kids by donating pajamas for the duffel bags. She hoped to get back to me within a week. And Willow called. She said the distributor she uses for her boxes is sending over a few samples for us to look at."

"That's incredible news."

"I know, and there's more. I found out that it can take anywhere from a few months to a *year* to set up a nonprofit, and then there's apparently a lot of red tape to get approved by the offices that govern the foster-care programs."

He winced. "That's a long time. I was kind of hoping we could get started sooner."

"Exactly. I know Bodhi offered to let us work through Hearts for Heroes, which is really generous, but they don't have the contacts and approvals for the right departments, so we'd be starting fresh with that part. CCF has worked through all of that already. They have contacts and approvals in every state for their programs. Parker offered to let us run the program through the foundation if we want to. It would still be ours to develop and run, but it would be under the CCF umbrella. Unless you'd rather work with Bodhi or open a foundation?"

"Are you kidding? CCF sounds like the way to go. The less red tape the better. Then we can focus on what really matters—getting things ready for the kids."

She popped to her feet and hugged him. "Are you as excited as I am?"

"Hell yes, and we make a damn good team, Princess."

"We do. Too bad we can't find some way to lure out the creepy guy without using me as bait."

He chuckled. "We'll find him without putting you at risk, but I do have a surprise for you."

"I *love* surprises."

"And dogs, apparently." He took her hand, leading her toward the living room.

"I think I am probably one of the few who prefers dogs to puppies."

"Why haven't you ever gotten one?"

She shrugged. "When I was younger Aiden had enough on his plate. He didn't need to worry about a pet, and then my schedule just sort of took over—" Remi stopped cold at the sight of an enormous tree filling the bay window in the living room. It had to be at least seven feet tall. "Mason? Is it Christmas in September? Is *this* what you and Porter were up to?"

"Something like that," he said as she walked over to the tree.

He'd hung two of the ornaments she'd made on it, and the boxes from her closet were lined up by the couch. "Mason . . . ?"

"The ornaments are important to you. They're too pretty and special to be hidden in boxes in your closet. Since you don't like to give them away, I thought you might like to display them, so we can enjoy them. I thought we could decorate the tree together. But if you'd rather not display them, I'll put them back in your closet, no hard feelings."

He flicked the light switch, illuminating bright red and white lights in the branches.

There was no holding back the happy tears spilling from her eyes as she wrapped her arms around him, too overwhelmed to speak at first. When she finally found her voice, she said, "Ever since my parents died, I've associated the things I've made with stress."

"Aw, Remi. I'm so sorry. I messed up."

She looked up at him and her heart swelled. "No, you didn't. I turned something special into something sad, and I didn't even realize it. But like with everything else, you did. Thank you. I would love nothing more than to decorate the tree with you."

As they decorated the tree, Remi told Mason stories about the ornaments. There were so many, he was amazed she could remember stories about each one. But as she shared her memories, he swore he saw weight lift from her shoulders.

None of the hearts on any of the ornaments were perfectly shaped. Some had flat ridges, others were lopsided, each one mirroring the emotions Remi relayed with her stories. She reached deep into one of the boxes and withdrew an ornament with a blue heart on the bottom, a smaller heart cut out of a book page, and on top, a third heart made of fabric with flowers on it.

Running her fingers over the flowers, she said, "Before Aiden packed up our parents' stuff and we moved to California, he said I could have anything I wanted. When my mom first taught me to make these, she took a page from one of my father's favorite books to use. I tried to stop her, because my father treasured his books. Some of my favorite memories are of him in his leather recliner. He'd pat his leg and say, 'I'll read you a story.' I'd scramble into his lap, excited to hear anything he'd read. I just loved his voice, and I felt so special when he did that, sharing his favorite books with me."

"The leather recliner in your room? Is that his?" Mason asked as she handed him the heart to hang on the tree.

"Yes. I bring it wherever I'm filming. It's comforting, and I feel less alone when I have some of our things with me. Before I met you, I was lonely, Mason. *So* lonely."

He crouched beside her and gathered her in his arms. "Me too, Princess."

"Don't make me cry," she said, pulling away and fanning her eyes. "This is a *happy* time. These are happy memories."

She pushed to her feet and began hanging more ornaments as she finished her story. "Anyway, my mom said my father knew she used pages from his books, and he didn't mind. One time when he was reading to me, we came to a missing page and he skipped right over it. When I asked him about that page, he looked at my mom with this secret expression I'll never forget, and he said, 'Don't worry about that page, sweetheart.'"

"It's nice that your parents had that type of relationship, with intimate secrets. It sounds like they were happy together."

"They seemed to be. I never did find out why she used pages from his favorite books, but he didn't mind, and he even seemed to like it. So when Aiden said I could take anything, I took my father's books and recliner, my mom's crafting supplies, and the blanket she and I used to cuddle under on the couch. The flowered one in my room. That's what that flowered heart is from. I cut off a piece to use on these and kept the rest for the blanket. We also used to make gift cards and invitations to birthday parties. Maybe I'll put an ornament into each birthday box, at least for the younger kids. We can make different shapes instead of hearts and write the year in glitter so they'll always remember when they received them."

"I think that's a great idea."

She hung an ornament on the tree and said, "Do you think it's silly for me to carry on doing something so childish? I mean, they are just paper ornaments."

"No. You're carrying on a family tradition. Traditions are nice."

He reached into the box for more ornaments, and she reached for his hand. "I'm sorry. I'm going on about my parents, and—"

"Don't, Remi. Don't think for one minute that hearing about your parents makes me feel bad about my own. I'm not a broken kid. I came to grips with my life a long time ago. I like hearing about your family and knowing you have good memories. Got it?"

"Sorry. I understand what's it like to have moved on. I don't like when people feel the need to pity me because I've lost my parents." She grabbed an ornament with a black heart on top and said, "There's a bunch in here with black hearts. I made them a lot as a teenager, when Aiden and I butted heads the most."

"Was he pretty strict?"

"Aiden was *interesting* with his strictness," she said as she hung ornaments on the tree. "He was never overbearing in the typical sense, where someone tells you what to do and how to think. He was, and still is, just overly cautious with me. If I was invited somewhere, he usually went with me. I remember one time a friend I knew through an acting club asked me to go bowling. Her mom was going to take us, but Aiden stepped in. He took us bowling and then out for ice cream. It was fun, but as I got older it bugged me, as you can imagine. I mean, who wants their older brother around *all* the time?"

"I don't know him that well, but don't you think it could have something to do with losing your parents and his not wanting to lose the only family he had left?"

"Yes. I'm sure it was. *Is.* I still get nervous when he travels, until I know he's arrived safely."

"What about dating? Did he let you date as a teenager?"

"I was too busy with auditions and schoolwork to pay much attention to boys. It wasn't until I was around nineteen or so that guys started playing a bigger part in my life. Aiden insisted on meeting anyone I went out with, and knowing Aiden, he probably did a full background check on them."

"Excellent man," Mason said with a grin.

She rolled her eyes. "No more Aiden talk. Let's make dinner and admire our gorgeous tree."

He smacked her ass as they headed into the kitchen. She squealed, trying to swat his butt, but he caught her around the waist and hoisted her over his shoulder like a sack of potatoes.

"Mason!"

He swatted her butt again, earning another squeal and giggles as she started using his butt like a drum. He gripped her around the waist, lifting her up over his head, and she beamed down at him.

"What's the matter? You don't like your butt swatted?"

"I just wanted to see your face." He lowered her at an angle, head down, kissing her lips as her feet flailed up toward the ceiling. He pressed her up again and then lowered her down for a kiss.

"You're bench-pressing me!"

"Gotta get my workout in somehow."

The next time he lowered his lips to hers, she grabbed his face with both hands and said, "I like you a lot, hottieguard."

He growled playfully at *hottieguard* and pressed her up toward the ceiling again, earning more laughter. Then he lowered her to the edge of the counter and wedged himself between her legs. He had no idea how things had changed so quickly, but as he gazed into her eyes, the fear that had swamped him when he'd heard her scream in the yard came rushing back.

"You scared me today, Princess. I'm so glad you were okay."

"I'm sorry. I was scared, too. But a very wise man told me that there are no take-backs, so let's not think about that. Let's think about happier things." She wound her legs around his waist, trailing her fingers over his biceps, and said, "Such as how much I like your muscles. Your turn!"

The list of things he liked about her was quickly becoming a list of things he loved. "I'm crazy about your smile."

"I adore your heart." She wound her arms around his neck, her fingers brushing along his skin.

He touched his forehead to hers and said, "You got me, Princess. I wasn't even aware of that particular organ until I met you."

CHAPTER NINETEEN

THURSDAY SHOULD HAVE been a fantastic day. Remi was excited to film a pivotal scene in which she and Raz had a huge argument that ended with a breakthrough for Raz's character. It was her favorite scene in the entire movie, and after all of her commitments, she had something special planned for Mason that she hoped he'd love. But as she sat in the makeup chair with Tillie, the makeup artist, working her magic, she was unable to tear her eyes away from the tabloids on the table. Each boasted a picture of her and Mason. In one he was helping her out of the SUV in the parking lot. In another he was walking with her across the set, and in a third they were walking out of La Love Café. That one was taken last night, when they'd gone into town to grab dinner, with Porter and Merrick standing nearby. The headlines boasted WHO IS REMI DIVINE'S NEW BEAU? and REMI FALLS FOR HER BODYGUARD, and IS THIS LOVE FOR REMI DIVINE?

Thursday was turning out to be anything *but* fantastic.

Mason's phone had blown up before dawn from his IT guys about the pictures, and he'd sprung into action, making sure his team was apprised of the situation. Remi had received urgent messages from Shea and Naomi shortly after. While Remi strategized with her team, Mason put his army on high alert, which wasn't much different from their regular hypervigilant mode, except that now they, and Mason, were chewing on nails, worried the headlines would draw the stalker into a new level of crazy.

Unfortunately, they'd gotten nowhere with the drone footage. The camera had caught a man on her property, but the footage was grainy. His head was lowered, and his dark hoodie made it impossible to get even a glimpse of his face.

Another dead end.

And now *this*.

Remi was so mad she could spit. Tabloid headlines were nothing new, but with the stalker and their plans for later, the timing sucked. Not that there was ever a good time to be the focus of tabloids, but if there was no stalker, she'd own those headlines with all the fanfare her relationship with Mason deserved. She didn't want to cancel their plans, and Porter had assured her that she didn't need to, but she couldn't stop thinking about the picture of Mason with the angry red slash through his face.

If the stalker hurt Mason . . .

She couldn't even allow her mind to go there.

"Okay, gorgeous. I think you're ready," Tillie said, breaking Remi from her thoughts. "I haven't seen your brother around. He never misses a filming. Did the bodyguards scare him off?"

"No. He hired them, actually. He had business overseas." She'd spoken to Aiden earlier. He'd taken the headlines in stride, writing them off as propaganda to sell magazines. Remi hadn't corrected him, which came with a modicum of guilt, but she had enough to worry about. Aiden's sole concern had been for her safety, and she'd reassured him that Mason and his men had her covered.

"That's a shame." Tillie raised her thick dark eyebrows. "He's way more interesting to look at *and* talk to than most of the men hanging around here. Although your bodyguards have been the highlight of many conversations lately." She eyed the tabloids. "Any truth to the rumors?"

Biting back an excited *Yes!* Remi pushed to her feet and said, "When have you ever known the tabloids to need truth? Thanks for making me look good, Tillie."

Tillie wiped her hands on a towel and said, "You make it easy. Break a leg."

Remi stepped into the afternoon sun and was immediately whisked off to the set with Mason and Carl, Mason chewing on nails, Carl making sure she was okay to film in light of the heightened security.

Filming couldn't end soon enough.

One more week, and then she was free.

Who was she kidding? Freedom didn't exist when a crazy person was after her.

Just breathe, Remi. Everything will be okay.

Once they started filming, Remi poured all of her frustrations into her character, which worked well for the angsty scene. Raz was on top of his game, too, and the director was elated with their performance. She'd give anything to be able to run into Mason's arms and celebrate her job well done. Instead, she forced herself to act casual as she approached him and Porter, who were deep in conversation.

"Is everything okay?" she asked, trying to read Mason's expression, which was a mix of confusion and irritation.

"Porter was just filling me in on a change to your schedule," Mason said. "Did you know Shea scheduled an appearance at the theater in town? Apparently they're doing a special showing of that movie you made last summer."

"Shoot. I saw that in an email the other day when I was making calls for the foster-care project. It totally slipped my mind. When is it?"

"In fifteen minutes." The muscles in Mason's jaw jumped.

"Okay. I just need to change my clothes."

"I've already had the theater and attendee list checked out," Porter said as they headed for Remi's trailer. "It's a short list, only fifteen attendees. Sorry I didn't get to you sooner, boss. Merrick is covering the front entrance. I'll cover the back, which is where you'll enter. I'm heading over now."

Remi quickly changed her clothes. Mason didn't say a word as they crossed the lot to the SUV. He drove with both hands on the wheel, his jaw clenched. Remi's heart raced. She knew he was pissed. He had every right to be.

He parked behind the theater, his face a mask of irritation and concern as he turned toward her and said, "Remi, you've *got* to be more careful with your schedule. To keep you safe, I need to know what's planned at all times. I'm not trying to be controlling. I trust Porter, Merrick, and my other guys, but when it comes to your safety, I don't like relying on others to ensure we're doing everything necessary, especially with what the tabloids printed today."

"I know. I'm sorry. I totally forgot, and it won't happen again."

With a curt nod, he exited the car. She blew out a breath, wishing she could say something to ease his tension. She watched him talking with Porter, who was standing guard by the back door, as promised. Mason's entire body looked *at the ready*, muscles taut, eyes scanning their surroundings, hands flexing. She got anxious just seeing him in that state.

He strode to her door and helped her out, abruptly taking her elbow and using his body to shield her as he walked her to the door.

Mason was livid, not at Remi specifically, but at the situation. The last thing he needed was for the asshole who was harassing her to slip through the cracks. He'd seen hurt glittering in her eyes when he'd told her to be more careful with her schedule, but he hadn't been able to temper his tone, which was why he'd taken an extra minute to talk to Porter before helping Remi from the vehicle. She had enough to deal with. She didn't need to take the brunt of his irritation.

"Thanks, Porter," Remi said as Porter held the door open for them. Porter nodded, as professional as ever.

Mason kept his eyes peeled as they entered the back of the theater and followed a hallway through a set of double doors. They followed signs toward the lobby. He knew he had to give Remi room to do her job, but the idea of even fifteen fanatical fans coming at her at once bothered him.

He stopped before the doors that led to the lobby and said, "Ready, Princess?"

A practiced smile slid into place, and he fucking hated that. He hated knowing he'd caused her to *force* a smile when she had to put on a good face for her fans. She'd been working long hours on the set. Once they were home, the stress fell away because they were finally alone, but that didn't mean her day was over. They made calls for the foster-care project, cooked dinner, talked about everything from ideas for the projects to things they'd like to do together once the stalker was behind bars. Sometimes they took time to just relax, and they always fell into each other's arms, making love until they were too sated to move. Guilt tightened like a noose around his neck. He hadn't slowed down to consider how jam-packed her schedule really was. It was no wonder something slipped through the cracks.

He stepped closer and said, "I'm sorry I spoke to you so harshly. You didn't deserve that."

"It's okay," she said softly. "You didn't do anything wrong. I did. I'm making your job harder, and that's the last thing I want to do."

"No, you've got a lot on your plate, and you forgot to tell me *one* thing. I shouldn't have spoken to you like that. I'm just wound tight because of all the shit going down. I'll get it under control."

"I know. Let's get this over with so we can go home and unwind *together*."

Heat smoldered in her beautiful eyes, and though he wasn't sure he deserved it, he was damn glad to see her feelings hadn't changed.

He pushed through the doors, and the scent of popcorn hung in the air as he followed Remi in, scanning the empty lobby.

"Mason!"

He spun around at the sound of the sweetest little girl he knew. Brooklyn barreled into him as Krista came out of the ladies' room behind her, she and Remi both grinning like Cheshire cats.

Remi embraced Krista. "It's so nice to finally meet you in person."

Mason crouched to hug Brooklyn, and his heart took a perilous leap. The three females he cared most about were right there in that room, and Remi had made it happen.

"Are you surprised?" Brooklyn exclaimed, happiness shimmering in her big brown eyes, which were just like her mother's. Her long dark hair fell straight down her back from beneath her favorite black fedora. Some little girls loved jewelry. Brooklyn loved hats, and she had dozens of them.

"I sure am, kiddo." He looked at Remi, the smoldering heat of moments ago multiplying tenfold as he rose to his full height and said, "I had no idea."

"You didn't tell me you were helping *Remi Divine*! She and Mommy talked on the phone three times! She even FaceTimed with us once! I like her," Brooklyn said. "She's Mommy's favorite actress."

"It turns out, she's mine, too," he admitted as he stepped forward and embraced Krista.

Remi crouched to talk with Brooklyn, who hugged her just as hard as she'd hugged Mason.

"She's a special lady," Krista whispered. "I hope the tabloids are right."

Losing a battle with his emotions, he could only say, "Excuse me for one second. I need to have a word with Remi." *Before I lose my mind.*

He took Remi gently by the arm, leading her around the corner.

"I'm sorry," she whispered anxiously. "I knew you didn't want to divide your attention between keeping me and Brooklyn safe, but I hated the idea of you letting Brooklyn down, so I arranged it with Porter and Merrick. I should have told you—"

He crushed his mouth to hers, backing her up against the wall as he deepened the kiss. He wanted to kiss her until she knew just how *not sorry* she should be, but he knew Brooklyn well enough to realize they had only seconds before she poked her pretty little head around the corner looking for him.

"You deserve an Oscar for that performance."

Her eyes turned innocent, and she said, "You're not mad at me for keeping it a secret?"

"I fucking adore you." He started to lower his mouth toward hers for a quick kiss when he heard Brooklyn's voice, bringing him back to his right mind. "I'll thank you properly later."

"I look forward to it," she said as they went back to the lobby.

"There they are!" Brooklyn reached for Mason's hand, bouncing on the toes of her sneakers. She looked adorable in pink skinny jeans and a white T-shirt with black bow ties all over it. Around her neck hung her ever-present locket with her father's picture inside. "Guess what we're seeing. *Mary Poppins Returns!*"

"Sounds perfect." He couldn't take his eyes off Remi, chatting with Krista like they were old friends. Remi had gone from sneaking out to find freedom, to sneaking somewhere so *he* could keep a promise. He hadn't thought it was possible for him to fall harder or faster for her than he already was, but he'd been dead wrong. He wasn't just falling; he was propelling at breakneck speed.

"How about some popcorn or candy?" Remi suggested.

Brooklyn's eyes shot to Krista. "Can I, Mom?"

"Sure. Why not? Mason will eat half of it anyway," Krista said.

"Who, me?" Mason teased as Brooklyn dragged him toward the refreshment counter.

"You always do," Brooklyn said. "Can we get lemonade, too?"

"Sure." Mason looked around. "Who's running the concession stand?"

"I am." Remi went around the counter. "The only one here is the manager, and we can help ourselves." As she filled a bucket with popcorn, she said, "I had no idea Mason was a popcorn fiend."

"He also loves Skittles, but he never eats my Goobers, so if you want candy he won't eat, go for that." Brooklyn threw her arms around Mason again, smiling up at him as she said, "I'm *so* happy to see you. I missed your funky mug."

They were always teasing each other, and he hadn't realized how much he'd missed it. "I've missed your funky mug, too."

Brooklyn carried her drink in one hand and reached for Remi's hand with her other as the two of them went to find seats. At ten, she was fearless and outgoing, just as her late father had once described Krista. Krista was still outgoing . . . *to a point.* She was guarded in ways Mason understood all too well. As far as fearless went, she'd lost too much and hadn't yet regained that level of confidence. He never thought he'd fall in love, and now that he'd found Remi and knew how the right person could change everything, he had hope that maybe one day Krista would open her heart again, too.

Krista sidled up to him, stealing a handful of popcorn as they followed Brooklyn and Remi through the doors. "Brook thinks Remi's the cherry on top of a really great sundae. I have to agree, and the way you're looking at her tells me you might, too. So . . . ? What's the *real* scoop with you two?"

Mason tried to remain stone-faced, but Krista was the only woman other than Remi he'd ever spent any amount of time talking to about real things, like the death of her husband and how it might impact Brooklyn and how losing his buddies had impacted him. "This can't go further than this room right now."

They stood just inside the doors as Brooklyn dragged Remi up and down the aisle, looking for the perfect seats.

"I think the tabloids have already outed you, Mase."

"We're not owning up to that. They do that shit all the time with celebrities. You know that. Did Remi tell you about her stalker situation?"

"Yes. She was very honest about the risks of getting together, but with you and the other two guys, I think we're okay. You're great at changing the subject, but, Mase, I've talked to Remi several times in the past couple weeks, and she's a doll. She's great with Brooklyn, and she thinks the world of you. When she first reached out to me, she said, 'I'm the reason Mason can't see your daughter, and I want to fix that.'"

Mason looked at Remi, remembering her reaction when she'd found out he was putting off their visit. "She knows what it's like to miss seeing someone you care about. She didn't want me to let Brooklyn down."

"She didn't want you to miss out, either. She thought it was just as important for you to see Brooklyn and that you count on these visits as much as Brook does. She *sees* you, Mason, and that can only mean that you've let down those rock-hard walls of yours enough to let her in."

"It's new, but, Kris . . ." He shook his head. "I'm crazy about her, which makes this gig a million times harder. I want to be with her night and day, and I can't even fathom a day without her. Is that nuts? You *know* me. I've never let anyone in. How can I feel this way so fast?"

The spray of freckles across Krista's nose spread with her grin. "I'm the last person to ask about falling too fast. I knew I loved Shelton the night we met, and we were married four months later."

Mason looked at Remi, chatting animatedly as Brooklyn pulled her down a row of seats in the middle of the theater. Remi glanced over, their eyes connecting with newfound depth. She winked just as Brooklyn plunked into a seat and pulled her down beside her, breaking their connection. In those split seconds he knew that it wouldn't matter if she'd said he couldn't, or shouldn't, fall fast, because he was already there.

"We've started a project together to help foster kids." He told Krista about what they'd been working on all week, and then he said, "We should probably go sit down."

"Sounds like Remi was meant to be your other half." As they walked toward the row where Remi was sitting, Krista whispered, "Mase, listen to me. You and I both know there's no guarantee of tomorrow. I had true love and I don't want you to miss yours. If you're falling for her, then dive in with both feet and hold on with both hands. Life's too short for hesitation."

"Can I sit between you and Remi?" Brooklyn called out.

There went his chance to hold Remi's hand in the dark theater. *Christ, I'm reverting to a teenager.* Though the Harmony Pointe theater was small, it had large reclining seats, and he couldn't stop himself from picturing Remi straddling him in one. *Nope, not a teenager . . .*

"Sorry, Krista," Remi said, pulling him from his fantasy. "We're having fun talking, but I didn't mean to take your spot."

"It's all good," Krista said. "I'll sit beside you so we can chat, too."

"Mom, Remi's going to teach me to make invitations for my birthday party! And she and Mason are going to make birthday boxes for kids! Can we help? *Please?*"

"Absolutely." As Krista took a seat beside Remi, she looked up at Mason and mouthed, *Hold on tight.*

Remi gazed lovingly up at him as he walked past. Letting go wasn't even on his radar.

CHAPTER TWENTY

"EMILY BLUNT MAKES a good Mary Poppins, but she's got nothing on you, Remi," Krista said after the movie. "I can't thank you enough for setting this up. It was really special."

"Thank you." Brooklyn hugged Remi and said, "I can't wait to do the invitations."

"We'll have to coordinate with your mom on a date for that," Mason said, remembering Remi's desire to go away after filming. Brooklyn's birthday wasn't for another few months, so they had plenty of time.

"I'm looking forward to it, and I'm glad you and your mom will help with the birthday boxes." Remi glanced at Mason and said, "That means we'll all get to spend more time together."

He liked the sound of that.

"Maybe by then Mason will catch the bad guy who's bothering you," Brooklyn said hopefully.

That was the extent of what Remi and Krista had told Brooklyn about Remi's situation, and at ten, that was enough.

"If anyone can, it's Mason. Remi, since you're going to be in Harmony Pointe for a while, maybe we can all go to the Christmas tree lighting together in Chiffon Park." Krista eyed Mason with the nudging look she'd been giving him all afternoon. "What do you think, Mase?"

"Sounds great." He'd never been to a Christmas tree lighting, but the thought of doing anything with Remi sounded good to him.

He embraced Brooklyn and then he put his hand on her hat, angling her head back so she was looking up at him. "I'm really glad I got to see your funky mug."

A wide smile appeared on her adorable face, and she said, "I'm glad I got to see your funky mug, too." She hugged him tight and said, "I love you, Mason."

"I love you, too, kiddo."

"I'll call you," Krista said to Mason, and then to Remi, "I'll call you, too. Thank you again. This was a lot of fun, and I appreciate all the effort that went into making it happen."

After Brooklyn and Krista left through the front door, where Merrick was waiting to see them to their car, Mason drew Remi into his arms. They were alone in the theater, and even though they weren't out in public, it felt damn good to hold her outside of their house. "You are an amazing woman, Remi Aldridge, and I'm so glad you're mine."

"The feeling is mutual, Mr. Swift. Now, how about you kiss me like you'll never get another chance?"

He lowered his lips to hers and did just that, kissing her so thoroughly, it didn't take long before they were both breathless and groping for more. He reluctantly tore his mouth away and said, "I need to get you home before I take you right here."

She fluttered her long lashes and hooked her finger into the waistband of his jeans. "I've never messed around in a dark theater before, and we *do* have it all to ourselves until six."

"What about the manager?"

"He had strict orders to leave right after the movie ended, which Porter knows. I asked Porter to text me when he was gone, and . . . he's gone." She dragged her finger down the center of his chest. "Aiden's not the only one who knows how to give strict orders."

"My sweet Princess, you are *divine*." He recaptured her mouth as he lifted her into his arms and carried her into the dark theater.

Euphoric wasn't a big enough word to describe how Remi felt as they drove home after their secret tryst. "You know what I want more than anything else in the world?"

"Tell me." Mason's smile was soft and sated, the kind of smile that told her he was just as blissed out as she was.

"To be a regular couple with you, to walk down these streets holding hands, kissing when we want to, walking through the park. I know it's a tall order until everything is over, but please tell me you've figured out a way we can at least go to my cabin after filming and have a few days alone together."

He stopped at a red light and lifted her hand to his lips, kissing the back of it. "It's already set up, Princess. Piper and her friend Harley are going to come over to the house the evening filming ends. You and I are going to swap clothes with them, and Piper bought a blond wig for you to wear. Then we're going to take Harley's truck and head up to your cabin. If anyone's watching the house, they'll think we're still there."

"That's a great plan. But why Harley and not Bodhi? How do you even *know* Harley?"

The light turned green, and he turned off the main road, heading home. "Bodhi and Bridgette need to run their flower shop, so Bodhi helped me set it up with Piper and Harley. I haven't met Harley yet, although I spoke to him on the phone and did a complete background check. The problem is, they can't be seen around town while we're gone, because if we're pretending to be them when we leave, they have to pretend to be us. If they're spotted in town and the stalker is around here, it could tip him off. Piper made arrangements for her father to run her jobs from Wednesday through Sunday, and Harley has someone covering the bar. He was all too happy at the prospect of spending time alone with Piper."

"Oh, you have no idea how happy he probably is. He's had his eye on Piper for years. I'd love to be a fly on the wall when they're in the house together. Poor Harley will probably get turned down fifty times."

Mason cocked a grin. "Or maybe he won't get turned down . . ."

"For his sake, I hope he doesn't, but don't count on it. I don't know what's up between them, but he's got a heck of a long-lasting crush. But *yay*, because now we get time together. I'm excited! I'll contact the woman who takes care of my cabin and let her know we're coming."

"Shirley?"

"Yes. I forgot you knew my entire life history and everyone I have ever been in contact with. She'll give the cabin a good scrub down and get it ready for us, stock up the fridge, clean the sheets . . ."

A sharp sound blared from his phone. Mason pulled it out and opened a notification. He pushed the gas pedal to the floor, his jaw clenched tight.

"What is it?" Panic flooded her chest.

"Someone's by the front gate," he said through gritted teeth as they squealed around a corner, racing down their road.

"Mason! Is it *him*?"

He poked at the screen on the dashboard and instructed, "Call Porter." The phone rang through Bluetooth.

"I just got it," Porter said. "I'm on my way."

He poked at the screen again and an image appeared of a guy in a dark hooded sweatshirt in front of the gate. The hood blocked his face as he pushed something through the gate, then took off running into the woods across from it. Mason sped down the road white-knuckling the steering wheel, shoulders hunched forward. He slammed the vehicle into park and fumbled with the keys, unlocking the glove box. He took out a gun.

Remi pressed back against her seat, panic consuming her. "Mason!"

He shoved the keys into the ignition. "Get in the driver's seat and lock the doors. Do *not* get out of this car under any circumstances. Porter will be here in a minute, but I've got to go after this guy." He kicked open his door. "Lock the doors. Wait for Porter, or drive to Bodhi's and wait for me there, but do *not* get out of this car for anyone else."

He slammed the door closed and bolted into the woods in the same direction the guy had run. Fear rioted inside Remi—for Mason's safety, for her own, and knowing Mason had a gun with him, for the stalker who was running from him. That was crazy. She should *want* the guy to get shot, but she couldn't hope someone got killed.

Oh God, what if the other guy has a gun?

She put Mason in danger.

He could get hurt. *Killed.*

Her chest constricted.

Breathe, Remi. Just breathe.

She forced herself to move to the driver's seat and locked the doors. She gripped the steering wheel, but her heart was beating too fast, making it hard to breathe. Her mind raced. Should she drive to Bodhi's? She hated driving, and she didn't want to leave Mason. *Mason, oh God, please don't hurt Mason!*

Just breathe . . .

It seemed like hours that she sat there with her heart in her throat, gripping the steering wheel like a lifeline, before Porter showed up, but in reality, it was probably only three or four minutes.

She opened the door, her entire body shaking. "Is Mason okay?"

"He's safe. He's still trying to find the guy. Let's get you inside."

"I can't . . . Can you drive?"

"Of course." Porter helped her into the passenger seat and grabbed something out of the glove box.

She watched as he opened the gate and crouched to pick up whatever the guy had put through the gate. He put it into a plastic bag, which she realized he'd taken from the glove box, and then he got back into the SUV and drove up to the house.

"Mason's the best, Remi. He's going to be fine. We've got two more men scouring the woods, hunting this guy down, and another three guys on the way. Let's get you safe inside. I need to look at the footage."

She watched the gate close behind them, feeling too far away from Mason. She knew she had to be on *this* side of the gate, but she hated knowing anything could happen to him out there while he was protecting *her*. She leaned back against the seat, fisting her hands to try to stop them from shaking as she threw a prayer up to the powers that be, hoping with all her might that the universe wouldn't be cruel enough to take away another person she loved.

Remi paced the living room, her heart still hammering inside her chest. She thought Mason would be back by now, or at least call to give them an update. It had been more than an hour since he'd taken off, and almost as long since Porter went downstairs to the control room. Every time Remi looked at the tree she and Mason had decorated, she panicked and was hit with fresh tears. She couldn't bear the thought of something happening to Mason, and yet that was *all* she could think about—the stalker guy getting ahold of him. Even though she knew in her heart that if the guy got close, Mason would tear him apart. Which was why her stupid head kept taking her to darker places, places with unexpected guns and knives, pummeling her with images of Mason lying in the woods unconscious and bloody.

Breathe, breathe, breathe.

She'd been avoiding going downstairs in case Mason came in. She wanted to be right there waiting the second he came through the door to be sure he was okay, but she couldn't take it anymore. She ran down the steps and hurried down the long hallway to the steel door at the end. When Aiden had told her there was a security control center when he'd first rented the fortress, she'd told him he was crazy, that she was going to be just fine.

She was an idiot.

As she pushed open the heavy door, she was glad Aiden wasn't there to be as freaked out as she was, but equally glad that he'd taken such strong measures to keep her safe.

Porter turned as she walked in, his face a mask of seriousness. It was the face that had been ingrained in her mind during his time as her bodyguard. He stood in front of a wall of monitors. She could see him struggling to form the smallest of smiles as he said, "Hi. Are you okay?"

"No," she said honestly. "Did you see anything on the videos?"

"Nothing helpful. The guy kept his face shielded from the camera, and he was quick. He tossed the letter through the gates and took off. I've checked all the perimeter cameras. He hasn't been anywhere else on the property." His eyes darted to a letter on the desk, lying on top of the plastic bag she'd seen him put it in earlier.

She reached for it and he grabbed her wrist. "It's evidence. You can't touch it."

"Let go, Porter," she demanded.

"It's dark stuff, Remi. I sent a picture of it to Mason. I think he'll want to be with you when you read it."

Her stomach plummeted. "You talked to Mason? Is he okay?"

"He's fine." He nodded to one of the monitors on the far side of the wall. Mason was talking with several other men, including two policemen, down by the front gate. Several vehicles crowded the street in front of the house. "I've already sent copies of the footage to the police."

She was so relieved to see Mason, her words came out too soft. "Did they get the guy?"

The regret in Porter's eyes conveyed the answer before he said, "No, but we've got men canvassing the area."

Anger boiled inside her. "Porter, show me the letter."

"Remi—"

She lunged for it, but he was too fast, moving between her and the desk.

"Do you want to mess up this investigation?" he said sharply. "You get your fingerprints all over this and we're screwed."

"This is *my* life this guy is messing with!" She couldn't keep from yelling. "Show me that damn letter or I'll kick you so hard in your privates you won't walk for a week!"

With his jaw clenched tight, he picked up two pens and held the paper down on either side with their edges so she could read it and said, "Never let your opponent know what you'll do. Take action—don't threaten."

"I'll remember that," she said, shocked that even after she'd snapped at him, he was teaching her about safety. She glanced at the letter, recognizing the sloppy, tilted handwriting. "That's the same handwriting as the letters I got in LA."

"I know," he said with a bite of anger.

Bile rose in her throat as she read the letter.

Remi, every day without you is torture. Did you like my other letters? Have you been thinking about me as much as I've been thinking about you? Waiting to be together? Not a day goes by that I don't see your face. We were so close the other day, I thought our time had finally come! But you let that bastard bodyguard steal you away. I can't wait to tear off your panties with my teeth and use them to bind your wrists. I'm going to make that bastard watch while I fuck you in every way possible. He's going to regret the day he ever put his mouth on you. And you'll regret the day you let him. Our time is coming, my love.

Remi looked away, feeling sick and angry. Porter carefully folded the letter and slid it into the bag.

"I feel like I'm going to throw up," she said.

Porter took her by the shoulders, guiding her into the chair. "I'll get you some water."

"No. What I want is someone to get this sick person and put him behind bars. He's threatening me *and* Mason. How psychotic do you have to be to write those things to a stranger? To even *feel* them?"

"He's a stalker, Remi. The guy's clearly unstable."

She looked up at Porter. His features were soft and hard at once, like he wanted to kill someone but knew he should be empathetic for her. "I'm sorry I was such a shit to you and Merrick."

"You've already apologized, and you weren't a shit. You were in a difficult position."

"Well, I'm sorry. You were just doing your jobs." She pushed to her feet. "I *hate* this. I hate that *anyone* has the power to make me feel like this, and to take over my entire life. I mean, look at us. Mason chased a guy through the woods with a gun, we're in this . . . *room* that is right out of a suspense movie, and—"

The shrill ring of Porter's phone interrupted her. She held her breath as he answered it.

"Boss?"

Mason. She looked at the monitor and saw Mason pacing with the phone pressed to his ear.

"Yeah, she's right here. Okay. Got it." He ended the call and grabbed the plastic bag with the letter in it.

"What'd he say?" she asked anxiously.

"He's on his way in. The police are leaving. They need the letter."

She followed him out the door and up the stairs. "Did they find anything? What's the plan?"

"Mason will fill you in."

Mason came through the door looking even angrier than Porter. The veins in his neck and arms bulged like thick snakes, and his shoulders rode high, muscles corded tight.

"Mason!" She ran to him and wrapped her arms around him. He embraced her, but stood rigid, not hugging her the way he usually did. She felt his holster on his waist, and a chill ran down her back. He must have put that on after he got back to the SUV.

He pressed a chaste kiss to the top of her head, then pried her from his body, his eyes locked on Porter. "That it?"

Porter nodded curtly, then motioned with his head for Mason to follow him.

Mason grumbled, "Be right back," and followed him out the front door.

A second later she heard Mason hollering. "What the fuck, Porter?" She stumbled back as more shouts rang out. The door flew open, and Mason stormed past her, straight down the stairs.

"Mason?" She followed him. "What happened out there?"

His long legs ate up the distance to the control room. He pushed through the door and stalked to the desk, pounding at the keys, angrily shoving a mouse around, his eyes glued to the monitors. His jaw was clenched so tight it had to hurt.

"Would you talk to me? Please? Why were you yelling at Porter?" She studied the monitors, trying to figure out what he was doing—and then she saw it. The image of the stalker pushing the letter through the gate. Mason zoomed in on his face, shielded by the hood and shrouded in shadows.

"Porter had no business showing you that letter," he seethed, zooming in on the guy's body, his chest, then his jeans, and last his sneakers.

"This is *my* life, Mason. I need to know what's going on."

"Fuck!" He shoved the keyboard away and punched the keyboard tray, snapping it in half. He spun around with rage in his eyes and grabbed her by the arms, his fingers digging into her muscles, nostrils flaring. "Not like *that*. Not without me."

"How would you being here change *anything*? I needed to see it!"

His eyes bored into her. "Because *I'm* the one who loves you! *I'm* supposed to be there to protect you from shit like that. I should have been there when you read that disgusting letter from the sick fuck, not Porter!"

Her jaw dropped, and tears flooded her cheeks. Love and anguish battled for dominance in his eyes as he pulled her trembling body against his hard frame, cocooning her within his arms.

"I *hate* that you had to read something so demented. The bastard slipped right through my fingers." He released her abruptly, pacing, his hands fisting. "I was only two minutes behind him. I should have *had* him." He twisted his fist in the air, baring his teeth like a rabid dog. "And that goddamn letter. I'm going to tear that fucker to pieces."

Her heart was going to beat right out of her chest. How could such an awful event spur the most magical moment of her life? Did he even realize he'd said he loved her? Or was he just caught up in the moment?

"Mason?" she said just above a whisper.

He stopped pacing and blinked several times, as if he had to clear the fog of rage from his eyes.

She went to him with her heart in her throat and said, "Breathe, Mason. Just breathe."

He scrubbed a hand down his face, then gathered her in his arms with a gentler touch, with the warmth and protectiveness she'd come to love and expect. There were so many emotions coursing through her she couldn't separate them, but one rose above the fear, above the anger and confusion.

"I'm sorry, Princess," he said vehemently, his cheek resting on the top of her head, his hand moving soothingly up and down her back.

"You *love* me?" she asked shakily.

He framed her face within his hands, and a smile pushed the anger from his eyes as he said, "I'm not making a great case for you to love me back right now, but I do, Remi. I love you, and it kills me that this is happening to you."

"Happening to *us*," she said softly. "I love you, too, and I'm sorry for dragging you into this."

"*Shh.* Don't say that."

He sat on the chair and guided her onto his lap. She wound her arms around his neck, and he buried his face in her chest. They held each other as the fear and anger shifted, allowing their love to fill the silence.

After a long while, Mason gazed lovingly into her eyes and said, "Before you, I was just existing. I'd rather be living through this mess with you than spend another day without you."

CHAPTER TWENTY-ONE

MASON STOOD AT the bedroom window late Sunday morning with his cell phone pressed to his ear, updating Aiden, as he'd done every day since they'd found the letter. "The handwriting matched the letters received in LA, but we're coming up empty at identifying the perp. We've tried to identify everything we could, from the manufacturer of his hoodie to the tread of his sneakers, but you know New York woods in September—the ground is covered with leaves. We've canvassed the surrounding homes, looking into anyone who matched the height description and didn't have an alibi, but it's like searching for a needle in a haystack."

"How's Remi really holding up? Is she giving you any more trouble?"

He glanced at Remi sprawled across the bed, her pink panties peeking out from beneath the T-shirt of his she'd slept in. He'd taught her to play strip poker last night, and she'd played him like a violin, *purposely* losing. His chest swelled with love—and guilt for not telling Aiden the truth about them.

"Your sister is braver and stronger than any woman I've ever met."

"She's a pistol, but don't let her fool you, Mason. Beneath all that gusto, she's as vulnerable as a kitten."

"I know," he said, remembering the way she'd tried to hold it together the night they'd found the letter, but once they were lying in bed and she was safely nestled within his arms, she'd surrendered to the relentless fear that she'd been holding back all evening and sobbed her sweet little heart out. "Don't worry. I'm taking good care of her."

"Thank you, Mason. She's all I have in this world, and I'd like to kill the bastard who's doing this to her."

"You and me both. When are you coming back?"

"Next Sunday."

He knew Aiden owned several houses, and he was curious about what *home* meant to the man who had raised the woman he loved. "Where is *home* for you, Aiden?"

Aiden didn't hesitate to say, "Wherever my sister happens to be at the moment. This month it's Harmony Pointe."

For me, too.

When Mason had bought his loft in the city, he'd thought he'd finally put down roots, but he worked so much it wasn't anything more than a place to rest his head. After only three weeks, the fortress felt like more of a home than any other structure ever had, and he knew it was because of the beautiful woman he shared it with.

"Remi's wrapping up filming on Wednesday. She wants to head to her cabin for a few days. Think you can meet us there? I know she'd like to see you."

Between filming, soliciting donations for their project, and coordinating with the staff of CCF to bring the effort to fruition, Remi's schedule was bursting at the seams. She needed that time off. She needed a hell of a lot more time than that.

He couldn't shake the image of the guy at the gate, and he fought the anger it sowed with everything he had on a daily basis. He never wanted Remi to bear the burden of his wrath again. He was looking forward to spiriting her away for a few days, knowing that Porter and Merrick would be staying nearby and accompanying them wherever they went, while the rest of his men would keep an eye on things in Harmony Pointe and alert him if anything suspicious popped up.

"Of course. But that's pretty remote. Are you sure it's safe?"

Remi rolled over, arching her back and stretching like a cat, toes pointed, arms over her head. She looked sleepily at Mason and mouthed, *Who's that?*

He mouthed, *Aiden.*

She scowled and stepped from the bed, sauntering over to him with a seductive look in her eyes. Her hair was messy and tangled, and his T-shirt hung nearly to her knees. She was stunning. Ever since he'd confessed his love for her, he'd been seeing images in his mind of the two of them years from now, with children underfoot. He had visions of Remi teaching their little girl to make ornaments and a little trouble-making boy wreaking havoc, the little girl chasing her brother as he scampered away with her supplies, giggling. For a man who had never imagined being in love, much less having a family, the images were as overwhelming as they were enticing. For the first time in his life, Mason was looking at a future with hope and inspiration.

"We wouldn't be going if I didn't think she'd be safe," he said to Aiden.

As he told Aiden their plans to get Remi out of town without anyone other than Piper, Harley, and Bodhi knowing, Remi did her best to distract him.

She kissed his chest, trailing her tongue along his nipple. He gritted his teeth as she kissed a path lower, slowing to trace the ridges of his abs with her tongue.

"Sounds like you've thought of everything," Aiden said. "How long will you be at the cabin?"

Remi hooked her fingers into the hips of Mason's briefs and drew them down to his ankles, palming his cock with a boastful look in her eyes. She teased the head with her tongue. Mason clenched his teeth, and said, "Through the weekend."

She mouthed, *Hang up*, then lowered her mouth over his cock, taking him to the back of her throat. He inhaled sharply and fisted his hand in her hair, tugging her head so she couldn't miss his warning glare.

Her eyes went dark and predatory as she again mouthed, *Hang up!*

He loved when she got demanding. "Aiden, I've got to run. We'll see you Sunday?"

"For sure. Thanks, Mason."

He ended the call, and in one quick move he lifted Remi up and tossed her on the bed, coming down over her. She laughed as he shoved his phone to the other side of the mattress and tore off her panties. When she bit his shoulder, he growled with pleasure.

"You think you're funny?" He trapped her hands beside her head, nudging her legs open with his knees.

"*Hilarious!*" She wiggled to align their bodies with a self-satisfied smirk. "You should have seen your face."

"Forget mine. I can't wait to see *yours*."

He buried the head of his cock in her tight heat, fighting the urge to thrust in deep. She lifted her hips, trying to take him deeper, and he rocked back, withdrawing completely.

"Mason!" she pleaded.

He kissed the edges of her lips, teasing her with just the tip, then withdrawing again.

She rocked up as he pushed in a little deeper, and she hissed, "*Yes.*"

He pulled out, enjoying the way her eyes filled with determination.

"You promised to keep Aiden *out* of our bedroom, remember?" she said heatedly.

"He called, and I didn't want to leave the room. Can you blame me for wanting to be close to you?"

He repeated the exquisite torture, pushing in just enough to drive them both wild with desire. She whimpered, and the sweet sounds tore at his heart. *Fuck*, it was hard to deny her. He covered her mouth with his, and she wound her legs around his hips as he sank deeper into her. She felt so good, so *right*, a moan tore from his lungs.

He gazed into her victorious eyes and said, "I want to disappear into you, Princess."

She grinned as she said, "I think you already have."

His forehead fell to her shoulder with his chuckle. "God, I love you."

Their mouths came together as their bodies took over, and they moved to their own private beat. Their lovemaking had become richer since they'd said those three little words. The knots from holding back had loosened, and then those heartstrings had tangled between them. Now, as they loved each other with all they had, Mason lost himself in the feel of her softness against him, her sweetness swallowing every inch of him. He quickened his efforts, kissing her more passionately, and her thighs tightened around him.

Her head fell back, and she panted out, "Don't stop."

"Never—"

Heat skated down his spine, and he struggled to stave off his own release as he pounded into her. He pushed his hands beneath her bottom, angling her hips to take him deeper the way they both craved. Instantly, her inner muscles tightened, and her nails dug into his flesh. Electricity scorched through him as his name sailed from her lips like a plea—"*Mason!*"

He stayed with her, determined to feel her come again, thrusting faster, loving her harder. Her desperate, sexy sounds took him higher. When she cried out his name a second time, a rush of heat shot down his spine, and he surrendered to his own powerful release. They lay clinging to each other, riding their waves of passion, until Remi lay limp and panting beneath him, and Mason tried to remember how to breathe.

"Let's disappear together," she whispered against his neck, "and never come up for air."

He shifted beside her and cradled her against him, burying his face in her neck. She smelled fresh as summer rain. He pressed a kiss there and said, "I'm right there with you," earning a warm, appreciative sound.

"For real, Mason," she said. "I'm sick of hiding and living a life fraught with fear. After Aiden comes back—"

"Uh-uh," he teased. "No *A-name* in the bedroom, remember?"

She huffed out a small, adorably frustrated sound. "After we tell *him* everything, I just want to be with you. I don't care if I have to pay Porter and your team to follow us everywhere until the stalker is caught. I want to go out together and not care about headlines or any of that. I want to hang out with our friends, go into the city and have dinner with Chuck and Estelle so I can get to know the man who changed your life and the woman he loves. I just want what we have right here and now to fill up every aspect of our lives."

"I want that, too, Princess, more than anything."

"But you're Mr. Protector." She ran her fingers down his arm. "Do you think you'll love me when the threat is gone? When I'm just a regular woman, without a stalker and when I'm not filming a movie? Because the more I get involved with CCF, the more I think I might want to take additional time off just to *be . . .*"

"Is that a serious question?"

She shrugged.

"My sweet, sexy, challenging girl, you could never be *just a regular woman*. You're Remington Aldridge. You were born to be extraordinary, no matter what you're doing." He kissed her softly. "And in case you don't believe me, I plan on cherishing you every minute of every day, reminding you just how extraordinary you are."

Later that afternoon, Remi lay sprawled over Mason's delicious body on a lounge chair on the patio, relaxing after days of nonstop stress. They'd already gotten their workout done for the day—in bed and in the gym.

The sun beat down on them, but Remi was under no misconceptions about her burly bodyguard actually relaxing. His laptop sat beside him, showing live feeds from the outside cameras, and he'd barely taken his eyes off it. It had taken practically an act of God to get Mason to allow himself to be close and try to relax with her outside, but in the end, she knew he needed it as much as she did.

Her phone vibrated on the table, and Mason snagged it, eyeing her with a cocky grin. "It'll cost you."

"After last night and this morning, I should have quite a tab built up."

He pressed his lips to hers and said, "I'll never get enough of your kisses, Princess."

He handed her the phone, and she kissed him again. "Me either. I might have to ask friends to text more often."

She opened the text and said, "It's from Piper," and then she read it aloud. "'Hey, *horndogs*.'" Remi rolled her eyes. "'Think you can come up for air long enough to come to Willow's for a barbecue at five? We need your hottieguard for a sixth.'"

"Sixth?" Mason asked.

"No idea. It's *Piper*. Lord only knows." She thumbed out, *6th?* and pressed *send.*

Piper's response rolled in, and Remi read it aloud. "'Basketball team. He owes me for my upcoming slumber party with Harley.'"

"Piper plays basketball?"

"With the guys, believe it or not. I hope you can shoot hoops, because they're really good."

"There's nothing I can't do, beautiful, and she's right. I do owe her for taking all that time off when we go away."

"I love how sneaky you are."

"Only when we've got to be, Princess." He kissed the tip of Remi's nose and said, "What should we bring to the barbecue?"

"For a guy who doesn't host parties, you're very knowledgeable about party etiquette." She crawled over him, smiling down at the man who had single-handedly changed her life, and said, "I'm bringing my hottieguard. I think that's enough, don't you?"

He tickled her ribs and she collapsed onto him in a fit of laughter. "Am I ever going to live down that name?"

"Nope. I love having my own hottieguard."

He swept her beneath him, laughing right along with her as he said, "And I love *you*, beautiful."

His lips met hers in a luxurious kiss, showing just how much he did. Remi's favorite times were when it was just the two of them like this. There was no better feeling than letting their emotions run free. She loved waking up in Mason's arms, knowing she could straddle him on the workout bench and tease him until he was too aroused to walk away, kiss him when she walked by, or make love to him on a blanket on the floor surrounded by candles.

Assuming Ben and Aurelia were going to the barbecue, Remi and Mason wouldn't be able to snuggle on a lounge chair, hold hands, or kiss. A sense of loss moved through her. She debated declining the invitation, because lying in the sun with Mason without having to hide anything about their relationship sounded better than any amount of time with friends ever could. But Piper was right—they owed her, and it would be well worth it. In a few days they'd have Remi's cabin all to themselves. Even though Porter and Merrick would be staying nearby *just in case*, the idea of being together an hour away from where the threats had gone down felt a heck of a lot like a much-needed vacation.

CHAPTER TWENTY-TWO

"NICE SHOT, BABY!" Willow cheered across her backyard as Piper and the guys played a game of three-on-three, while the girls and Roxie sat around the patio table nibbling on snacks and admiring the view. It was shirts—Mason, Piper, and Zane—versus skins—Ben, Bodhi, and Derek. Louie was playing on both teams, adorably darting between the players, trying to be like one of the big guys, and Dan was refereeing the game, which really meant he was walking around the edge of the court cheering them on.

The girls were mooning over their men, and Remi was doing her fair share of that, too, though she reluctantly kept her comments to herself, which sucked.

Talia leaned her chin on her palm, gazing dreamily at her fiancé. "Derek is really beautiful, isn't he?"

"Listen to my proper sister gushing over her man," Bridgette said. "Derek might be beautiful, but Bodhi is the hottest guy out there. Look at all those muscles just waiting to be touched."

Sorry, Bridge, but not even Bodhi can hold a candle to Mason.

"Sorry, girls," Aurelia said, bouncing Bea on her lap, "I know he's your brother, but there is absolutely nothing sexier than Ben Dalton shirtless, sweaty, and kicking butt on a basketball court. Except maybe Benny boy changing Bea's diaper. There's definitely something to be said about a man taking care of his baby. Right, sweet pea?" She rubbed noses with Bea.

Remi eyed Mason in his black shorts and tank top. His powerful legs carried him swiftly across the court, his muscular arms waving as he covered Bodhi, who was trying to take a shot.

"Come on, Bodhi!" Bridgette hollered. "Get around that hottie-guard!" She turned an apologetic expression to Remi and said, "Sorry."

"Don't be." *My man won't let him get by.* "I doubt anyone can get past Mason."

Bodhi took a shot, and Mason jumped, knocking the ball to Piper, who dribbled like a pro. She wove between the burly men and took a shot, which fell effortlessly through the hoop, and cheers rang out.

Remi threw her arms up. "Nice pass, Mason! Great shot, Piper!"

"That's my girl!" Roxie hollered.

Piper high-fived Mason and Zane, who then high-fived each other.

"Nice play, Piper," Derek said, earning a scowl from Ben.

"Lucky shot," Ben grumbled, and took the ball out of bounds.

"Lucky my ass, loser." Piper scoffed.

"You've got this, Ben!" Aurelia called out as the players moved into position.

Bea babbled, "*Dadadadada.*" She looked sweet in tiny pink-and-white-striped leggings and a pink shirt.

"That's right, baby girl, cheer for Daddy." Roxie tickled Bea's chin, earning a drooly smile.

On the court, Zane nudged Mason and said, "You're not so bad, *hottieguard,*" with a chuckle.

Mason shook his head. "Keep it up, buddy."

"No probs in that department," Zane said.

"That's right!" Willow hollered. "My man is badass, on the court and in the—"

"Willow!" Roxie glared at her.

"What? I was going to say in the . . ." Willow bit her lower lip, her brow furrowing. "Oh, come on, someone help me out."

"Boardroom?" Aurelia suggested.

"Nope, Zane's not a boardroom guy," Bridgette said. "How about in the loft? Since he used to stay in yours above the bakery?"

"That works. Mom, you okay with that?" Willow teased.

Roxie smiled. "Honestly? I'm not even sure why I interrupted you like that. Everyone here has sex."

"Mom!" Bridgette snapped. "We don't want to think about that with you and Dad!"

Roxie pointed at her daughters and said, "One day you're going to be my age, and I hope you'll still be having sex then. *Sheesh*. I'm human just like you."

"Stop," Willow said. "Now I need to erase that visual from my brain." She looked pointedly at Zane. "Ah, that's better."

Remi loved their banter. Mason looked over, and their eyes caught, electricity eating up the space between them.

Aurelia's and Roxie's brows lifted curiously.

"It looks like your hottieguard might have more than basketball and bodyguarding on his mind," Aurelia said.

Willow and Bridgette turned knowingly toward Remi, and a hint of jealousy prickled her spine, because they could publicly claim their men, while she had to pretend hers was only with her for his job. It was hard enough keeping their relationship a secret on set. She hated keeping secrets from close friends like Ben and Aurelia.

Roxie pushed to her feet and said, "Remi, while these ladies drool over their men, why don't you help me bring dessert out?"

Glad to get out from under the cloud of guilt hanging over her, Remi said, "That sounds great. Should we bring out some drool cloths, too?" She followed Roxie inside.

"Those girls are something else." Roxie went to the counter and opened the Sweetie Pie Bakery box. "Can you please get a platter from the cabinet, sweetheart?"

"Sure." Remi set the platter on the counter.

As they transferred pastries from the box to the platter, Roxie said, "I snuck a peek at the sample boxes Willow brought for your project from her distributor. They're really adorable. I can't wait to see the duffel bags."

They'd sent several sample boxes, decorated with images of teddy bears, sports items, hearts, books, and even skateboards. They clearly had a wide selection for all ages.

"We hope to get them next week," Remi said. "But we've requested solid colors for those, since the kids could use them for years."

"That was smart. I'm putting together a special happiness and positivity potion for the soaps, shampoos, and body washes I'm going to donate. Nothing wrong with adding a little extra sparkle to their days, right?"

"You can say that again. Mason and I are excited to get started. We're just waiting for CCF to get some administrative things in order before we can finalize the logistics. I can't get over how much support we're getting from your family and *everyone*. We've already confirmed donations of pajamas from JRB Designs, toothpaste from Sparkle White, hairbrushes and combs from Groom Me, and a bunch of other personal items for the duffels. And several toy manufacturers, including Stackables, which was Piper's brilliant idea, have agreed to donate to the birthday boxes."

Roxie set a pastry on the platter and said, "Piper has always marched to her own beat. She never wanted anything to do with dolls or dresses."

"Well, you did something right raising her. I'd give anything to be as tough as she is."

"You are every bit as tough as Piper, sweetheart." Roxie's voice softened as she turned her attention from the pastries to Remi and said,

"You're under a lot of pressure, and I'm sure you miss your parents a lot at times like these. I'm here if you want to talk."

"Thank you. I appreciate that."

"I can only imagine how difficult it is with those awful threats coming when you least expect them and Aiden so far away. Not to mention suddenly having a handsome, virile man watching over you."

Remi walked over to the window to escape Roxie's knowing eyes and said, "I've had other bodyguards, remember?"

Outside, the girls were cheering as Louie zipped between Bodhi and Mason, clutching the basketball against his belly. Mason scooped him up and held him beside the basketball hoop. Louie dunked the ball and threw his hands up victoriously. Then he wrapped his arms around Mason's neck, hugging him tight. Mason returned the embrace with a smile that shot straight to Remi's heart.

"Yes, I remember the men you ran away from." Roxie glanced out the window as Mason set Louie on the ground and fist-bumped Bodhi.

As if Mason felt the heat of Remi's gaze, he looked over, his eyes trained on Remi, until Zane swatted him on the back. Mason lunged toward Zane, laughing when Zane took off running.

"It looks to me like this one is here to stay."

Shock at Roxie's words snapped Remi's thoughts back in line. Roxie arched a brow with a matronly expression that told Remi she had seen what Remi had felt. She shouldn't be shocked. Roxie had a sixth sense for love.

"Oh, Roxie." Remi sat down at the kitchen table and lowered her face to her hands. "Aiden's going to kill me."

Roxie stroked Remi's head. Remi lifted her face from her hands as Roxie sat down beside her and said, "Honey, why would Aiden kill you for finding happiness?"

"Maybe because he's *Aiden*," she said sarcastically. "You know how his mind works. To him I'm still a broken little girl. No matter how often I prove I can handle myself, he will always see me that way. Plus, he *hired* Mason, and Mason's nine years older than me. Aiden is going to twist everything around and say Mason took advantage of me." She sat back with a long exhalation.

"So you *haven't* told Aiden about the fire brewing between you two?"

"Are you crazy? Aiden would have been on the first plane home, blown his business deal, *and* ruined my chance to be with Mason. We're telling him when he comes back this Sunday. I haven't even said anything to Aurelia because I'm afraid Ben will find out, and I can't ask him not to tell Aiden."

Roxie patted Remi's hand and said, "Honey, I understand why you're nervous about telling Aiden, but he's a caring brother. He might have a hard time with it, but he loves you above all else, and he'll come to grips with it."

Remi glanced out the patio doors, and her pulse quickened. Mason was heading in their direction. "Ever since we lost our parents, we've been Aiden and Remi, a *unit*, like peanut butter and jelly. And now I want so badly to be Mason and Remi, a *couple*. But I have no idea how to tell Aiden."

"I have a feeling that when the time comes, you'll take one look at Mason and you won't be able to hold it in."

Mason came through the door and put a hand on Remi's shoulder, bending down like he was going to kiss her. Her heart skipped a beat. He stopped short, clearing his throat as he straightened his spine, awkwardly patting her shoulder, and said, "Everything okay in here?"

Roxie pushed to her feet and said, "Very much so. Is the game over?"

"No. I just wanted to check on Remi." He hiked his thumb over his shoulder. "Mind if I use the bathroom?"

"Not at all." A mischievous look rose in Roxie's eyes as she picked up the tray of pastries and said, "Remi, why don't you show him where it is."

"Sure. It's right down the hall," Remi said, hurrying Mason toward the bathroom.

"What was that about?" he asked.

"This."

She pushed him into the bathroom, shutting the door behind them, and plastered her lips to his. He deepened the kiss, loosening the knots that had formed when she was talking about Aiden. Mason's arms circled her, crushing her against his familiar, broad chest, tying those unknotted strings into pretty little bows. He leaned back against the door, widening his stance, and guided her between his legs as he slid lower, bringing them face-to-face.

He tucked her hair behind her ear and said, "Hello, beautiful. I've missed you."

"Only you could make a bathroom feel romantic." She pressed her lips to his and said, "Roxie knows. I didn't tell her—she just *knew*."

"I'm not surprised. I can't keep my eyes off you." He kissed her cheek and bowed his head, speaking low, directly in her ear. "It's getting harder every day, and when we were out there, I wanted to tell everyone you're mine."

A hard rap at the door startled them. Remi pressed her finger over her lips, shushing Mason as he moved slowly away from the door.

"I'm going to be a minute," she said loudly. "You might want to use another bathroom."

She tried not to laugh as Mason pulled her into his arms and whispered, "That was brilliant."

She gave him another long, loving kiss. And then she flushed the toilet and ran the faucet. "But you haven't gone to the bathroom yet. I'll go out, and you can act like you snuck in before the next person. Ready?"

She opened the door, and they found Ben, with his arms crossed and an annoyed look in his dark eyes. "Are you shitting me?"

"Mason was just helping me—"

"Don't even try to cover it up, Remi." He scowled at Mason. "The look in your eyes tells me everything I need to know."

Mason stepped forward and said, "Ben, it's not what you think. I love Remi. This isn't a meaningless hookup."

"But you can't tell Aiden," Remi said anxiously. "We're going to tell him next Sunday when he gets back."

Ben scoffed. "Remi, come on. I'm not going to lie to your brother. I don't work that way, and you know it."

"Benjamin Dalton!" Roxie strode down the hall, pointing up at her son as she said, "First of all, we don't tattle on family, and Remi is family. And second, you lied to yourself for years about your feelings for Aurelia. I think you can bite your tongue for one week."

"*Seriously*, Mom? Aiden's my business partner." Ben ground out a curse.

"Watch your language and go take care of your lovely soon-to-be wife and adorable daughter, and leave these two lovebirds alone. They have enough stress keeping Remi safe." Roxie nudged Ben down the hall, winking at Mason and Remi.

Mason said, "I love that woman."

As he pulled Remi into his arms, Aurelia came rushing down the hall toward them, eyes wide. "You two are a *couple* and I have to find out from Ben grumbling about not telling Aiden? What the heck, Remi? I share my grandmother with you!"

"I'm sorry!" Remi pleaded. "But I've got a crazy stalker threatening me *and* Mason. The last thing I wanted was for Ben to find out and tell Aiden!"

"Oh, don't worry about that. Roxie and I will make sure he keeps his mouth shut." She wrapped her arms around both Remi and Mason, earning the cutest confused expression from Mason as she said, "I'm so happy for you guys!"

"Aurelia?" Ben appeared at the end of the hall. "Oh, hell *no*. This is not happening. Jesus, Mason, you've got your own woman." He hauled Aurelia down the hall, all of them laughing as he looked over his shoulder and said, "Seven days, Aldridge. That's all you get before I come clean to Aiden!"

"That's all I need," Remi called after him. Then she grabbed the front of Mason's shirt, tugging him down to her height, and said, "But I need a *lot* more than that with you . . ."

CHAPTER TWENTY-THREE

"I CAN'T BELIEVE how fast this last week has flown by," Remi said as she and Mason took one last look around her trailer to make sure they hadn't left anything behind. She'd already packed up her belongings and Porter had taken them back to the house, but as with everything else, Mason was being thorough, giving the place a last once-over.

Filming had wrapped on schedule, and thankfully, there had been no more threats from the stalker. They'd both hoped the stalker would be caught by now, and Mason had worried that the stalker might get bolder as filming wound down. He said he might see it as his last chance to get to her, which not only scared Remi for her own safety, but for Mason's.

She watched Mason checking beneath cushions, muscles strewn tight, expression serious, and wished she could take the weight of their world from his shoulders. She knew Mason was frustrated. It wasn't his fault all the leads had led to dead ends, but she knew he took it as such. Earlier that morning, he'd met with his team to go over instructions one last time before they left for the cabin. Porter and Merrick were set to follow them out of town and stay nearby.

"Hey, you." She put her arms around him from behind, pressing a kiss to his back, and felt him relax a little. "I think we've checked and rechecked enough times."

He turned, and his gaze softened in the way it did only when he looked at her.

"Come here." She took his hand and led him to the couch. When he sat down, she straddled his lap in her shorts and long-sleeve shirt, earning a heated look and the cocky grin she loved. She put her arms around his neck, bringing their faces closer. "This wasn't where we had our first kiss, but it's where we had our first best kiss."

His big hands slid up her back and his fingers threaded into her hair. "I'll never forget either of those kisses." He pressed his warm lips to her neck, and then he opened his mouth, sucking just hard enough to make her hot all over.

"You always drive me crazy," she said breathlessly.

He tugged her mouth down to his and shifted her onto her back on the cushions as he had the very first time, moving his hard body over her. His hands tangled in her hair, holding her as his willing captive for him to devour. She craved this closeness, the feel of his weight bearing down on her, his love consuming her. She'd waited her whole life for their love, their kisses. Their love wasn't just passionate. It was safe and empowering, mind-numbing and demanding. It was all-consuming and possessed a dreamy intimacy so luxurious, she wanted to crawl inside it and burrow down for the winter.

A greedy noise rumbled up his chest and she rocked beneath him. She couldn't get enough of him, and she knew she never would. She tugged up on the back of his shirt, pushing her hands beneath, feeling his glorious muscles flex, drawing hungry moans from both of them. A knock at the door startled her, and she jerked beneath him, but Mason didn't relent. He held her tighter, kissing her harder, and she surrendered to him as he took and gave in equal measure.

Another knock sounded, and Mason reluctantly drew back, biting out, "I hate coming up for air."

She was right there with him as he kissed her softly and they both got up. "The quicker we get out of here, the faster we can leave town and be alone."

He answered the door. "Hey, Raz. What's up?"

Remi peered around Mason at Raz, wearing his favorite hoodie and jeans. He looked more like the boy next door than a movie star. "Hi, Raz. We were just getting ready to leave. Are we all set, Mason?"

"Yeah. We're good to go." Mason followed her out of the trailer, standing protectively beside her, his keen eyes taking in their surroundings.

There was a flurry of activity as tents and canopies were disassembled, equipment was moved and secured for transport. People rushed from one location to the next, moving in and out of trailers, gathering in small groups, talking animatedly as the weight of filming lifted. Fans lined up along the sidewalk with cell phones, taking pictures and videos, calling out to the actors as they passed by. Remi had become adept at tuning them out.

"I just wanted to say goodbye," Raz said. "It was a lot of fun filming together again."

"Where are you going?" Remi waved to Carl and Tillie, who were heading their way.

"Home to Peaceful Harbor to see my family. You know I always need a good dose of normalcy after filming."

"I hear ya. I'm escaping, too, heading to my cabin," she said as Carl and Tillie joined them. "Thanks for everything, you guys. You make my life so much easier."

"Are you coming to the wrap party tonight?" Tillie asked.

"I'm heading out," Raz said.

"Me too. Sorry I'll miss it, though," Remi said.

Tillie grinned and said, "We'll have a good enough time for both of you."

"Safe travels," Carl said, and they walked off.

"Any news on the asshole who's harassing you?" Raz asked.

"Not yet," Remi said.

"You know if you ever need a place to hide out, you're always welcome to hang with me." He hugged Remi.

"Thanks, Raz. I appreciate it, but I'm in good hands."

"Mason, it was nice to meet you." Raz shook Mason's hand. "I hope you catch the guy before our promotional events start, but if not, then I'm sure I'll see you again."

Mason nodded. "We're doing our best to nail him. Have a safe trip home."

Remi and Mason made the rounds of the lot, saying goodbye to the cast and crew, before heading home.

As they drove off the lot, Remi realized this would be the last time she'd be leaving a film set for a very long time. She reached for Mason's hand, looking forward to discovering another side of herself, one she'd happily spend years exploring.

Remington Aldridge, *girlfriend.*

By late afternoon, Operation Identity Swap, as Remi had deemed it, was underway. Remi and Mason were dressed identically to Piper and Harley, and hopefully, they would soon slip out of town unnoticed. Remi looked hot in tight faded jeans, work boots, a gray T-shirt that had LET'S GET HAMMERED written across the chest, and a red-and-gray flannel shirt with the sleeves folded up to just below her elbows.

"How do I look as a blonde?" Remi patted her straight blond wig, fluttering her lashes.

"Princess, you could have blue hair—or no hair at all—and you'd still be the hottest woman on the planet." Mason hauled her against him and pressed his lips to hers. "But for the record, I prefer you *au naturel.*"

"Okay, guys," Piper said. "Can you leave now? Seriously, all this mushy shit is making me a little sick."

"I'll break her of that by the time you get back." Harley smirked as he picked up the cardboard box containing Remi's and Mason's belongings for the trip. He was a grizzly of a man, solid and thick, with brown hair and deep-set blue eyes that had been looking hungrily at Piper since they'd arrived. He and Mason were dressed in navy Henleys, dark jeans, and black leather boots. Harley's hair was a little longer than Mason's, but before they left, Harley would give Mason his Dutch's Pub hat. With that on, Mason would look close enough to pass for Harley.

"In your dreams, Dutch, especially now that you've shaved that beard. That took you down a notch on the hotness meter." Piper tapped the box and said, "Get that thing outside so they can get out of here."

Harley rubbed his clean-shaven chin and said, "I'll grow that puppy back in a few days. Trust me, you'll enjoy the scratch of scruff on your thighs."

Piper rolled her eyes.

Mason reached for the box. "I'll take that out."

"Nah, I've got it," Harley said as he headed for the door. "This is the last time I'll get outside until Sunday night."

Mason had covered all their bases. He'd given Piper and Harley a rundown on the security system and the control room. They were armed with phone numbers for each of Mason's guys who were remaining in the area, as well as Porter, Merrick, and Mason's IT specialist in case they had trouble with the security system.

"I can't believe we packed in a cardboard box," Remi said. "But honestly, I'd go without bringing a single scrap of clothing. It'll be great to get away from the place where most of the stalker stuff has gone down."

"I doubt you'll *need* more than a scrap of clothing." Piper chuckled and said, "I do think the box is genius, though. If that creepy freak *is* watching, it would look weird for anyone to carry a suitcase out. But a cardboard box? That's about as normal as life gets."

When Harley came back inside, he relinquished his hat and keys to Mason, swung an arm around Piper's shoulder, and said, "Have fun, kids."

Piper shrugged him off. "Mason, you set up the cage in the basement, right?"

Harley waggled his brows. "Cool. Didn't realize you were into kink."

"*Oh my gosh.*" Remi blushed. "I can see you two are going to have an interesting time." She hugged Piper. "I can't thank you enough. You have no idea how much I'm looking forward to a few days without worrying about every move we make."

"If I were you, I'd never leave the cabin." Piper handed Remi an oversized bag she'd carried in with her. "I got you a few things for your road trip."

"Aw, thank you," Remi said, digging through the goodies. "M&M's, Skittles, protein bars. All our favorites." She pulled out a strip of condoms, eyes wide. "Um . . . ?"

They all laughed.

Remi handed the condoms to Harley and said, "Good luck with that."

"He'll need more than luck," Piper said.

Remi hugged Harley, looking tiny in his arms, and said, "Thank you. We owe you both big-time."

"After what you've been through, it's payback enough knowing you'll finally get a few days of peace," Harley said.

Piper gave Remi and Mason a playful shove toward the door and said, "Now, get out of here so we can raid your cupboards and make good use of that media room."

"Don't forget to lock the doors," Mason said as he put on Harley's hat. "And call if you notice anything out of the ordinary."

Remi and Mason headed out to Harley's shiny red dual-cab truck. As Mason drove down the long driveway, he squeezed Remi's hand and said, "Like this ride better than my *overkill* SUV?"

"I like any vehicle if you and I are in it."

"Me too, Princess. Here's to our clandestine escape."

Mason drove through the gate, waiting in the road as it closed. "Hey, Princess . . ." His eyes caught on movement out the tinted window, in the woods. The hair on the back of his neck stood on end as he leaned forward to get a better look.

"What are you looking at?"

Remi turned to look out her window at the same second the silhouette of a man came into focus. She gasped as the man turned and ran deeper into the woods.

Mason slammed the truck into park, threw his door open, and yelled, "Call Porter!"

He bolted into the woods, running over fallen logs and dodging trees, his lungs burning as he closed in on the guy. The asshole jerked to the left, sprinting toward the road. Mason's lungs burned and the forest blurred as he lunged, grabbing the man by the shoulder and throwing him to the ground. Mason was on him instantly, twisting his arm up behind his back.

"Stop! *Fuck*, man! I was just out bird-watching!"

"Bird-watching my ass." Mason used his free hand to search the guy for a weapon.

"Dude, seriously. I'm going to sue your ass."

"You do that." Mason dragged him to his feet, recognizing the fucker as the fan who had grabbed Remi. He shoved him back against a tree, and a piece of paper fell from the pocket of the guy's hoodie.

"I was taking a walk!" The man sneered. "You're fucking *dead*."

Mason grabbed him by the front of his shirt and shoved him down with him as he bent to retrieve the folded paper. He glowered as he shook open the paper, roiling at the familiar slanted handwriting. Remi's name stood out like a neon light in the twisted love letter. Hatred seared through Mason's veins as he slammed the asshole against a tree. The guy was shaking like a leaf, eyes wide and terrified. *Good.*

"You're a sick fuck," Mason snarled as sirens broke through his rage. It took all of his control not to smash his head in. He got right in the bastard's face, seething through gritted teeth, "I should snap your neck for fucking with Remi."

"I'm going to have her," the guy choked out. "We're meant to be together!"

The scent of fear seeped out of the fucker's pores as Mason leaned into him, crushing him against the tree, and seethed, "Over my dead body, motherfucker." He glowered, his hand shaking with the need to throttle the dirtbag's neck. "The only thing you're going to have is a long hard look at the world from behind bars."

CHAPTER TWENTY-FOUR

REMI FELT LIKE she was in a trance as she and Mason thanked the police and Mason's team. She couldn't believe it was finally over. Almost two hours after catching Ken Kantes, they had enough evidence to file charges and had verified that he had been in Los Angeles at the time of the break-in, which meant he could face charges there, too. Mason's team had already gotten the rundown on him. He was a basement dweller from the city, a computer genius and gamer working as an IT consultant from home, with a history of obsessive behavior. He'd woven an intricate and elaborate web of false identities and proxy servers, skillfully evading detection. He'd been arrested nine years ago for stalking and threatening an ex-girlfriend. Apparently he had seen Remi arrive at a premiere earlier in the year, and when she'd waved to the fans and said, *Thank you! I love you!* he'd twisted it in his mind to mean she was talking directly to him.

With the police and his team gone, Mason pulled Remi into his arms. "You're safe now, Princess. He'll go in front of a judge soon. He might get bail, but with his history, I doubt it."

"I can't believe it's over," Remi said.

"No shit," Piper said, finally coming to a halt. She'd been pacing the floor like a caged tiger. She was so protective, she'd insisted on staying until the police left, which meant Harley had stayed, too, since he'd driven them both.

"Hopefully they'll lock him away for many years," Harley said.

"I have to call Aiden and let him know it's over," Remi said. "I hate to say this, but I feel guilty. If I hadn't said I love my fans, maybe none of this would have happened."

Piper scowled. "Are you fucking kidding me? Do not even *try* to go there. That guy is so messed up in the head, all you had to do was look in his direction and he'd probably go psycho."

Harley put his hat on and said, "I think I'd better get Piper out of here before she wears a path in your floor." He embraced Remi. "I'm glad you're safe, darlin'."

"Thanks. Sorry you and Piper didn't get to be locked in the fortress together."

"One day she'll step off that high horse of hers and realize everything she needs is right here." Harley slapped his broad chest with both hands.

Piper shook her head. "Why do you insist on egging him on?"

"Because I like Harley and I like you," Remi said. "*And* he might be the only man on earth who can handle a strong woman like you."

They walked Piper and Harley out, and as Mason grabbed the box of their belongings from Harley's truck, Piper said, "Are you still going to your cabin?"

"God, *yes*," Remi said. "Once the media gets wind of the arrest, they'll be swarming me again."

"Smart. I didn't think of that." Piper hugged her and said, "I'm glad you're safe, and I'm glad you have Mason."

"Will you fill in Willow and everyone for me? I really just want to get out of town and not think about this."

"Absolutely."

Piper hugged Mason and said something Remi couldn't hear.

As Piper and Harley drove off, Mason said, "Looks like it's just you and me, Princess. For *real* this time."

"I'm pretty sure it was always supposed to be just you and me." That light inside her that brightened around Mason became even brighter as relief gave way to happiness. "Guess what? We can kiss and hold hands and be a couple!"

His arm circled her waist, and he crushed his mouth to hers. "Best." *Kiss.* "News." *Kiss.* "Ever!" *Kiss.*

She couldn't stop grinning. "In case I haven't said it enough, thank you for never letting your guard down even when I thought it was silly to be worried, and thank you for putting your life on the line to save mine."

"I'd take a bullet for you, Remi." He kissed her tenderly and said, "Do you want to repack your things in a suitcase?"

"No way. Load that box in the *overkill* vehicle and let's get out of here. It feels like I've been waiting forever to have time as a normal couple, away from the stress. Did you tell Porter and Merrick they don't have to follow us? They must be relieved."

"Yes, but it's their job. They wouldn't have minded. They're just happy you're safe, and Porter said he's glad we can openly be a couple now. He said I was like a cocked gun ready to go off these past few weeks."

"I like your *cocked gun*," she said seductively. "Let's get out of here so we can get to the cabin and *unload your magazine* as often as we'd like. I'll call Aiden on the way." As he loaded the box into the SUV, she said, "What did Piper say when she was hugging you? I hope she didn't threaten you again."

"She said she thinks you're still in shock and to watch you carefully. She said I should be ready for tears, and if I can't handle it, to call her and she'll drive to the cabin to be there for you."

"She said all that?"

"Well, in her own way. What she really said was, 'The girl's gonna crash at some point. You've got my number. Use it if she needs me.'"

Remi climbed into the SUV and said, "Now, *that* sounds like Piper."

They were both in lighter moods as they drove out of Harmony Pointe toward the cabin. Remi called Aiden and filled him in. For a moment Aiden went silent, and in those quiet seconds, Remi felt his relief as if he were right next to her. She pictured his serious eyes closing, the finely engraved tension lines around his eyes and mouth easing.

"Thank God," he finally said. "And you're okay?"

"I'm fine. Great actually. We're on our way to the cabin."

"Good. I'll be there Sunday afternoon."

"Okay. And, Aiden, I know I was a pain at first about having bodyguards, and I'm sorry for that, and for ditching them. Thank you for insisting and for hiring Mason. He's an amazing man, and I think if you were here, you'd be really happy with how careful he's been with me."

"He's kept you safe, Remi. That's all I've ever wanted," Aiden said. "Can I talk to Mason for a moment?"

"Yeah, hold on." She handed Mason her earpiece. "Aiden wants to speak to you."

"Hi, Aiden. How are you?" Mason listened. "Mm-hm. Yes. Don't worry. I'm not leaving her side. Yes, there will be an arraignment . . ."

As they talked, Remi closed her eyes, thankful for each of the two most important men in her life. In a few days everything would be out in the open and they would truly be free.

It was after seven o'clock when Mason turned off the highway, following winding narrow roads to Remi's private one-hundred-forty-two-acre rural mountain estate. He wasn't like other men who could shut down their worrying brains and disappear into a good book, thinking about nothing other than the next chapter, or play eighteen holes of golf wondering if he'd make par. Even though the threat to Remi had been cleared, Mason was still in warrior mode, noting the distance to the main roads, the lack of nearby properties, and the relaxed, gorgeous smile on his girlfriend's face.

There was something to be said about shutting down one's mind, and that smile sure made him want to learn how.

He drove down the long driveway and focused on the lush woods bordering it. Vibrant and colorful fall leaves brought a sense of freedom and privacy.

Remi rolled down the window, and the scents of autumn wafted in. "Every time I come here, my stress just falls away, and life feels less complicated."

"How often do you get up here?"

"Usually twice a year, at least for a few days. Same with the Cape if I can fit it in."

"Alone?" He hated the idea of her up there in the mountains without anyone to protect her.

"Well, before I met the Daltons, I could have counted my *real* friends on one hand, one of them being Naomi, my assistant. So sometimes Naomi would come with me, and if I dared come alone, Aiden usually showed up. You know how he hates it when I'm alone."

"I'm glad you have the Daltons." Mason cocked a grin as he parked out front and said, "You know, the more I hear about Aiden, the more I like him."

"Let's see how much you like him when he hears you're sleeping with his baby sister, because in his eyes, I'm afraid that's who I'll always be." She opened her door and jumped out. Then she popped her head back in and said, "But I've been taking a crash course in forming effective boundaries, and I think it's time I set some up with my big brother. Come on. I'm excited to show you the cabin!"

"It is gorgeous here," Mason said as he climbed out and grabbed their box. "How come you've never put roots down closer to your friends in Harmony Pointe or Sweetwater?"

They climbed the steps on the side of the house up to the wide wraparound porch. The entrance was on the side of the cabin, and three French doors faced a clearing in front of the driveway.

"I don't know. I guess because my schedule has always been crazy, and between Willow, her sisters, and Aurelia, I've always had a place to stay. I was thinking about that when we were at Willow's house for the barbecue. I love Sweetwater and Harmony Pointe, and I don't like LA. Maybe I should sell my LA house. It's not like I ever considered it home. It was just a place for me to stay when I was in the area." She dug her keys from her bag and unlocked the door. "I could always buy the fortress. It has some stressful memories because of the letters and what happened today." She turned smiling eyes to Mason as she said, "But it *is* where you and I came together, which is one of my happiest memories."

He pressed his lips to hers. "Mine too. I'm not trying to get you to buy a house or sell your LA house. I was just curious."

"I know. But if I owned the fortress, we could host the birthday bashes there. It's plenty big enough, and there's a pool and a great patio and room for the kids to run around. It might be worth considering."

He followed her inside, and as Remi disarmed the alarm, he took in the two-story ceilings, the floor-to-ceiling stone wall surrounding the fireplace to the right, and the cozy peach-colored couches and chairs by the French doors. To their left, there was a small round table in the dining area, bookshelves, and pictures of Remi's family hanging on the wall. A bar separated the kitchen from the rest of the living space. He knew the hall to the right of the kitchen led to three bedrooms and two full baths.

"The master's at the end of the hall," Remi said. "Why don't you put our stuff in there, and then we can go into town and get dinner. I'm so excited, I can barely stand it! I actually get to hold your hand and kiss you in public!"

271

"I'm excited, too, Princess." He headed down the hall, passing a bedroom on either side and a full bath on the right.

The master suite spanned the width of the cabin, and it felt like Remi, light, breezy, and understatedly elegant. The king-sized bed had an ornate brushed wrought-iron headboard with florid designs and fancy posts with decorative finials. The comforter was buttercup yellow, which complemented the pale blue glass bedside lamp and the pale blue-and-yellow armchair by the French doors that led to a large screened-in porch, complete with a fireplace.

Mason set the box down beside the bed and dug out his sweatshirt. Then he checked the locks on the windows and doors, wishing she had a freaking ten-foot wall around her property after the nightmare she'd just been through.

"Okay, Mr. Swift, it's time we had a little chat."

Mason turned and found Remi standing in the doorway with a smirk on her gorgeous face, arms crossed, tapping the toe of her boots. She crooked her finger, beckoning him to her, and his heart turned over in his chest. This beautiful, smart, playful woman was all *his*.

He wrapped his arms around her waist and said, "*Chat*, my love."

"Tonight, can you just be my boyfriend and not my bodyguard? I can see the gears in your head churning, but I need you to be with me tonight as Remi, not as the girl with the stalker."

"The stalker is behind bars, but your safety will always be in the forefront of my mind."

"I know, and I appreciate that. But just for one night, take a deep breath and just *be* with me."

He shook his head. "Do you even know who you're with? I warned you, remember? I can't turn it off that easily." He lowered his voice and said, "But for you, I'm going to try *really* hard to dial it down."

"Oh, you'll be *hard* all right—*later*, after we celebrate our freedom and coupledom." She gave him a chaste kiss and tugged him out the bedroom door.

As they drove into Auburn Grove, Mason said, "You know you're still Remi Divine, right? Or are you so excited about the stalker being caught that you've lost sight of the fact that you might have fans all over you tonight?"

She lifted her chin and said, "I'm *that* excited, yes, but I also had a fantastic teacher these last few weeks. If anyone recognizes me, which they might not in this getup, I'm going to *wow* you with my boundary-setting prowess." She'd touched base with Naomi and Shea on the drive up to let them know she wanted a week without interruptions unless it was urgent. She'd passed those boundaries lessons with flying colors.

"I look forward to it."

Auburn Grove was smaller than Harmony Pointe, and equally charming. There were rocking chairs on front porches and children playing in yards, despite evening rolling in. They parked by the clock tower in the center of town and held hands as they crossed the street to the brick-paved courtyard that spanned the area between two rows of shops. Mason loved the feel of Remi's delicate hand in his, but it wasn't enough. He tucked her beneath his arm, wanting her closer.

Moonlight reflected in her eyes as she said, "This is pretty awesome, isn't it?"

"The town?" he teased. "Yeah, it's cute."

She swatted his stomach, and he lost his mind for a minute, his guard slipping completely away as he lifted her into his arms and twirled her around, pressing his lips to hers. He'd never felt what he'd call *giddy*, but at that moment he was damn close.

He set her feet on the ground, keeping her close, and said, "Being with you like this, out in the open, is better than pretty awesome, Princess. It's *everything*."

They walked along the courtyard, scoping out the shops for tomorrow, when they'd come back and check them all out, and found a cute eclectic café called Hot Eats. Ivy crawled up the sides of the redbrick walls, giving it a rustic feel. Like the Italian restaurant and the deli they'd passed at the other end of the courtyard, the café had seating out front. Unlike those other venues, none of the seating matched. Customers sat on wooden benches with thick red cushions beside big drums used as tables and in iron chairs surrounding a large farm-style table. Others sat in wicker, wooden, and upholstered chairs with mismatched tables for one or two. At the far end of the eating area, two couples sat cross-legged atop colorful striped blankets on an open futon, with a pizza between them. Lanterns with candles lit up the bricks around the futon.

Just outside the eating area was a fountain. A long-haired guy sat on a knee-high stone wall around the fountain playing his guitar.

Remi swayed to the music. She leaned closer to Mason and said, "Best first date ever."

They were greeted by a bubbly blonde, who asked if they wanted to sit in the lovers' chair. Remi practically squealed with delight when she saw the chair for two beneath a canopy surrounded on three sides by pretty white sheers flowing in the breeze. The glass table was adorned with a red tablecloth, a vase of wildflowers, and candles. They ordered drinks, salads, and tomato-basil chicken, and then Remi rested her head against Mason's shoulder as they listened to the music and snuggled together on the chair. Mason couldn't remember a time when he'd been happier or more at ease. He was thankful Remi hadn't been recognized, and though he was still watching the people around them, being able to hold her while watching over her made everything that much sweeter.

The waitress brought their food, and they talked while they ate. Even though they'd eaten together every day for weeks, this felt different. *Better.* Remi snagged bites of tomatoes from his plate and peppers from his salad, reminding him of the very first time they'd cooked together. It felt like a lifetime ago, and at the same time, it was such a bright memory, it felt like yesterday.

When they were done eating, Remi lifted her glass and said, "Here's to the end of a nightmare. I'm so happy being with you, out in the open. I don't think I've ever been this happy in my whole life."

He tapped his glass to hers, then set it down. He slid his hand beneath her hair, drawing her lips to his, loving the peaceful look in her eyes. "I have a feeling I'll be kissing you a lot more now that I can do it whenever I want to, so if it's too much, you need to tell me."

"I'm a glutton. I hope you never stop."

He pulled her in for a long, slow kiss, and then he brushed his nose along her cheek, breathing her in. "You've changed my world, Princess. With you I feel things I never thought possible. I see every day through new eyes. I just need to know one thing: Where do you want to go from here? After we tell Aiden, do you want to go to the city and stay at my loft? Spend time there enjoying the lights, see a show or two? Or do you want to stay in Harmony Pointe?"

"I want to be wherever you are. Where do you want to be?"

"With you, Remi. That's all that matters to me. But you've been told what to do and where to go for so long, I want this decision to be yours."

"You can't imagine how much that means to me."

"Oh, I think I can. A certain strong-willed woman ditched some of my best men, and even tried to ditch me."

"No, I didn't. It was either get out of the house or throw myself at you, because you were strutting around all hot and sexy and looking at me like you are right now."

The guitarist started playing "She Is Love." Mason threw a wad of way too much money on the table to cover the bill and a nice tip and rose to his feet, bringing Remi up with him. "Come on, beautiful. He's playing our song."

He led her over by the fountain, and there beneath the stars, with dozens of people all around them, he held his love in his arms for all to see, and then he kissed her, just because he could.

They continued dancing to several more songs, some fast, some slow, every single one as joyful as the last. The longer they danced, the more couples joined them. An hour later, the middle of the courtyard was so crowded it looked more like a dance floor, making the evening feel like even more of a celebration.

When the guitarist took a break, applause broke out—for him, not for Remi and Mason, though the way Remi was looking at Mason, it was as if the applause were meant for him. They walked hand in hand toward the clock tower, the old-fashioned light posts casting a romantic glow around them.

They passed a tattoo parlor, and Mason said, "Were you serious about getting a tattoo?"

"Only if you'll hold my hand."

"Aw, Princess. You're the cutest. I'll hold your hand, but how about if you sleep on it, since tattoos are forever?"

"Okay, but I won't change my mind." Remi leaned into his side and said, "This night couldn't get any more perfect. The town, the food, the dancing, my *man* . . ."

"Hold that thought." Mason took her hand, tugging her into an alley between two buildings. "Come on," he whispered, and helped her up onto the fire escape he'd spotted.

"What if we get caught?" she whispered, but the light of mischief in her eyes told him she was loving every second of their impromptu escapade.

"I'll take the heat and say I forced you to do it."

He followed her up to the rooftop, and she wrapped her arms around herself, like she had when he'd taken her onto the roof of the building where he'd once lived in the city. She turned in a circle, taking in the lights of the small town, so different from the big city and yet so beautiful.

"I know where I want to go after we tell Aiden," she said.

"Where's that?"

"I want to go to the city. I want to see where you live and spend some time in your world. But I really want to go see Chuck and get to know him, if that's okay."

He didn't think his heart could feel any fuller than it did right then. "That's more than okay. I was serious when I said I was going to make changes in my life, Remi. When I spoke to my team earlier, I told them I'm going to be delegating a lot more of the jobs I normally take on. I want to dedicate time for our foster-care project. That's *ours*, sweetheart, and I want to be involved every step of the way, helping to get people to donate and putting together boxes, holding fundraisers. I want to see those smiling faces at the birthday bashes and know that we made it happen together."

He sat down and guided her to sit between his legs, her back resting against his chest. She snuggled against him, shivering a little. He pulled off his sweatshirt and helped her put it on.

She ran her hands over his forearms and said, "This reminds me of the first night we met, when I maimed your arms."

"I wanted to hold you like this that first night, but you hadn't yet taunted me into crossing the uncrossable line between us."

"I hadn't *taunted* you into it? Like I was some kind of seductress?" She turned her face, so he could see the scowl she was feigning.

She was so adorable, he had to laugh. "Don't worry, babe. I take all the blame, and given the chance, I'd do it all over again."

CHAPTER TWENTY-FIVE

MASON AWOKE TO the sound of soft music and a cool breeze brushing over his legs. He climbed from the bed, grabbed a pair of boxer briefs from the box, which they had yet to unpack, and put them on. The doors to the screened porch were open, but Remi wasn't there. The music floating in from the living room told Mason where she was. He washed his face and brushed his teeth, then followed the trail of clothes they'd left on the floor last night, remnants of how hungry they'd been for each other, out to the living room.

The French doors were all open. Remi stood on the deck wearing his sweatshirt, which hung low on one side but bunched around her other hip, exposing one perfect, creamy butt cheek. Her honey hair lay over one shoulder. The toes of her right foot rested on the bottom rung of the railing. He'd never get used to the way his heart stumbled every time he saw her. It hadn't been that way at first glance. He'd been physically attracted to her, of course—she was gorgeous. But he'd had her pegged all wrong, thinking she was a diva. His feelings had sure developed quickly, starting that first night at the fundraiser as he'd watched her with her friends and Aiden. As he'd gotten to know her, there was no stopping them. He'd never known love, much less anything like the inescapable and insatiable adoration they shared. The depth of emotions she continued to unearth often sent him reeling, and he knew in his soul that would never change. She was his own private miracle.

She could do anything, go anywhere, and yet she wanted to share *his* world. Did she know she made that world so much brighter than he'd ever imagined? They were so deeply connected, he didn't even have to ask what she was doing out there all alone. He already knew.

She was finally free.

Almost, anyway. She was still putting on a brave face about Aiden, though he knew his bighearted girl was carrying guilt over not having told her brother about them, the same way he was. Just a few more days and hopefully that would ease, too, and then she could truly be free. He had an inkling that there was even more to Remi than either of them realized and that other parts of her might not appear until years after she climbed out from under Aiden's caring wings. That just gave Mason even more to look forward to.

He stepped outside and said, "Hey, beautiful." He wrapped his arms around her and kissed her cheek.

She made a soft purring sound, turning in his arms. "Can you believe we have *all* day to do whatever we want?"

He slipped his hands beneath the sweatshirt, taking hold of her bare bottom. "And what would you like to do?"

"*You*," she said saucily. "And I have a very long *to-do* list." She pressed her kiss to the tattoo on his chest and said, "I think I'm addicted to being in your arms."

"That's funny," he said, his fingers grazing the warmth between her legs. "Because I'm addicted to having you there."

He lowered his mouth to hers, and she bowed against him, grabbing his butt. He loved when she claimed him. It spurred him on to tease between her legs, dipping his fingers inside her. She moaned into their kisses, amping up his arousal.

"God, baby, you own me," he said heatedly.

He reclaimed her mouth more demandingly, his fingers moving in and out of her slick heat, teasing over the spot that elicited sharp little gasps with every stroke. She ground against his hard length. She felt so good, he wanted to wrap her sexy little hands around the railing and take her from behind until she cried out his name so loud it echoed in the forest. But the sweet, sinful noises she was making, and the way she felt rubbing against him, was too good to stop. He teased her until she went up on her toes, grinding against his hand.

She tore her mouth from his, whimpering against his cheek. "*Please*, Mason. Make me come," she pleaded.

He dropped to his knees and sealed his mouth over her center.

She fisted her hands in his hair. "Yes," she panted out, her thighs flexing. "Don't stop. Right there . . . Oh . . . Oh . . . *Oh! Mason!*"

Fireworks went off inside him as her sex pulsed around his thrusting tongue. She bucked against his mouth, a stream of sexy sounds sailing from her lips. God, he loved to pleasure her.

"Again, again, *again*," she pleaded.

That was another thing he loved about her. The closer they became, the more she dropped her sexual boundaries. He quickened his efforts, loving the low, surrendering moans he elicited as she climbed toward the clouds, gasping and pleading until she shattered, *gloriously*—and then collapsed, boneless and beautiful, against him.

"Kiss me," she whispered.

He crushed her to him, kissing her with all he had as he lifted her into his arms and carried her through the living room and into the bedroom. He lay her on the bed, making quick work of stripping off her sweatshirt and then his briefs.

He came down over her, and as their bodies became one, he breathed against her neck, "*God*, I fucking love you, Remi. You've become the very air I breathe."

"I want to be so much more," she said.

He kissed her then, soft and lovingly. "We're one being, Remi. Don't you feel it?"

"Yes, with every piece of my soul."

The first touch of their lips was sensual and soft, but as he'd come to expect, their hearts took over, their movements synced, and their kisses became passionate proclamations of their love. Remi wrapped her legs around his waist, holding him so tight, he knew she felt as swept away as he did.

"Harder," she pleaded.

He thrust harder, gritting his teeth to hold back his mounting release.

"Come with me," she said against his neck.

The love in her voice sent a surge of desire through him. He held her tighter, loved her deeper, and they spiraled over the edge together. He clung to her, panting out her name like a prayer, staying with her as their bodies jerked with aftershocks, until they were both too spent to move.

She melted against him as they came down from the clouds. They lay tangled together for a long time, the morning air cooling their heated flesh.

Mason pressed a kiss to her temple. "Love you, Princess."

She slicked her tongue along his neck, sending prickles of heat to his core, and teased him with her hands, turning him into a greedy bundle of lust and love.

"I love you, Mason," she said softly, and then she straddled him. Her silky hair fell like a curtain around their faces as she whispered, "Let me show you how much . . ."

CHAPTER TWENTY-SIX

PIPER'S SUGGESTION OF not leaving the cabin had been a good one. After the most exquisite day spent relaxing in the sun and loving each other, followed by an evening cuddled up by a warm fire where they made love long into the night, they were greeted Friday morning with the same rejuvenating feelings—and excitement over getting Remi's first tattoo. Yesterday they'd researched local tattoo artists, and once Mason was sure they were safe and skilled, they found the font Remi wanted for her tattoo and made an appointment.

They lounged around the cabin all morning, and then went into town and treated themselves to a delicious pizza.

As Remi bit into her third slice, Mason said, "I'm so glad to see you aren't afraid to eat when you're not filming."

"I told you. I'm just a normal person doing what I have to in order to maintain my career. I have plenty of time to lose any weight I might gain before the promotional tour for the movie starts."

Mason's phone rang, and he glanced at the screen. "It's Porter." He held up one finger as he answered the call. "Hey, Porter, what's the update?" He nodded. "Good. Of course he is. Go over all the case docs one more time, just to be sure we haven't missed anything. Yes. Great. Thanks for keeping me in the loop."

"Well?" she asked as he pocketed his phone.

"The judge denied bail, which means the guy will be in jail until the trial. He's denying having broken into your house in LA, but they have proof that he was in LA at the time, so he's probably just trying to get out of that charge."

Relief swept through Remi like a gale-force wind. She threw her arms around Mason's neck, hugging him tight and counting her blessings. "I didn't realize how worried I was that he might get out. I'm *so* relieved."

"I think we can all breathe a little easier now."

"I'll say! We should get down to the tattoo shop. It's almost time for my appointment."

"Do you want to call Aiden first?"

"I'll text him and the girls on the way. I don't want to be late, and they'll all be glad to hear the news."

She texted Aiden and her friends as they walked along the courtyard. The girls' responses rolled in one after another, excited that the man who had harassed her would remain behind bars.

"Aiden must be in a meeting," she said as they entered the tattoo shop.

Her gaze swept over the seating areas on either side of the doors, with black leather couches and tables covered in tattoo books and magazines. A guy with short dark hair, thick forearms covered in ink, and large ear gauges sat behind a desk. Red walls decorated with framed pictures of tattoos and dark-themed artwork surrounded three workstations, where tattooists hunkered down over their current clients, tattoo guns in hand. Each station was separated by a half wall, giving Remi a clear view of the artists at work.

The persistent buzz of the guns made her pulse quicken. "I've never actually been inside a tattoo parlor," she said nervously.

Mason put his arm around her. "You've got this, babe, but if you want to back out, now's the time." He was so supportive, gently nudging her when she needed it and never pressuring her to do things she might not want to.

"I want to do this, and I'm glad you're here with me. I couldn't do it alone."

He flashed that devastating smile that had first caught her eye and said, "There's nothing you can't do."

"Maybe, but I've wanted this forever, and never got up the guts to do it until you came into my life."

"Can I help you?" the guy behind the desk asked.

Mason stepped up and said, "We have an appointment for Swift."

It was silly, but her heart did a little happy dance knowing he'd used his name for her appointment.

"Right. I'll need a copy of your driver's license, and you'll need to fill out this paperwork. Crish will be doing your tattoo." He pointed to a bearded guy wearing black-framed glasses and a beanie, currently tattooing a woman's shoulder. "He should be done any minute."

Remi gave him her driver's license.

"Remington Aldridge. Cool name. I'm just going to make a copy of this. You can sit down and fill out the paperwork."

"Guess he doesn't go to the movies," Mason said as they sat down.

"Good," Remi whispered. "I love that no one here has recognized me. It makes it easier to relax."

Twenty minutes later she was sitting in a black chair beside Crish as he put a transfer of the tattoo she wanted on the inside of her wrist. He was a nice guy with colorful inked sleeves, the name *Gloria* tattooed on the left side of his neck, and a tiny anchor tattooed behind his right ear. Mason stood beside her, arms crossed, brows knitted. She was sure he looked as imposing to Crish as he was *reassuring* to her.

"Take a minute to be sure this is exactly what you want," Crish said as he lifted the transfer paper off her skin. "There's no rush, and if you'd like to adjust the placement, it's no big deal." He began preparing his tattoo gun.

Remi looked at the simple cursive script on her wrist—*Just Breathe*—and her mother's voice whispered those words through her mind. Unexpected emotions floated up inside her. She reached for Mason's hand.

"Are you okay?"

"Yeah," she choked out. "I just heard my mom's voice." Her eyes teared up, and she looked up at the ceiling, trying to blink them dry.

Mason sat on the edge of the chair, facing her. "We don't have to do this. We can leave right now."

"No, that's just it. I *know* it's right. These are happy tears."

Crish handed her a wad of tissues and said, "I was going to ask you if you had a stressful job and that was why you were getting this tattoo. But I guess it's much more personal than that."

Remi dabbed at her eyes, sharing a secret smile with Mason over not being recognized. "It is. My mom died when I was young, and she said that to me."

"It's a nice tribute to her." Crish sat back and said, "Take your time."

"I don't need time. This is exactly what I want." She looked at Mason, glad for his support, and said, "I'm ready."

"You picked a pretty painful place for your first tattoo," Crish said. "Try not to jerk your arm."

"Okay." She squeezed Mason's hand so tight his fingers turned red as Crish began tattooing. "Okay, *yeah*, that hurts."

Crish stopped, his face empathetic. "You okay? Need a break?"

Mason kissed the top of her head in silent support.

"No, I'm good." She closed her eyes as Crish began tattooing again, and a few seconds later she mustered the courage to watch. "Mason, can you take a picture? I want to remember this. Wait. Crish, I'm sorry, but can you stop for a sec?" He stopped, and she said, "I know this is going to seem silly, but can we ask someone to take a picture of the three of us while you do it, with Mason holding my hand?"

"That's not silly. This is a memorable occasion. Ink's addicting, too. Before you know it, you'll have three more tats, and you should always remember your first." Crish called up to the front, "Hey, Taylor! Can you take a pic for us?"

The guy from the front sauntered back, and Remi gave him her phone. As Crish tattooed her wrist, Taylor took a few pictures, and then he gave the phone to Mason.

"Thank you," Remi said. "This feels like a big step in the right direction, but I still wish I had said goodbye."

"Me too, Princess," Mason said.

Crish sat back with a thoughtful expression, his dark eyes lifting to Mason as he said, "Did you lose someone, too?"

"Brothers-in-arms," Mason answered tightly.

"Right," Crish said. "Thanks for your service, man."

Mason nodded curtly. Remi wasn't surprised that Mason didn't reveal the loss of his mother. She blew him a kiss, earning that sexy smile she loved.

"My friend Gertie has a place down the street, Gertie's Gifts," Crish said. "She sells wire-free sky lanterns that you light and release. When I lost my dad, it was sudden, and there were no goodbyes. A buddy of mine set up a goodbye ceremony for him. We went to my dad's favorite place, and we each said something, and then we released the lanterns. It was life changing for me. *Freeing.*" He shrugged, and as he began tattooing again, he said, "Just an idea."

"I love that idea, and I know the perfect place. What do you think, Mason?"

"Sounds like a plan. Private and meaningful."

A while later they walked out of the shop with tattoo-care instructions in hand and Remi's new tattoo safely covered with a sterile bandage.

"You were so brave." Mason hugged her as they headed down the street toward Gertie's Gifts.

"You're dating a tattooed badass now."

He laughed. "I've got news for you, Princess. You've always been badass. Tell me about the place you want to release the lanterns."

"I'll do better than that. I'll show you when we get home. It's not far from the cabin. I'd really like to have the ceremony at the break of dawn. Is that okay? I know that doing this won't be a miracle cure, but it feels like it could be a stepping-stone toward letting go of some of our painful pasts and moving forward with a little less guilt and longing on our minds. It would be symbolic to do it as a new day rises. New day, new outlook."

"I love the way your mind works, and dawn sounds *perfect*. Just like you."

CHAPTER TWENTY-SEVEN

MASON SCANNED THE area out of habit as he carried their shopping bags into the cabin, but it was just as quiet and peaceful as ever. After picking up lanterns at the gift shop, they'd meandered through several other stores, picking up matching Auburn Grove sweatshirts and a few scented candles that Remi said reminded her of *all things happy*.

She flitted around the cabin in the chunky black boots she'd worn to Decadence, opening the French doors in the master bedroom and living room, letting the fresh air in. She looked gorgeous in a flouncy floral miniskirt with an oversized gray sweater that had slipped off her shoulder so many times it had quickly become one of his favorites—giving him better access to kiss her there.

Mason was filling a glass with ice water when Remi grabbed a belt loop on the back of his jeans, tugging him toward the doors.

"Come on, I want to show you the place for the ceremony."

He guzzled the water and then swept her into his arms for a hard kiss. "You're like a whole new person."

She held up her wrist, which was now bandage-free, showing off her tattoo, and said, "You mean I'm a *badass babe*, right?" She smirked. "It's amazing what knowing the stalker is behind bars does to a girl. Now, come on, let's go!"

She dragged him by the hand out the door and down a trail by the side of the house. "My dad and I used to come out here early in the mornings, before anyone else was awake. He'd drink coffee and make up stories about the most outrageous things, which was funny, because my father was as serious as Aiden. Risky business was *not* in his repertoire." She plowed through long grass, hopping over rocks and logs with renewed energy. "Anyway, he'd tell me about the time he supposedly wrestled a bear or rode an elk." She laughed softly. "I really miss that time with him."

"I bet you do."

They weren't but five minutes away from the cabin when they came to the crest of a hill where the woods fell away, exposing the most incredible views. Tall trees covered the mountainside, giving way to a valley below. In the distance, the tops of mountains kissed the sky.

Remi dropped Mason's hand and spread hers out to her sides. "What do you think? Isn't it perfect?"

He stood at the edge of the clearing, hands on his hips, filling his lungs with crisp mountain air. "If I were to pick a place to say goodbye, this would be it."

"Really?" She launched herself into his arms, lifting her feet off the ground. She kissed him, and as she slid back down to her feet, she said, "I'm so glad you like it. I feel closer to my parents up here. One day I want to have kids and bring them here and tell them ridiculous stories that could never have happened. I want them to have nothing but great memories." She shaded her eyes from the setting sun and said, "Do you want a family someday?"

"I've always wanted a family. I just never thought I'd have one." He moved beside her and said, "Maybe one day that dream will come true for both of us."

Her eyes brightened and her voice softened as she said, "I can only imagine a little Mason running around with your serious blue eyes, making sure his baby brother or sister is safe."

He wanted that more than she could ever know, and he imagined that a baby sister would look just like Remi, with gorgeous honey-brown hair and unforgettable hazel eyes.

But he was getting ahead of himself, and he didn't want to scare Remi off, so he cleared his throat and said, "Did I ever tell you about the time I caught a moose?"

She took his hand. "No, but is it true that moose love muffins?"

His brow furrowed in confusion.

"You don't know that story?" she asked, unable to hide her astonishment.

"Can't say I do."

"Oh boy. You need to have kids just so you can learn the stories. Tomorrow we're hitting the bookstore so you can read about moose and muffins, pigs and pancakes, cats and cupcakes . . ."

He laughed and hugged her. "Okay, how about boyfriends and steaks?"

"I can get on board with that, right after you tell me about the time you caught a moose."

"I lied. It was a *fox*." He swept her off her feet, kissing her again, her feet dangling beside him as he headed back down the path toward the cottage. "A beautiful fox with hazel eyes and a killer ass."

"And she loved pizza?" she asked with a giggle as he set her on her feet.

"Nah, that's a different story," he teased. "This fox was *wild*, and she wanted only one thing. It was big and thick and—"

Her eyes widened. "Your fox is a slut!"

"Why? Because she craves Loverboys? I hear they're a great mix of cupcakes and éclairs."

"Nice save." She swatted his arm. "Now I want a Loverboy."

"You're out of luck." He draped an arm over her shoulder and said, "How about a lover *man*?"

They both laughed, and then he said, "You're pretty cute, foxy girl."

"You're not so bad yourself, lover *man*."

He was grinning like a fool as they followed the trail back to the cabin. "Why don't I start up the grill and throw a few steaks on?" His phone rang, and he pulled it from his pocket and saw Porter's name on the screen. "It's Porter."

Remi lowered her voice and said, "If you decide you'd rather have *fox* than steak, I'll be waiting in the bedroom." She took off her sweater as she ascended the porch steps, tossed it over her back, and strutted into the cabin.

Holy fuck.

He put the phone to his ear. "Hey, Porter, what's up?"

"I've got another update."

Mason heard tires on gravel and said, "Hold on, Porter," as a black sedan pulled up beside the SUV. "I've got to call you back."

Mason ended the call, eyeing Remi's sweater on the ground a few feet away as Aiden stepped from the car with an angry expression. *Fuck.* "Hey, Aiden. We weren't expecting you until Sunday."

"Clearly," he seethed, stalking toward Mason. "Shea texted when I was on my way up the mountain. In case you've forgotten, I'm Remi's business manager. Shea couldn't reach Remi and she wanted to know how to handle *this*." He shoved his phone in Mason's face, showing him TMZ's Instagram feed with a picture of Remi and Mason walking arm in arm and kissing, taken earlier today by the shops. Beside it was a picture of them dancing the other night in the courtyard.

Damn it. "Listen, Aiden, we were going to tell you what was going on when you got here. We didn't want to screw up your business trip."

Aiden fisted his phone, speaking through gritted teeth. "Screw up my *business trip*? I'm not paying you to fuck my sister, Mason."

Mason got in his face, hands fisted to keep from grabbing Aiden by the collar. "Don't you ever talk about Remi like that. You've got it all wrong."

"Yeah?" Aiden hollered. "Looks pretty damn clear to me. Do you have any idea how *old* she is?"

"I know *exactly* how old she is," Mason shot back. "I also know that she was in the car with your parents when they were killed, how goddamn scared she was, and that you've been there for her ever since. But she's not that kid anymore, so back off." He tried not to sound threatening and forced a calmer tone. "I'm in love with Remi, Aiden, and every penny you paid me is coming back to you, so whatever you're thinking—"

The sound of glass shattering cut him off. Mason bolted inside with Aiden on his heels, flying over Remi's boots and skirt. He pushed the bedroom door open, and his heart stopped at the sight of Remi in her lingerie, gagged and tied to the bed, her terrified eyes staring back at him. Standing beside the bed, Carl spun around with a gun in his hand aimed directly at Aiden. Mason lunged in front of Aiden at the same time two shots rang out. Mason felt searing pain in his chest and stomach a second before he connected with Carl's body, taking him down with him.

Blinded with rage, Mason punched him in the jaw, yelling, "Get Remi!" to Aiden as his fist connected with Carl's face time and time again. Blood poured from Mason's wounds, splattering from the force of Mason's fist connecting with Carl's jaw.

"Mason!" Remi screamed. "Aiden! Call 911! Oh God! Mason!"

Her cries jarred Mason from his storm of fury enough to realize Carl had gone limp beneath him, out cold. Mason rolled off him, trying to catch his breath as blood gushed from his chest and stomach. Aiden spoke frantically into the phone as Mason pushed to his knees, pain fracturing his ability to see and speak.

Remi leapt from the bed to the floor. "Oh my God! There's too much blood." She grabbed the sheet, pressing it to Mason's chest and stomach. "Aiden, help me!"

Mason slumped against the wall, his vision blurring as his eyes swept over Remi. "Are . . . ?" He gasped for air. "You hurt?"

"No! Oh God, Mason. Hang on! Help is coming." Tears flooded her cheeks. Her hands were covered in his blood as she futilely tried to stop his bleeding.

"I'm fine," he said weakly, though he was anything but.

"The police and ambulance are on the way," Aiden said frantically as he fell to his knees and pressed a towel to Mason's chest and another to his stomach.

Pain clutched Mason as he grabbed Aiden's wrist, trying to drag air into his lungs. "Get the cuffs . . . my glove box. Keys . . . by the door."

"Remi, push on these. *Hard.*" Aiden's face was a mask of terror as he switched places with Remi. "I'll get the cuffs!" He ran out of the bedroom.

"Carl was here when I came inside," Remi cried. "He grabbed me and shoved something in my mouth. I tried to scream. Oh, *Mason!* The blood . . . I can't lose you. You have to be okay."

Aiden flew back into the room. "Got 'em."

Mason had only one thing on his mind, keeping Remi safe. He struggled to fill his lungs, but the pain was too intense. He finally choked out, "Roll him . . . over . . . cuff . . . wrists." The room began to fade in and out, sounds muffled, and his sight blurred.

"Mason!" Remi pressed the drenched towels against him, sobbing. "Don't close your eyes, Mason! Stay with me! I love you! Please! You have to be okay . . ."

Mason tried to focus on her, to shake the darkness that was overtaking him. "I can't . . ."

"I'm not letting you go!" she sobbed. "Mason! *Aiden!* We have to do something! Help me!"

Mason's vision went black, and Remi's voice carried him into the darkness.

CHAPTER TWENTY-EIGHT

PLEASE BE OKAY screamed through Remi's mind as she paced the hospital waiting room, followed closely by *Just breathe* in a never-ending cycle of hurt. The hospital staff wouldn't tell her or Aiden anything because they weren't family, and she feared the worst. Time passed in a blur. Aiden had been on and off the phone since they got there, alternating between talking with Porter and trying to get her to calm down. As if calming down was even possible.

He ended a call and approached her again. Remi held her hand up. "If you tell me to sit down one more time, I swear I'll lose it."

"I won't. I was going to tell you what Porter said about Carl."

Fresh tears fell. "I can't . . . I *trusted* him . . ."

Aiden pulled her into his arms. "We all did."

"Why would he do this? It's his fault Mason might die!" Sobs overcame her. "I can't lose him, Aiden. I *can't*. He has to be okay."

"I know, honey."

"Do you?" She pushed from his arms. "Do you know about us? Me and Mason?"

"He told me, but if he hadn't, the way you ran off that bed to him . . ."

He drew back, looking down at her with hurt and anger she didn't want to see, knowing she'd caused both.

"Remi, why didn't you tell me?"

"Because I thought you'd lose your mind," she said honestly, too upset to try to soften the truth.

"I *did* lose my mind. You're my sister, and my responsibility. I want what's best for you. You've never even had a long-term relationship. How can you know you love him?"

The way he said it wasn't judgmental. It was inquisitive, and it struck her that he *really* didn't understand. "Because I can't imagine a single day without him, and even though it's a completely different kind of love, it's also similar to the way that I can't imagine a life without you in it. I just *know*, Aiden. In here." She put her fist over her heart.

"He's not much younger than me."

"I know, and he's been through war and too many other types of hell. He's a good man, Aiden, a great man, and I love him with every ounce of my soul." Tears flowed down her cheeks, and her breathing hitched as her frustrations poured out. "You have to stop seeing me as the terrified little girl you pulled from that accident. I'm *not* her anymore, and I can't spend my life trying to prove to you that I can handle myself. I know I acted childishly by ditching my bodyguards, but it was all too much. I was *smothered*. I love you, Aiden. You've spent your whole adult life taking care of me, and I appreciate that, but you've *got* to get a life. You *deserve* to have a life separate from mine, to find someone who loves you as much as Mason and I love each other. You and I, we might be broken because of what we've gone through, but we're *fixable*, Aiden. We can *love* and we can *be loved*."

She swiped at her tears, and Aiden grabbed her wrist, turning it over. There were red marks from the rope Carl had used to bind her, but Aiden wasn't looking at them. He'd already made sure she was okay when the EMTs had arrived. He was looking at the tattoo, which was still red and raw.

He brushed his thumb just below it, lifting sad eyes to Remi. "Please tell me this isn't some sort of rebellion."

She laugh-sobbed and shook her head. "It's just the opposite. You've been my breath for so long, Aiden. It's time for me to breathe on my own. But if I lose Mason, I'm going to need you to be my breath again, because I've only just found him, and . . ." Sobs swallowed her voice.

Aiden pulled her into his arms. "*Shh.* I know."

Porter burst through the doors, and Remi ran to him. "They won't tell us anything! He got shot, Porter. Twice! I'm so scared."

She threw her arms around him and he embraced her, though rigidly, and said, "I'll find out what's going on."

"Thank you!"

As he strode away, Aiden put his arm around her. "He's a good man, too. I'm sorry for making you feel smothered. I just . . . I can't lose you, Remi."

"I know," she choked out.

"Mason saved both our lives tonight. If he hadn't been there . . ."

"Don't go there. I can't . . . Why would Carl do this? I thought they caught the stalker."

"Porter said the other guy sent the letters and emails. Carl was the one who broke into your LA house. According to his wife—"

"Oh God, poor Samantha! Did she know?"

"Porter said she didn't. When he called earlier, he said the police were questioning Carl. Carl said he was trying to scare you so you'd quit acting. He had some convoluted fantasy that you stole his wife's success."

"*Ohmygod.* I love Samantha. I'd never . . ." She wrapped her arms around herself. "He had a *gun*, Aiden. He shot at you. He shot Mason *twice*. That's not just scaring me. It's trying to take *everything* away from me."

Life passed in slow motion, but at the same time, minutes seemed to race by. Remi was sitting with her face in her hands beside Aiden, praying Mason would be okay, when Porter returned.

She sprang to her feet. "What did they say?"

"Mason's going to pull through," Porter said.

The air rushed from Remi's lungs, and she leaned against Aiden for support. "Thank God."

"One bullet hit his lung. The other missed his vital organs. He's going to be in ICU for observation for at least twenty-four hours before he'll be moved to a regular patient room."

Remi closed her eyes, sucking air into her lungs for what felt like the first time since their nightmare began. Her eyes flew open and she said, "What about Carl?"

"He's under arrest," Porter assured her. "He has a concussion, and they're running tests to look for bleeding and facial injuries, but you don't have to worry. He'll be released directly into police custody."

"Thank God," Aiden said.

"Can I see Mason?" Remi asked.

Worry filled Porter's eyes. "Yes, but you should take a minute to prepare yourself. He has a chest tube, and he's just had surgery. He's weak, and he's not going to look like the man you expect."

"None of that matters. He's alive. That's all I care about."

Porter glanced at Aiden and said, "The media is out front. Merrick is holding them off. Do you want to make a statement?"

"I can't deal with them," Remi said anxiously. "I need to be with Mason."

"I'll call Shea to strategize, and then I'll make a statement," Aiden reassured her.

"Thank you. Aiden, I want the world to know that I'm with Mason, that we're a couple. I'm done hiding, and if it's all the same to you, I'm done with this public life for a while, too."

"Of course."

The guilt on Aiden's face cut her to her core, but she didn't want to waste another second talking, and went to see Mason.

The nurse at the desk tried to prepare Remi, just as Porter had, but between her racing heart, the blood rushing through her ears, and her dire need to be with Mason, she barely heard a word of it. She pushed through the door to Mason's room. A blond nurse was standing beside the bed doing something Remi couldn't see. Mason was hooked up to machines, eyes closed like he was sleeping. An oxygen tube snaked beneath his nose, a thicker tube led from some sort of rectangular machine directly into Mason's side, and there were more tubes attached to his arm. There were bandages on his chest, and though he was covered with a sheet, she knew his stomach would also bear the proof of his surgeries. She couldn't hold back tears.

Porter was wrong. Mason didn't look weak. He'd taken two bullets to save her brother and her. He was the strongest man she knew, and no matter what happened to him, he'd always look like *her Mason*.

The nurse turned with a warm expression and said, "Hi, I'm Leisa, Mason's nurse. Are you by chance Remi?"

Remi's throat thickened, and she nodded. "Yes" came out as a whisper.

"When they first brought Mason in, he came to, struggling to get off the gurney. He kept saying he needed to get to you."

Her chest tightened, drawing more tears as she went to him. "Can I touch him?"

"Yes. Just be careful of the tubes and his injuries."

"Of course. Thank you for taking care of him."

"My pleasure. If you need me, just push that button." She pointed to a call button on the bed rail.

After Leisa left, Remi stepped closer to the bed, on the side without the chest tube, and sobs consumed her.

Just breathe. Breathe, breathe, breathe.

She carefully held Mason's hand. His knuckles were raw, and she realized it was the hand he'd used to hit Carl. Her stomach clenched. Even shot, he'd continued to protect her. She pressed her lips to his hand.

"I'm so scared, Mason," she said shakily, just above a whisper. "I know they said you'll be okay, but I need to see your eyes. I need to hear your voice." Sobs silenced her again. "I need . . ." *To be closer.* She was trembling all over. She took off her boots and climbed carefully into bed beside him, lying on her side and holding his hand, her head close to his. "You once told me not to let anyone or anything stand in my way of getting everything I want and deserve. I want only *you*, Mason, and I don't know if I deserve you, but I sure hope so."

She must have dozed off, because she awoke sometime later to Mason's fingers curling around hers, and her heart raced. "Mason? Oh, Mason! I love you! Can you hear me, Mason?"

His eyes opened slowly, and "Princess" came out scratchy and full of relief. "Thank God you're safe."

"Because of you." She cried happy tears. "Thank goodness you're okay. I love you, Mason. I was so scared."

"Don't be afraid. I told you I'd always keep you safe."

"I wasn't afraid for me. I was afraid I'd lose *you*."

"I'm the best, remember?" he said groggily, flashing a half-cocked grin, drawing even more of her tears. "It'd take a lot more than a couple of bullets to keep me from you."

She pressed her lips to his, her tears slipping between them like bittersweet secrets.

"I love you, Princess, and I'm never letting you go."

CHAPTER TWENTY-NINE

AFTER SEVERAL DAYS of camping out in the hospital and nearly three weeks of taking it easy, Mason was beyond ready to stop being treated like he was convalescing. The truth was, he'd been ready to stop being pampered the moment he'd woken up to find Remi lying in his hospital bed, safe and sound. They'd stayed in the cabin in Auburn Grove during his recovery, away from prying eyes and the media. Porter, Krista and Brooklyn, Chuck and Estelle, the Daltons, and their other friends had come to visit. Last week Bodhi and Bridgette had their baby, a beautiful little girl they named Emerson. Although Mason and Remi hadn't seen her in person yet, they'd FaceTimed, and both melted at the sight of their tiny little blessing. Even Flossie had come to visit with Ben and Aurelia, and she'd brought enough food to last a lifetime. Several friends had offered to stay and help, but Remi continued to be her strong, brave self, refusing any help at all. She had taken phenomenal care of him, seeing to his every need, even the naughty ones, which had taken some creativity given the location of his injuries.

He looked across the room at Remi and Aiden standing by the tree Porter and Merrick had brought from the fortress with all of Remi's ornaments. Aiden had been giving them space, staying at the fortress and visiting rather than staying with them at the cabin. He'd been overwhelmed when he'd seen the tree. Aiden said he'd always known that Remi made ornaments when she was stressed, but that Mason had thought to display them for her had touched him deeply. In a strange way, Mason thought that might have been even more of an indicator to Aiden of Mason's love for his sister than anything else had been.

Aiden and Remi were laughing as they gathered the paper lanterns in preparation for their goodbye ceremony. It was five thirty in the morning, and they were heading up to the trail shortly. Remi had asked Aiden to join them, hoping it would help him move forward, too. Mason was glad the two of them were finding a *new normal*, building a relationship with boundaries, which was hard for both of them. He and Aiden were also building a new relationship. Mason knew it was difficult for Aiden to fully let go of his role as Remi's sole protector, and he respected that. It wasn't every day a young man of twenty-four gave up his freedom to raise his younger sister, and Aiden had done a hell of a job. Remi was a remarkable woman.

Remi blew Mason a kiss. Her oversized rust sweater hung past her wrists and covered the top of her black leggings. She called it her cuddle-up sweater. He'd discovered she had many cuddle-up sweaters, as almost every night when they lit a fire in the fireplace, she'd declare, *Look! I'm wearing my favorite cuddle-up sweater! You know what that means!* She was a different person now that there were no threats to evade or reasons to hide their relationship. She'd become even more loving, funnier, and more relaxed.

Their relationship had only recently stopped taking up the headlines, and they were both overwhelmed by the outpouring of well-wishes on social media, get-well cards, and gifts that had been sent to Remi's publicist for them. While their relationship wasn't taking up as much landscape in the tabloids, the stalker situation continued to persist in the headlines. Ken had been sentenced to two years in jail, and Carl was looking at many more, given the severity of his crimes. The police had interrogated Carl's wife, Samantha, and they were convinced she had no idea what Carl had been up to or the hatred he'd harbored toward Remi. Remi was inclined to believe her. They were all shocked when Carl wrote a letter of apology to Remi. It had taken her two weeks to get up the nerve to read it. He'd professed his love for his wife and his sorrow for what he'd done to Remi, but no words could make up for the pain he'd caused. She'd burned the letter in the fireplace and said, "There are no take-backs. I only hope Samantha and Timmy can escape from under his dark shadow."

"Ready, Romeo?" Aiden asked with a smirk.

"Always." Mason helped Remi with her coat before putting on his own.

"You know, the fortress is still up for sale," Aiden said. "Have you thought more about buying it?"

"Actually, I think we want to find someplace of our own," Remi said as they headed outside, into the brisk dawn air.

After the ceremony, Mason and Remi were going to the city for two weeks, to stay at his loft, spend time with Chuck and Estelle, see a show or two, and get things underway for their foster-care project. Parker had been wonderful, continuing to make arrangements for the birthday boxes and the first birthday bash, which they had decided to hold in Harmony Pointe right after New Year's.

"*You* could buy it," Mason suggested to Aiden. "Finally put some roots down."

"I have a feeling Remi might want a little more space than that," Aiden said as Mason locked the door.

Remi reached for Mason's hand and said, "I'm cool with you living nearby, Aiden. Besides, then I can play matchmaker. You haven't met Krista yet."

Mason chuckled as they headed up the trail. His chest constricted with memories of the last time they'd taken that particular walk, and as he'd had to do several times when they'd first come back to the cabin, he pushed those thoughts down deep.

Remi leaned closer with a loving look in her beautiful eyes and said, "Breathe, hottieguard. Just breathe."

Remi knew just what was going through Mason's head, because the memories of that terrible afternoon when their worlds were turned inside out were weighing on her, too. She was determined not to allow what had happened to them to steal her joy of being at the cabin, or her hope for the ceremony to help them all move forward.

Pushing those thoughts away was a struggle, but she was with the two most important people in her life, and they were getting ready to start their new lives together *and* separately. With Mason and Aiden by her side, she knew anything was possible, including moving past the horrid memories.

They stepped into the clearing, and the breathtaking view of the sun rising in the distance, spreading flares of bright reds and oranges over the mountains, drew a moment of silence among them—as if the universe was telling them to pause, take a breath, and enjoy the moment.

"Wow," Aiden said. "It's been years."

Remi knew he almost never went up there. "That's what makes it so perfect."

Aiden handed her a lantern, with the expression she knew so well, the one that pulled his brows up just a little and brought tension lines around his mouth. It was the look of her brother trying to appear more relaxed than he felt. No matter what Aiden went through, he never failed to look distinguished, and today was no different. His dark-brown hair was brushed away from his face, and his tan cashmere turtleneck and suede coat made him look like he'd walked off the pages of *GQ*.

"How do we do this?" Aiden asked as he handed Mason a lantern. "Is there an order to who goes first?"

"We thought we'd each say something and then release our lantern," Mason said. He'd let his scruff grow out the last few weeks, though he kept it neatly trimmed. The short beard gave him an even tougher look. In his black cable-knit sweater and coat, he looked deliciously rugged. "But we can do it however you'd like. I'm not sure there's a right or wrong with something like this."

They both looked at Remi as if she had the answers. It was a first for Aiden to turn to her for help, and she knew how hard it was for him not to take control and dole out directions.

"How about if we just take turns," she suggested. "Who wants to go first?"

Aiden looked at Mason, who looked at Remi. She said, "I'd kind of like to go last, if that's okay?"

"I'll go first," Mason offered. He lit his lantern and held it up, his jaw clenching a few times before he said, "To my brothers-in-arms, I have endless respect, honor, and love for you. To my mother." His muscles in his jaw bunched again. "I know you tried, and I appreciate that. I wish things could have been different, but everything I've been through, and everyone I've lost, has led me to this moment and to Remi. For that I can only be grateful. Rest in peace."

He released his lantern, and Remi put her arms around him. He held her tight, kissing her head as he often did when his mind was far away.

"I guess it's my turn?" Aiden said.

"Is that okay?" Remi asked. Aiden had never been comfortable showing emotions, and she had no idea what to expect. She hoped for his sake he could say whatever would set him free.

"Yes. I'd like to do this," Aiden said. "I'm glad you included me."

He lit the lantern and held it up toward the sky, inhaling deeply. "Mom, Dad, you made me the man I am, and not a day goes by when I don't hear your voices and see your faces. I would give anything to go back in time to that night and ask you to meet me someplace other than at home."

Remi's heart broke. She'd never known Aiden blamed himself. She let go of Mason and put her arm around her brother. "It's not your fault," she said through tears.

She wasn't sure he heard her, because he didn't even look over. He just continued talking to their parents.

"I hope I've made you proud," Aiden said solemnly. "I love you, and I don't know how to say goodbye, so I hope you're waiting for me when my number comes up."

He released the lantern, and then his arm circled Remi, and she wrapped both of hers around him, holding him tight. "The accident wasn't your fault," she cried. "We were going home anyway. It was the deer, not you, Aiden."

"Thanks." He stepped back, his glassy eyes shifting away from her as he said, "It's your turn, Remi."

How could she say goodbye to her parents when she was so heart-broken over Aiden?

"Remi?" Mason put a hand on her lower back.

"I know." She looked at Aiden and said, "Tell me you don't blame yourself, Aiden. Not for all these years."

Aiden shrugged one shoulder. In all her life she'd never seen him shrug. Aiden was a very clear communicator. There was no gray area in his answers, only black and white. He cleared his throat and said, "I know it's not my fault, Remi, but guilt is hard to erase."

"Will you try? For me?" She knew he'd do anything for her, and she hoped he would agree to do this if not for himself, then for her. "Talk to someone about it? Do something so I know you have a chance to let go of it at some point?"

"I can recommend a good therapist. Krista saw her when she lost her husband," Mason said.

Aiden swallowed hard, lowered his eyes for a beat, and when he finally met her gaze, she saw as much love as anguish as he said, "Sure, okay."

Remi hugged him. "Thank you. That means a lot to me. Mom and Dad wouldn't want you suffering when none of it was your fault and you've done so much for me."

"Okay," Aiden said. "Now, how about we let you say your goodbyes and get off the *Aiden truth train*?"

She half laughed, half cried, feeling a little better knowing he would talk to someone.

Mason lit her lantern, and she held it up, looking at the sky, her chest tight and achy. "I've thought a lot about what I want to say and how to say goodbye, but a wise man told me there are no do-overs, so instead of saying goodbye, I want to say thank you." Tears flooded for the hundredth time in as many days as she said, "Thank you for loving me and showing me what true love looked like. Thank you for raising Aiden to be the man he is. Without him, I would be so lost. Daddy, thank you for the stories and for supporting my dreams and keeping our lives real. Mom, I'm still making ornaments, and I know you had a hand in Aiden finding Mason, because I'm his Princess, too. Thank you for him."

She paused to try to regain control of her emotions.

Mason put his arm around her, kissed the top of her head, and said, "Just breathe, Princess."

His support gave her strength. She steeled herself against her tears and said, "I love you both, and I miss you every day, but I know you're smiling down on all of us, just like we're smiling up at you. And, Mom, I know if you were here, you'd be pushing Aiden to find love, too, so don't worry—I'm on it."

Aiden made a strangled sound, and she glanced over and saw tears sliding down his cheeks.

"Help me with this?" she asked Aiden, and he stepped closer, putting one hand on the lantern. She turned to Mason. "You too? Please?" Mason put his hand beside hers on the lantern, and she said, "On the count of three? *One.* I love you all. *Two.* When this lantern flies, it'll take the hurt and guilt of not saying goodbye with it. *Three.*"

They let go, and Remi called out, "I love you, Mom and Dad!"

As the sun kissed the sky and the lanterns floated away, their glimmering flames turning to flickering specks in the distance, Remi took hold of Mason's and Aiden's hands.

"Here's to the start of our new family. I love you guys so much."

"This was a good idea, Remi. Thank you," Aiden said. "But I need a minute alone. I'm going to head back to the cabin. You two take your time."

"Are you sure you're okay?" Remi asked.

"Yeah, better than okay. I think you're right. It's time I talked to someone."

She watched Aiden walk down the path and said to Mason, "Do you think he's okay?"

"Yes," he assured her. "Everyone handles grief differently. I've talked a lot with Aiden these past few weeks. I know the changes between you two are hard for him, but they were necessary. They opened old wounds for Aiden, but he's trying to deal with them."

"You guys must have *really* talked to know that much."

"It's not like females have a monopoly on deep discussions. Besides, Aiden and I had other things to talk about, too."

"Really?"

"Oh yes. *Important* things." He dropped to one knee and pulled a jewelry box from his coat pocket.

Her heart skipped. "Mason! What are you doing?"

"Hopefully starting our new family." He opened the box, and a gorgeous diamond ring shimmered in the sunlight.

"Oh my gosh, *Mason!*" Her pulse sprinted so fast she could barely breathe.

His lips curved up and he said, "My beautiful Remi, I never knew love until I met you. I'm not even sure I believed in it. But you changed that. When I was shot, as my vision blurred and everything faded to black, my only thoughts were of you. I want a life with you, Remi, a *full* life, raising our children to be strong little girls and boys, and helping foster kids have special birthdays, and who knows what else the future will hold. But I want it, whatever it is, with you."

She couldn't stop nodding. "I want that, too. And maybe we can foster a child and give them everything you never had?"

He rose to his feet with tears in his eyes and said, "Yes. *God yes.* Remington Aldridge, Princess, will you marry me? Let me be the man you deserve for the rest of our lives? I promise to—"

"Yes!" She launched herself into his arms and kissed him. "I love you, Mason! Yes, yes, *yes!*"

He laughed between kisses. "You didn't hear my promise."

"I don't have to. I don't need promises. I just need you."

"God I love you."

He slid the most gorgeous diamond ring she'd ever seen on her finger, and as he lowered his lips to hers, Aiden came out of the woods, aiming his phone at them with a big grin on his face.

"I thought you went to the . . . Wait. You *knew* he was proposing?"

Mason and Aiden shared a conspiratorial glance.

"Is this how it is now? Two against one?" she teased, bubbling over with happiness that Mason had shared such a special moment with Aiden.

"You don't think I could ask for your hand in marriage before first talking with Aiden, do you?" Mason asked.

"You did?" She looked at her brother with tears in her eyes. "Aiden?"

Aiden winked and said, "Congratulations, little sister. You've got one hell of a future husband here. Now, let's give the press a winning engagement-kiss photo."

"We might need to take a few to get it right," she said, her arms circling Mason's neck. Their mouths came together with the swift softness of a never-ending breeze, lifting her right up to the clouds.

"Nice one," Aiden said.

"I love you, Princess," Mason whispered against her lips. "Today, tomorrow, and forevermore."

She pulled him in for another kiss and couldn't imagine ever letting go.

EPILOGUE

REMI SMOOTHED THE last bit of frosting on the birthday cake and pushed the candles, numbers three and five, securely in place. It was Mason's birthday, and she'd gotten up before dawn to decorate their new house and make his cake. Nahla, their two-year-old golden retriever rescue, brushed against Remi's leg, wagging her tail. Remi had decorated Nahla, too, with a big blue ribbon around her neck. Mason had surprised Remi with Nahla for Christmas right after they'd gone to the Christmas tree lighting in the center of town with Krista and Brooklyn. Nahla was the most loving dog Remi had ever known, and she was great with children and other dogs. Bridgette and Bodhi came over often to let Louie love her up, and of course they brought Nahla's bestie, Dahlia. The two dogs loved to chase each other around the yard, and Remi couldn't get enough of their sweet baby girl, Emerson.

"You can't have cake until Daddy does," she said to the eager pup. "But you know he'll give you some if you give him kisses."

She patted Nahla's head, and Nahla *woof*ed.

They'd gotten lucky and found a cute four-bedroom Victorian on the outskirts of Harmony Pointe, situated on ten acres, with a barn big enough to host the birthday bashes, the first of which was taking place later today. Mason had immediately had a ten-foot iron fence installed around the property and a state-of-the-art security system put in. Remi was okay with all of it. Even though she'd decided to put acting on hold for a while and focus on their work with CCF, and Carl was behind bars serving a ten-year sentence, after everything they'd been through, she didn't want to take any chances. Piper and her crew had renovated the barn, adding heat and air-conditioning, as well as a full kitchen and two bathrooms. They'd completed it just in time for today's party.

Remi slipped Mason's gift into the pocket of her short silk robe, excited to make his birthday extra special. He was also focusing more on their charity, and although he'd delegated much of his work over the holidays, he was planning to take on clients in the spring, with limited to no travel. She couldn't imagine a life where he wasn't doing what he did best, taking care of others. But this morning was all about Mason.

She carried the cake upstairs to the master bedroom with Nahla beside her. Mason was fast asleep, naked, the sheet bunched around his hips. The pink scars from his surgeries no longer gave her painful pangs. Instead they reminded her of how strong Mason was. Though with his broad, muscular chest and arms on display, she hardly needed reminding.

She set the cake on the dresser to light the candles, and then she picked it up and began singing. "Happy birthday to you, happy birthday to you."

Nahla leapt onto the bed with a low *woof*, giving Mason sloppy kisses all over his face.

"Good morning to you, too, Nahla." Mason tousled her fur, pushing up to sit against the headboard. His eyes raked down the length of Remi's body, leaving shivers of heat in their wake. "And good morning to you, gorgeous. You made me a cake?" His gaze swept around the room, lighting up at the sight of streamers and the birthday banner she'd put up while he slept. "Remi . . . ? When did you do this?"

"You were sleeping pretty hard after last night's lovefest." She sat on the edge of the bed, holding the cake, and sang, "Happy birthday, my beautiful soon-to-be husband, happy birthday to you!" They'd decided to get married in early summer, when the weather was warmer, in an intimate ceremony there at the house. *Their* house. *Our home.* "Make a wish and blow out your candles."

"What could I possibly wish for? Everything I want is right here in this room."

"I'm sure you'll think of something."

"How about if we make a wish together?"

Oh, how she loved that he wanted to share his special wish with her. But this was his wish to make. "It's your birthday, not mine, and don't tell me what you wish for or it might not come true."

"My last wish did. You said *yes* to my proposal."

Nahla pushed her nose between them to sniff the cake and pressed her nose into the frosting.

"Nahla," Remi said with a laugh.

Nahla licked the sweetness off her snout.

"Better make your wish quick or the cake will be full of nose prints."

"This takes some thought. I'm not prepared," he teased. "But seriously, I've got a fiancée I'm crazy about, the best friends a guy could want, a project I'm beyond proud of—"

Nahla licked Mason's arm.

"And a dog I adore. What else could I want? Wait, can I wish for something for others?" he asked.

"Of course. It's your wish."

"Got it." His face went serious for a second, and then he blew out the candles.

"Yay!" Remi cheered, which caused Nahla to bark. She set the cake on the dresser and sat beside Mason on the bed again. "I got you a little something."

"Princess, you got me way more than a little something. You made a cake and you decorated our room."

"You should see the rest of the house. This is just the beginning of your new birthday traditions. From here on out, every birthday will be more special than the last."

He pulled her in for a kiss, which Nahla decided to join in on with her wet nose and sloppy tongue, causing them both to chuckle.

"This birthday is already more special than any other because I'm sharing it with you," Mason said. "How much time do we have before everyone shows up?"

"An hour and a half. The party starts at ten, but everyone's coming to help set up at eight. Parker and Grayson should get here around nine. I'm excited for you to meet them in person and see their baby girl. She's so stinking cute!" Parker and her family were staying with them for the week, to visit and to talk about the future of their endeavor.

Mason swept her into his arms and rolled her beneath him with a boyish grin. "Then we have enough time to play?"

Nahla *woof*ed, tail wagging, paws and snout flat on the bed. Nahla loved to play, and so did Mason—tossing balls for Nahla *and* playing sexy games with Remi.

Mason rolled his eyes.

Remi whispered, "You said the *p*-word."

He eyed Nahla, who licked his face. "Okay, we'll play, too, Nahla."

"After I give you your present," Remi said.

Mason pulled the tie on her robe open and pushed the silk to the sides, exposing her nakedness. "Now, *that's* a present."

"That's not your present! You can have me *after* I give you your real gift." She reached into the pocket of her robe and pulled out the wrapped box. "Happy birthday, Mason."

"You didn't have to get me a gift," Mason said as they sat up. He pulled her into his arms and said, "Thanks, Princess," sounding choked up.

"You're welcome. Don't you want to open it?"

He continued holding her and said, "Yeah," against her neck, embracing her for a moment longer. Then he sat back with a long inhalation, his eyes drifting from the gift to her. "You're really something."

He unwrapped the gift and lifted the top of the box. His eyes teared up again, and he put the top back on.

"You don't like it?" She feared she'd made a big mistake. "I can return it. I'm sorry."

He shook his head, tears welling, his jaw muscles jumping double time. "Remi, this is . . . *God* . . ." He pulled her against him again, breathing hard. "This is just like the pocket watch I lost from my mother. It even has the same initials."

"I'm ninety-nine percent sure it's the same one."

He sat back, gazing into her eyes.

"I put out a reward online. This woman was going through her father's things after he passed away and she found it. Her son had bought it at a pawnshop and had given it to his grandfather two years earlier. I don't know how it got to the pawnshop or how many other times it had been pawned. Porter tried to trace its history for me, but after tracking two owners and two pawnshops, he tracked it to a third pawnshop that had closed, so it was a dead end. I had Chuck come with me when I went to see it, because he said you'd described it to him, too."

She'd loved spending time with Chuck and his wife, Estelle, when they were in the city, and they'd even gone to shows and dinners together. He'd told her all sorts of stories about Mason's surly teenage attitude when he was younger and how Chuck had known that beneath the anger and the attitude was a good man waiting to be set free.

"You took *Chuck*? When?" Mason cleared his throat, regaining control of his emotions.

"One day when you thought I was going to visit Flossie with Aurelia. They actually went with me to see the watch, too. The four of us went together. Now you have something to pass down to our children. A family tradition."

"Christ, Princess. I can see life with you is going to be full of surprises."

"So, you like it?" she asked hopefully.

"I love it, almost as much as I love you." He set the box on the dresser and said, "Nahla, *down*."

Nahla whimpered and jumped off the bed.

"Aw, poor girl," Remi said.

"She'll be fine. I can't get a gift like that without properly thanking my favorite girl." His lips came coaxingly down over hers, and then he proceeded to thank her in the most toe-curling, exquisite way possible.

By ten thirty the birthday bash was in full swing, celebrating the special days of twenty-one foster children who had birthdays during the first quarter of the year. It was cold outside, but the barn was warm and festive, with colorful balloons and streamers hanging from the rafters. All of their friends had shown up to support the event. Music played from a stereo, and kids of all ages were doing arts and crafts and playing birthday games. Nahla was in her heyday, being loved up by children and adults everywhere she went.

Mason looked across the barn at Remi, who was helping a group of girls make ornaments. Patrice, an adorable four-year-old with pigtails, sat on Remi's lap, where she'd been practically since the moment she'd arrived, and beside Remi was Olive, a fourteen-year-old girl who also hadn't left Remi's side since she'd arrived. Mason had never seen Remi look happier. He had thought the birthday boxes would make a huge difference in children's lives, but seeing the celebration they'd been working on for months come to fruition was a gift in and of itself.

Aiden sidled up to him and followed his gaze to Remi. "She's meant for this, isn't she?"

"I'll say. She's a natural with kids."

"You've made a world of difference in her life, Mason. I just want you to know that I recognize that. I think I was holding her back, and you set her free."

"Or maybe she set me free," Mason said as Brooklyn barreled through the barn doors and crashed into Mason.

She beamed up at him. "Mason, look!" She patted her fur hat as Krista joined them. "I'm wearing the hat you and Remi got me for Christmas! Don't I look cool?"

"You sure do." Before he finished speaking, Brooklyn darted off to greet Remi.

"Sorry," Krista said, her eyes moving to Aiden. "She's . . . um . . . She's . . . a little excited to celebrate with the kids."

Mason had never seen Krista at a loss for words, and Aiden looked a little starry-eyed, too. "Aiden, this is my friend Krista. She's a photographer, among other things, and she's going to take pictures of the event. Would you mind showing her where the coatroom is?"

"Absolutely," Aiden said. "Right this way."

As Krista followed Aiden, she glanced at Mason over her shoulder and mouthed, *Wow, he's hot!*

"Playing matchmaker?" Piper asked as she came to his side, gnawing on a Twizzler.

"Just being nice," he said as Porter came through the doors with his eight-year-old nephew. "Hey, Porter's here with Lucas."

"That delicious dish is married?" Piper sighed. "Figures."

"That's his nephew. His sister is a nurse and a single mother. He helps her out with Lucas when he can." He nudged Piper and pointed to Harley, who was heading their way. "Besides, I think someone else has his eye on you."

Piper arched a brow and said, "Nephew, huh? I'm good with a nephew."

She headed for Porter and Mason headed for Remi, but Bodhi cut him off before he got halfway there.

"Hey, Mason, can you do me a favor?" Bodhi asked with Emerson in his arms.

"Sure. What do you need?"

"Would you mind taking Em for a minute? Willow needs my help getting a few things from her van." Willow was providing the birthday cakes for the event.

"No problem." He cradled Emerson in his arms and couldn't resist pressing a kiss to her forehead, breathing in her sweet baby scent. She had Bodhi's serious dark eyes and light hair like her mama.

"I hear if you smell them, you're ten times more likely to have one in the next year." Roxie brushed her fingers down Emerson's cheek. "Isn't that true, sweet baby girl? And how cute would a little Masi be?"

"Masi?" Mason arched a brow.

"Haven't you seen the latest rag magazines? I've seen *two* new nicknames for you and Remi—*Remson* and *Masi*. You know, Mason and Remi combined. The press loves to do that. I prefer Masi. Oh, and apparently Remi's pregnant, too."

"*What?*" His gaze shot to Remi, and he warmed with the thought.

"That picture of her at the Christmas parade made her look a little heavier than normal, which of course means you're having a baby." Roxie laughed. "You need to keep up with the gossip."

"I guess so. I never got a chance to thank you for your apricot potions."

"My pleasure." She looked at Remi, who was watching Mason with a dreamy look in her eyes. "I'm really happy for you two. I can bring some *fertility* potions by if you'd like."

"How about we get married first?"

"Okay, but if you ask me, that baby in your arms is proof that babies come on their own schedules." Emerson had been conceived after Bodhi and Bridgette were engaged but before they were married. Roxie pressed a kiss to Emerson's head and said, "I think I'd better go see how Shira's doing. Last I saw, she was drooling over Aiden."

"He's popular today."

Roxie lowered her voice to a whisper and said, "I gave him a special shaving cream, too. Let that be our little secret." She winked and walked away.

Mason arrived at the table where Remi was working with the kids just as Grayson Lacroux, Parker's husband, rang a cowbell and announced, "Who's ready to watch a magic show?"

Remi set Patrice on her feet and said, "Go with Olive. I'll be right there."

Olive, a shy brunette, took Patrice's hand, and they joined the other kids and the adults gathering for the magic show.

Mason sat down beside Remi and said, "Hey, beautiful. Having fun?"

"I want to keep them all. Every last one of them." She brushed her lips over Emerson's head. "Think Bridgette will let us borrow Emmy for a night?"

"You have Miriam to play with for the next week."

"I know, but look how cute Emmy is. I think we need a bigger house."

He chuckled. "You can't keep all these kids. They have foster families."

"I know, but looking at them and thinking of what you went through, I can't make sense of it. I just want to love every last one of them." She motioned toward their crowded barn and said, "Can you believe we helped pull this together? Look how happy the kids are."

"It's pretty incredible." He saw Aiden talking with Krista and said, "Did you see Aiden and Krista? They're sort of gaga over each other."

"Aiden doesn't do gaga. He probably has gas," she teased.

"You know, nobody thought I would get all mushy over a woman, either, and look at me now."

"When I met you, I thought everything I wanted was just out of reach, and now I have you, and we have this, and a future, and . . ." Her eyes teared up.

He nuzzled against her neck and kissed her beside her ear, whispering, "I'm crazy about you, Remi Aldridge."

"Talk dirty to me, baby," she teased.

And he did, until her cheeks flamed red. She rolled her lower lip between her teeth, and her gorgeous hazel eyes brimmed with desire. Then he leaned closer and whispered, "*Just breathe, Remi.* Together we'll make all your dreams come true."

A NOTE FROM MELISSA

I have been waiting to write Remi's story since I first met her in *The Real Thing* (Sugar Lake series). When I met Mason, I knew the charming, burly man had a huge heart and the right instincts to be Remi's hero. I hope you enjoyed their love story as much as I loved writing it. I'm looking forward to spending more time with Remi, Mason, Aiden, the Daltons, and all of their wonderful friends, and I am excited to bring you more Dalton and Harmony Pointe love stories soon. Ben and Aurelia's story, *Call Her Mine*, is available in digital, print, and audio formats. Willow, Bridgette, and Talia each have their own book as well and have found their happily ever afters in the Sugar Lake series, all of which are now available for your binge-reading pleasure. If you'd like to read more about Duncan "Raz" Raznick, he's mentioned in *Anything for Love*, the second book in my Bradens & Montgomerys series. Raz will eventually get his own love story.

Be sure to sign up for my newsletter to keep up to date with my new releases and to receive an exclusive short story (www.MelissaFoster.com/News).

If this is your first Melissa Foster book, you might enjoy the rest of my big-family romance collection, Love in Bloom. Characters from each series make appearances in future books so you never miss an engagement, wedding, or birth. A complete list of all series titles is included at the start of this book, and downloadable checklists, free series starters, and family trees are available on the Reader Goodies page of my website (www.MelissaFoster.com/RG).

Happy reading!

Melissa Foster

ACKNOWLEDGMENTS

I'm continually surprised and inspired by fans and appreciate all of your emails and messages on social media. It's wonderful to know that you're enjoying my worlds as much as I enjoy creating them. I often turn to fans while researching scenes, and would like to thank Leisa Cossey Cook and Stephanie Durboraw, who were kind enough to answer numerous medical and hospital-related questions. Thank you for your endless patience and expertise.

If you'd like sneak peeks into my writing process and to chat with me daily, please join my fan club on Facebook. We talk about our lovable heroes and sassy heroines, and I always try to keep fans abreast of what's going on in our fictional boyfriends' worlds. You never know when you'll end up in one of my books, as several members of my fan club have already discovered (www.facebook.com/groups/MelissaFosterFans).

Follow my Facebook fan page to keep up with sales and events (www.facebook.com/MelissaFosterAuthor).

A special thank-you to my patient, funny, and all-around awesome editor Maria Gomez and the incredible Montlake team for bringing Remi and Mason's story to life. As always, heaps of gratitude to editors Kristen Weber and Penina Lopez, and to my personal assistants who are always there to talk me off the ledge. And, of course, to my very own hunky hero, Les, and my youngest boys, Jess and Jake, who allow me to spend endless hours in front of my keyboard without complaint, thank you for understanding my need to create. I love you more than chocolate (most days, anyway).

ABOUT THE AUTHOR

Photo © 2013 Melanie Anderson

Melissa Foster is a *New York Times* and *USA Today* bestselling and award-winning author of more than sixty-five books, including *The Real Thing* and *Only for You* in the Sugar Lake series. Her novels have been recommended by *USA Today*'s book blog, *Hagerstown* magazine, the *Patriot*, and others. She has also painted and donated several murals to the Hospital for Sick Children in Washington, DC.

She enjoys discussing her books with book clubs and reader groups, and she welcomes an invitation to your event. Visit Melissa on her website, www.MelissaFoster.com, or chat with her on Instagram @MelissaFoster_Author, Twitter @melissa_foster, and on Facebook at www.facebook.com/MelissaFosterAuthor.

ABOUT THE AUTHOR